DARK FANG

EARTH CALLING

MILES GUNTER • KELSEY SHANNON

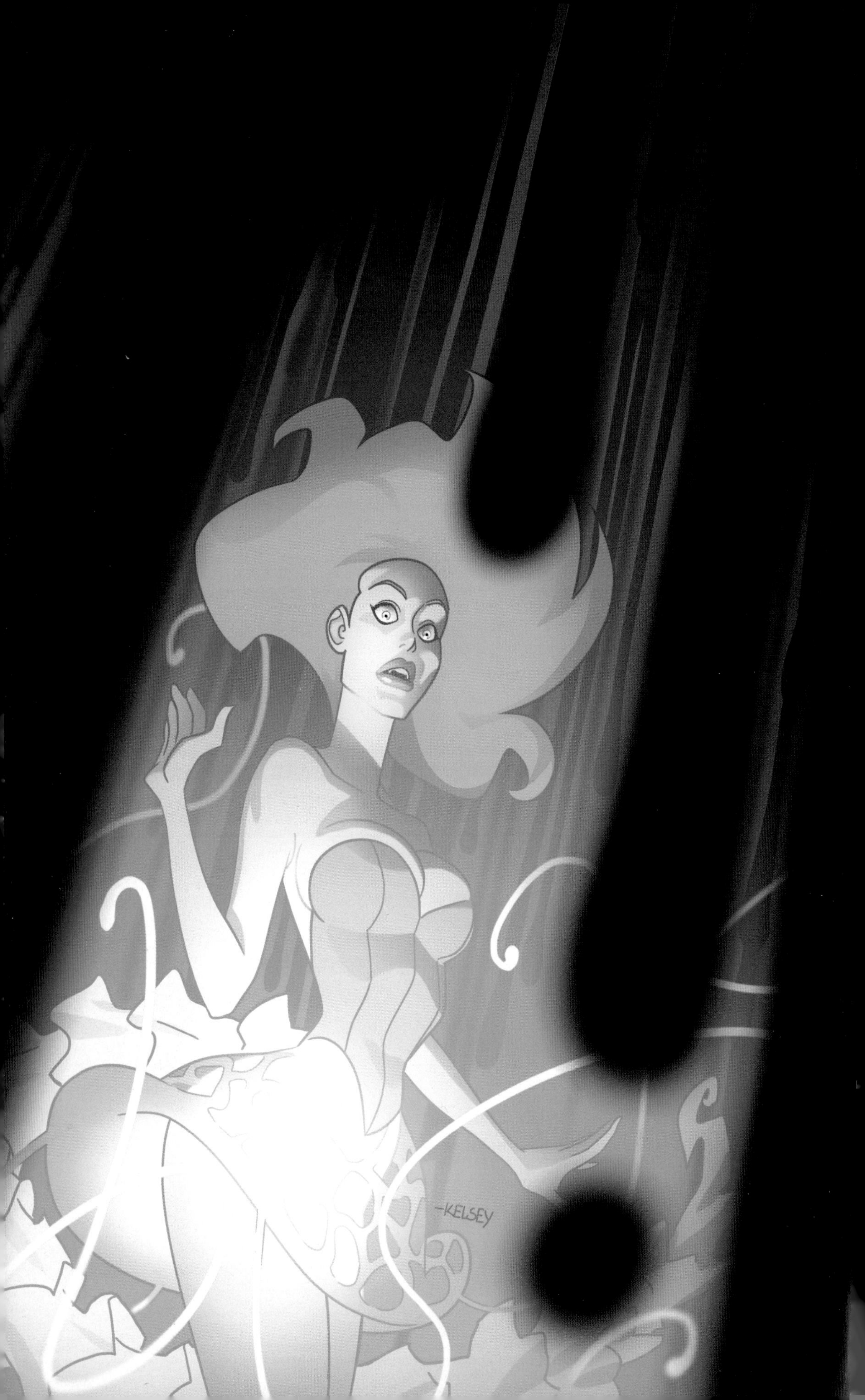
-KELSEY

(handwritten) Dark Fang V.01

DARK FANG
EARTH CALLING

WRITER
MILES GUNTER

ARTIST
KELSEY SHANNON

LETTERER
TAYLOR ESPOSITO

PRODUCTION
CAREY HALL

COPY EDITS
MELISSA GIFFORD

IMAGE COMICS, INC.

Robert Kirkman – Chief Operating Officer
Erik Larsen – Chief Financial Officer
Todd McFarlane – President
Marc Silvestri – Chief Executive Officer
Jim Valentino – Vice President
Eric Stephenson – Publisher / Chief Creative Officer
Corey Hart – Director of Sales
Jeff Boison – Director of Publishing Planning & Book Trade Sales
Chris Ross – Director of Digital Sales
Jeff Stang – Director of Specialty Sales
Kat Salazar – Director of PR & Marketing
Drew Gill – Art Director
Heather Doornink – Production Director
Nicole Lapalme – Controller
IMAGECOMICS.COM

I

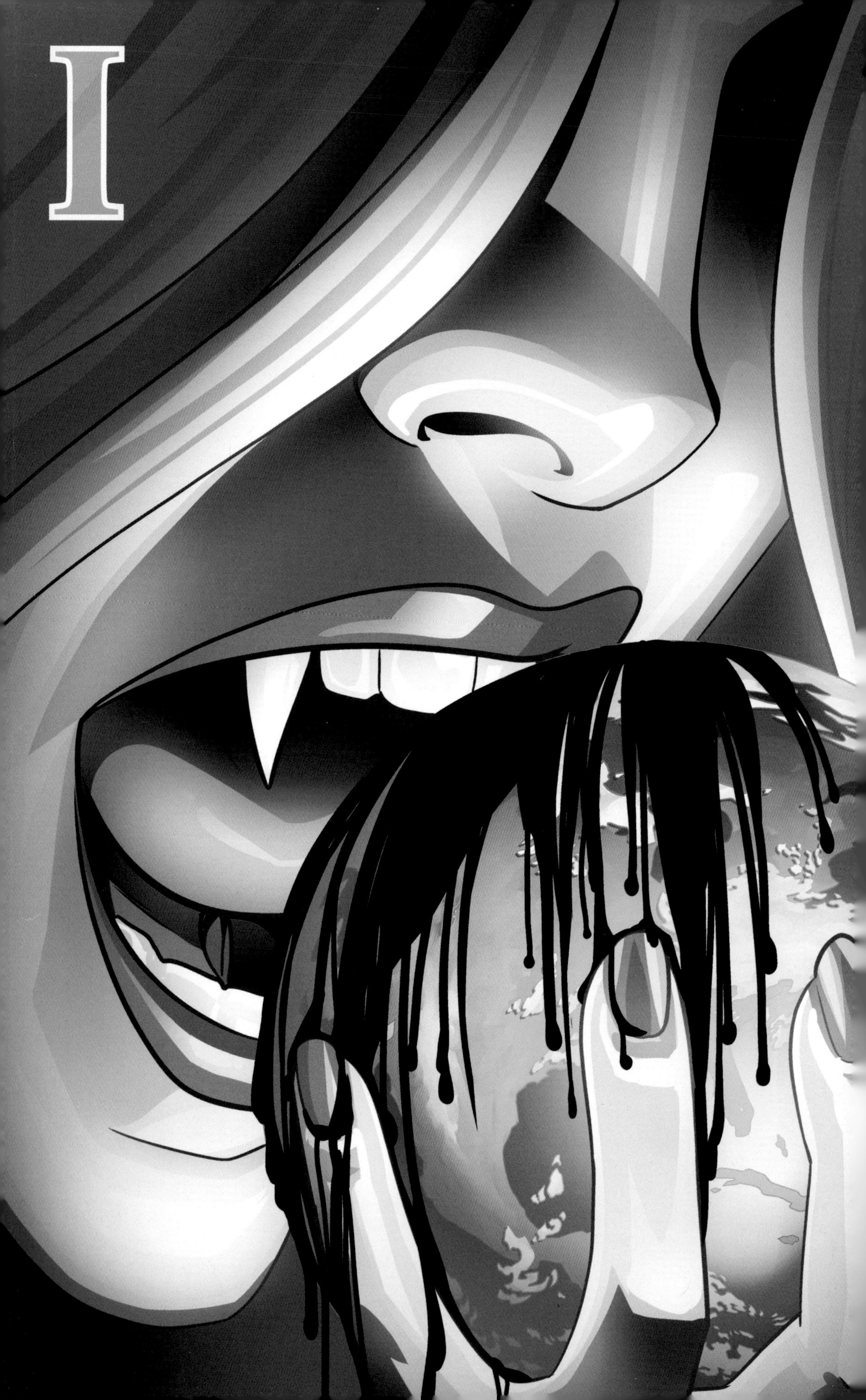

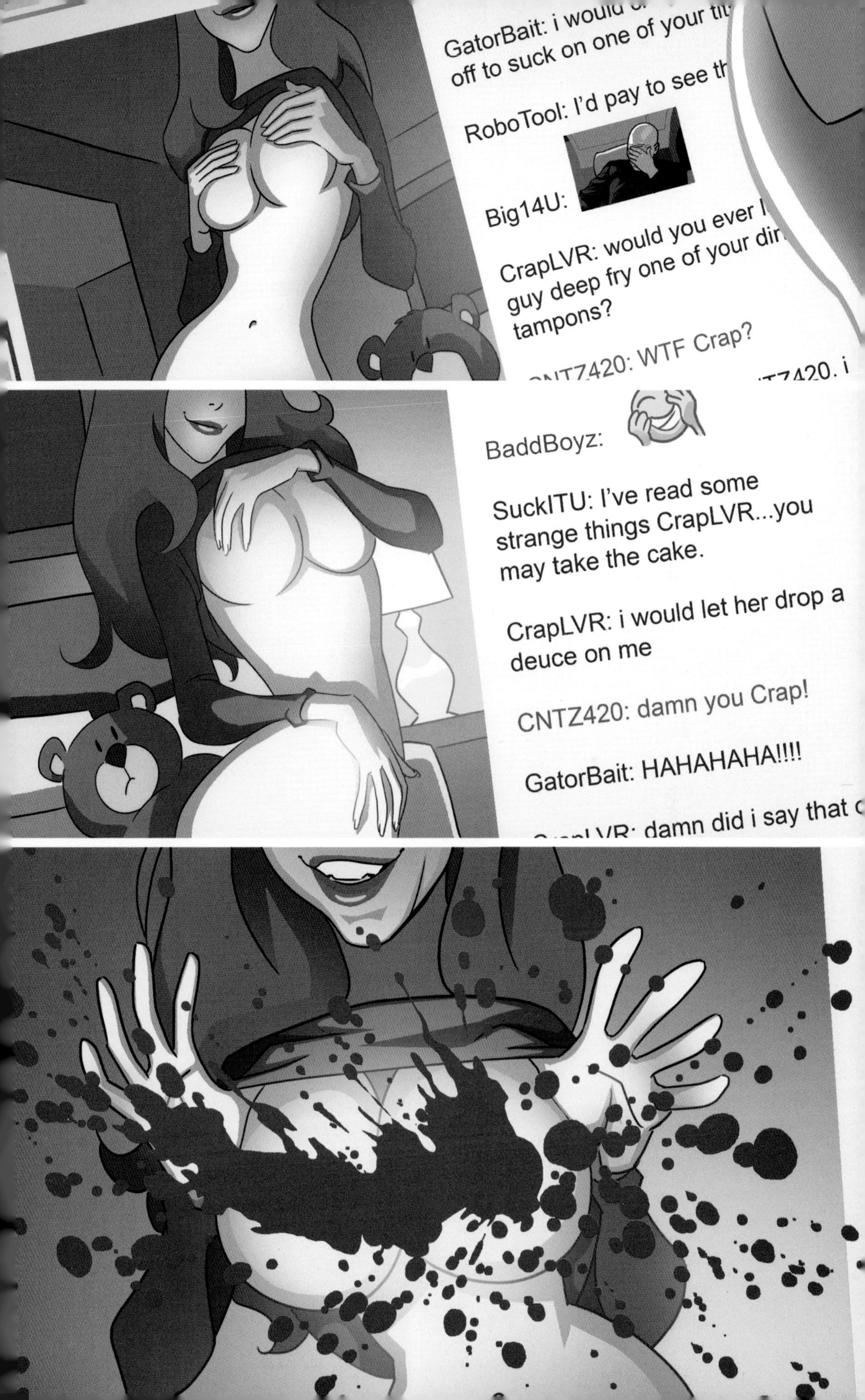
GatorBait: i would
off to suck on one of your tit
RoboTool: I'd pay to see th
Big14U:
CrapLVR: would you ever l
guy deep fry one of your dir
tampons?
CNTZ420: WTF Crap?
BaddBoyz:
SuckITU: I've read some strange things CrapLVR...you may take the cake.
CrapLVR: i would let her drop a deuce on me
CNTZ420: damn you Crap!
GatorBait: HAHAHAHA!!!!
damn did i say that

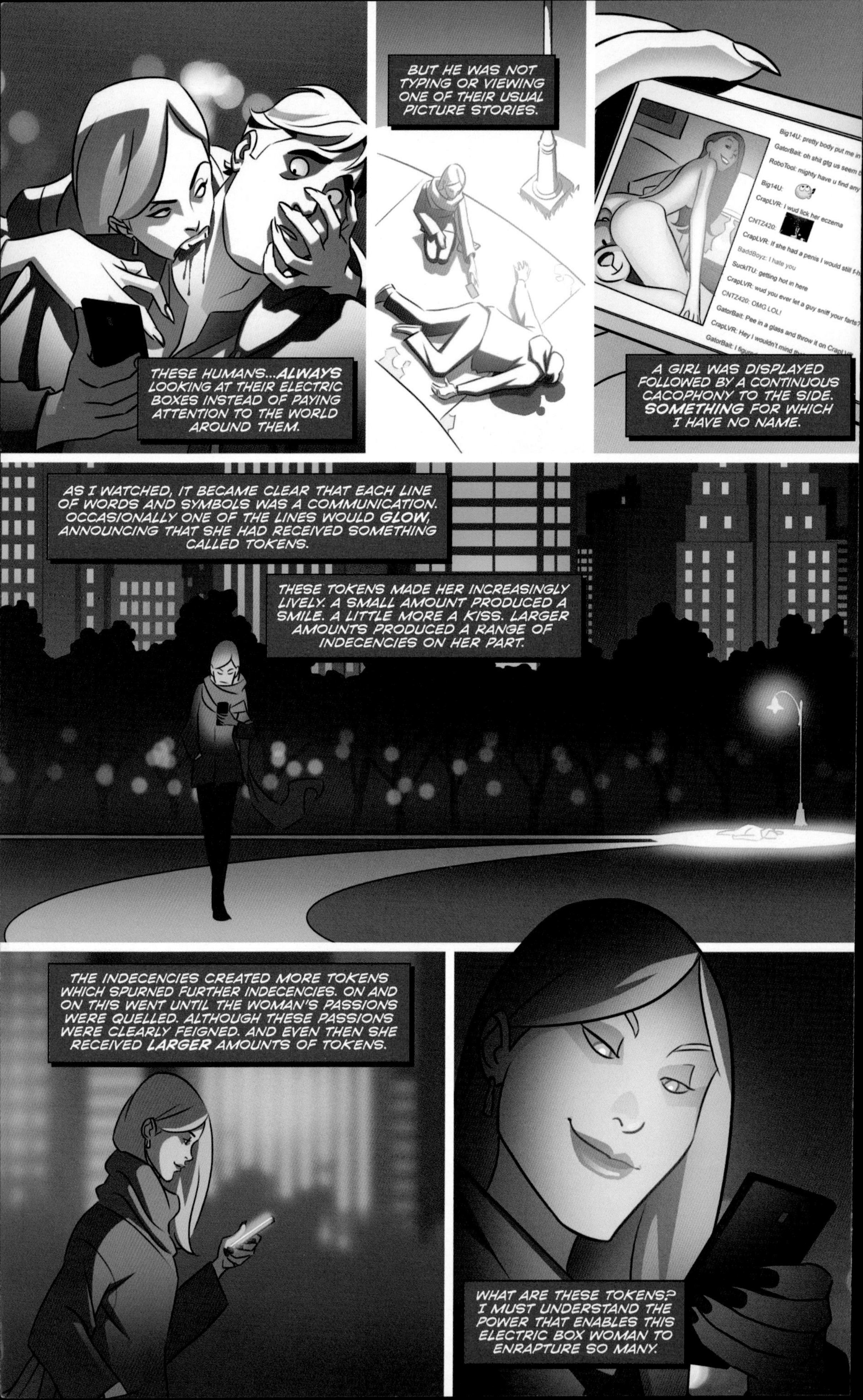

THESE HUMANS...**ALWAYS** LOOKING AT THEIR ELECTRIC BOXES INSTEAD OF PAYING ATTENTION TO THE WORLD AROUND THEM.
BUT HE WAS NOT TYPING OR VIEWING ONE OF THEIR USUAL PICTURE STORIES.
Big14U: pretty body put me in
GatorBait: oh shit gtg us seem
RoboTool: mighty have u find any
Big14U:
CrapLVR: I wud lick her eczema
CNTZ420:
CrapLVR: If she had a penis I would still
BaddBoyz: I hate you
SuckITU: getting hot in here
CrapLVR: wud you ever let a guy sniff your farts?
CNTZ420: OMG LOL!
GatorBait: Pee in a glass and throw it on
CrapLVR: Hey I wouldn't mind
A GIRL WAS DISPLAYED FOLLOWED BY A CONTINUOUS CACOPHONY TO THE SIDE. **SOMETHING** FOR WHICH I HAVE NO NAME.
AS I WATCHED, IT BECAME CLEAR THAT EACH LINE OF WORDS AND SYMBOLS WAS A COMMUNICATION. OCCASIONALLY ONE OF THE LINES WOULD **GLOW**, ANNOUNCING THAT SHE HAD RECEIVED SOMETHING CALLED TOKENS.
THESE TOKENS MADE HER INCREASINGLY LIVELY. A SMALL AMOUNT PRODUCED A SMILE. A LITTLE MORE A KISS. LARGER AMOUNTS PRODUCED A RANGE OF INDECENCIES ON HER PART.
THE INDECENCIES CREATED MORE TOKENS WHICH SPURNED FURTHER INDECENCIES. ON AND ON THIS WENT UNTIL THE WOMAN'S PASSIONS WERE QUELLED. ALTHOUGH THESE PASSIONS WERE CLEARLY FEIGNED. AND EVEN THEN SHE RECEIVED **LARGER** AMOUNTS OF TOKENS.
WHAT ARE THESE TOKENS? I MUST UNDERSTAND THE POWER THAT ENABLES THIS ELECTRIC BOX WOMAN TO ENRAPTURE SO MANY.

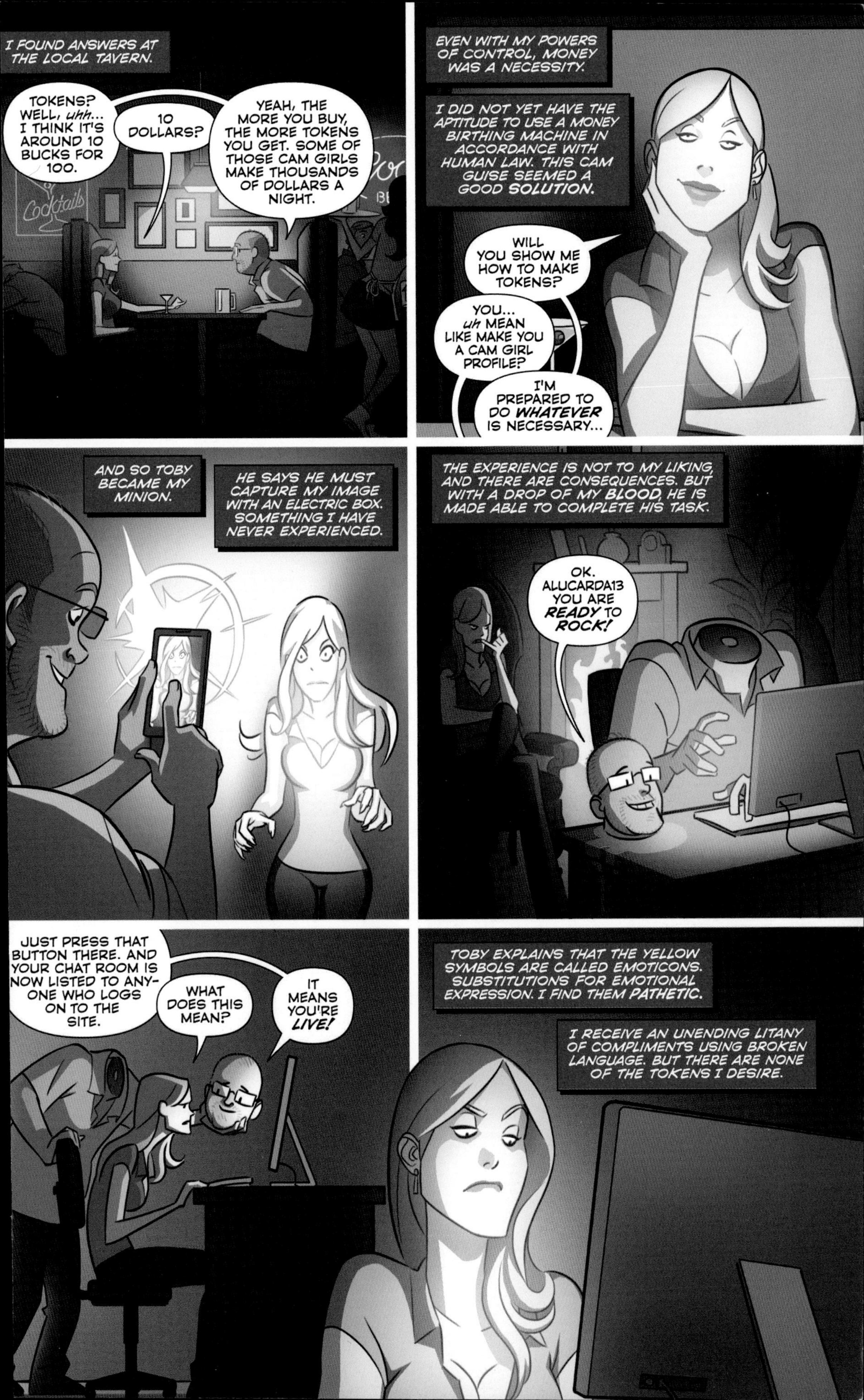
I FOUND ANSWERS AT THE LOCAL TAVERN.
TOKENS? WELL, *uhh*... I THINK IT'S AROUND 10 BUCKS FOR 100.
10 DOLLARS?
YEAH, THE MORE YOU BUY, THE MORE TOKENS YOU GET. SOME OF THOSE CAM GIRLS MAKE THOUSANDS OF DOLLARS A NIGHT.
Cocktails
EVEN WITH MY POWERS OF CONTROL, MONEY WAS A NECESSITY.
I DID NOT YET HAVE THE APTITUDE TO USE A MONEY BIRTHING MACHINE IN ACCORDANCE WITH HUMAN LAW. THIS CAM GUISE SEEMED A GOOD **SOLUTION**.
WILL YOU SHOW ME HOW TO MAKE TOKENS?
YOU... *uh* MEAN LIKE MAKE YOU A CAM GIRL PROFILE?
I'M PREPARED TO DO ***WHATEVER*** IS NECESSARY...
AND SO TOBY BECAME MY MINION.
HE SAYS HE MUST CAPTURE MY IMAGE WITH AN ELECTRIC BOX. SOMETHING I HAVE NEVER EXPERIENCED.
THE EXPERIENCE IS NOT TO MY LIKING, AND THERE ARE CONSEQUENCES. BUT WITH A DROP OF MY **BLOOD**, HE IS MADE ABLE TO COMPLETE HIS TASK.
OK. ALUCARDA13 YOU ARE ***READY*** TO ***ROCK!***
JUST PRESS THAT BUTTON THERE. AND YOUR CHAT ROOM IS NOW LISTED TO ANY-ONE WHO LOGS ON TO THE SITE.
WHAT DOES THIS MEAN?
IT MEANS YOU'RE ***LIVE!***
TOBY EXPLAINS THAT THE YELLOW SYMBOLS ARE CALLED EMOTICONS. SUBSTITUTIONS FOR EMOTIONAL EXPRESSION. I FIND THEM **PATHETIC**.
I RECEIVE AN UNENDING LITANY OF COMPLIMENTS USING BROKEN LANGUAGE. BUT THERE ARE NONE OF THE TOKENS I DESIRE.

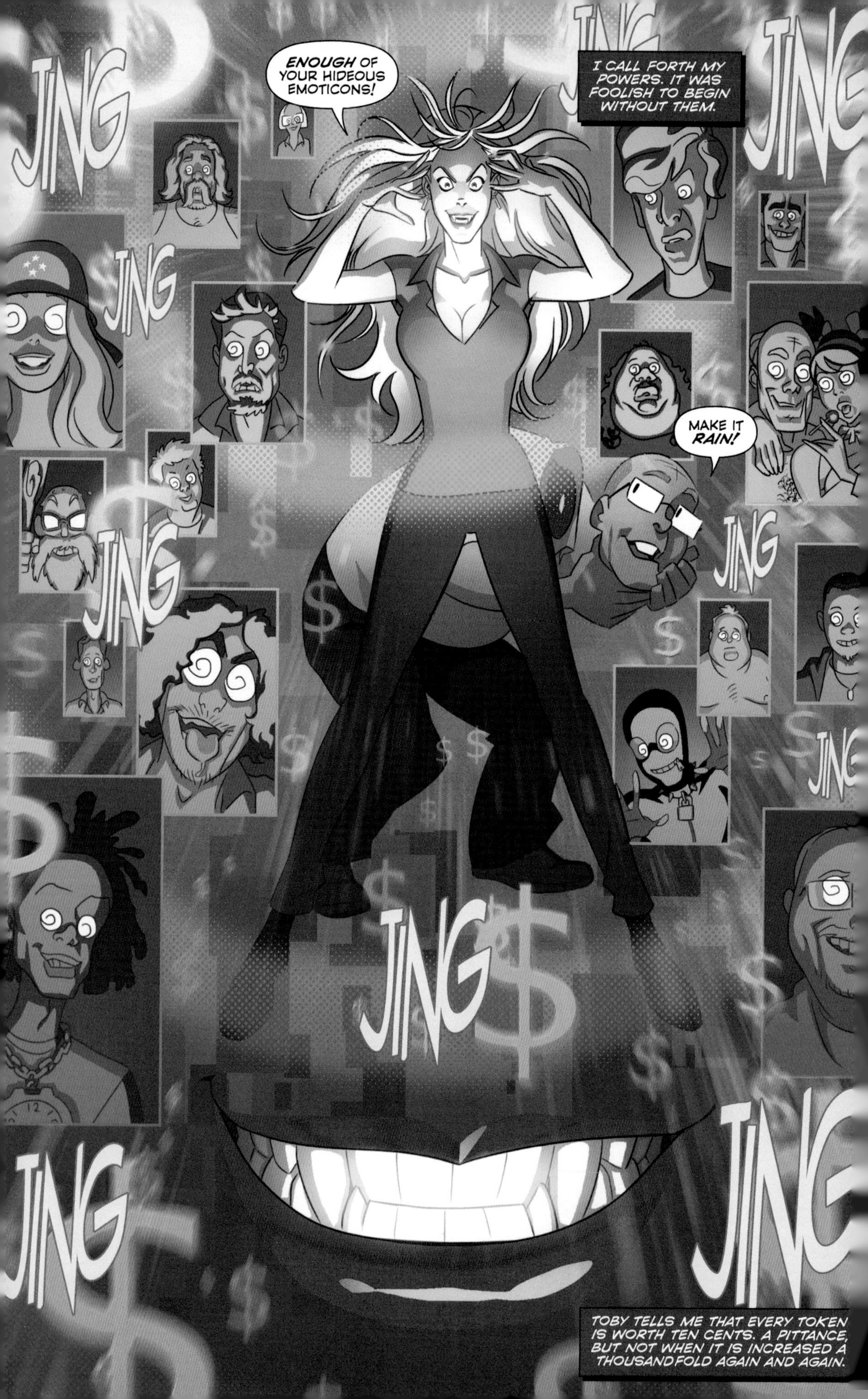
I CALL FORTH MY POWERS. IT WAS FOOLISH TO BEGIN WITHOUT THEM.
ENOUGH OF YOUR HIDEOUS EMOTICONS!
JING
JING
JING
JING
JING
MAKE IT RAIN!
JING
JING
JING
JING
JING
JING
TOBY TELLS ME THAT EVERY TOKEN IS WORTH TEN CENTS. A PITTANCE, BUT NOT WHEN IT IS INCREASED A THOUSANDFOLD AGAIN AND AGAIN.

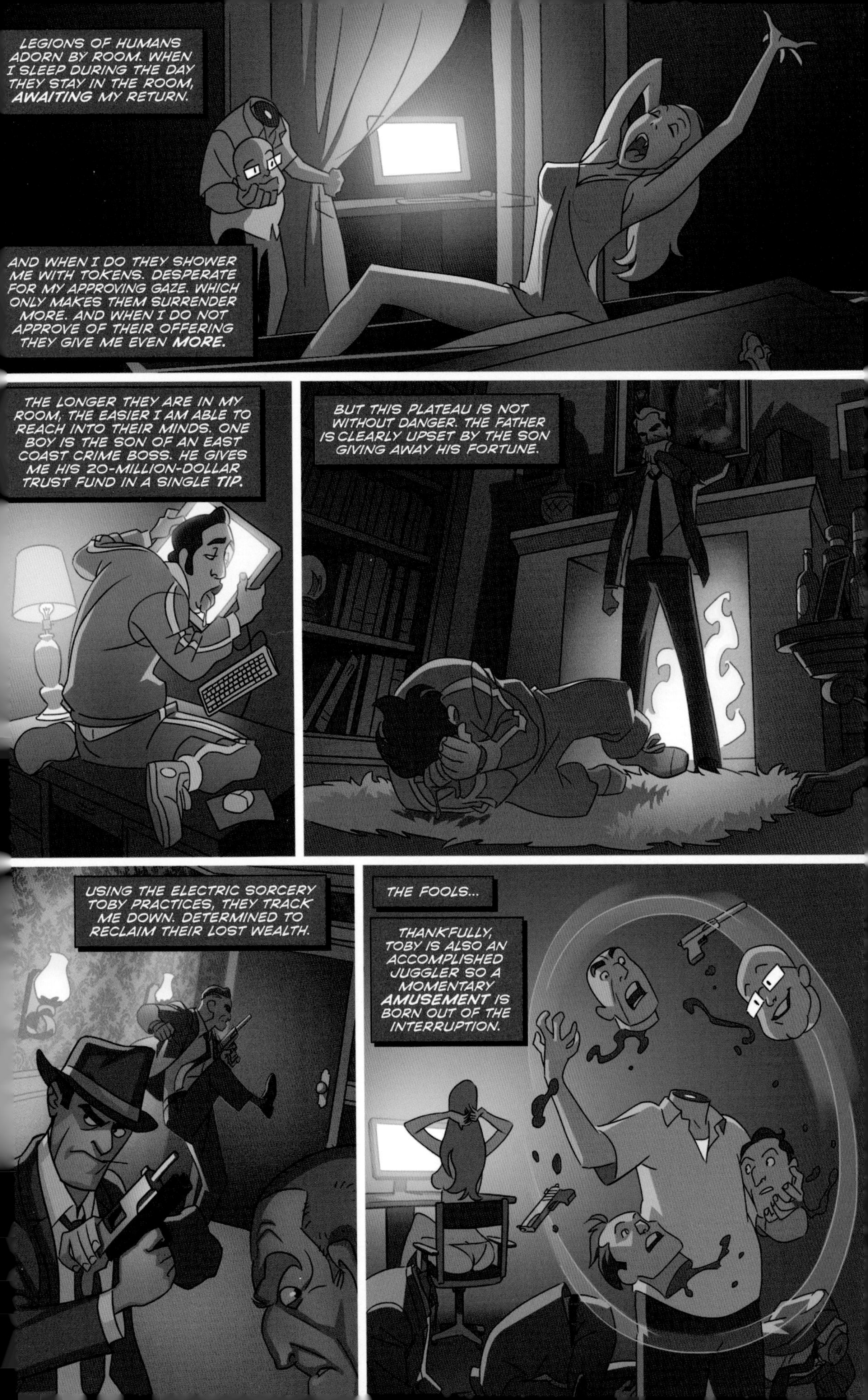
LEGIONS OF HUMANS ADORN BY ROOM. WHEN I SLEEP DURING THE DAY THEY STAY IN THE ROOM, AWAITING MY RETURN.
AND WHEN I DO THEY SHOWER ME WITH TOKENS. DESPERATE FOR MY APPROVING GAZE. WHICH ONLY MAKES THEM SURRENDER MORE. AND WHEN I DO NOT APPROVE OF THEIR OFFERING THEY GIVE ME EVEN MORE.
THE LONGER THEY ARE IN MY ROOM, THE EASIER I AM ABLE TO REACH INTO THEIR MINDS. ONE BOY IS THE SON OF AN EAST COAST CRIME BOSS. HE GIVES ME HIS 20-MILLION-DOLLAR TRUST FUND IN A SINGLE TIP.
BUT THIS PLATEAU IS NOT WITHOUT DANGER. THE FATHER IS CLEARLY UPSET BY THE SON GIVING AWAY HIS FORTUNE.
USING THE ELECTRIC SORCERY TOBY PRACTICES, THEY TRACK ME DOWN. DETERMINED TO RECLAIM THEIR LOST WEALTH.
THE FOOLS...
THANKFULLY, TOBY IS ALSO AN ACCOMPLISHED JUGGLER SO A MOMENTARY AMUSEMENT IS BORN OUT OF THE INTERRUPTION.

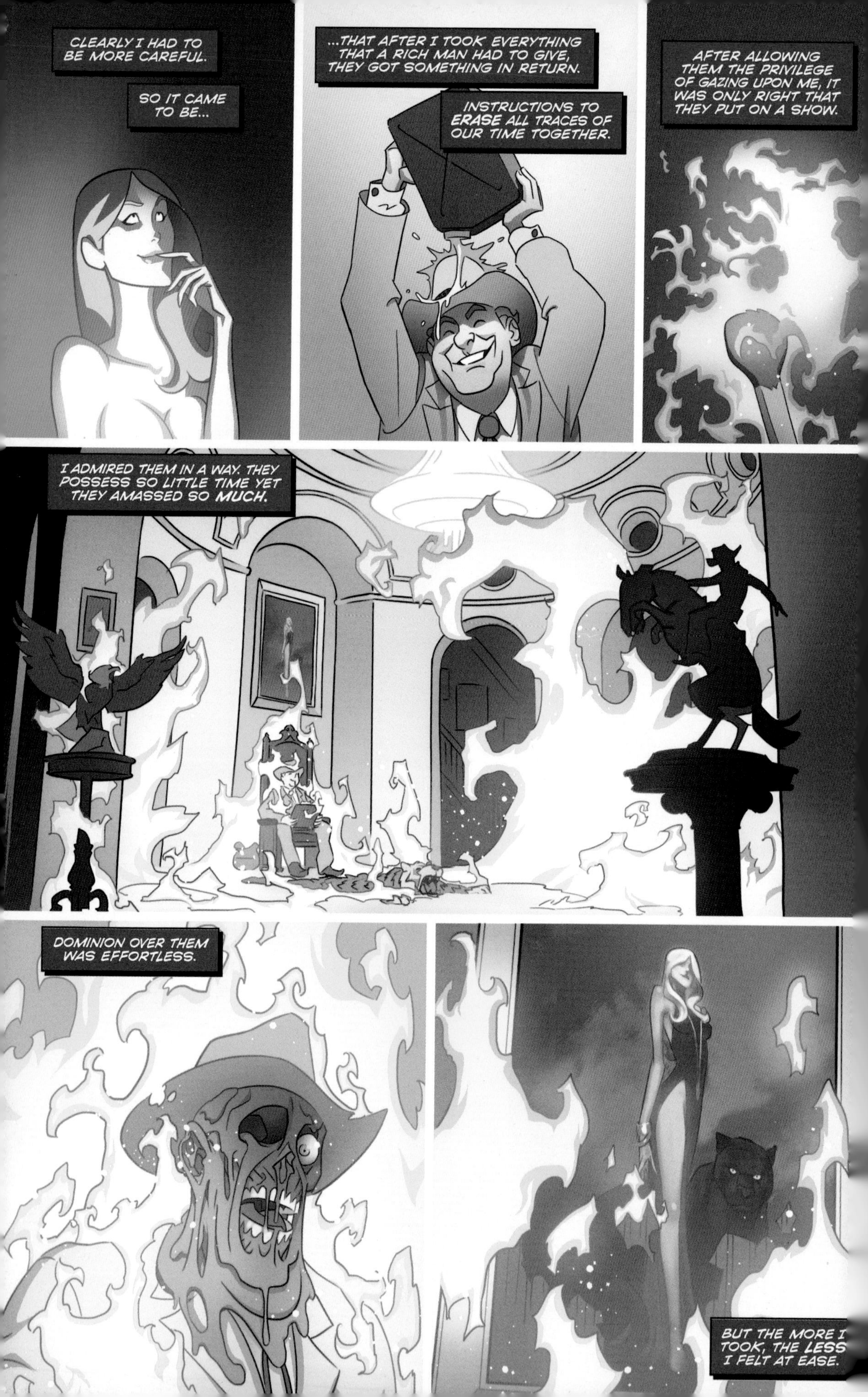
CLEARLY I HAD TO BE MORE CAREFUL.
SO IT CAME TO BE...
...THAT AFTER I TOOK EVERYTHING THAT A RICH MAN HAD TO GIVE, THEY GOT SOMETHING IN RETURN.
INSTRUCTIONS TO ERASE ALL TRACES OF OUR TIME TOGETHER.
AFTER ALLOWING THEM THE PRIVILEGE OF GAZING UPON ME, IT WAS ONLY RIGHT THAT THEY PUT ON A SHOW.
I ADMIRED THEM IN A WAY. THEY POSSESS SO LITTLE TIME YET THEY AMASSED SO MUCH.
DOMINION OVER THEM WAS EFFORTLESS.
BUT THE MORE I TOOK, THE LESS I FELT AT EASE.

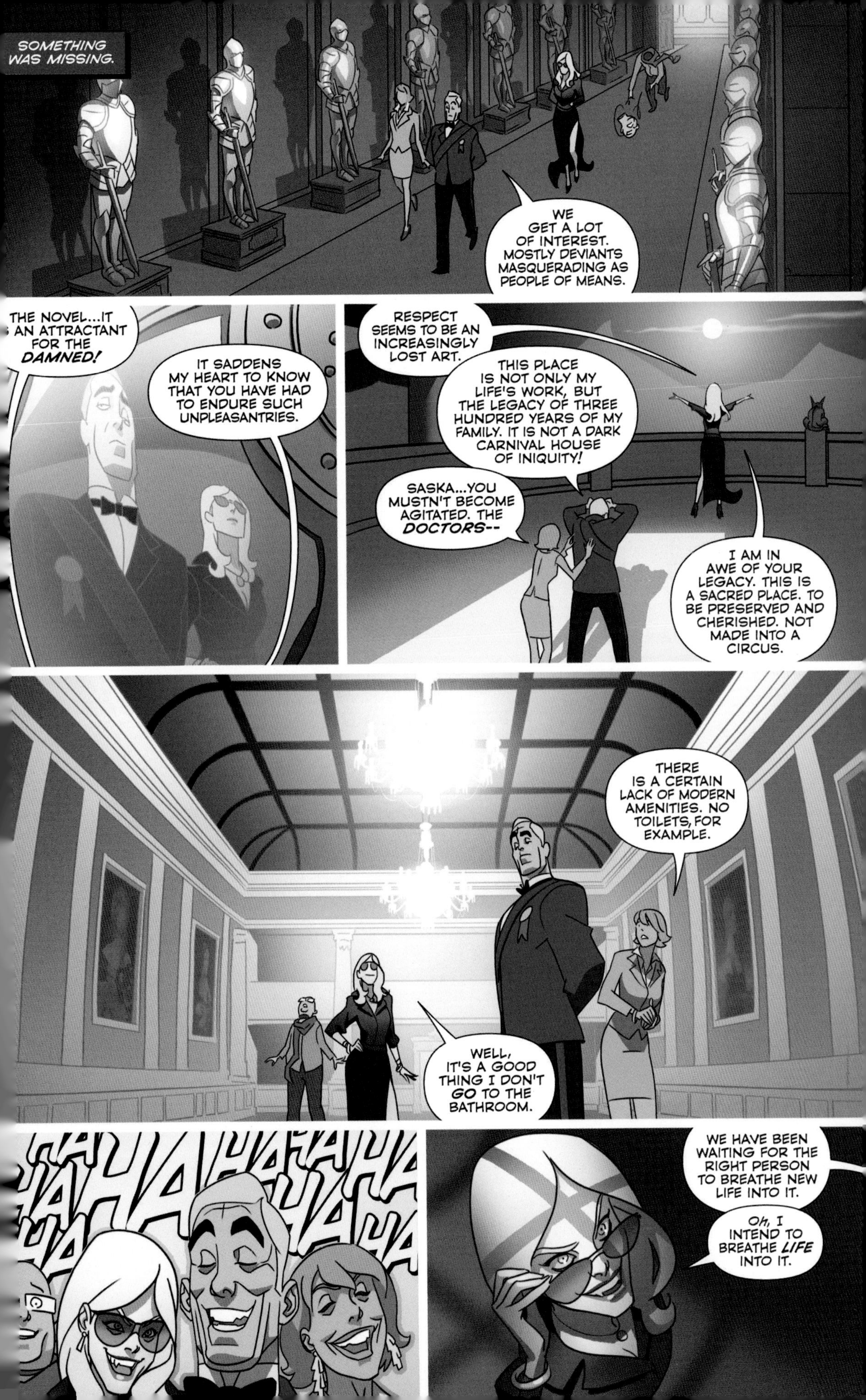
SOMETHING WAS MISSING.
WE GET A LOT OF INTEREST. MOSTLY DEVIANTS MASQUERADING AS PEOPLE OF MEANS.
THE NOVEL...IT 'S AN ATTRACTANT FOR THE DAMNED!
IT SADDENS MY HEART TO KNOW THAT YOU HAVE HAD TO ENDURE SUCH UNPLEASANTRIES.
RESPECT SEEMS TO BE AN INCREASINGLY LOST ART.
THIS PLACE IS NOT ONLY MY LIFE'S WORK, BUT THE LEGACY OF THREE HUNDRED YEARS OF MY FAMILY. IT IS NOT A DARK CARNIVAL HOUSE OF INIQUITY!
SASKA...YOU MUSTN'T BECOME AGITATED. THE DOCTORS--
I AM IN AWE OF YOUR LEGACY. THIS IS A SACRED PLACE. TO BE PRESERVED AND CHERISHED. NOT MADE INTO A CIRCUS.
THERE IS A CERTAIN LACK OF MODERN AMENITIES. NO TOILETS, FOR EXAMPLE.
WELL, IT'S A GOOD THING I DON'T GO TO THE BATHROOM.
HAHAHAHAHAHAHAHA
WE HAVE BEEN WAITING FOR THE RIGHT PERSON TO BREATHE NEW LIFE INTO IT.
Oh, I INTEND TO BREATHE LIFE INTO IT.

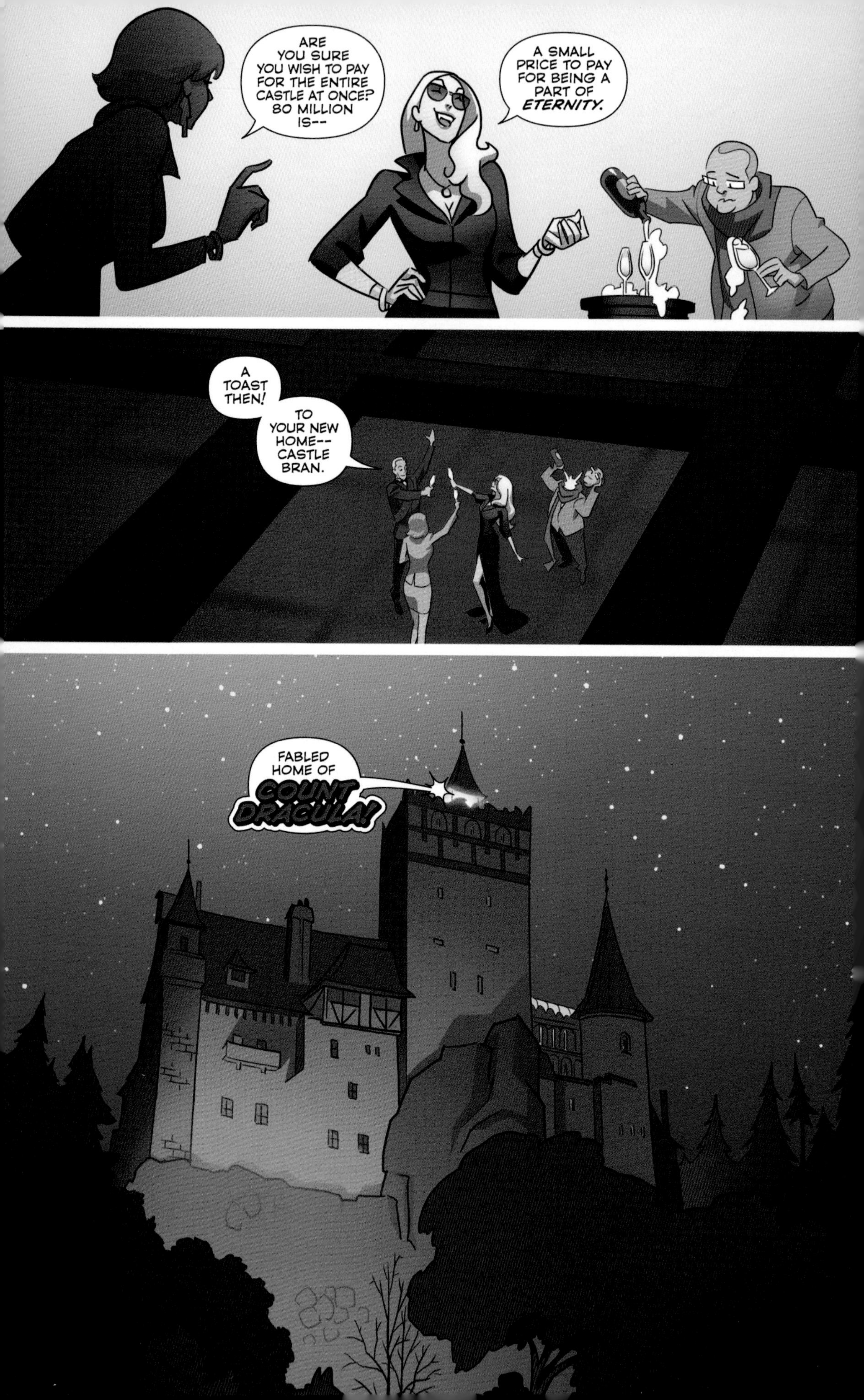
ARE YOU SURE YOU WISH TO PAY FOR THE ENTIRE CASTLE AT ONCE? 80 MILLION IS--
A SMALL PRICE TO PAY FOR BEING A PART OF *ETERNITY.*
A TOAST THEN!
TO YOUR NEW HOME-- CASTLE BRAN.
FABLED HOME OF
COUNT DRACULA!

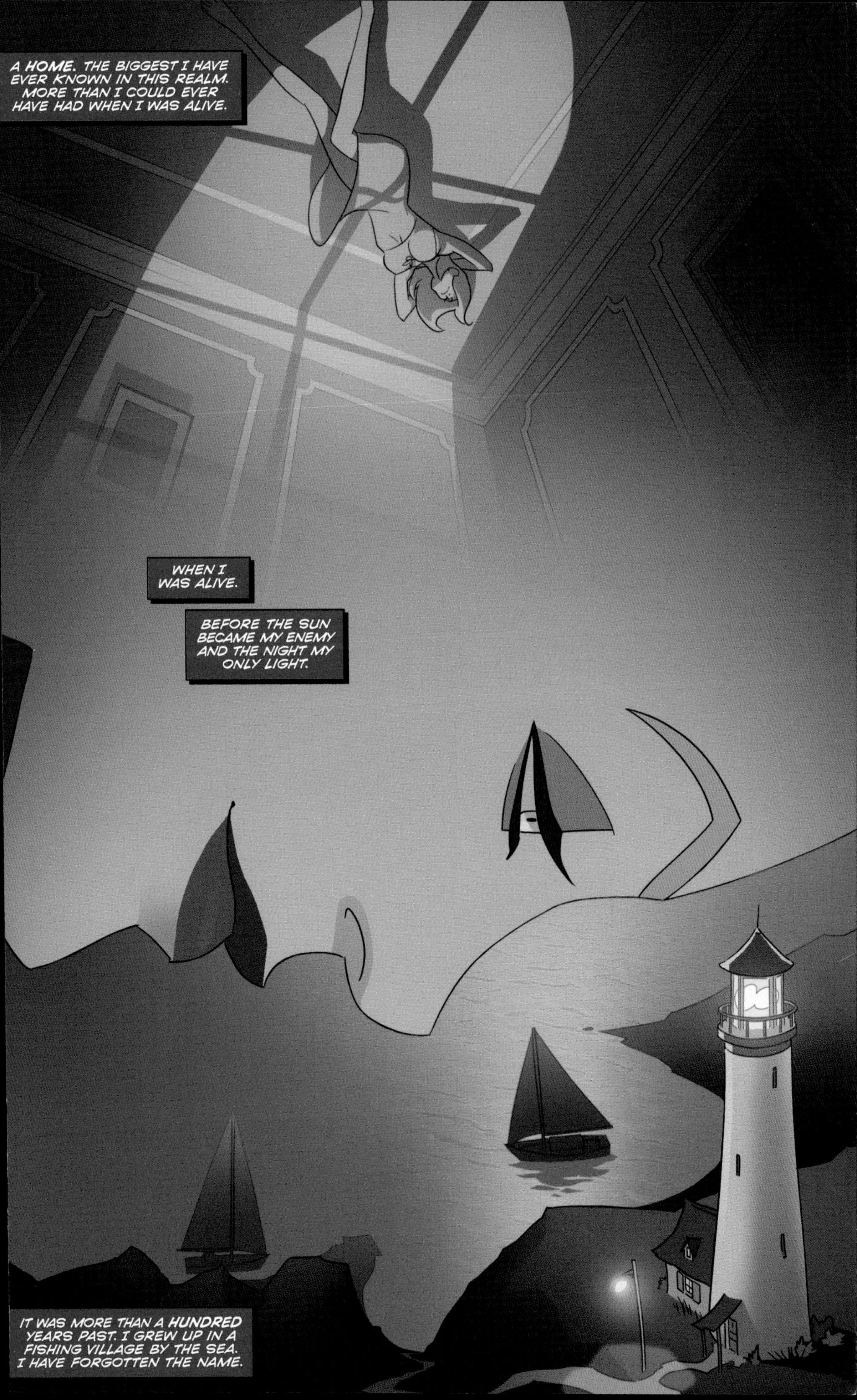
A HOME. THE BIGGEST I HAVE EVER KNOWN IN THIS REALM. MORE THAN I COULD EVER HAVE HAD WHEN I WAS ALIVE.
WHEN I WAS ALIVE.
BEFORE THE SUN BECAME MY ENEMY AND THE NIGHT MY ONLY LIGHT.
IT WAS MORE THAN A HUNDRED YEARS PAST. I GREW UP IN A FISHING VILLAGE BY THE SEA. I HAVE FORGOTTEN THE NAME.

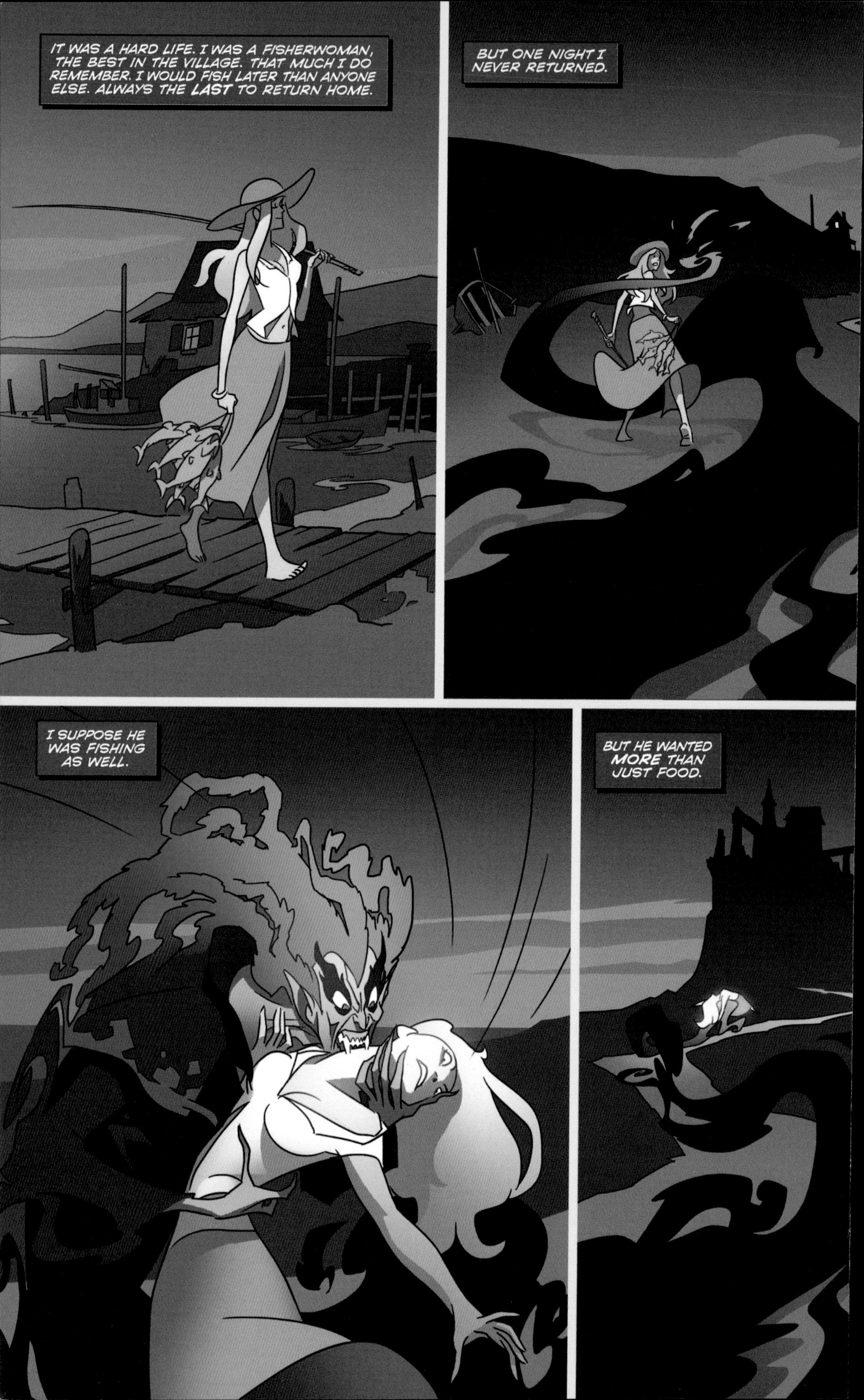
IT WAS A HARD LIFE. I WAS A FISHERWOMAN, THE BEST IN THE VILLAGE. THAT MUCH I DO REMEMBER. I WOULD FISH LATER THAN ANYONE ELSE. ALWAYS THE LAST TO RETURN HOME.
BUT ONE NIGHT I NEVER RETURNED.
I SUPPOSE HE WAS FISHING AS WELL.
BUT HE WANTED MORE THAN JUST FOOD.

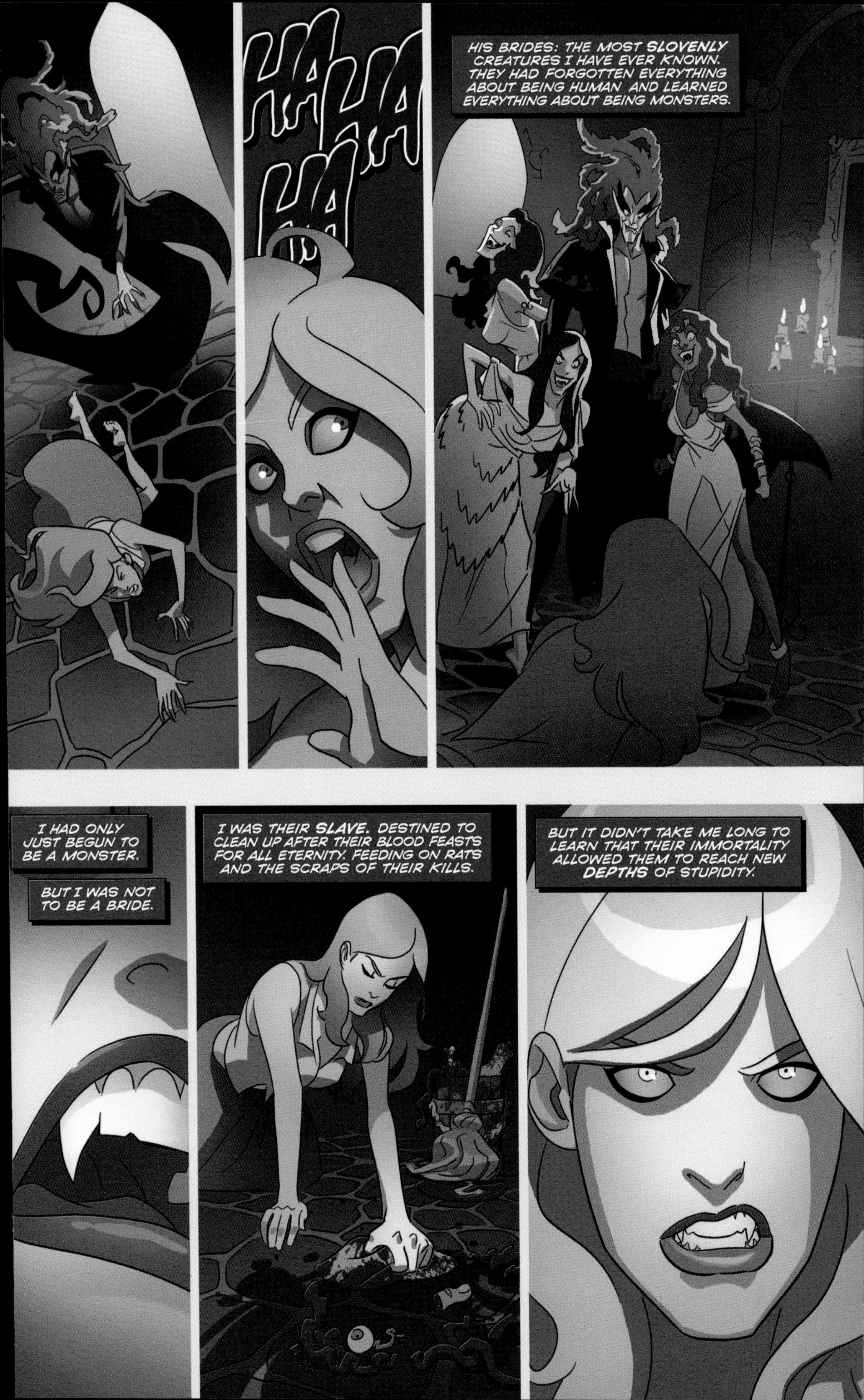

HA HA HA HA HA
HIS BRIDES: THE MOST SLOVENLY CREATURES I HAVE EVER KNOWN. THEY HAD FORGOTTEN EVERYTHING ABOUT BEING HUMAN AND LEARNED EVERYTHING ABOUT BEING MONSTERS.
I HAD ONLY JUST BEGUN TO BE A MONSTER.
BUT I WAS NOT TO BE A BRIDE.
I WAS THEIR SLAVE. DESTINED TO CLEAN UP AFTER THEIR BLOOD FEASTS FOR ALL ETERNITY. FEEDING ON RATS AND THE SCRAPS OF THEIR KILLS.
BUT IT DIDN'T TAKE ME LONG TO LEARN THAT THEIR IMMORTALITY ALLOWED THEM TO REACH NEW DEPTHS OF STUPIDITY.

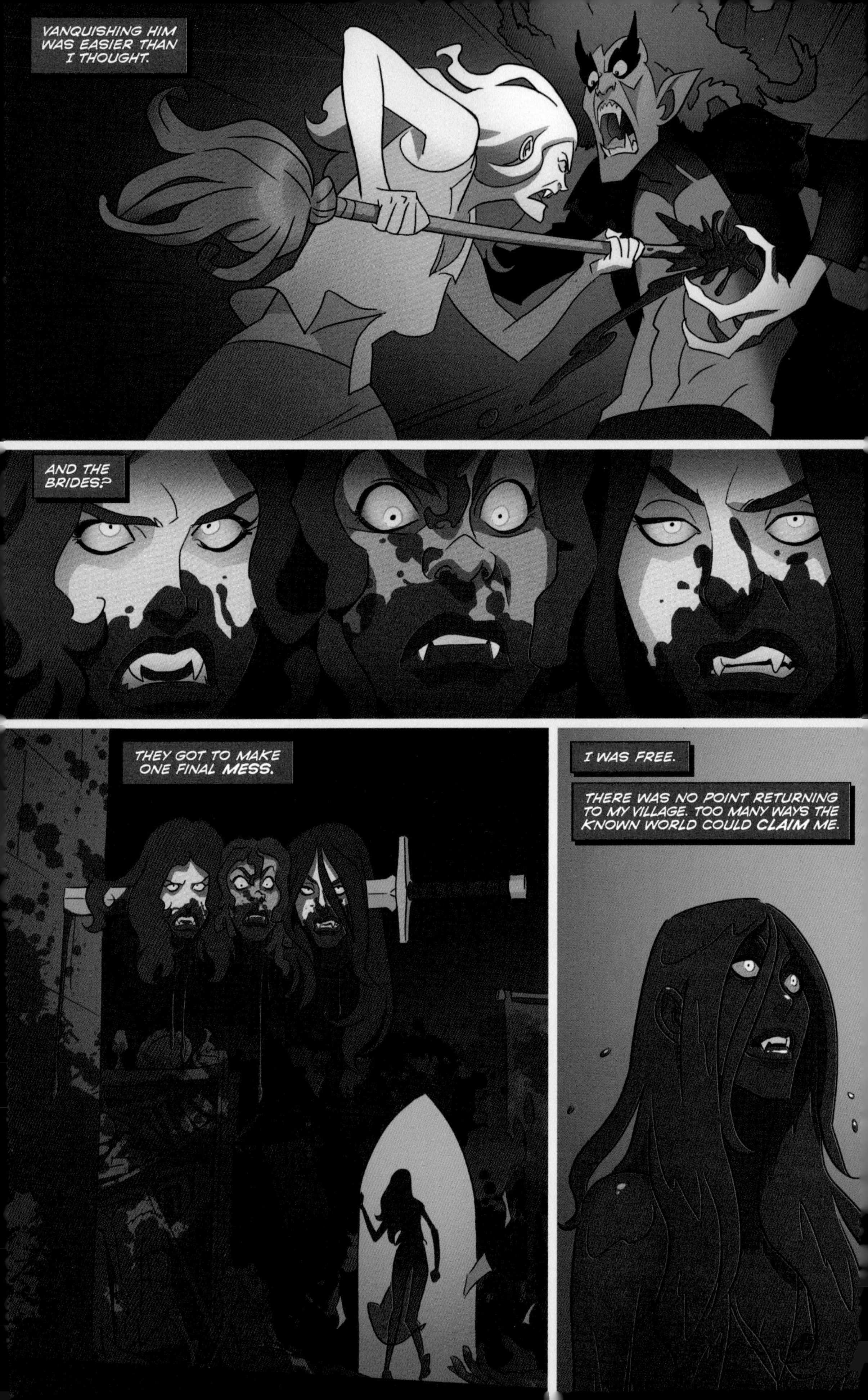
VANQUISHING HIM WAS EASIER THAN I THOUGHT.
AND THE BRIDES?
THEY GOT TO MAKE ONE FINAL MESS.
I WAS FREE.
THERE WAS NO POINT RETURNING TO MY VILLAGE. TOO MANY WAYS THE KNOWN WORLD COULD CLAIM ME.

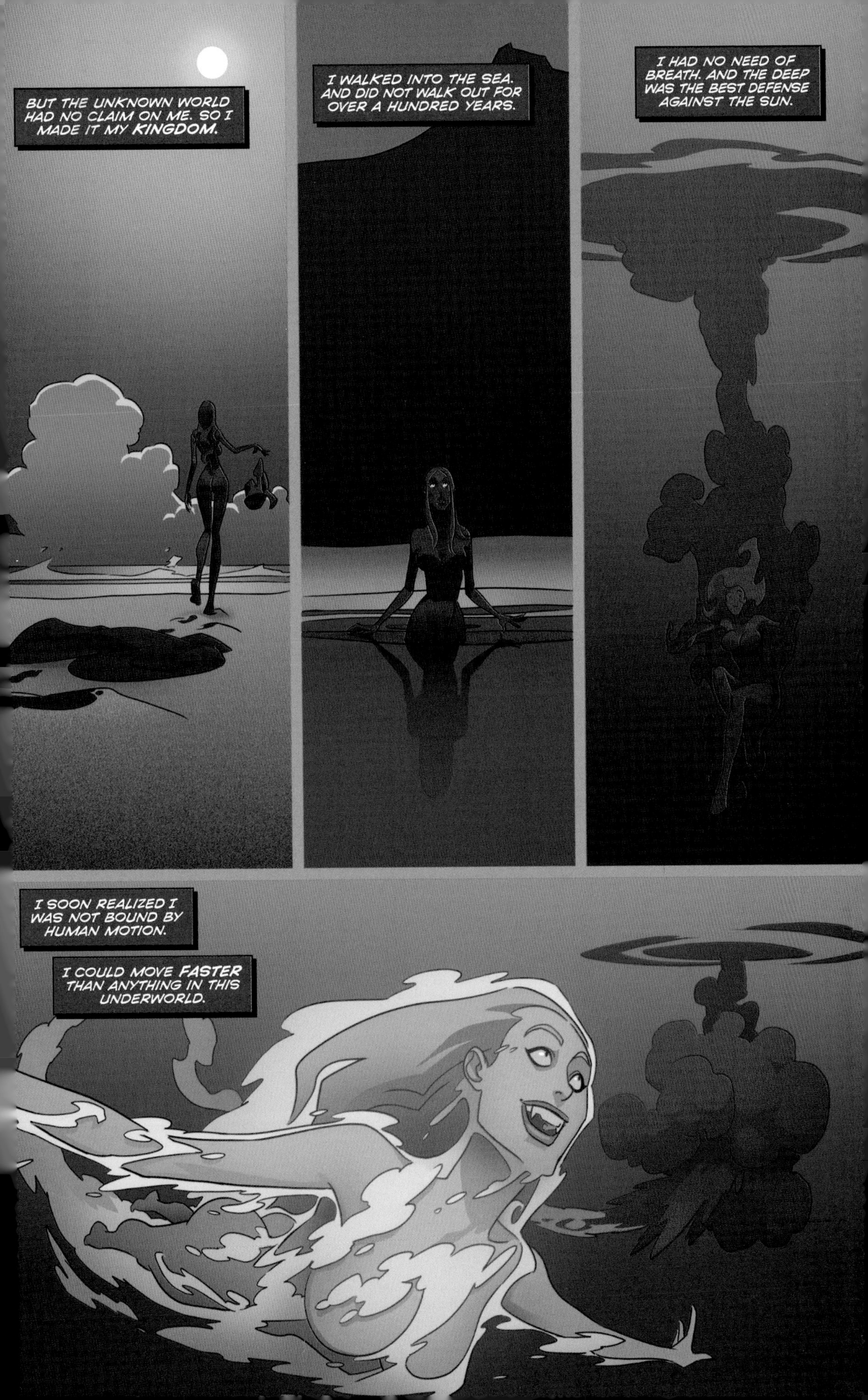
BUT THE UNKNOWN WORLD HAD NO CLAIM ON ME. SO I MADE IT MY KINGDOM.
I WALKED INTO THE SEA. AND DID NOT WALK OUT FOR OVER A HUNDRED YEARS.
I HAD NO NEED OF BREATH. AND THE DEEP WAS THE BEST DEFENSE AGAINST THE SUN.
I SOON REALIZED I WAS NOT BOUND BY HUMAN MOTION.
I COULD MOVE FASTER THAN ANYTHING IN THIS UNDERWORLD.

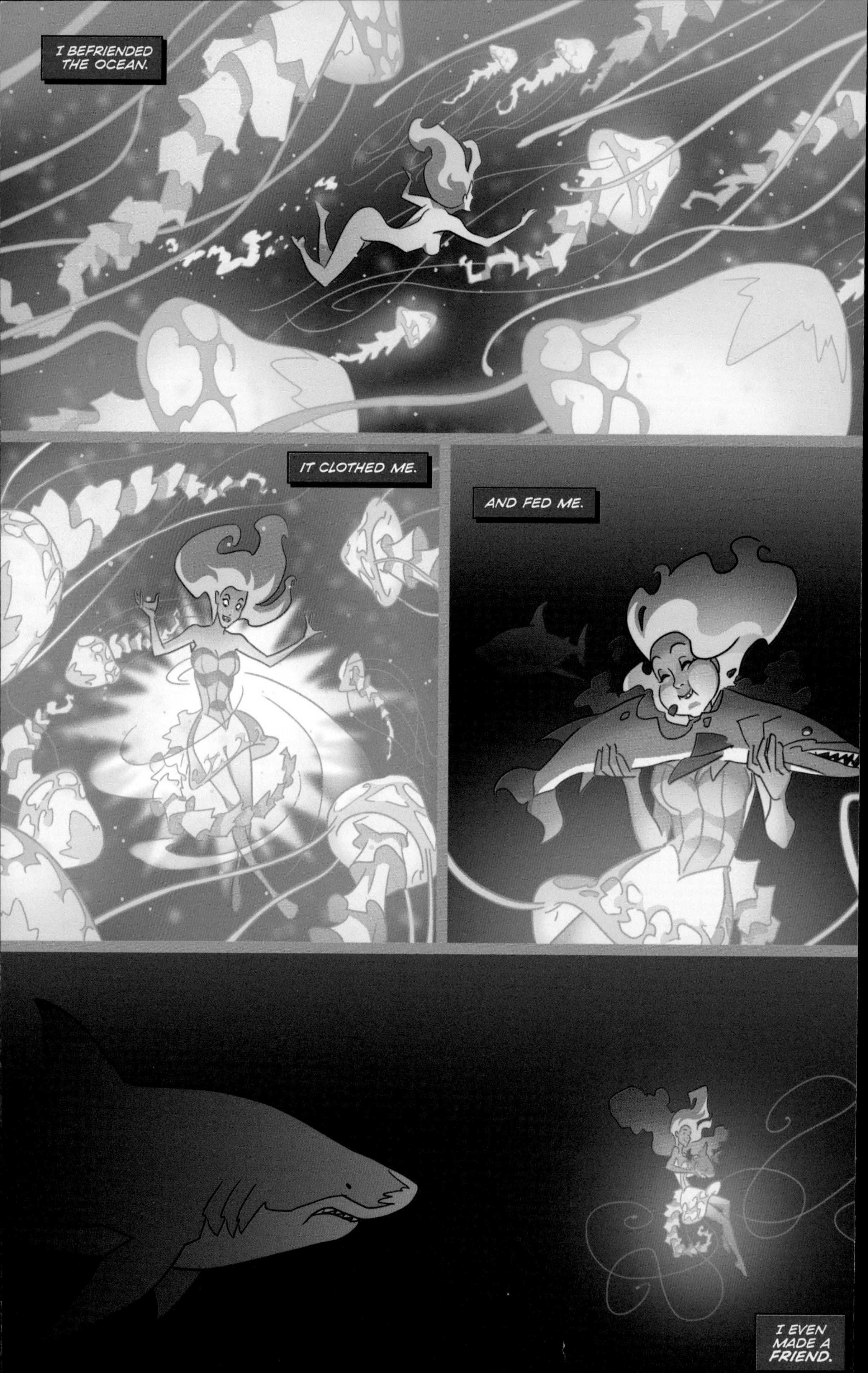
I BEFRIENDED THE OCEAN.
IT CLOTHED ME.
AND FED ME.
I EVEN MADE A FRIEND.

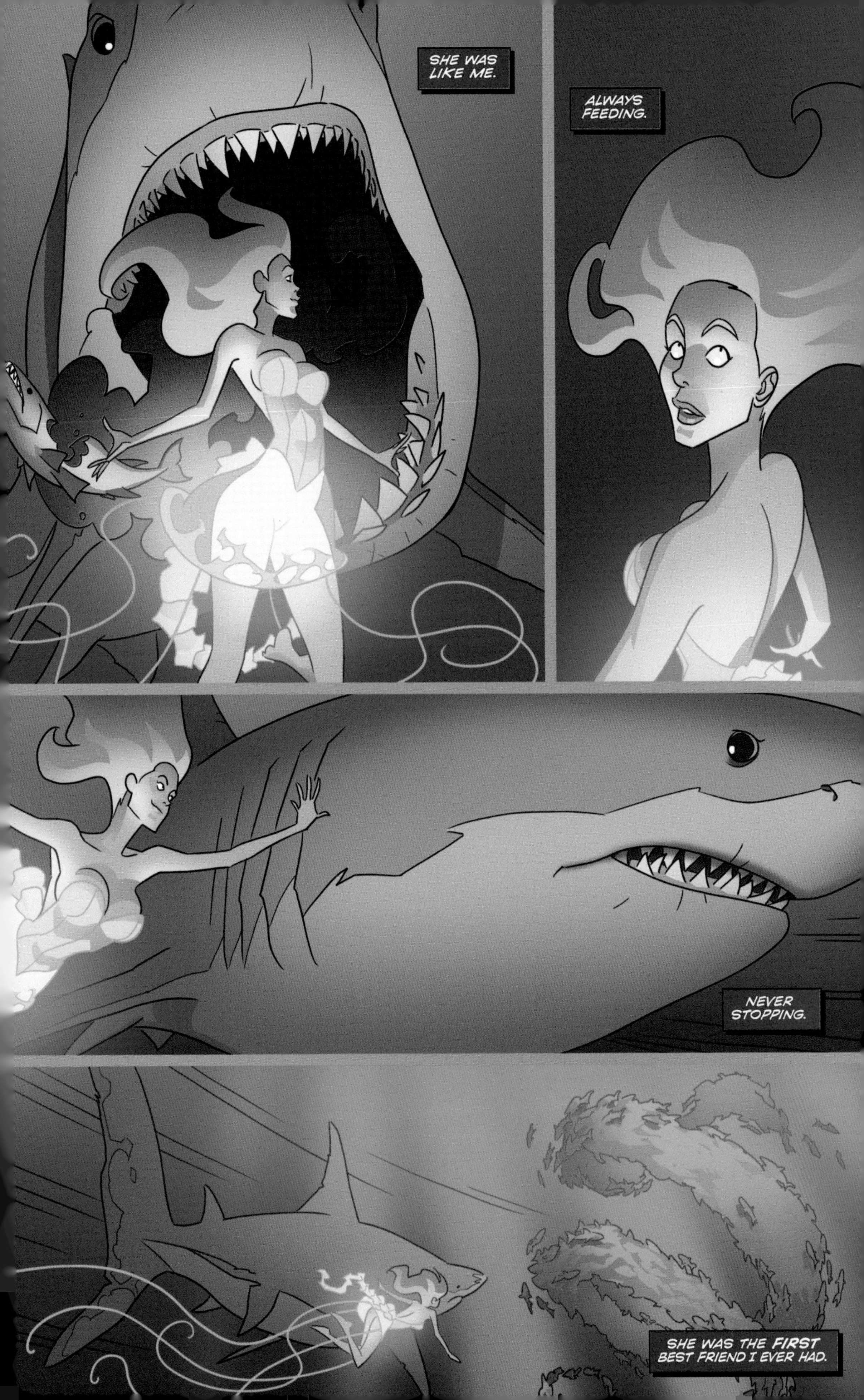
SHE WAS LIKE ME.
ALWAYS FEEDING.
NEVER STOPPING.
SHE WAS THE FIRST BEST FRIEND I EVER HAD.

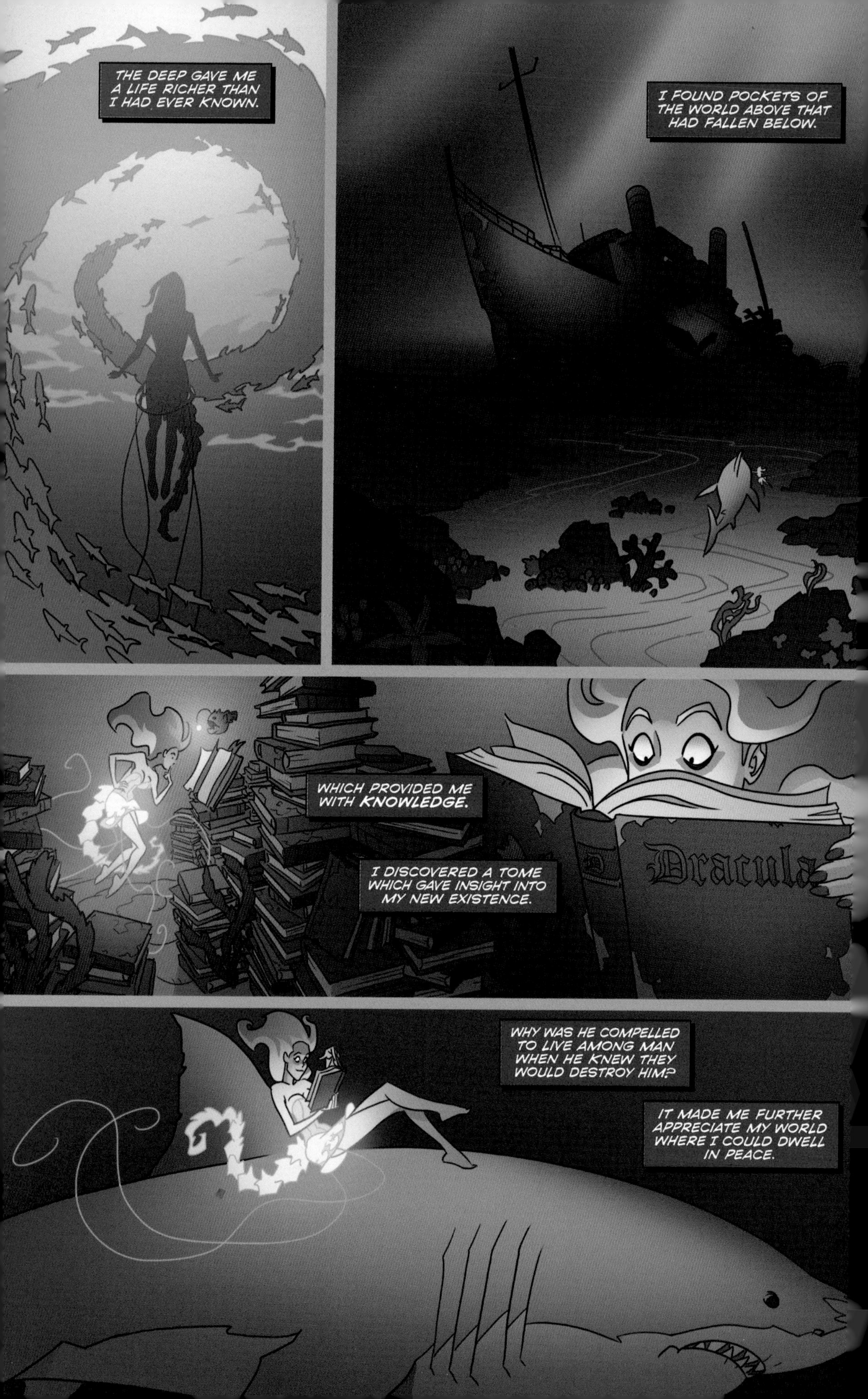
THE DEEP GAVE ME A LIFE RICHER THAN I HAD EVER KNOWN.
I FOUND POCKETS OF THE WORLD ABOVE THAT HAD FALLEN BELOW.
WHICH PROVIDED ME WITH KNOWLEDGE.
I DISCOVERED A TOME WHICH GAVE INSIGHT INTO MY NEW EXISTENCE.
Dracula
WHY WAS HE COMPELLED TO LIVE AMONG MAN WHEN HE KNEW THEY WOULD DESTROY HIM?
IT MADE ME FURTHER APPRECIATE MY WORLD WHERE I COULD DWELL IN PEACE.

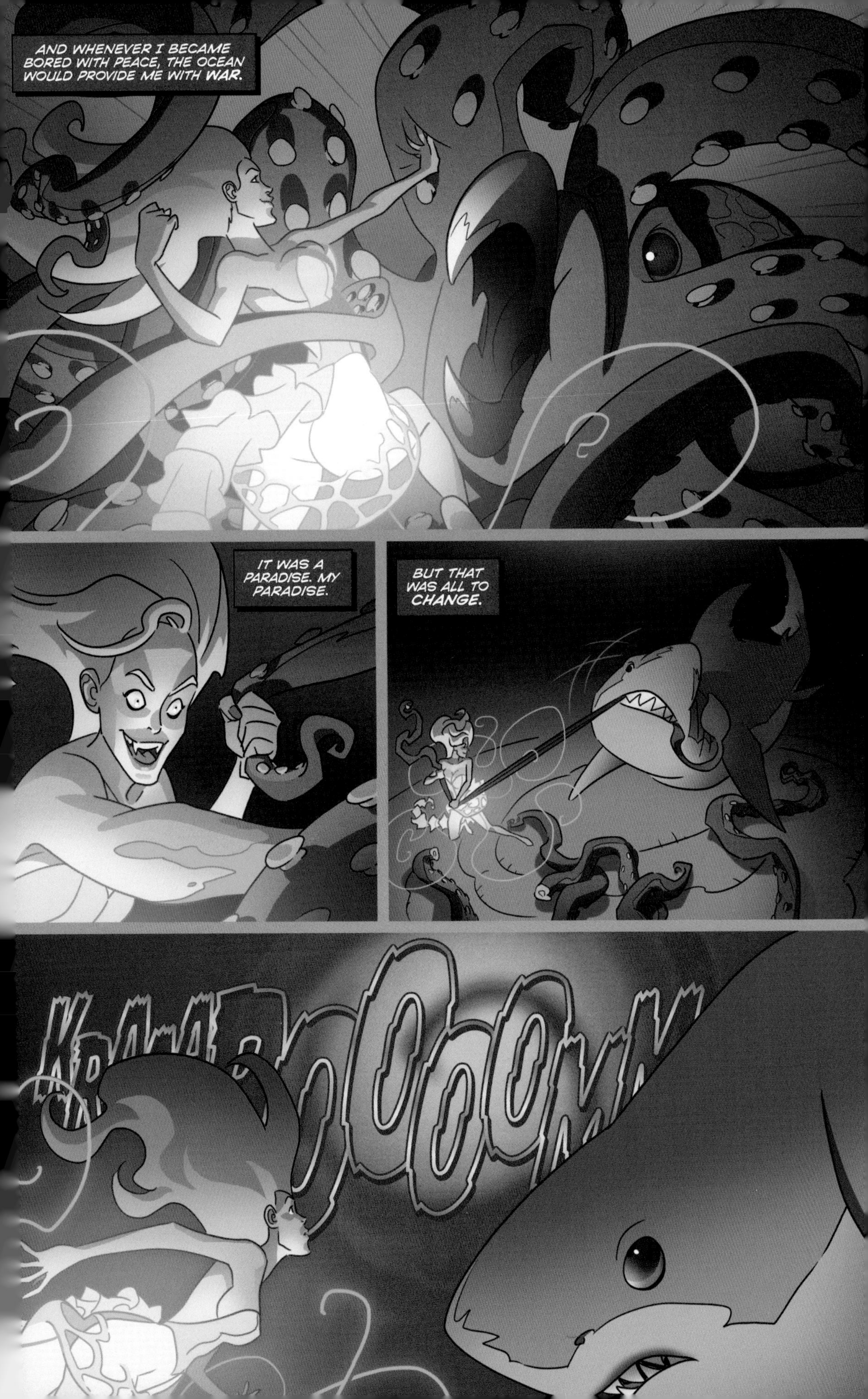
AND WHENEVER I BECAME BORED WITH PEACE, THE OCEAN WOULD PROVIDE ME WITH WAR.
IT WAS A PARADISE. MY PARADISE.
BUT THAT WAS ALL TO CHANGE.

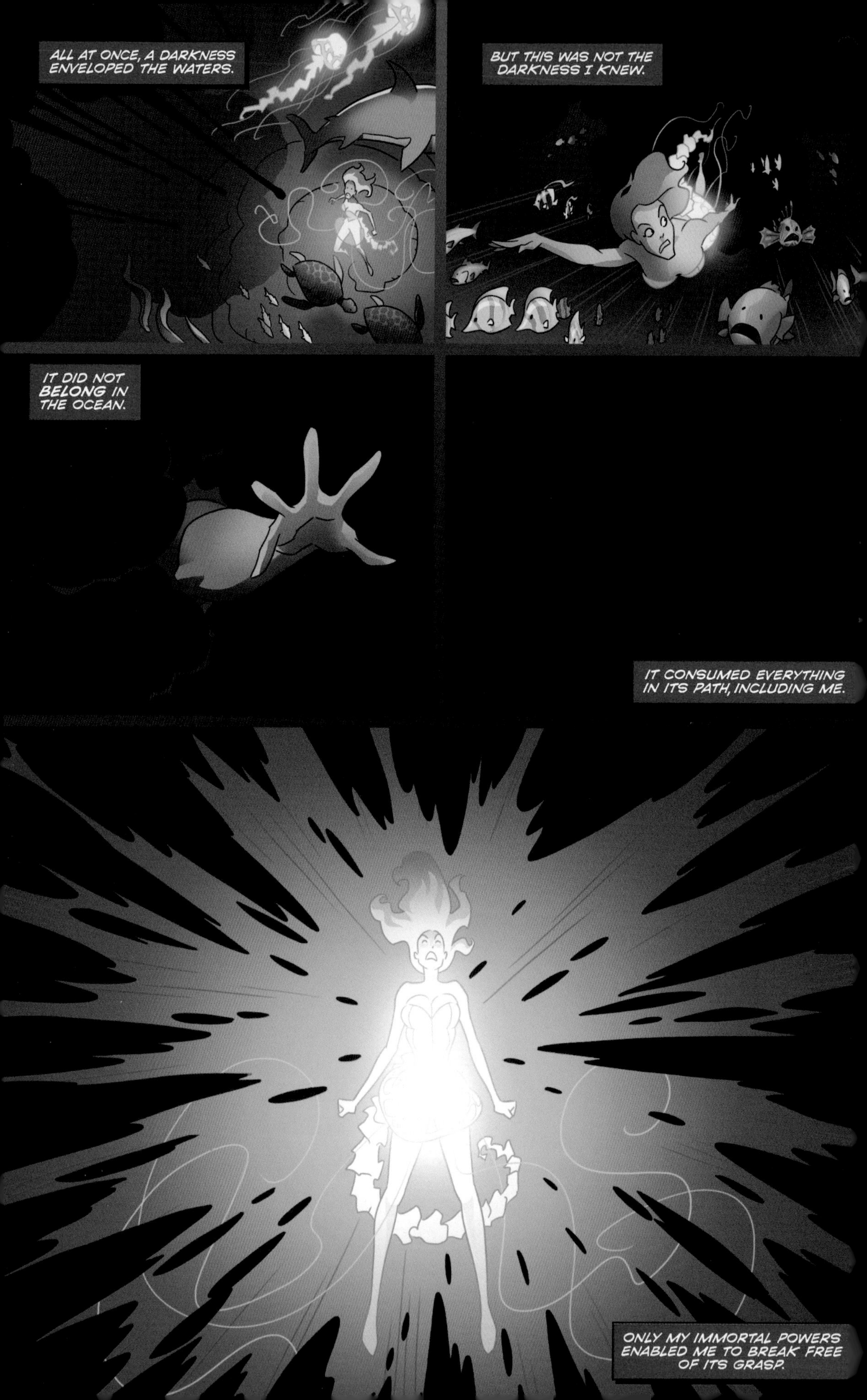
ALL AT ONCE, A DARKNESS ENVELOPED THE WATERS.
BUT THIS WAS NOT THE DARKNESS I KNEW.
IT DID NOT BELONG IN THE OCEAN.
IT CONSUMED EVERYTHING IN ITS PATH, INCLUDING ME.
ONLY MY IMMORTAL POWERS ENABLED ME TO BREAK FREE OF ITS GRASP.

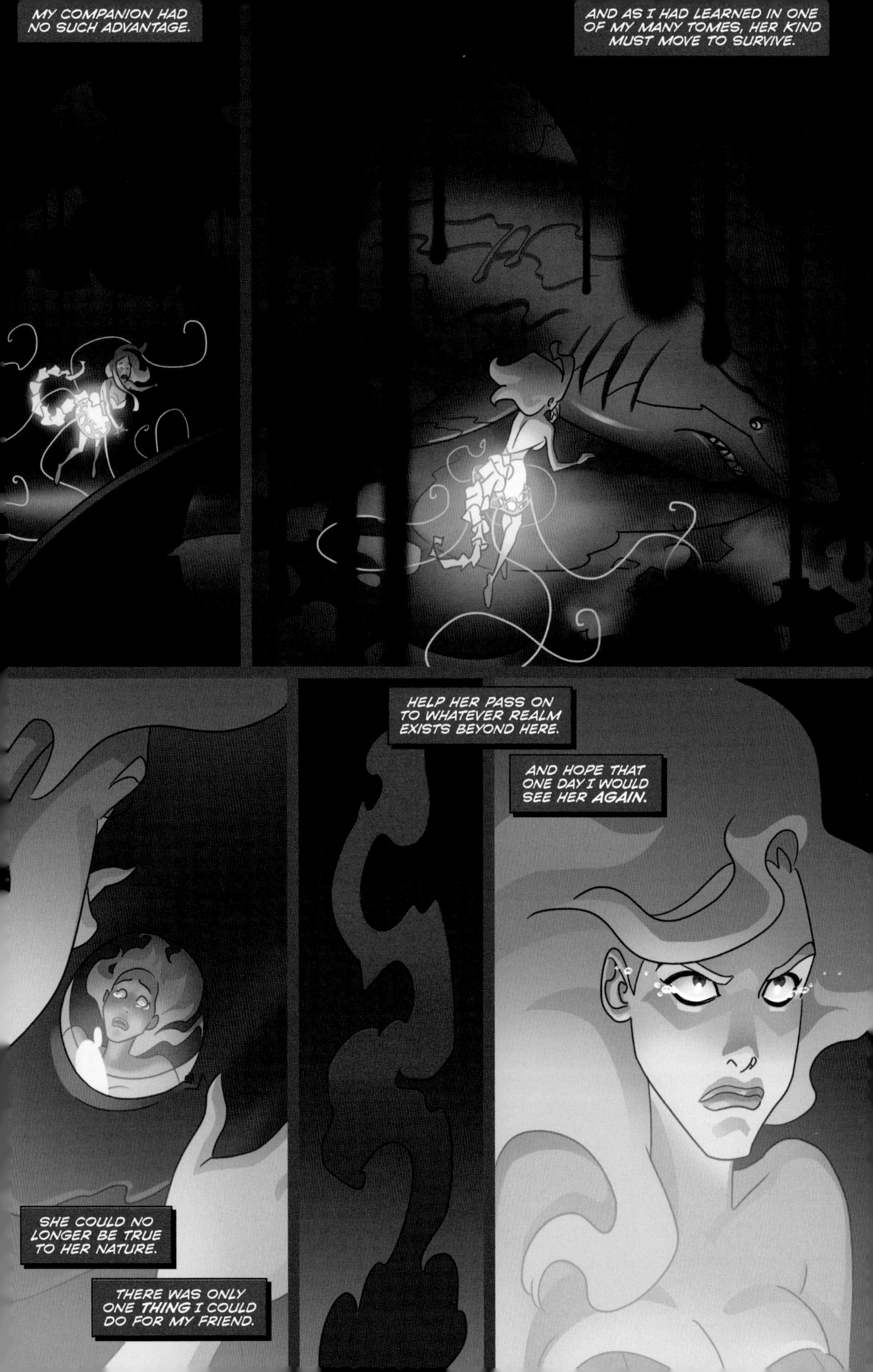
MY COMPANION HAD NO SUCH ADVANTAGE.
AND AS I HAD LEARNED IN ONE OF MY MANY TOMES, HER KIND MUST MOVE TO SURVIVE.
SHE COULD NO LONGER BE TRUE TO HER NATURE.
THERE WAS ONLY ONE THING I COULD DO FOR MY FRIEND.
HELP HER PASS ON TO WHATEVER REALM EXISTS BEYOND HERE.
AND HOPE THAT ONE DAY I WOULD SEE HER AGAIN.

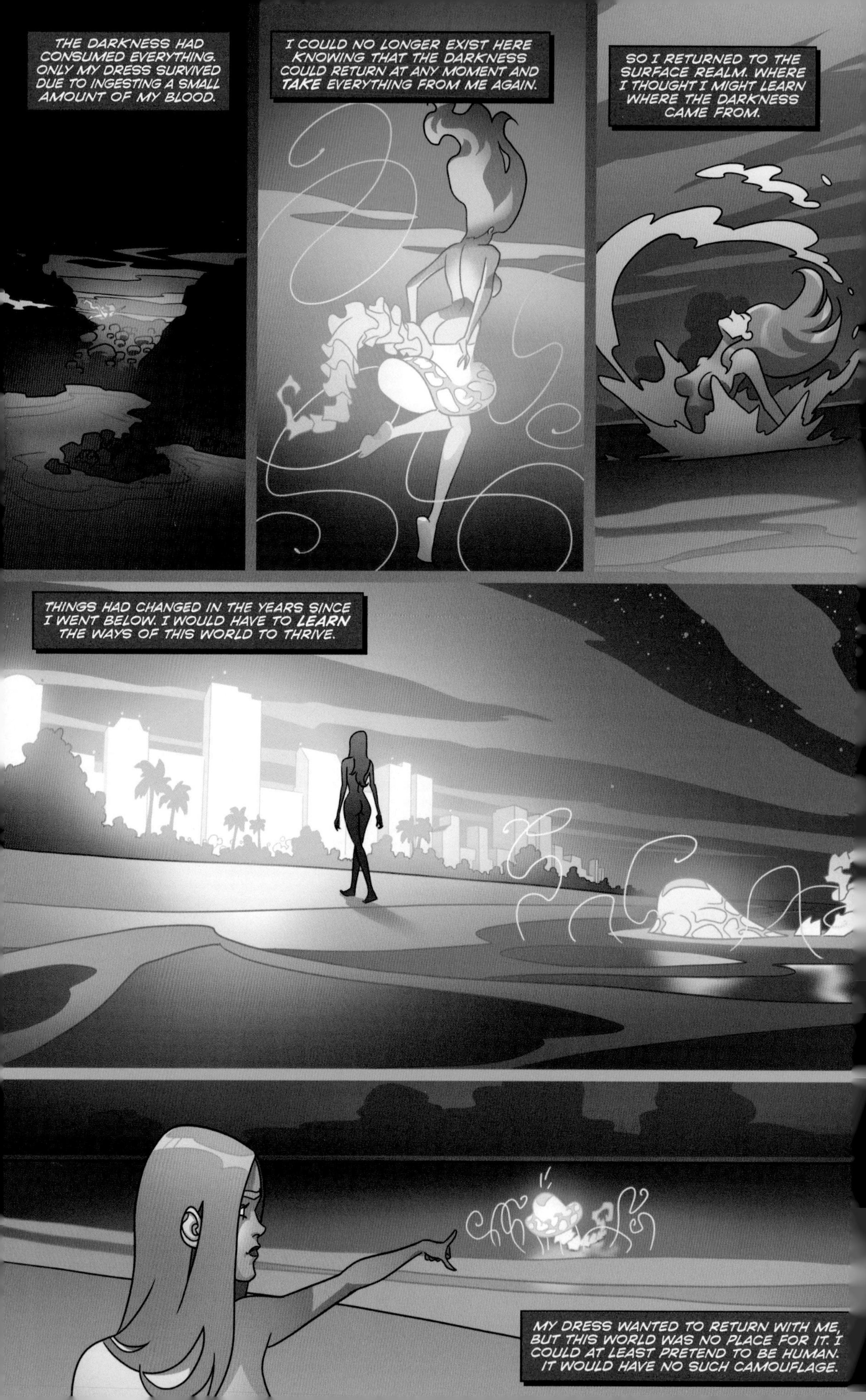
THE DARKNESS HAD CONSUMED EVERYTHING. ONLY MY DRESS SURVIVED DUE TO INGESTING A SMALL AMOUNT OF MY BLOOD.
I COULD NO LONGER EXIST HERE KNOWING THAT THE DARKNESS COULD RETURN AT ANY MOMENT AND TAKE EVERYTHING FROM ME AGAIN.
SO I RETURNED TO THE SURFACE REALM. WHERE I THOUGHT I MIGHT LEARN WHERE THE DARKNESS CAME FROM.
THINGS HAD CHANGED IN THE YEARS SINCE I WENT BELOW. I WOULD HAVE TO LEARN THE WAYS OF THIS WORLD TO THRIVE.
MY DRESS WANTED TO RETURN WITH ME, BUT THIS WORLD WAS NO PLACE FOR IT. I COULD AT LEAST PRETEND TO BE HUMAN. IT WOULD HAVE NO SUCH CAMOUFLAGE.

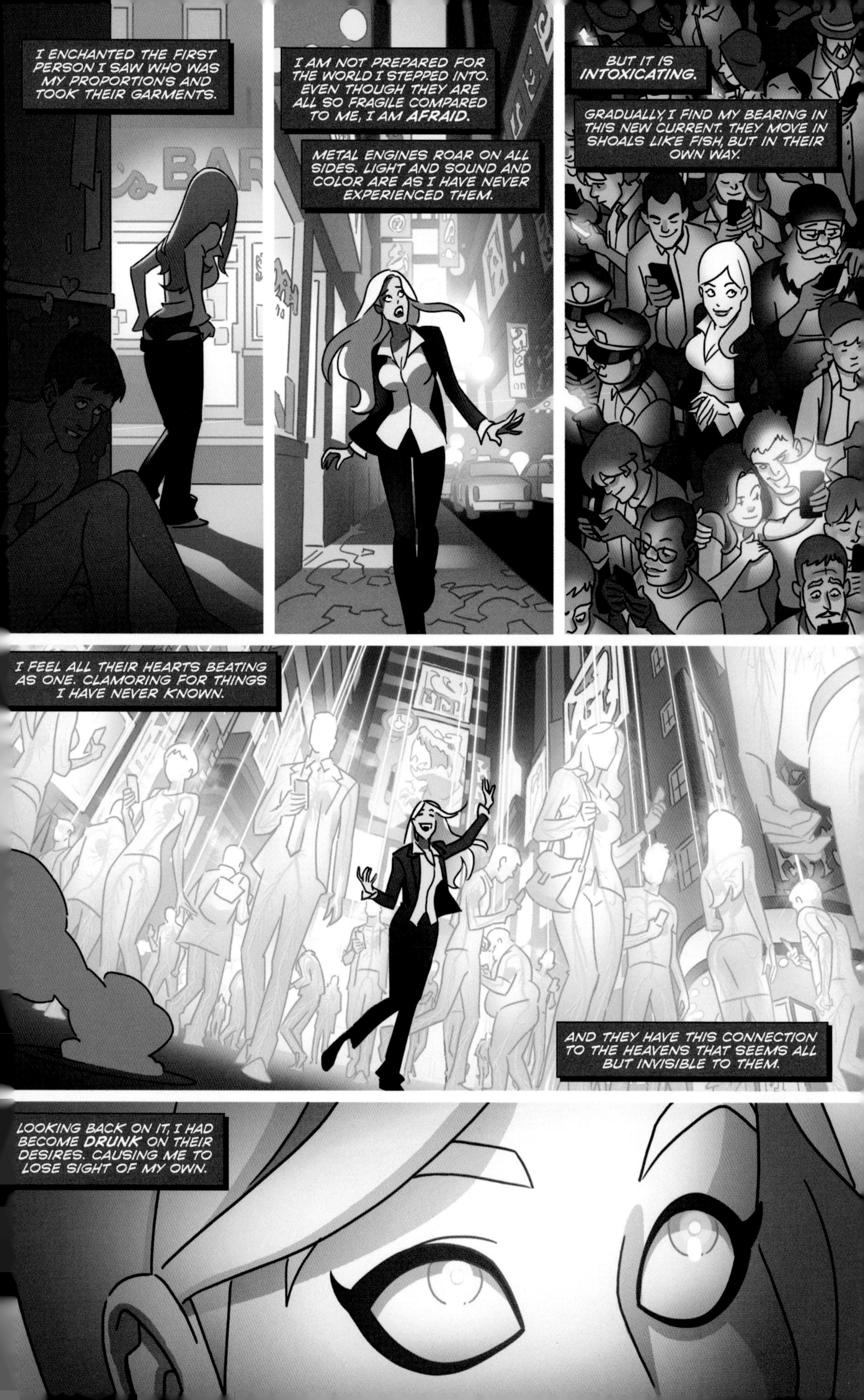
I ENCHANTED THE FIRST PERSON I SAW WHO WAS MY PROPORTIONS AND TOOK THEIR GARMENTS.
I AM NOT PREPARED FOR THE WORLD I STEPPED INTO. EVEN THOUGH THEY ARE ALL SO FRAGILE COMPARED TO ME, I AM AFRAID.
METAL ENGINES ROAR ON ALL SIDES. LIGHT AND SOUND AND COLOR ARE AS I HAVE NEVER EXPERIENCED THEM.
BUT IT IS INTOXICATING.
GRADUALLY, I FIND MY BEARING IN THIS NEW CURRENT. THEY MOVE IN SHOALS LIKE FISH, BUT IN THEIR OWN WAY.
I FEEL ALL THEIR HEARTS BEATING AS ONE. CLAMORING FOR THINGS I HAVE NEVER KNOWN.
AND THEY HAVE THIS CONNECTION TO THE HEAVENS THAT SEEMS ALL BUT INVISIBLE TO THEM.
LOOKING BACK ON IT, I HAD BECOME DRUNK ON THEIR DESIRES. CAUSING ME TO LOSE SIGHT OF MY OWN.

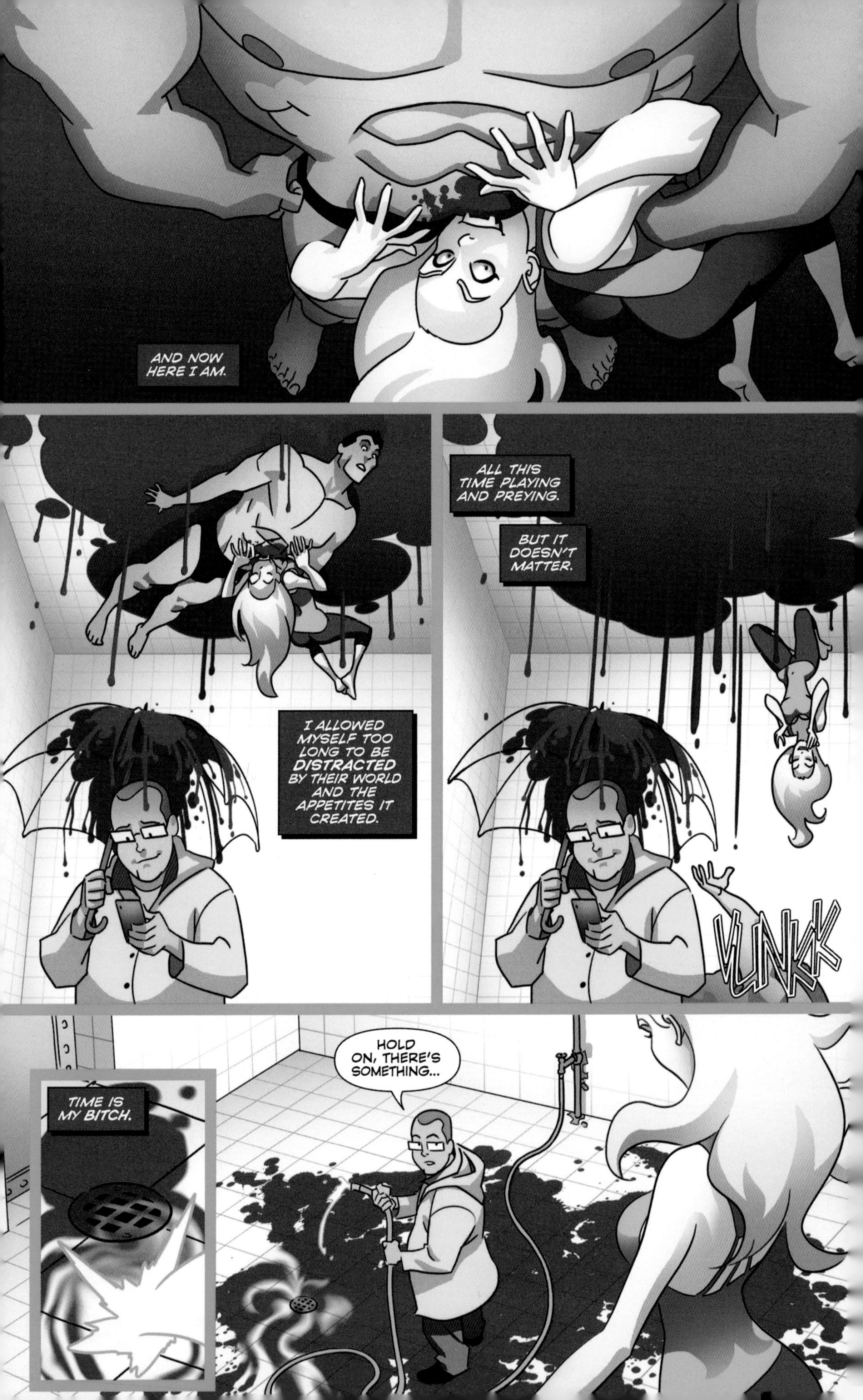
AND NOW HERE I AM.
I ALLOWED MYSELF TOO LONG TO BE DISTRACTED BY THEIR WORLD AND THE APPETITES IT CREATED.
ALL THIS TIME PLAYING AND PREYING.
BUT IT DOESN'T MATTER.
VLUNKK
TIME IS MY BITCH.
HOLD ON, THERE'S SOMETHING...

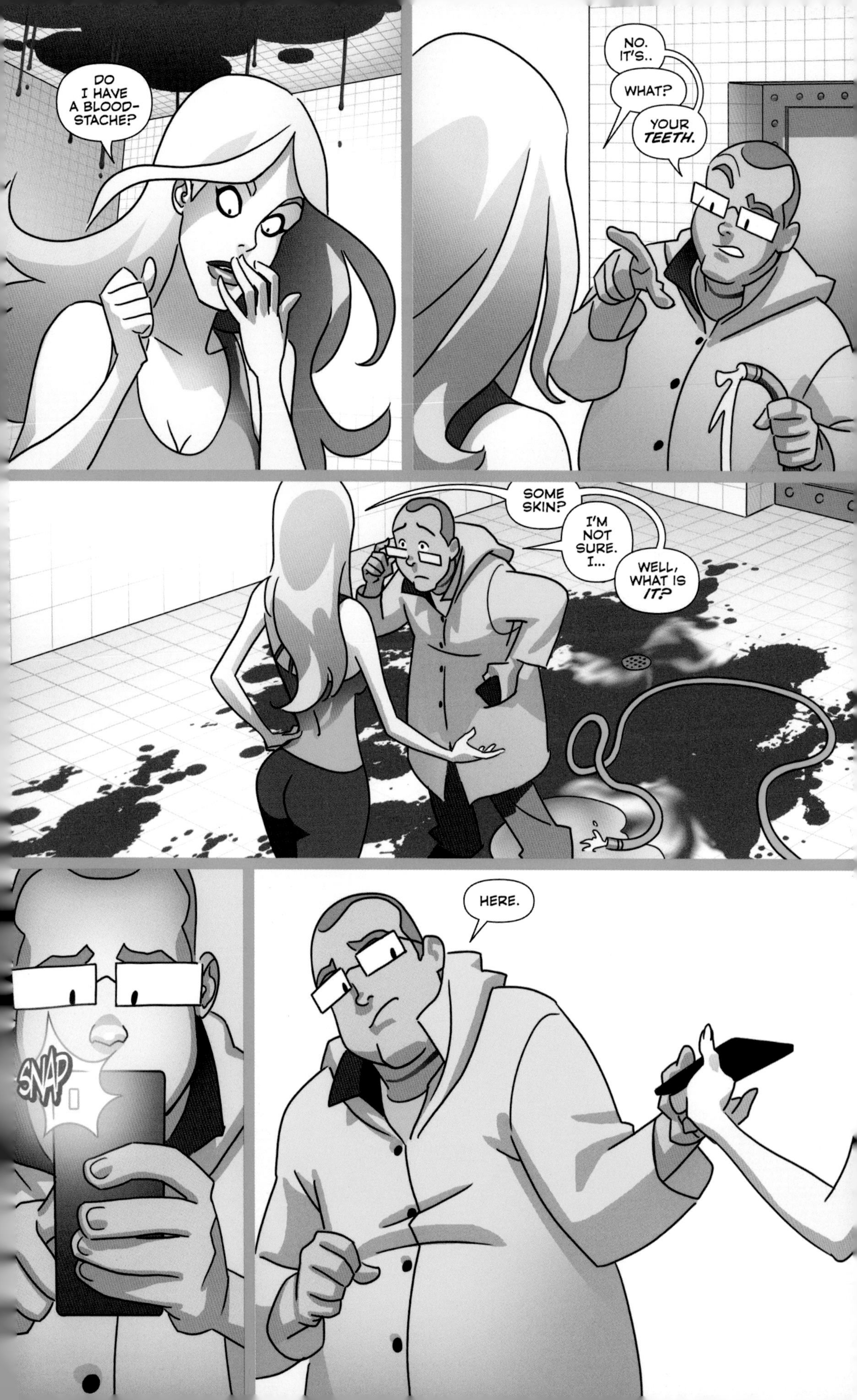
DO I HAVE A BLOOD-STACHE?
NO. IT'S..
WHAT?
YOUR *TEETH.*
SOME SKIN?
I'M NOT SURE. I...
WELL, WHAT IS *IT?*
SNAP
HERE.

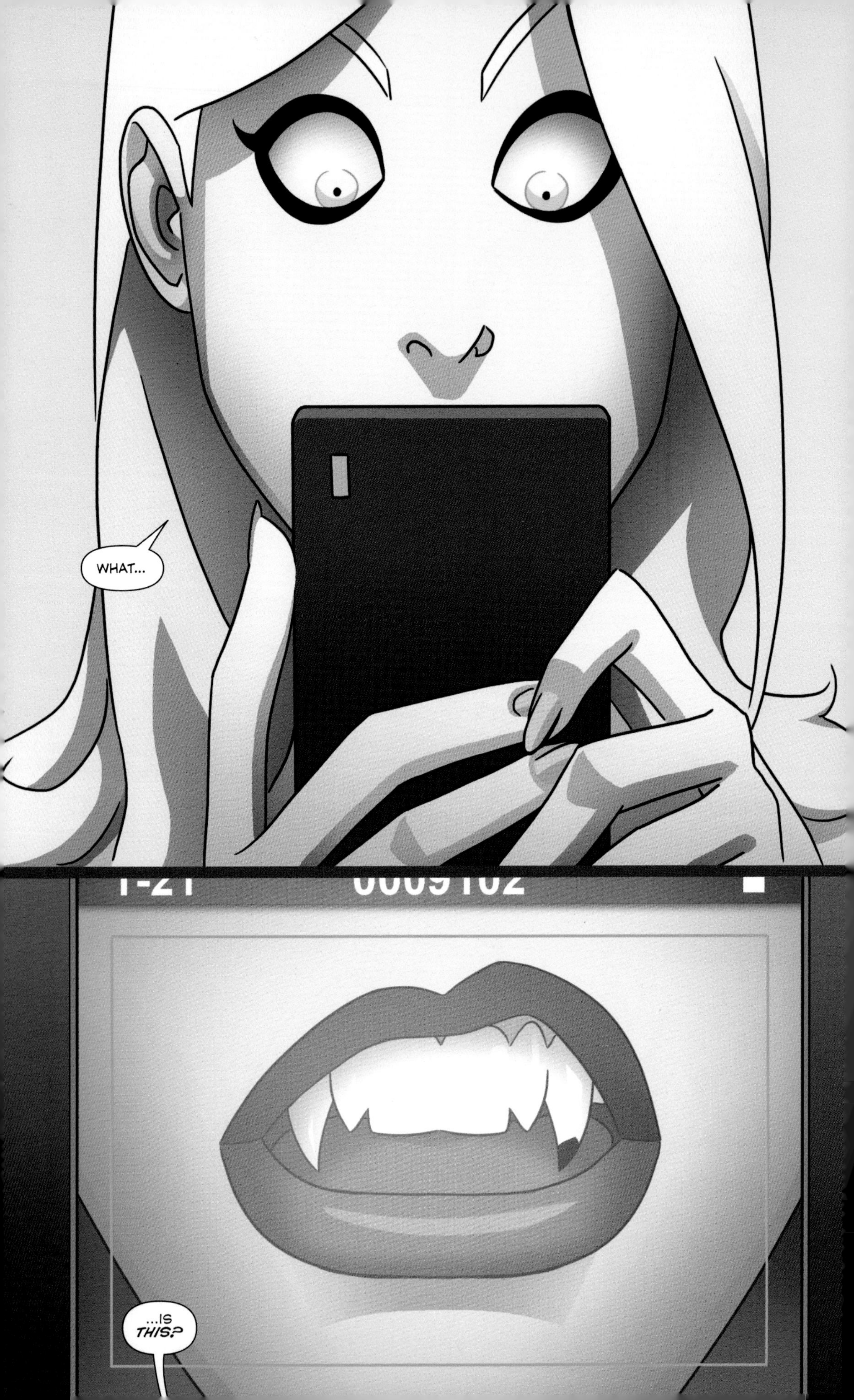
WHAT...
...IS THIS?

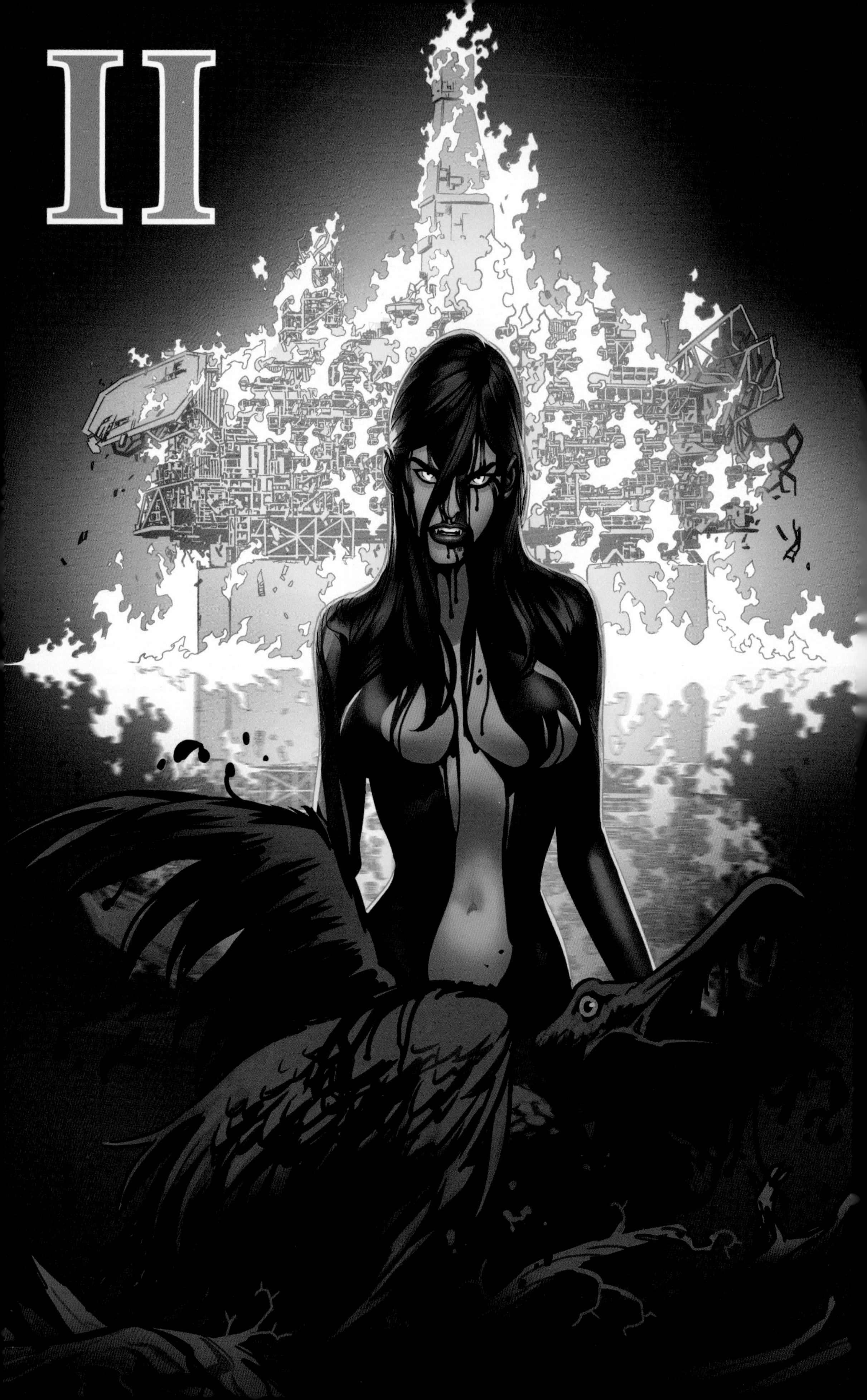
II

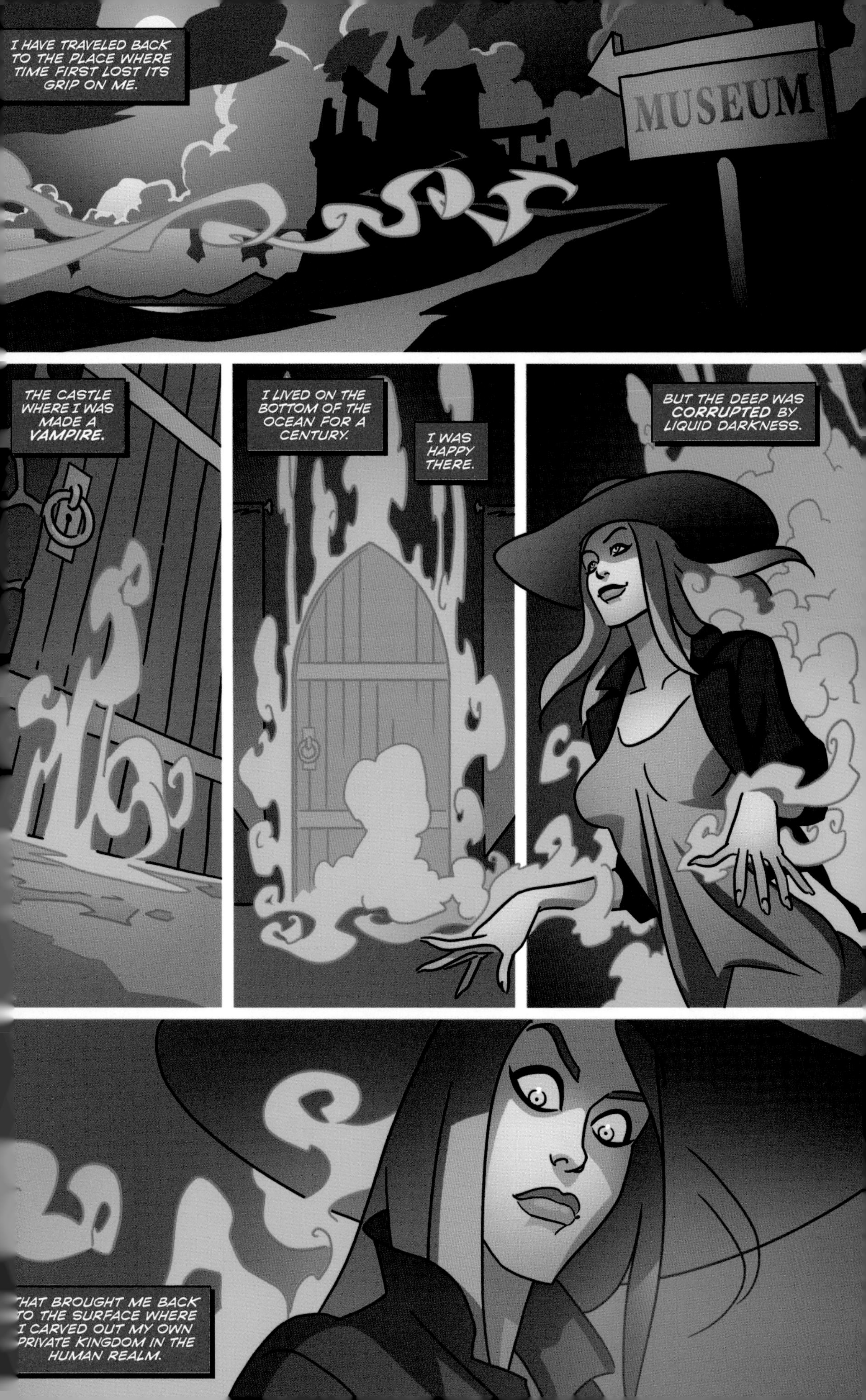
I HAVE TRAVELED BACK TO THE PLACE WHERE TIME FIRST LOST ITS GRIP ON ME.
MUSEUM
THE CASTLE WHERE I WAS MADE A VAMPIRE.
I LIVED ON THE BOTTOM OF THE OCEAN FOR A CENTURY.
I WAS HAPPY THERE.
BUT THE DEEP WAS CORRUPTED BY LIQUID DARKNESS.
THAT BROUGHT ME BACK TO THE SURFACE WHERE I CARVED OUT MY OWN PRIVATE KINGDOM IN THE HUMAN REALM.

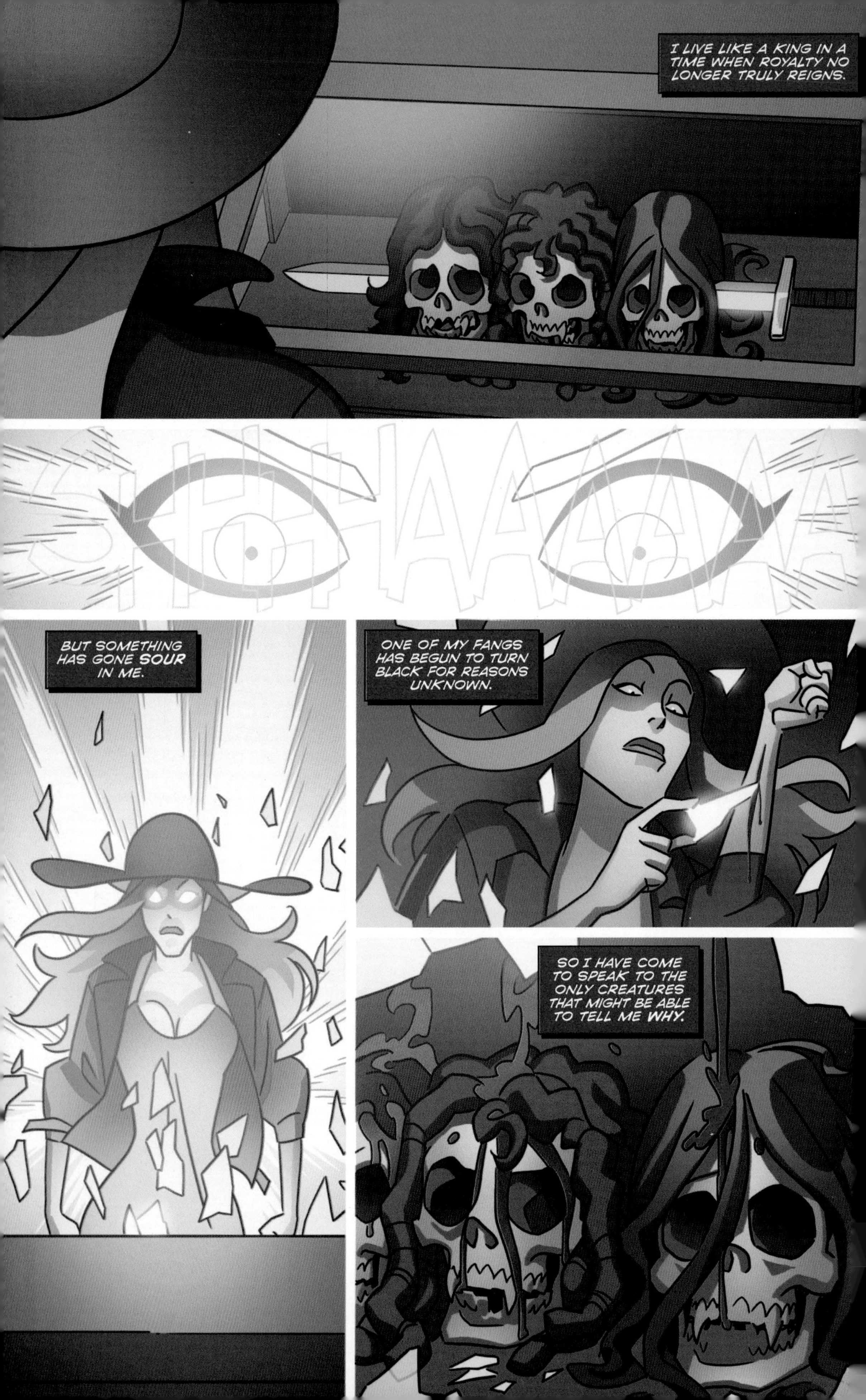
I LIVE LIKE A KING IN A TIME WHEN ROYALTY NO LONGER TRULY REIGNS.
SHHHAAAAAA
BUT SOMETHING HAS GONE **SOUR** IN ME.
ONE OF MY FANGS HAS BEGUN TO TURN BLACK FOR REASONS UNKNOWN.
SO I HAVE COME TO SPEAK TO THE ONLY CREATURES THAT MIGHT BE ABLE TO TELL ME **WHY**.

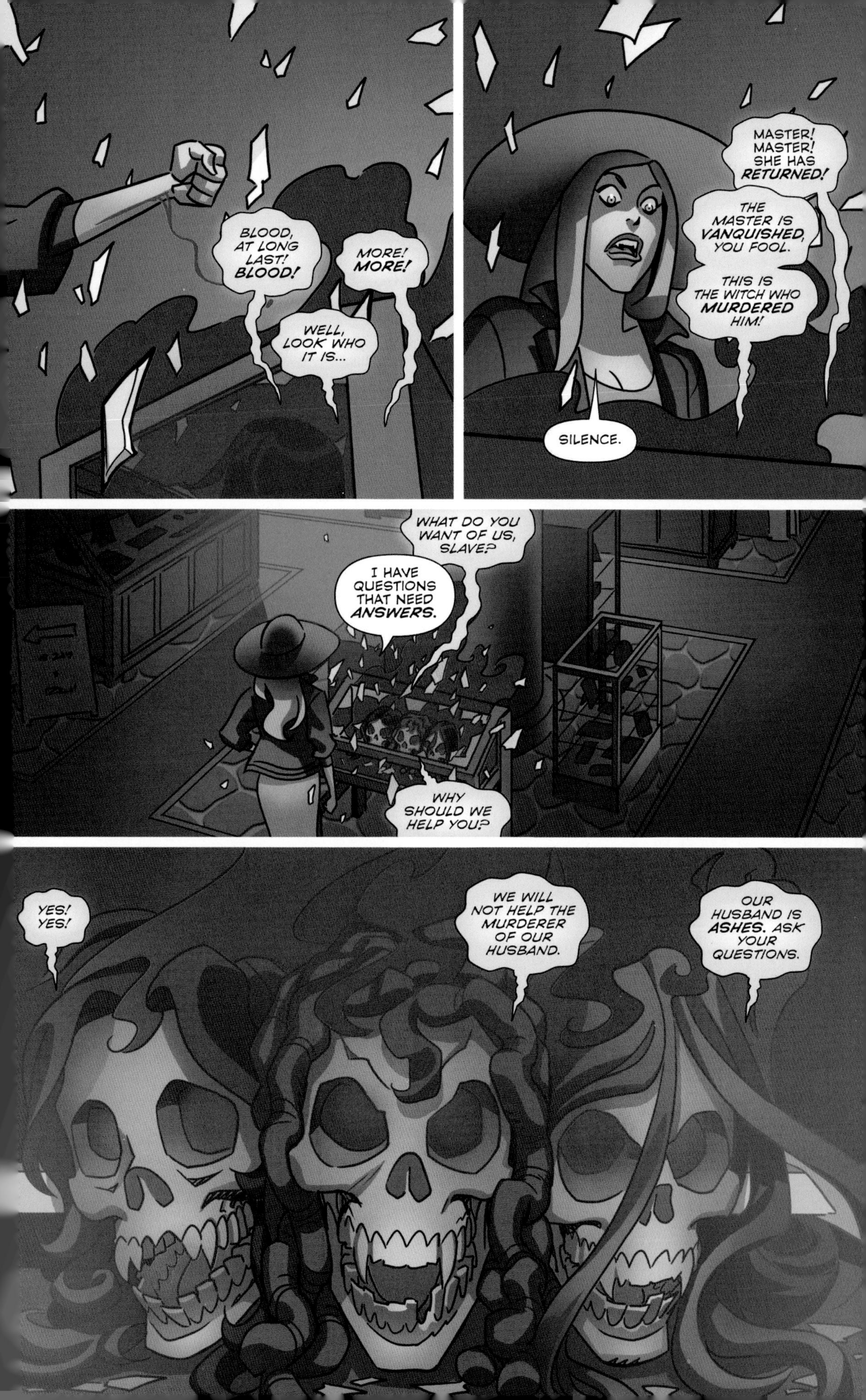
BLOOD, AT LONG LAST! BLOOD!
MORE! MORE!
WELL, LOOK WHO IT IS...
MASTER! MASTER! SHE HAS RETURNED!
THE MASTER IS VANQUISHED, YOU FOOL.
THIS IS THE WITCH WHO MURDERED HIM!
SILENCE.
WHAT DO YOU WANT OF US, SLAVE?
I HAVE QUESTIONS THAT NEED ANSWERS.
WHY SHOULD WE HELP YOU?
YES! YES!
WE WILL NOT HELP THE MURDERER OF OUR HUSBAND.
OUR HUSBAND IS ASHES. ASK YOUR QUESTIONS.

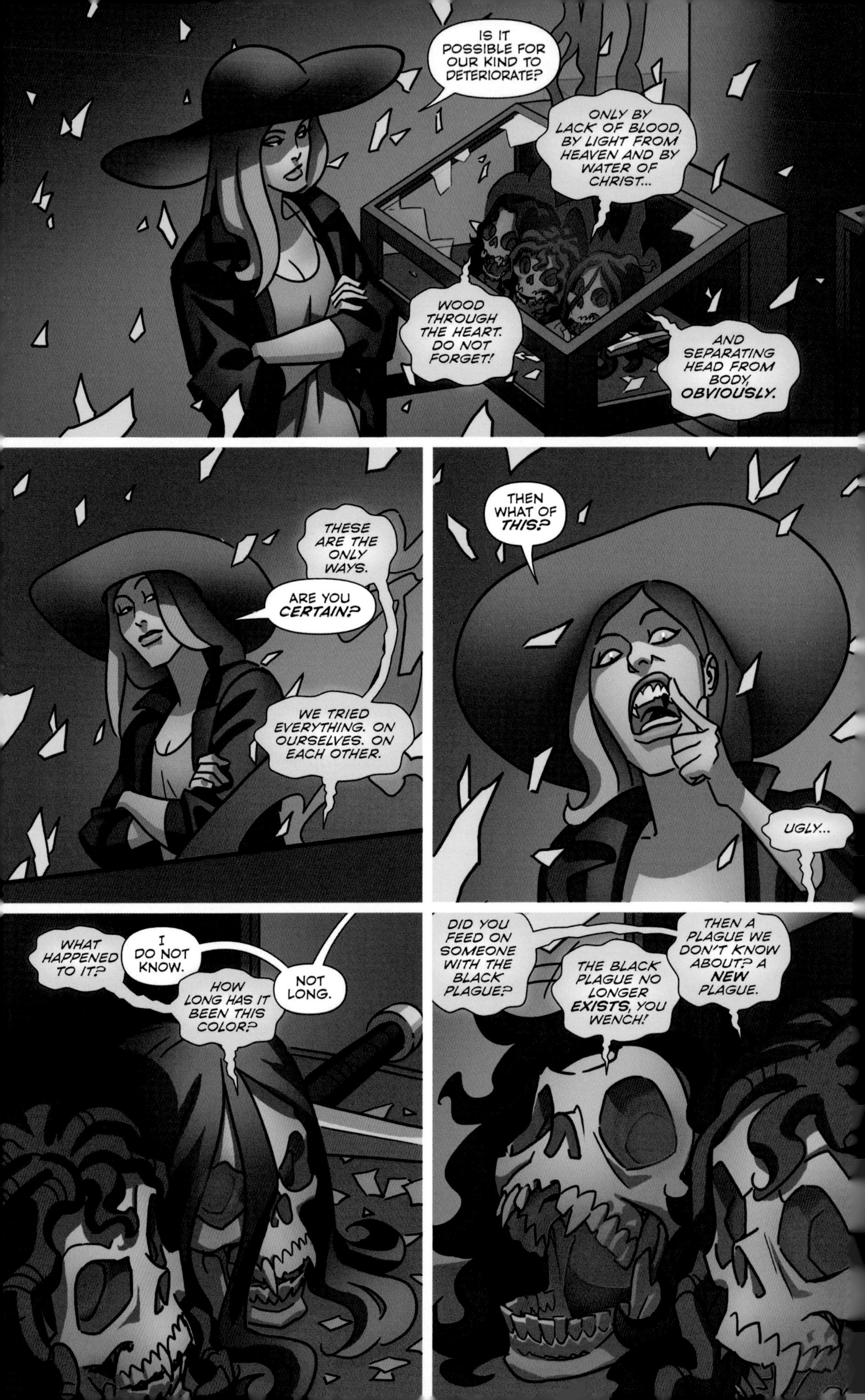
IS IT POSSIBLE FOR OUR KIND TO DETERIORATE?
ONLY BY LACK OF BLOOD, BY LIGHT FROM HEAVEN AND BY WATER OF CHRIST...
WOOD THROUGH THE HEART. DO NOT FORGET!
AND SEPARATING HEAD FROM BODY, OBVIOUSLY.
THESE ARE THE ONLY WAYS.
ARE YOU CERTAIN?
WE TRIED EVERYTHING. ON OURSELVES. ON EACH OTHER.
THEN WHAT OF THIS?
UGLY...
WHAT HAPPENED TO IT?
I DO NOT KNOW.
HOW LONG HAS IT BEEN THIS COLOR?
NOT LONG.
DID YOU FEED ON SOMEONE WITH THE BLACK PLAGUE?
THE BLACK PLAGUE NO LONGER EXISTS, YOU WENCH!
THEN A PLAGUE WE DON'T KNOW ABOUT? A NEW PLAGUE.

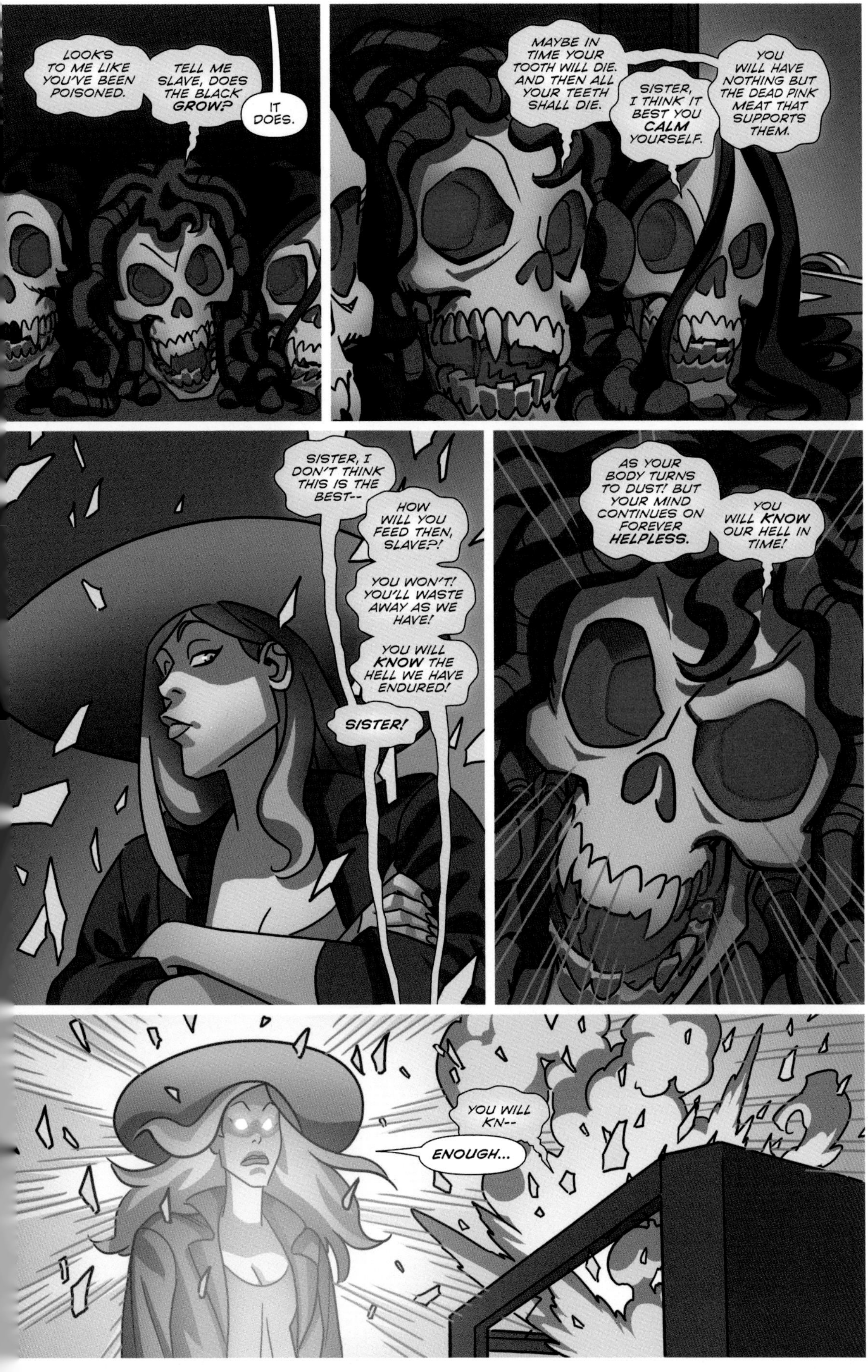
LOOKS TO ME LIKE YOU'VE BEEN POISONED.
TELL ME SLAVE, DOES THE BLACK GROW?
IT DOES.
MAYBE IN TIME YOUR TOOTH WILL DIE. AND THEN ALL YOUR TEETH SHALL DIE.
SISTER, I THINK IT BEST YOU CALM YOURSELF.
YOU WILL HAVE NOTHING BUT THE DEAD PINK MEAT THAT SUPPORTS THEM.
SISTER, I DON'T THINK THIS IS THE BEST--
HOW WILL YOU FEED THEN, SLAVE?!
YOU WON'T! YOU'LL WASTE AWAY AS WE HAVE!
YOU WILL KNOW THE HELL WE HAVE ENDURED!
SISTER!
AS YOUR BODY TURNS TO DUST! BUT YOUR MIND CONTINUES ON FOREVER HELPLESS.
YOU WILL KNOW OUR HELL IN TIME!
YOU WILL KN--
ENOUGH...

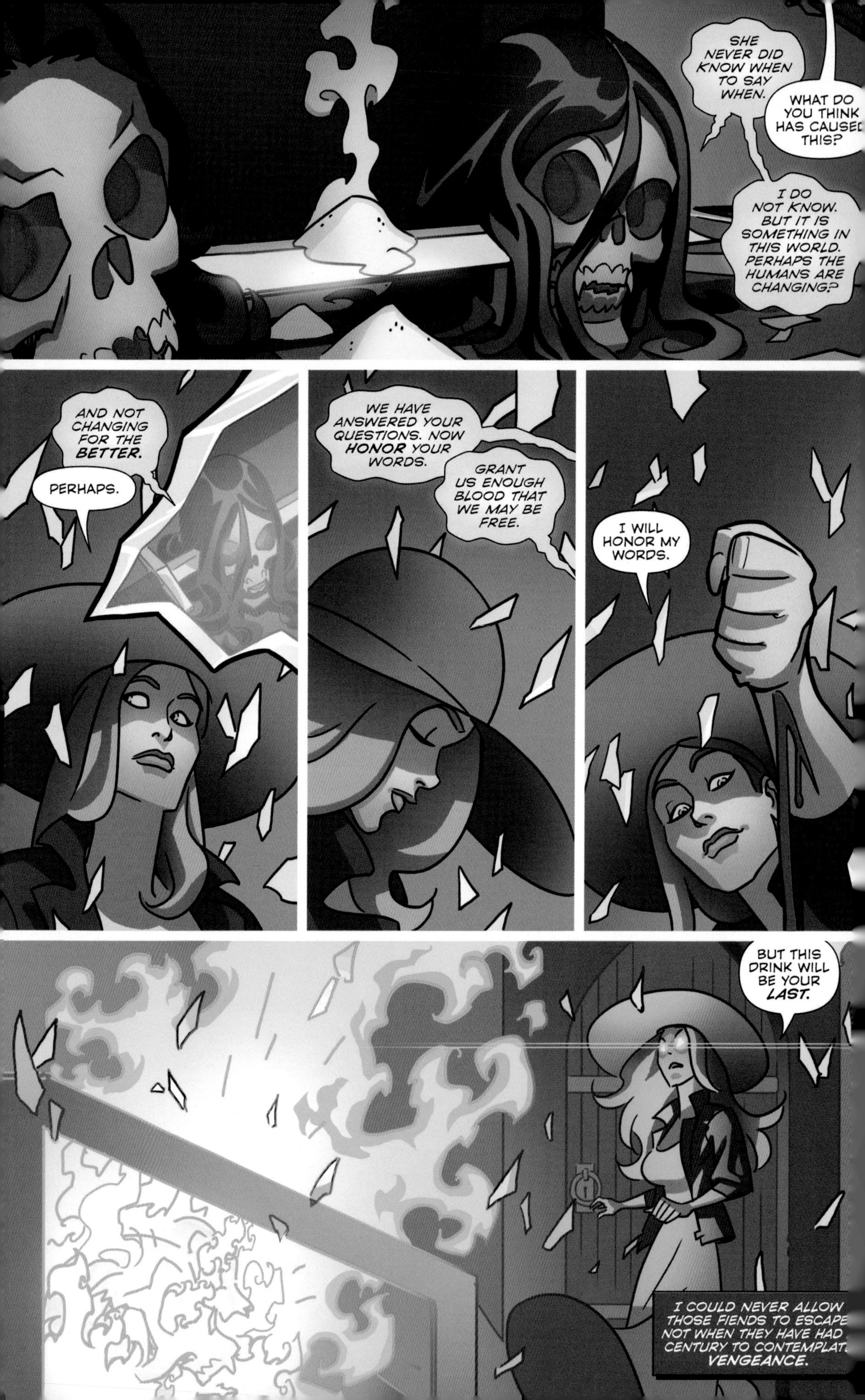
SHE NEVER DID KNOW WHEN TO SAY WHEN.
WHAT DO YOU THINK HAS CAUSED THIS?
I DO NOT KNOW. BUT IT IS SOMETHING IN THIS WORLD. PERHAPS THE HUMANS ARE CHANGING?
AND NOT CHANGING FOR THE BETTER.
PERHAPS.
WE HAVE ANSWERED YOUR QUESTIONS. NOW HONOR YOUR WORDS.
GRANT US ENOUGH BLOOD THAT WE MAY BE FREE.
I WILL HONOR MY WORDS.
BUT THIS DRINK WILL BE YOUR LAST.
I COULD NEVER ALLOW THOSE FIENDS TO ESCAPE NOT WHEN THEY HAVE HAD CENTURY TO CONTEMPLAT VENGEANCE.

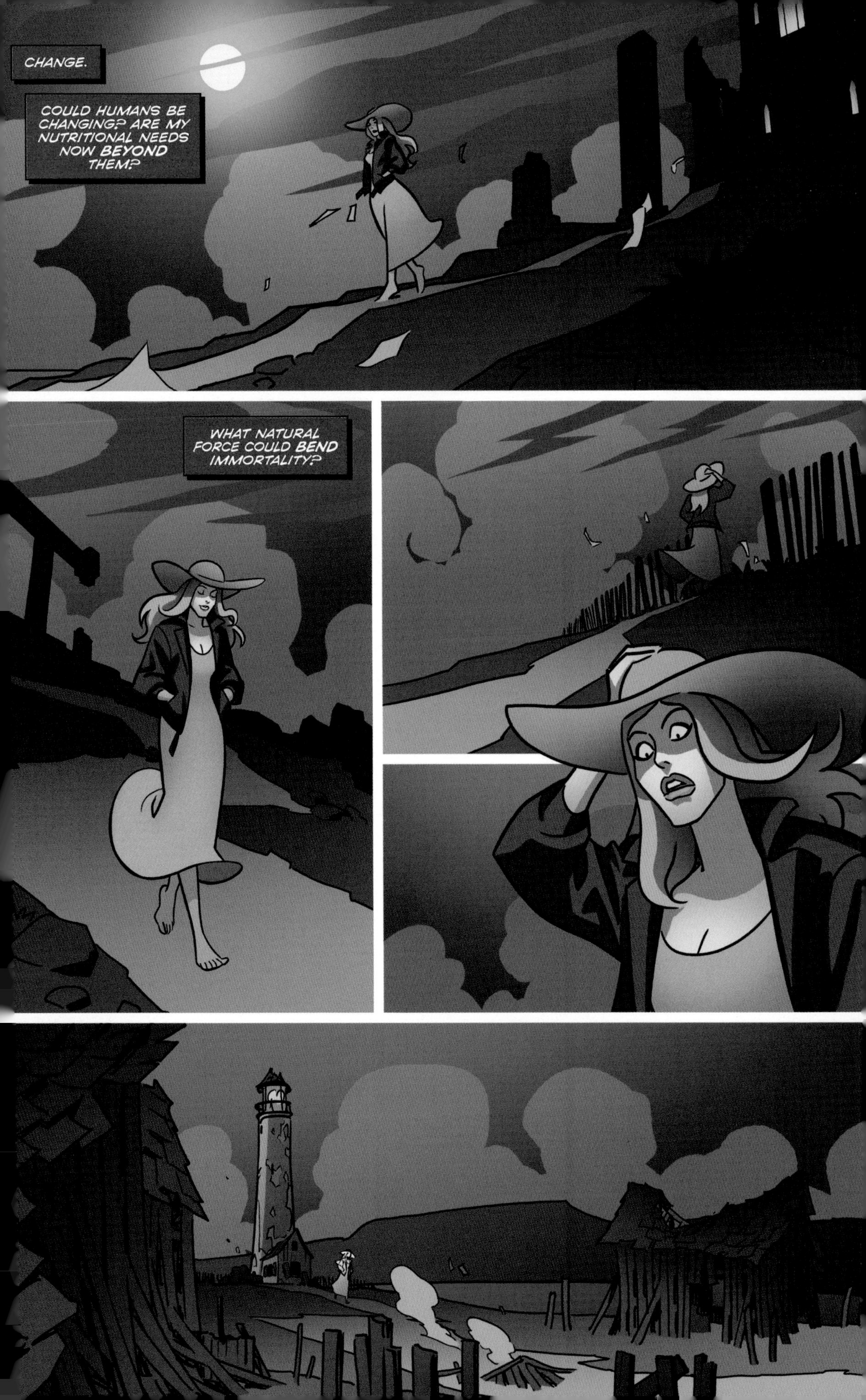
CHANGE.
COULD HUMANS BE CHANGING? ARE MY NUTRITIONAL NEEDS NOW BEYOND THEM?
WHAT NATURAL FORCE COULD BEND IMMORTALITY?

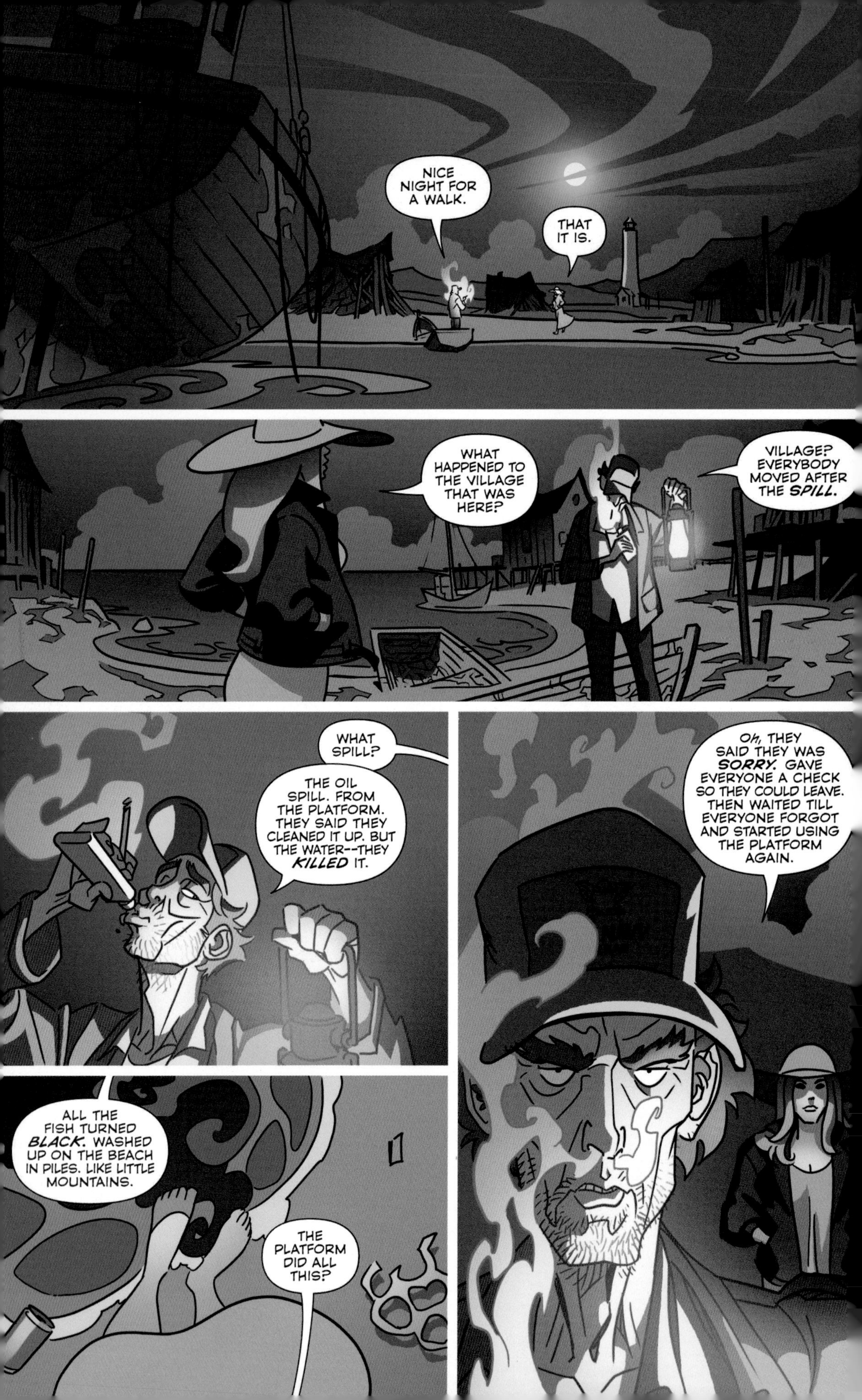
NICE NIGHT FOR A WALK.
THAT IT IS.
WHAT HAPPENED TO THE VILLAGE THAT WAS HERE?
VILLAGE? EVERYBODY MOVED AFTER THE *SPILL.*
WHAT SPILL?
THE OIL SPILL. FROM THE PLATFORM. THEY SAID THEY CLEANED IT UP. BUT THE WATER--THEY *KILLED* IT.
ALL THE FISH TURNED *BLACK.* WASHED UP ON THE BEACH IN PILES. LIKE LITTLE MOUNTAINS.
THE PLATFORM DID ALL THIS?
Oh, THEY SAID THEY WAS *SORRY.* GAVE EVERYONE A CHECK SO THEY COULD LEAVE. THEN WAITED TILL EVERYONE FORGOT AND STARTED USING THE PLATFORM AGAIN.

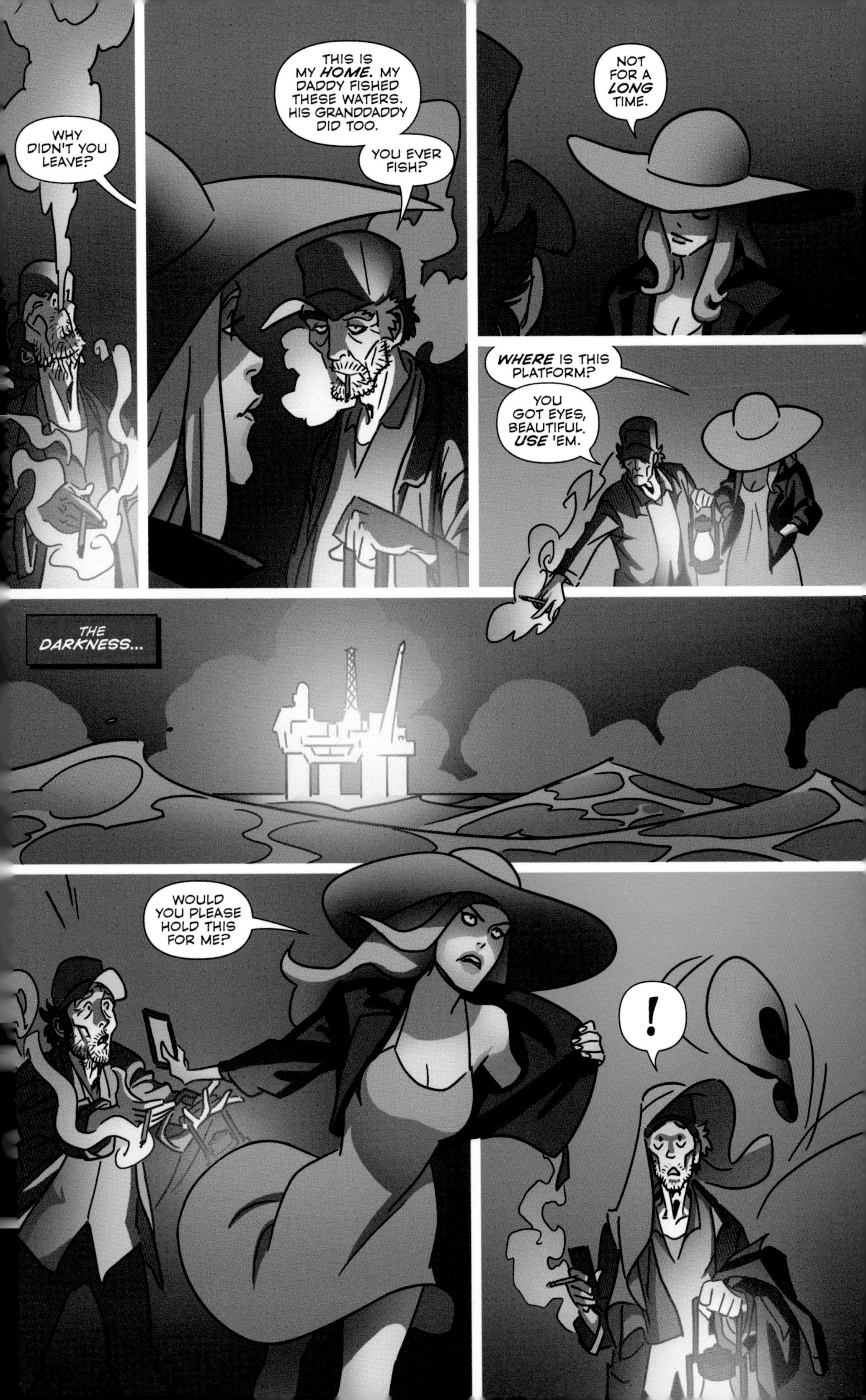
WHY DIDN'T YOU LEAVE?
THIS IS MY **HOME.** MY DADDY FISHED THESE WATERS. HIS GRANDDADDY DID TOO.
YOU EVER FISH?
NOT FOR A **LONG** TIME.
WHERE IS THIS PLATFORM?
YOU GOT EYES, BEAUTIFUL. **USE** 'EM.
THE DARKNESS...
WOULD YOU PLEASE HOLD THIS FOR ME?
!

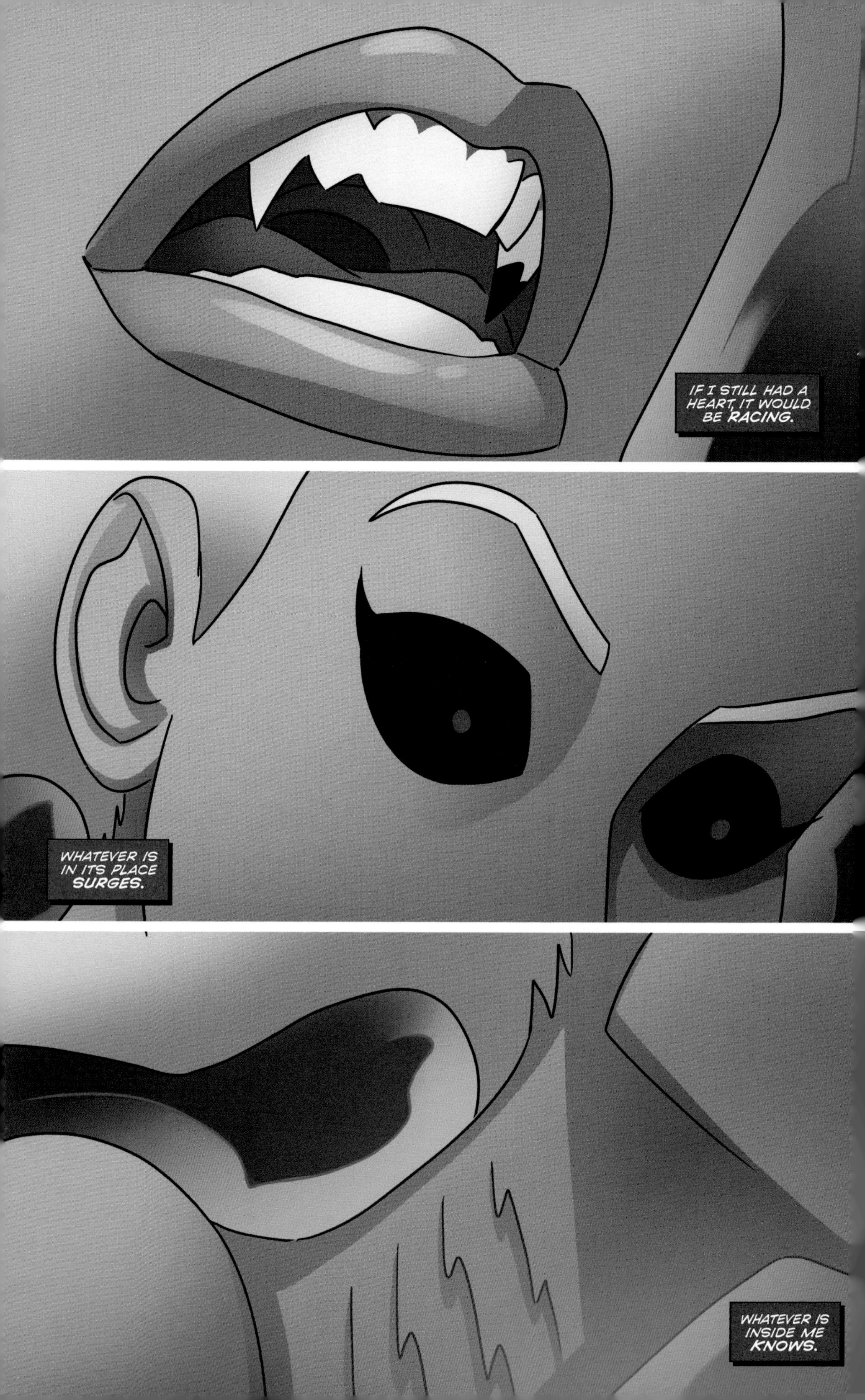
IF I STILL HAD A HEART, IT WOULD BE RACING.
WHATEVER IS IN ITS PLACE SURGES.
WHATEVER IS INSIDE ME KNOWS.

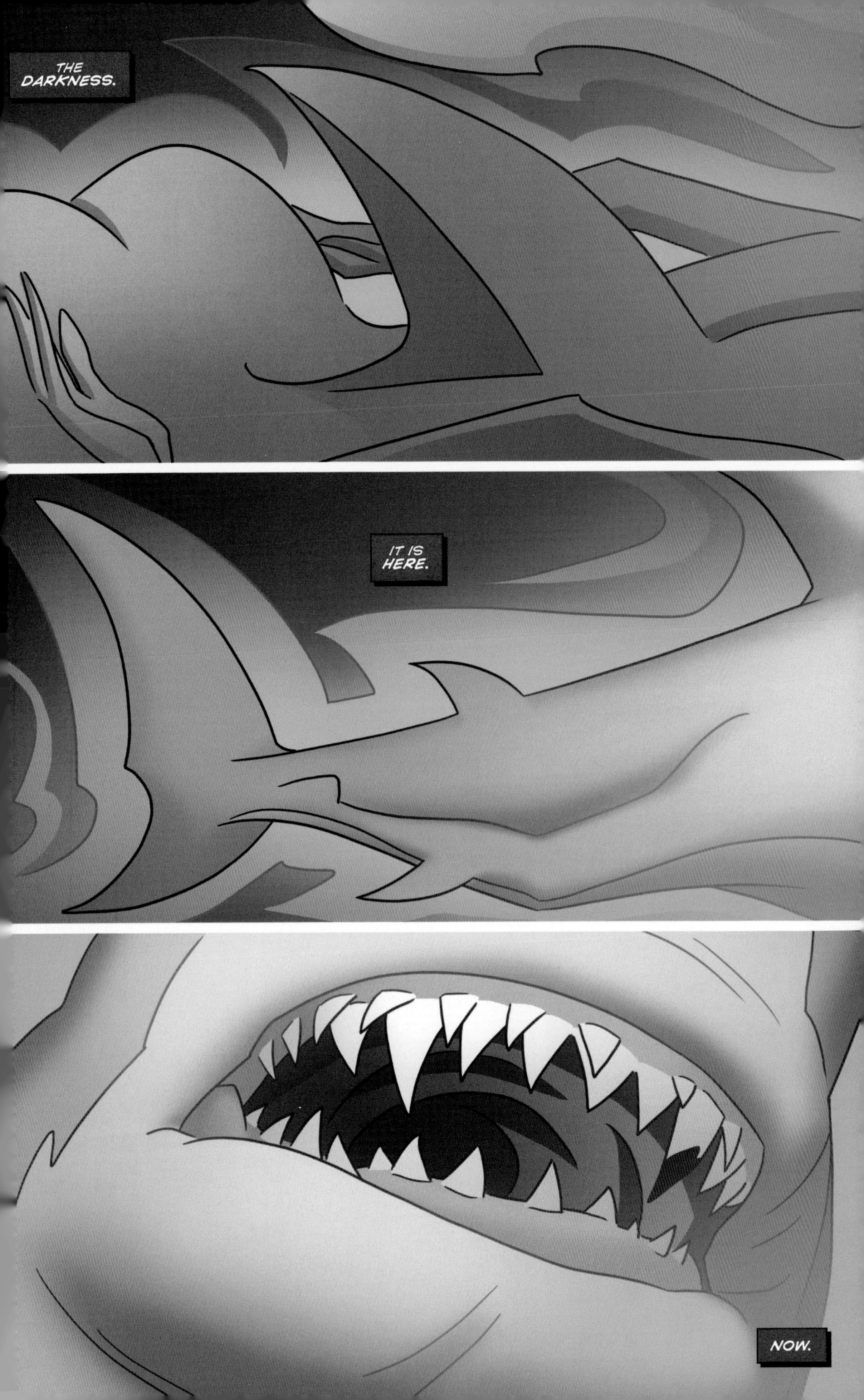
THE DARKNESS.
IT IS HERE.
NOW.

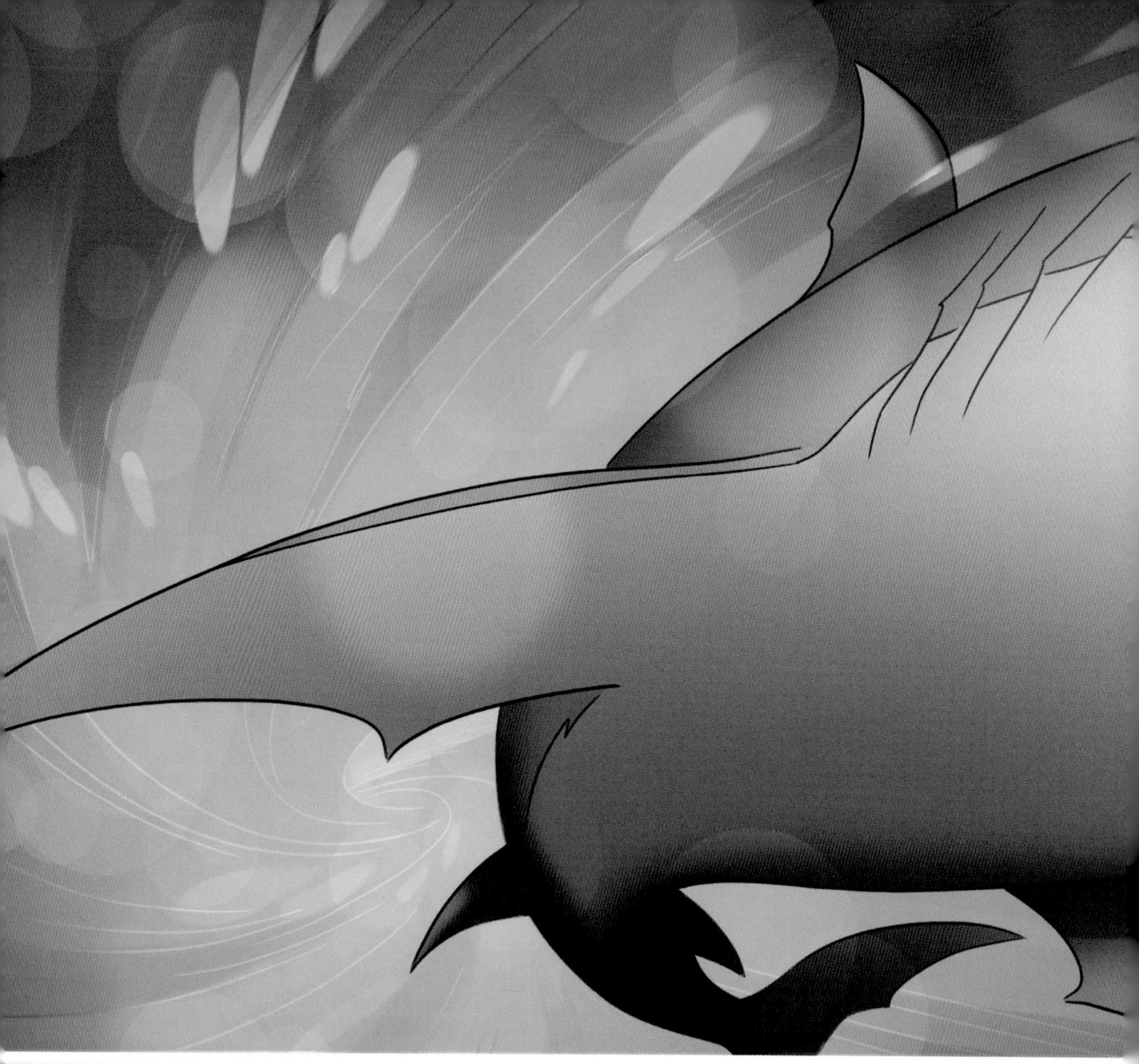

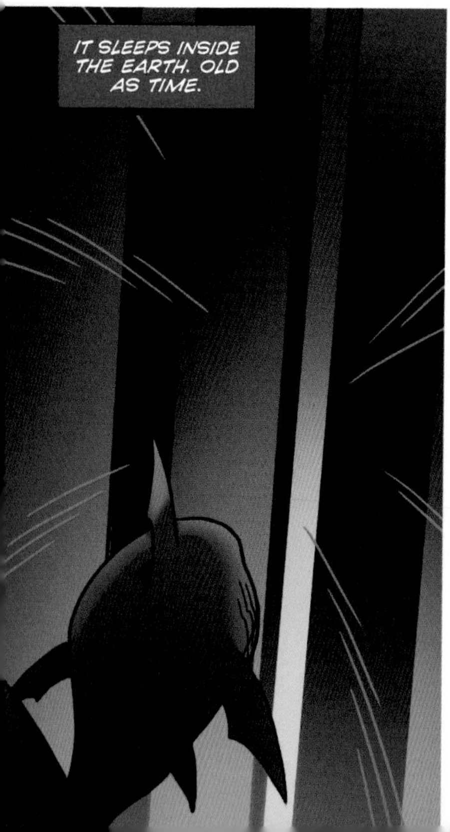

IT SLEEPS INSIDE THE EARTH. OLD AS TIME.

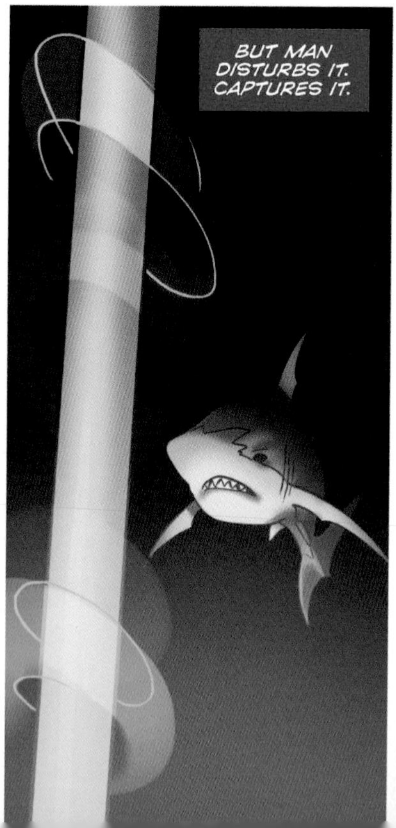

BUT MAN DISTURBS IT. CAPTURES IT.

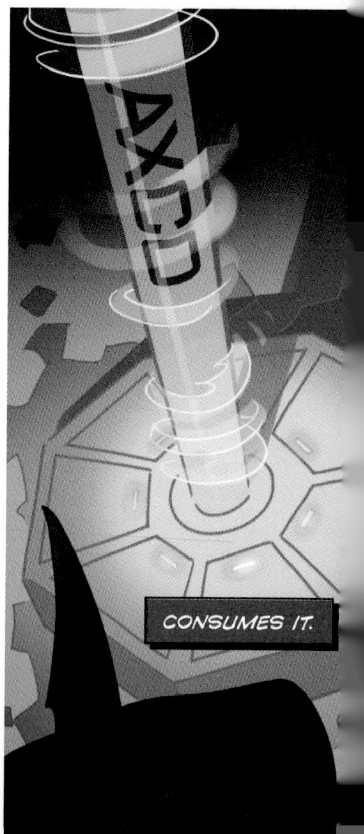

AXCO
CONSUMES IT.

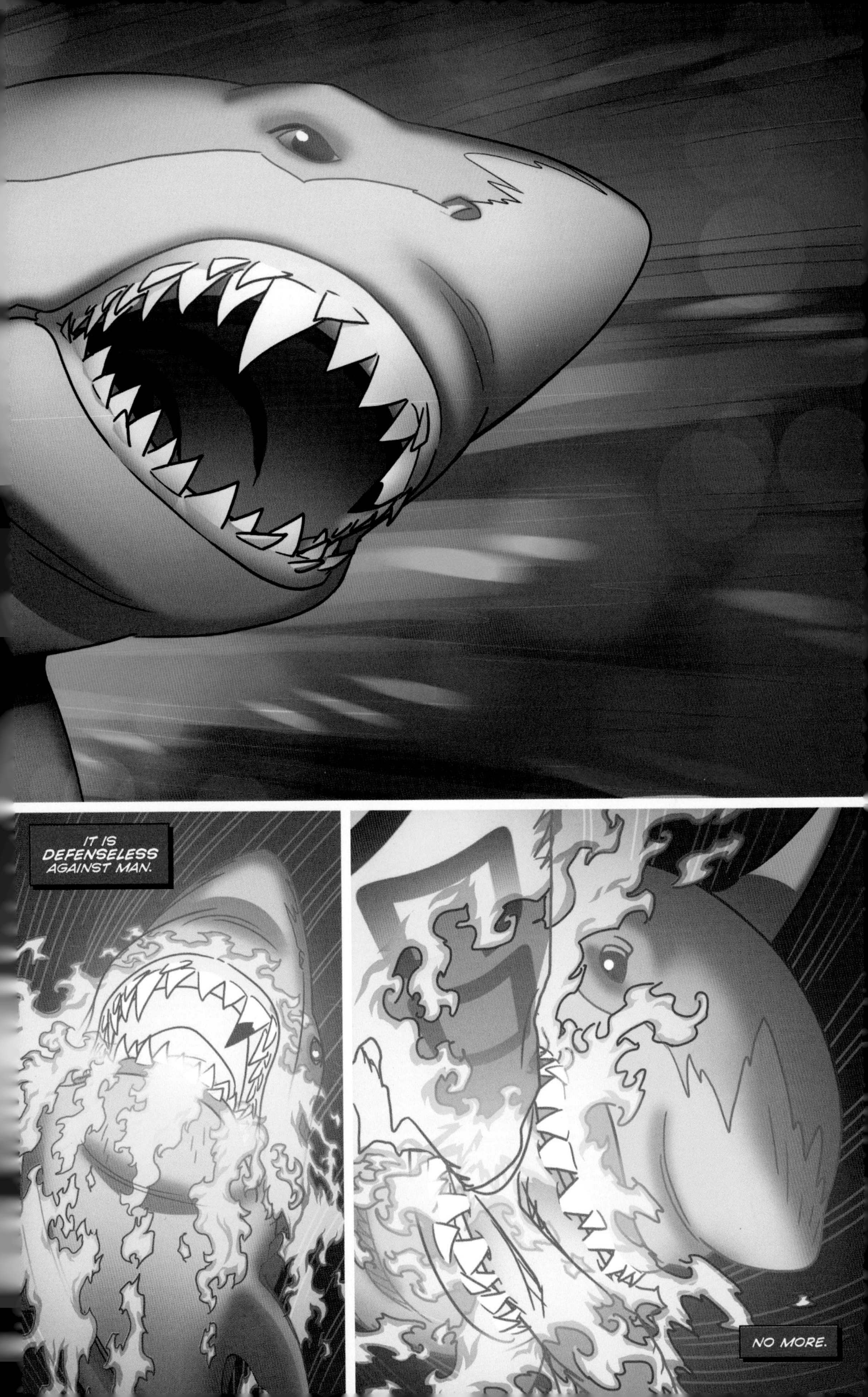
IT IS DEFENSELESS AGAINST MAN.
NO MORE.

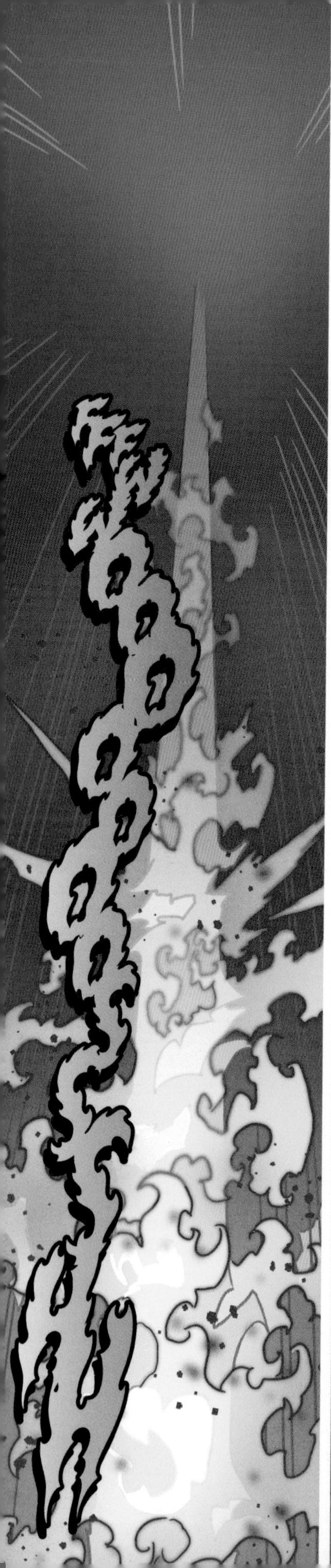
FWOOOOOOOOSH

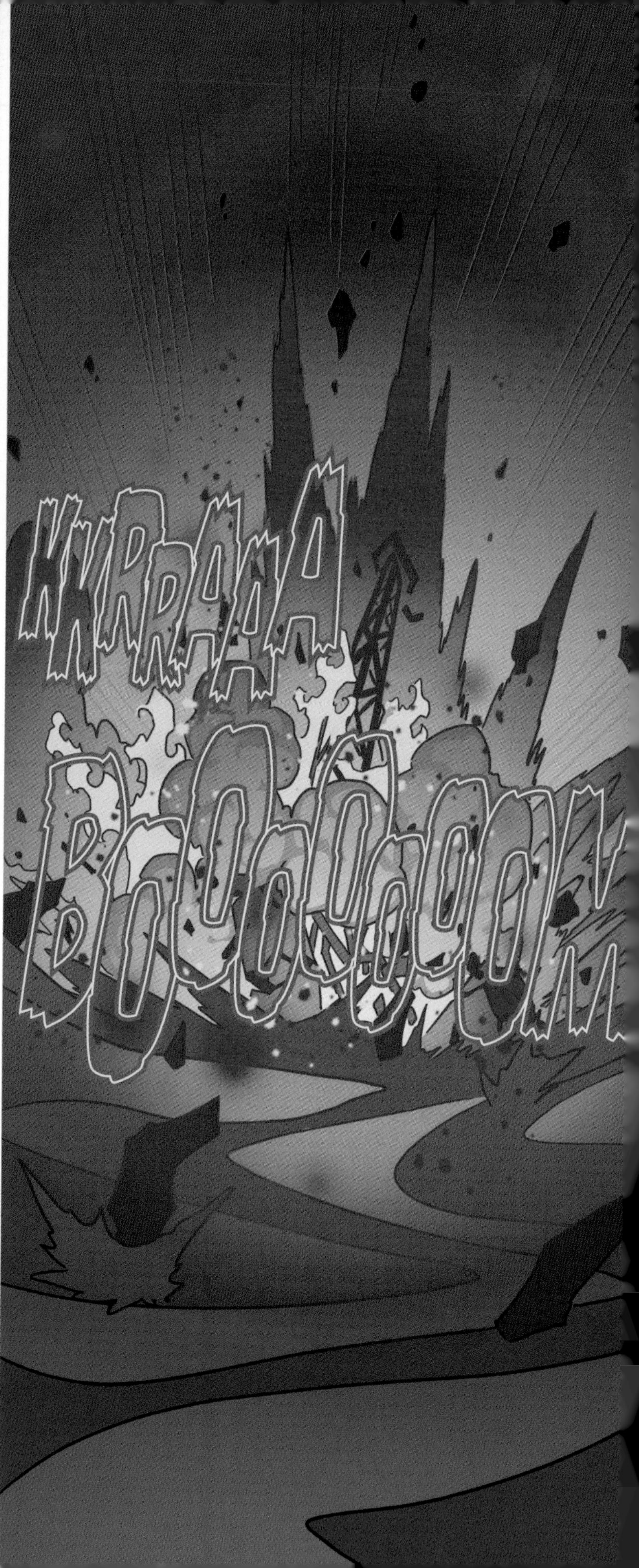
KKRAAAA
BOOOOOOOOOM

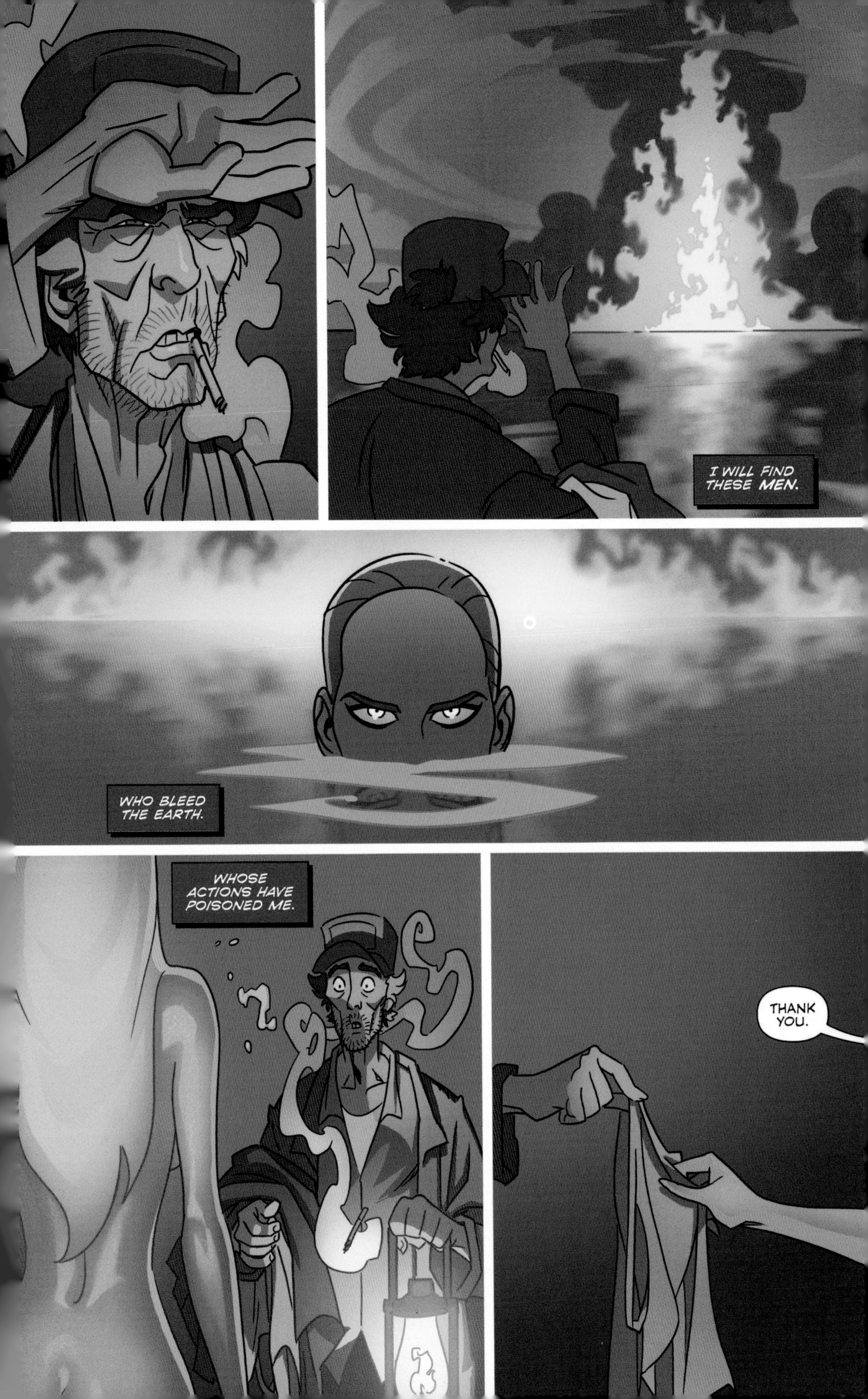
I WILL FIND THESE MEN.
WHO BLEED THE EARTH.
WHOSE ACTIONS HAVE POISONED ME.
THANK YOU.

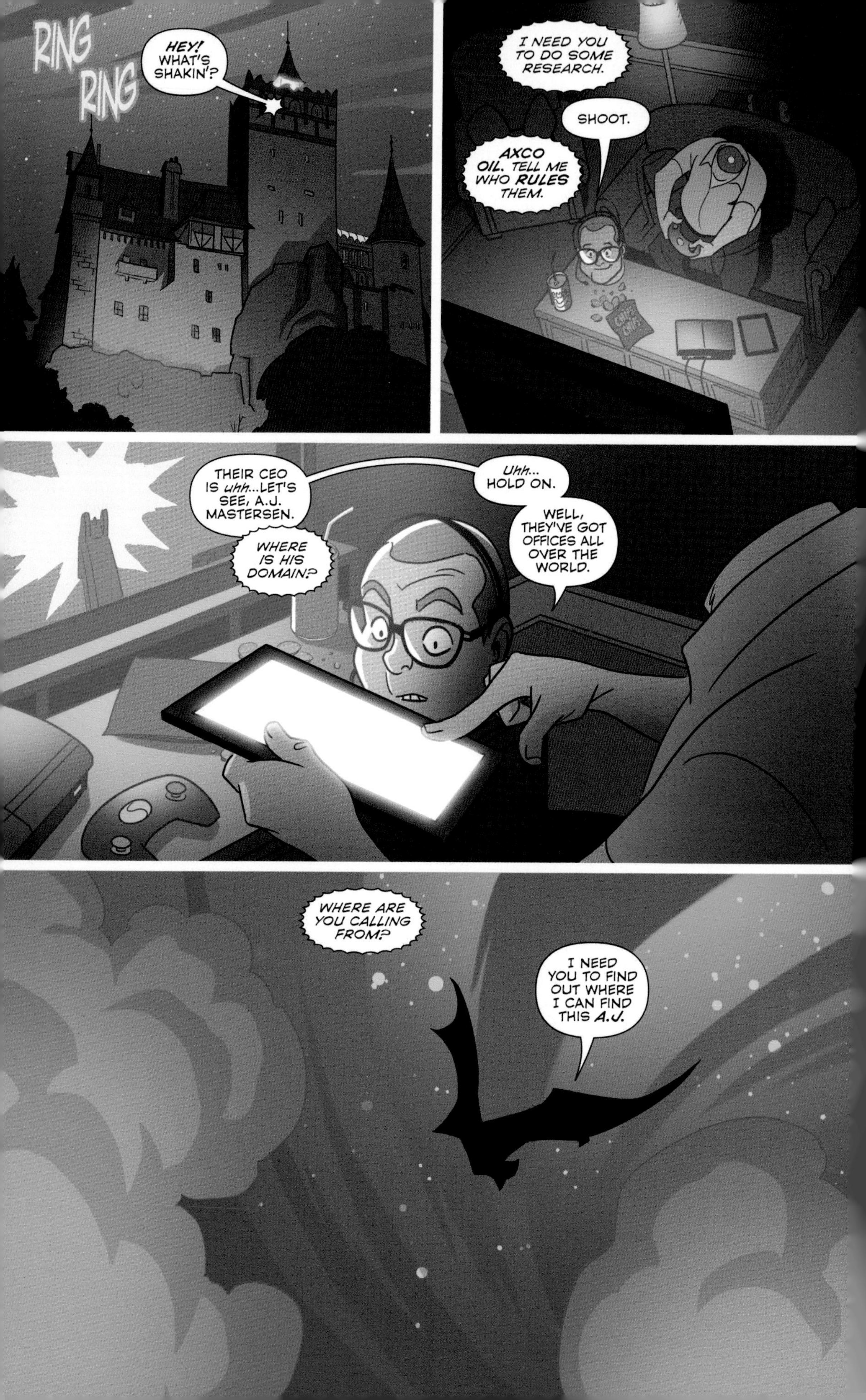
RING RING
HEY! WHAT'S SHAKIN'?
I NEED YOU TO DO SOME RESEARCH.
SHOOT.
AXCO OIL. TELL ME WHO RULES THEM.
THEIR CEO IS uhh...LET'S SEE, A.J. MASTERSEN.
WHERE IS HIS DOMAIN?
Uhh... HOLD ON.
WELL, THEY'VE GOT OFFICES ALL OVER THE WORLD.
WHERE ARE YOU CALLING FROM?
I NEED YOU TO FIND OUT WHERE I CAN FIND THIS A.J.

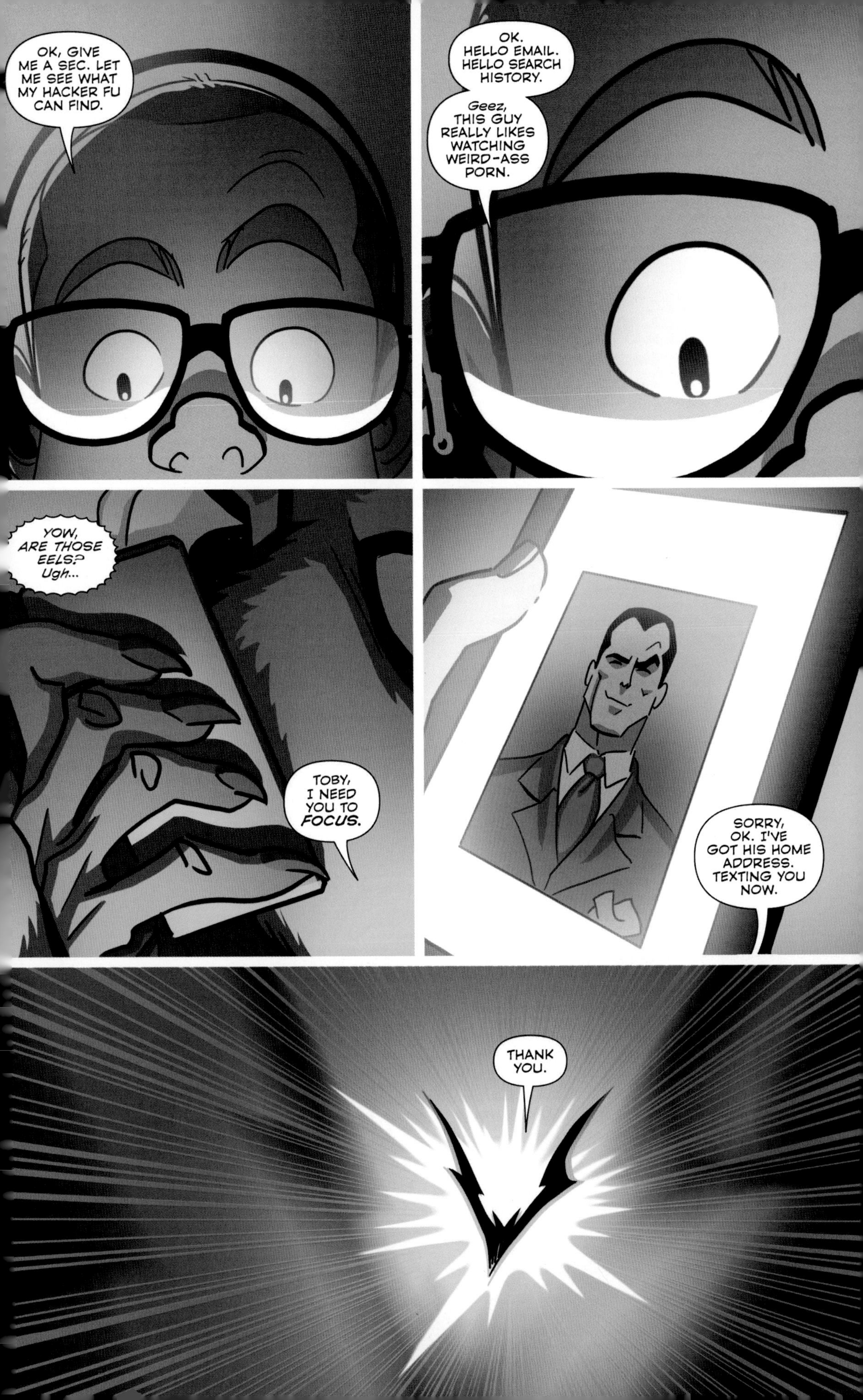
OK, GIVE ME A SEC. LET ME SEE WHAT MY HACKER FU CAN FIND.
OK. HELLO EMAIL. HELLO SEARCH HISTORY.
Geez, THIS GUY REALLY LIKES WATCHING WEIRD-ASS PORN.
YOW, ARE THOSE EELS? Ugh...
TOBY, I NEED YOU TO FOCUS.
SORRY, OK. I'VE GOT HIS HOME ADDRESS. TEXTING YOU NOW.
THANK YOU.

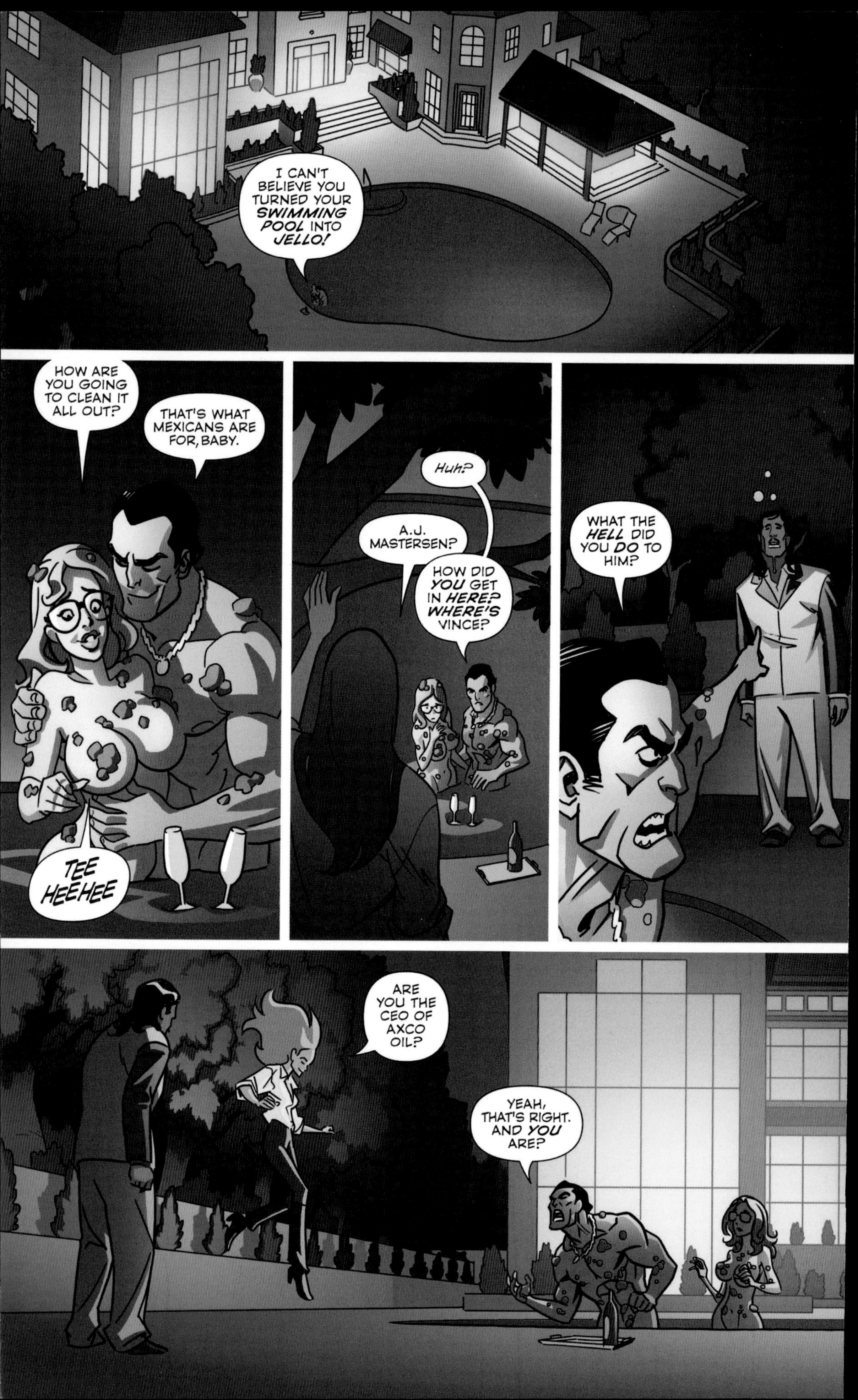
I CAN'T BELIEVE YOU TURNED YOUR SWIMMING POOL INTO JELLO!
HOW ARE YOU GOING TO CLEAN IT ALL OUT?
THAT'S WHAT MEXICANS ARE FOR, BABY.
TEE HEEHEE
Huh?
A.J. MASTERSEN?
HOW DID YOU GET IN HERE? WHERE'S VINCE?
WHAT THE HELL DID YOU DO TO HIM?
ARE YOU THE CEO OF AXCO OIL?
YEAH, THAT'S RIGHT. AND YOU ARE?

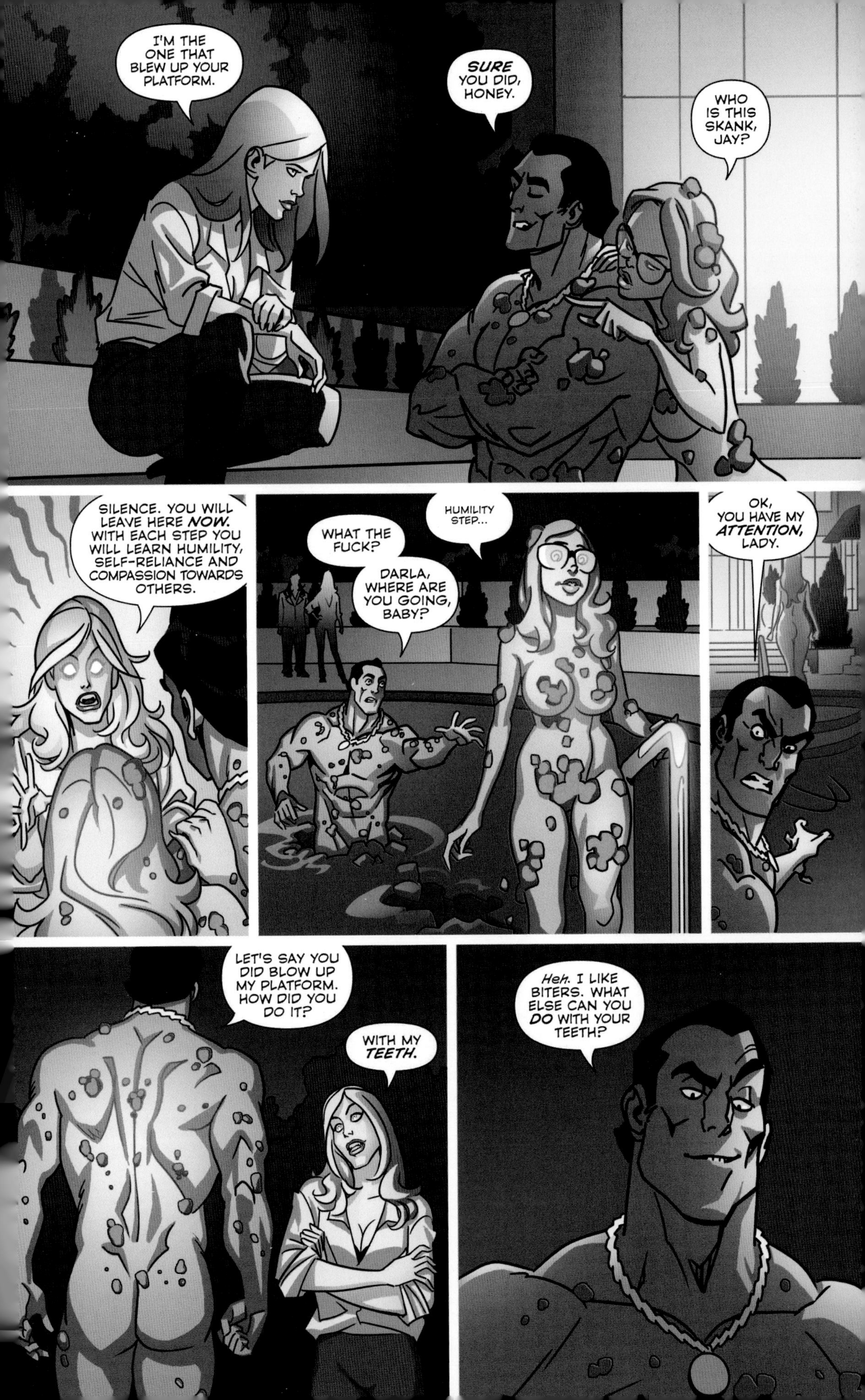
I'M THE ONE THAT BLEW UP YOUR PLATFORM.
SURE YOU DID, HONEY.
WHO IS THIS SKANK, JAY?
SILENCE. YOU WILL LEAVE HERE ***NOW.*** WITH EACH STEP YOU WILL LEARN HUMILITY, SELF-RELIANCE AND COMPASSION TOWARDS OTHERS.
WHAT THE FUCK?
HUMILITY STEP...
DARLA, WHERE ARE YOU GOING, BABY?
OK, YOU HAVE MY ***ATTENTION,*** LADY.
LET'S SAY YOU DID BLOW UP MY PLATFORM. HOW DID YOU DO IT?
WITH MY ***TEETH.***
Heh. I LIKE BITERS. WHAT ELSE CAN YOU ***DO*** WITH YOUR TEETH?

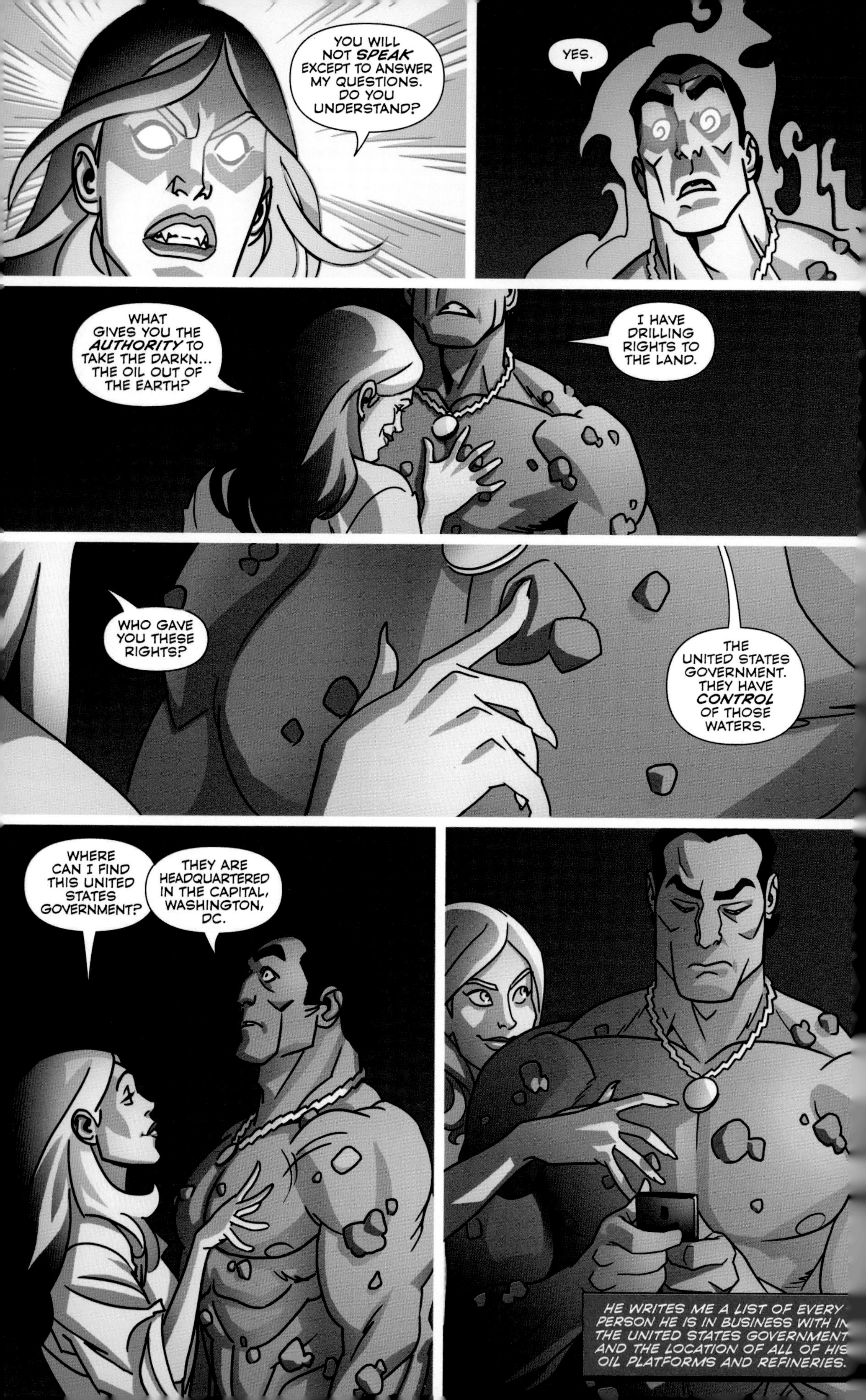
YOU WILL NOT SPEAK EXCEPT TO ANSWER MY QUESTIONS. DO YOU UNDERSTAND?
YES.
WHAT GIVES YOU THE AUTHORITY TO TAKE THE DARKN... THE OIL OUT OF THE EARTH?
I HAVE DRILLING RIGHTS TO THE LAND.
WHO GAVE YOU THESE RIGHTS?
THE UNITED STATES GOVERNMENT. THEY HAVE CONTROL OF THOSE WATERS.
WHERE CAN I FIND THIS UNITED STATES GOVERNMENT?
THEY ARE HEADQUARTERED IN THE CAPITAL, WASHINGTON, DC.
HE WRITES ME A LIST OF EVERY PERSON HE IS IN BUSINESS WITH IN THE UNITED STATES GOVERNMENT AND THE LOCATION OF ALL OF HIS OIL PLATFORMS AND REFINERIES.

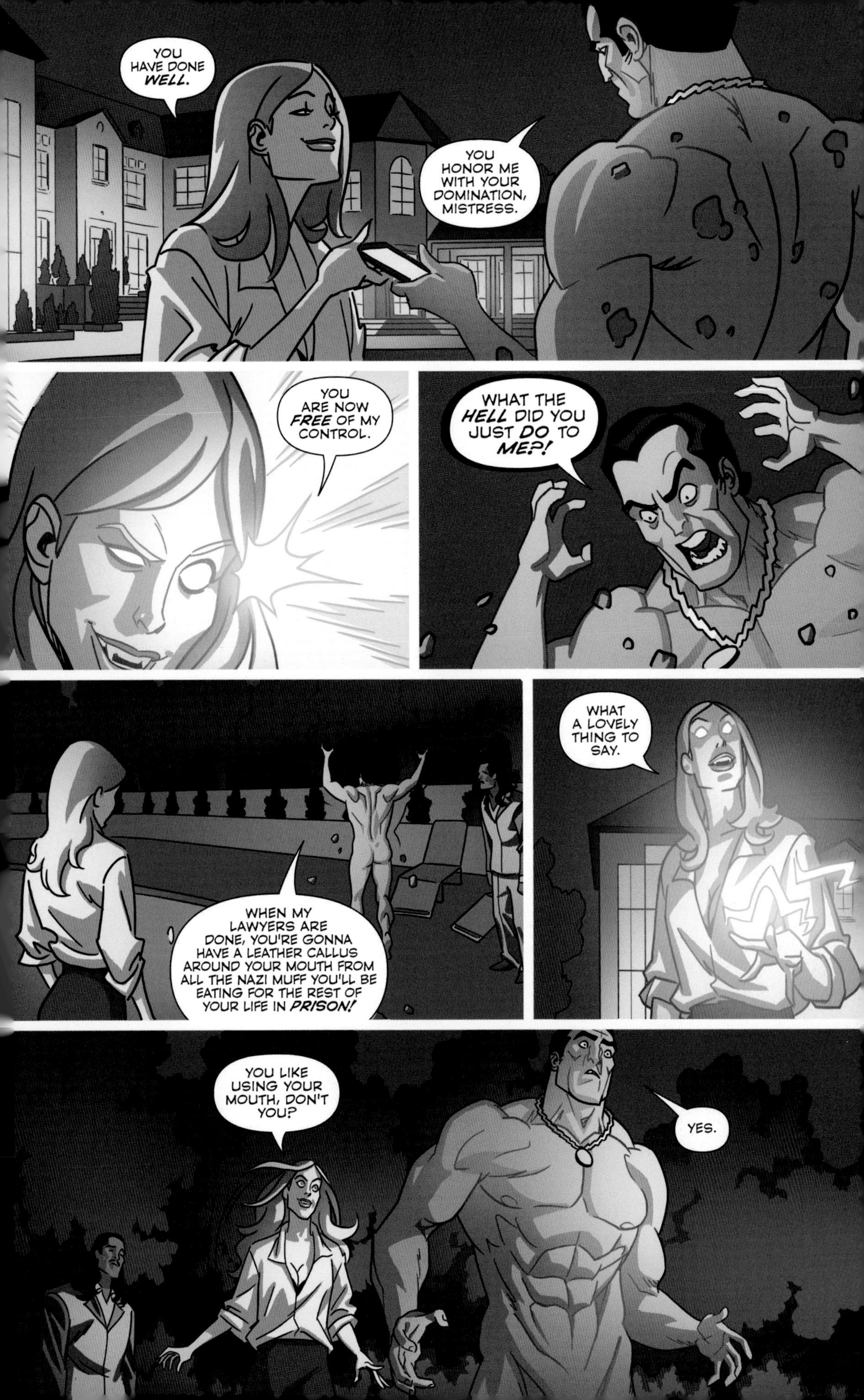

YOU HAVE DONE WELL.
YOU HONOR ME WITH YOUR DOMINATION, MISTRESS.
YOU ARE NOW FREE OF MY CONTROL.
WHAT THE HELL DID YOU JUST DO TO ME?!
WHEN MY LAWYERS ARE DONE, YOU'RE GONNA HAVE A LEATHER CALLUS AROUND YOUR MOUTH FROM ALL THE NAZI MUFF YOU'LL BE EATING FOR THE REST OF YOUR LIFE IN PRISON!
WHAT A LOVELY THING TO SAY.
YOU LIKE USING YOUR MOUTH, DON'T YOU?
YES.

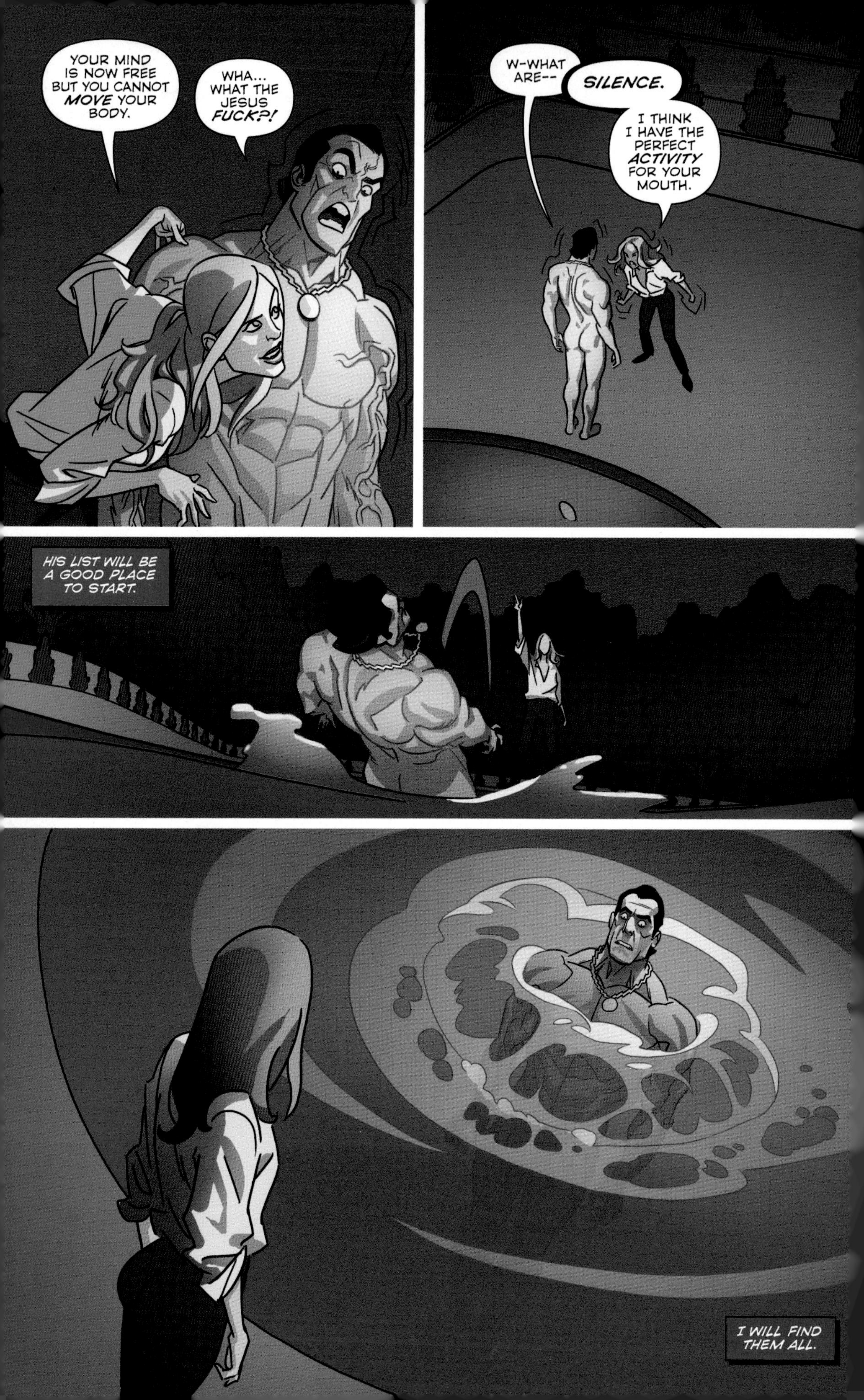
YOUR MIND IS NOW FREE BUT YOU CANNOT MOVE YOUR BODY.
WHA... WHAT THE JESUS FUCK?!
W-WHAT ARE--
SILENCE.
I THINK I HAVE THE PERFECT ACTIVITY FOR YOUR MOUTH.
HIS LIST WILL BE A GOOD PLACE TO START.
I WILL FIND THEM ALL.

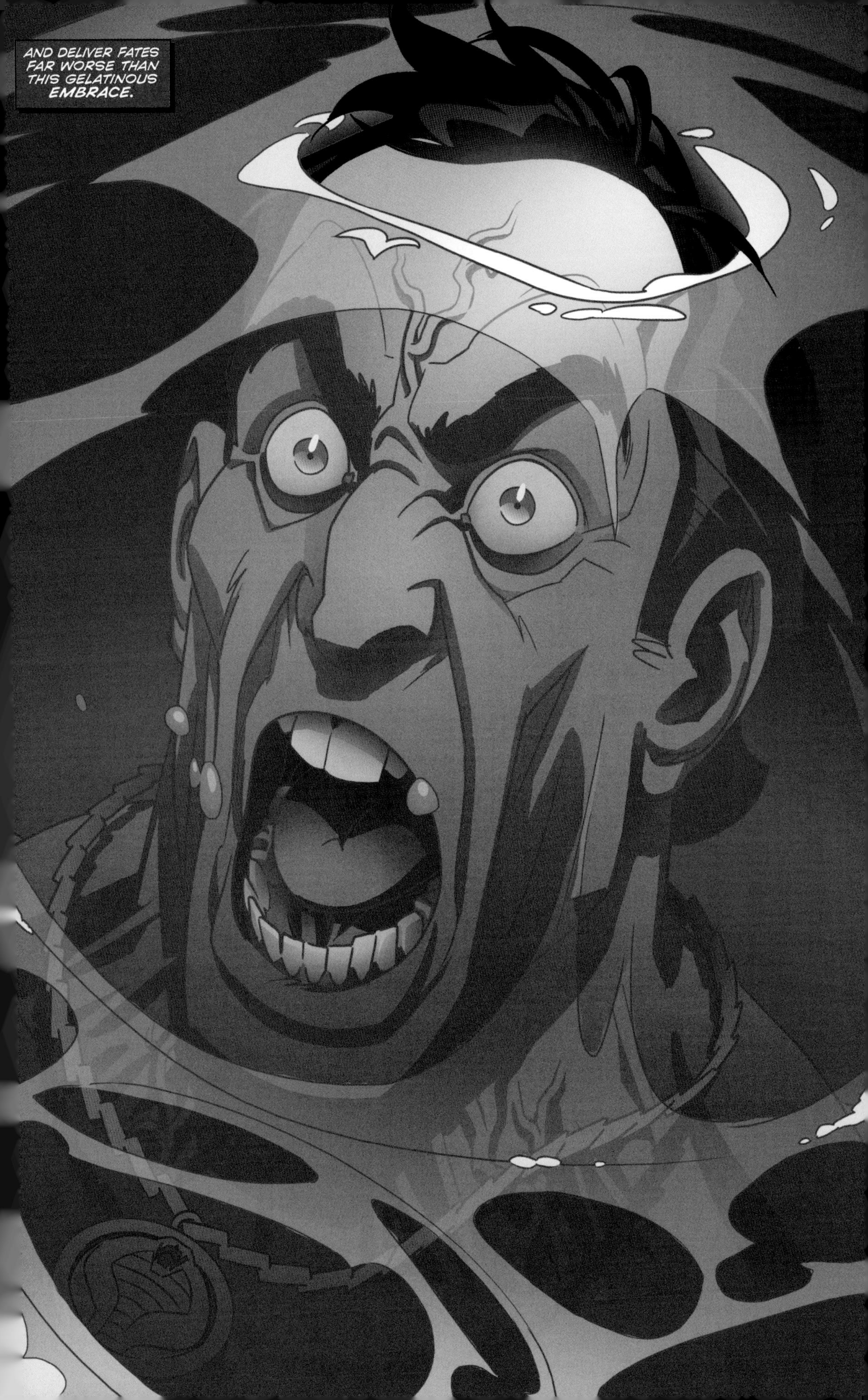
AND DELIVER FATES FAR WORSE THAN THIS GELATINOUS EMBRACE.

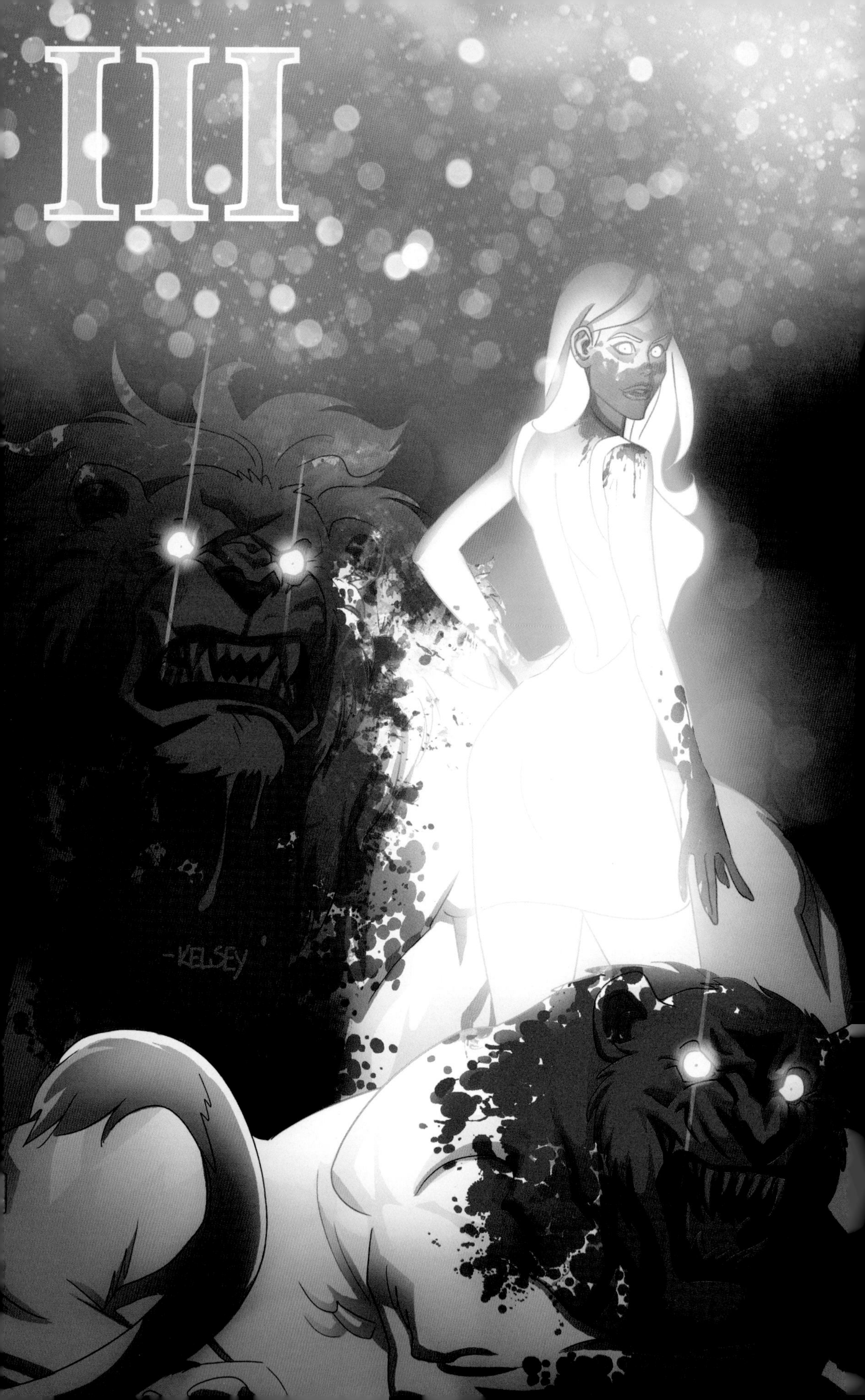
III
-KELSEY

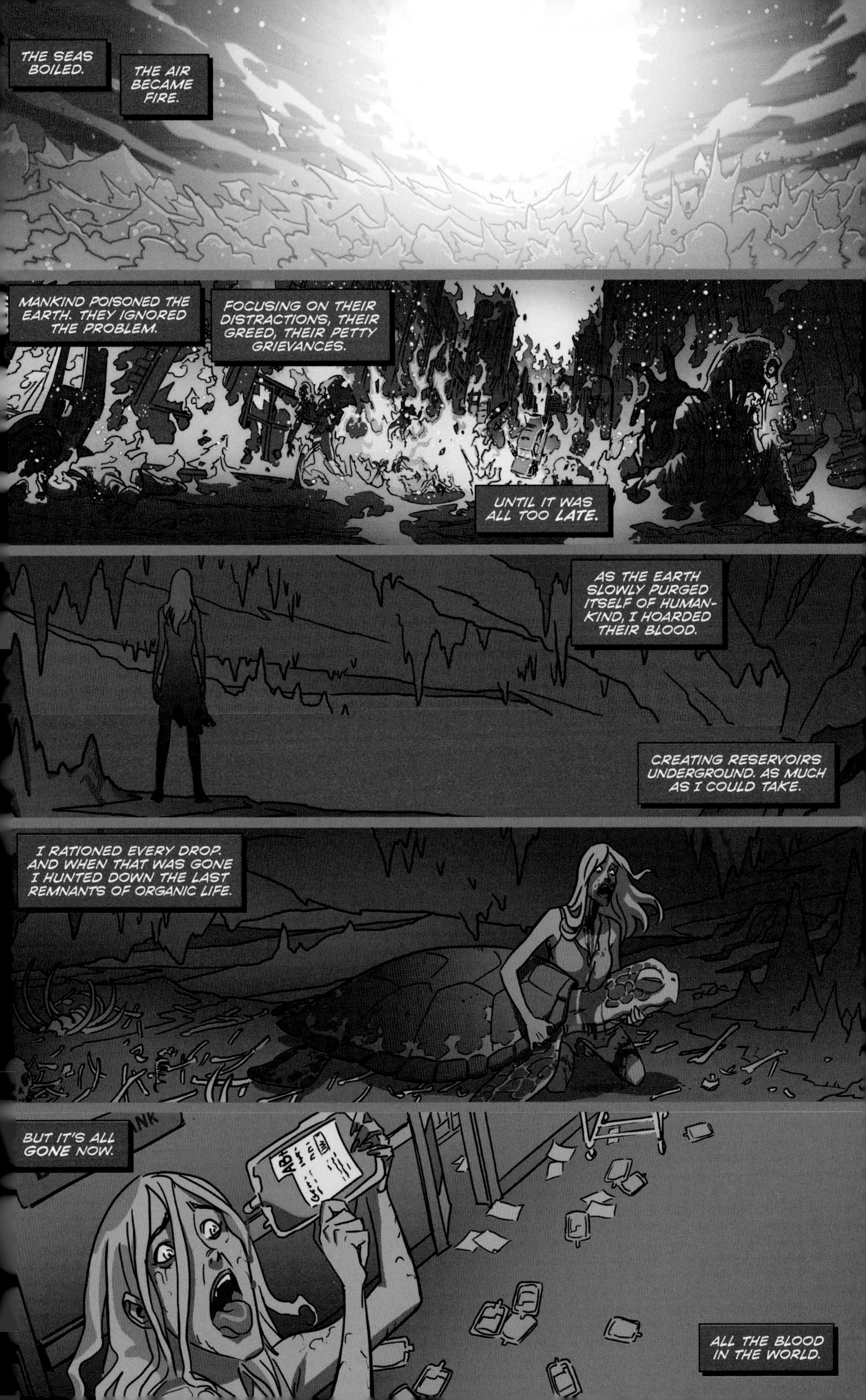
THE SEAS BOILED.
THE AIR BECAME FIRE.
MANKIND POISONED THE EARTH. THEY IGNORED THE PROBLEM.
FOCUSING ON THEIR DISTRACTIONS, THEIR GREED, THEIR PETTY GRIEVANCES.
UNTIL IT WAS ALL TOO LATE.
AS THE EARTH SLOWLY PURGED ITSELF OF HUMAN-KIND, I HOARDED THEIR BLOOD.
CREATING RESERVOIRS UNDERGROUND. AS MUCH AS I COULD TAKE.
I RATIONED EVERY DROP. AND WHEN THAT WAS GONE I HUNTED DOWN THE LAST REMNANTS OF ORGANIC LIFE.
BUT IT'S ALL GONE NOW.
ALL THE BLOOD IN THE WORLD.

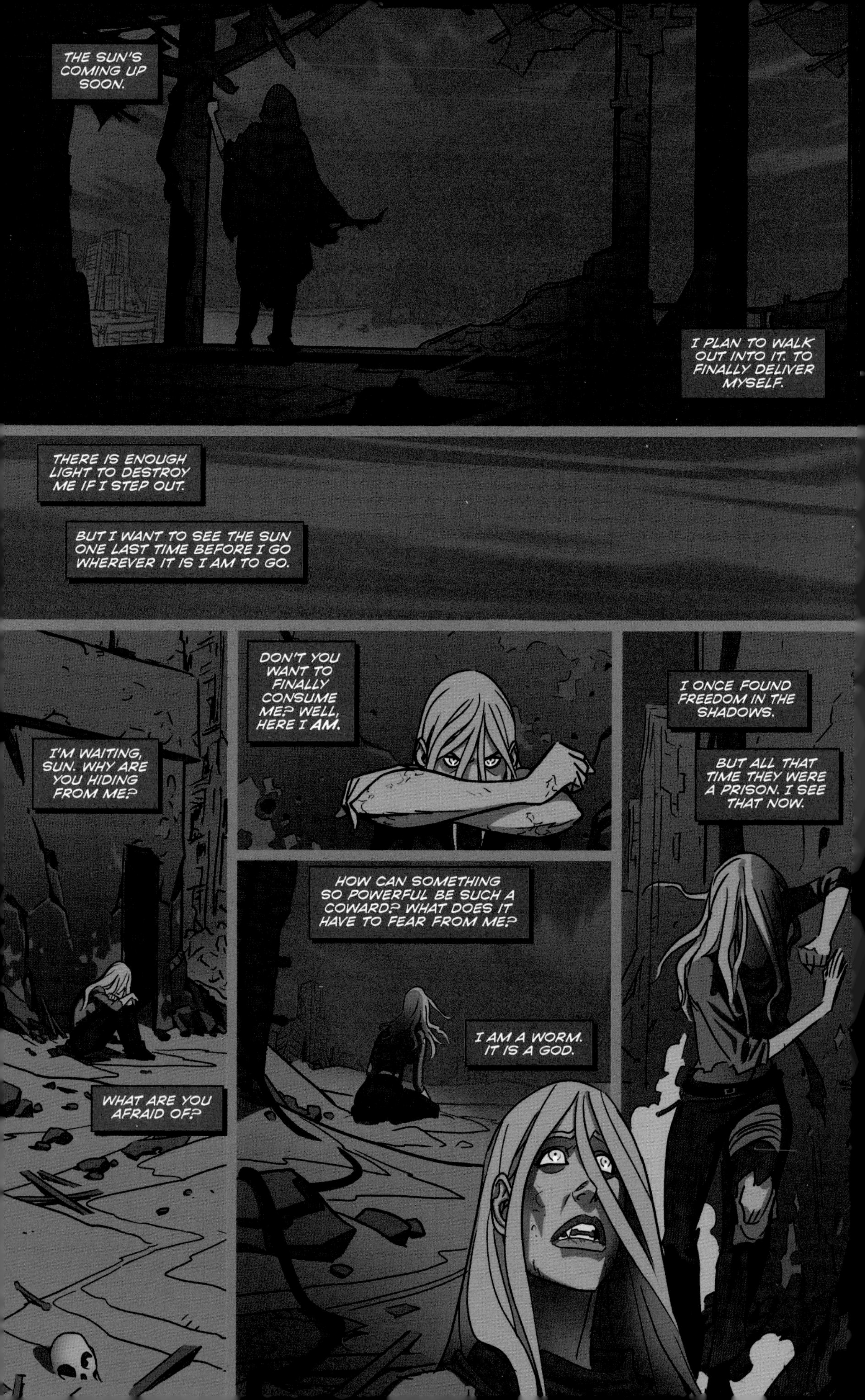
THE SUN'S COMING UP SOON.
I PLAN TO WALK OUT INTO IT. TO FINALLY DELIVER MYSELF.
THERE IS ENOUGH LIGHT TO DESTROY ME IF I STEP OUT.
BUT I WANT TO SEE THE SUN ONE LAST TIME BEFORE I GO WHEREVER IT IS I AM TO GO.
I'M WAITING, SUN. WHY ARE YOU HIDING FROM ME?
WHAT ARE YOU AFRAID OF?
DON'T YOU WANT TO FINALLY CONSUME ME? WELL, HERE I AM.
HOW CAN SOMETHING SO POWERFUL BE SUCH A COWARD? WHAT DOES IT HAVE TO FEAR FROM ME?
I AM A WORM. IT IS A GOD.
I ONCE FOUND FREEDOM IN THE SHADOWS.
BUT ALL THAT TIME THEY WERE A PRISON. I SEE THAT NOW.

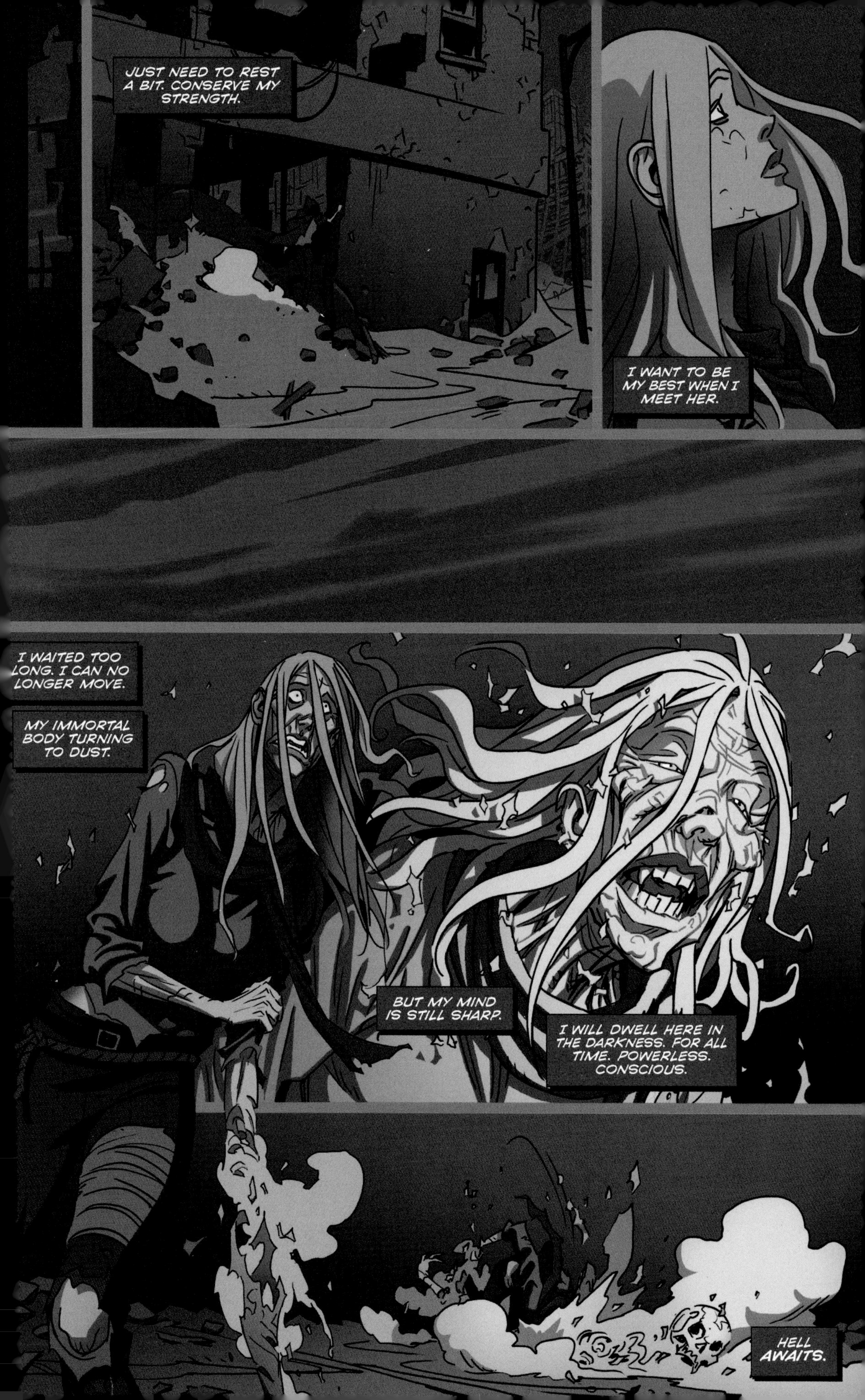
JUST NEED TO REST A BIT. CONSERVE MY STRENGTH.
I WANT TO BE MY BEST WHEN I MEET HER.
I WAITED TOO LONG. I CAN NO LONGER MOVE.
MY IMMORTAL BODY TURNING TO DUST.
BUT MY MIND IS STILL SHARP.
I WILL DWELL HERE IN THE DARKNESS. FOR ALL TIME. POWERLESS. CONSCIOUS.
HELL AWAITS.

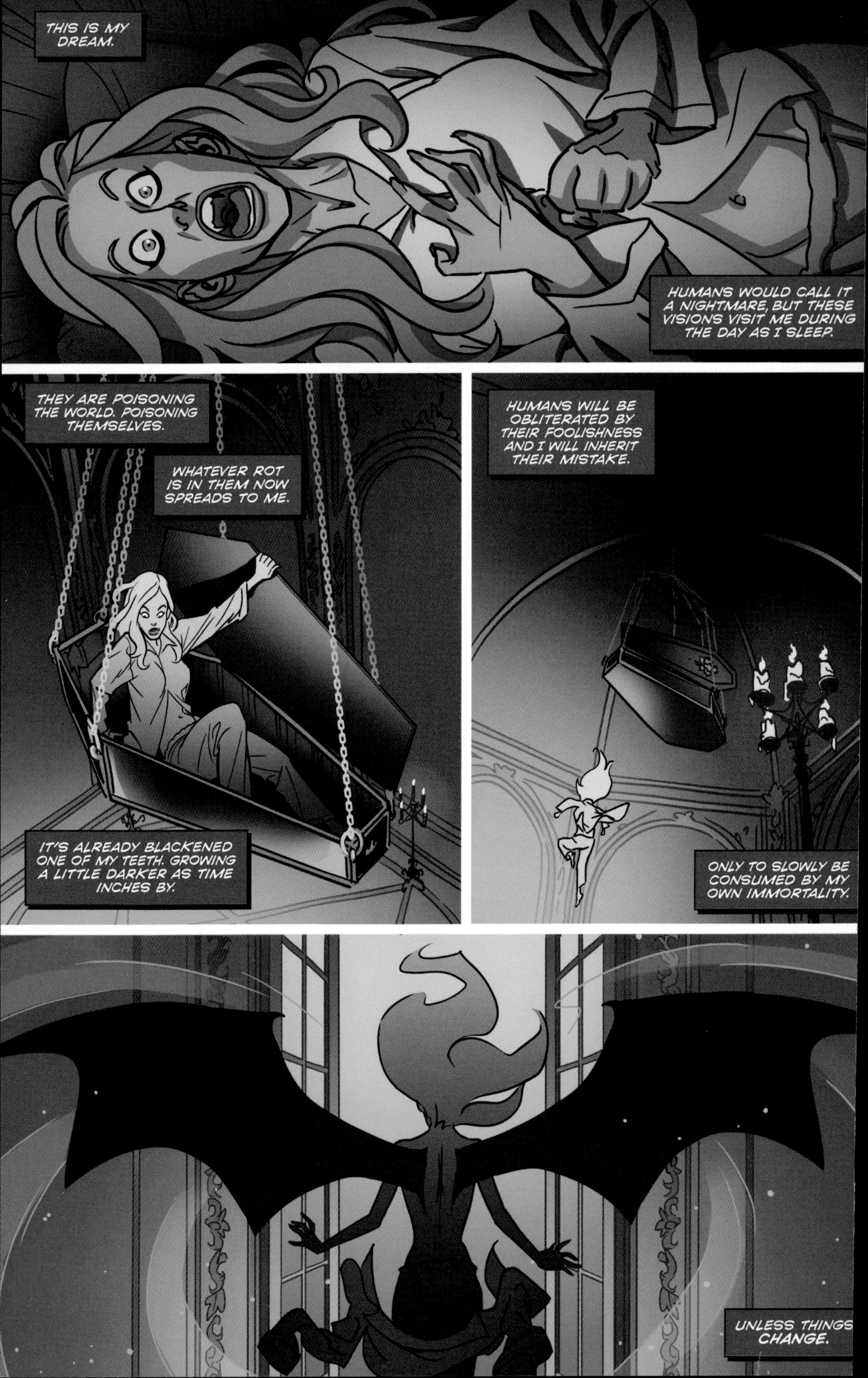
THIS IS MY DREAM.
HUMANS WOULD CALL IT A NIGHTMARE, BUT THESE VISIONS VISIT ME DURING THE DAY AS I SLEEP.
THEY ARE POISONING THE WORLD. POISONING THEMSELVES.
WHATEVER ROT IS IN THEM NOW SPREADS TO ME.
IT'S ALREADY BLACKENED ONE OF MY TEETH. GROWING A LITTLE DARKER AS TIME INCHES BY.
HUMANS WILL BE OBLITERATED BY THEIR FOOLISHNESS AND I WILL INHERIT THEIR MISTAKE.
ONLY TO SLOWLY BE CONSUMED BY MY OWN IMMORTALITY.
UNLESS THINGS CHANGE.

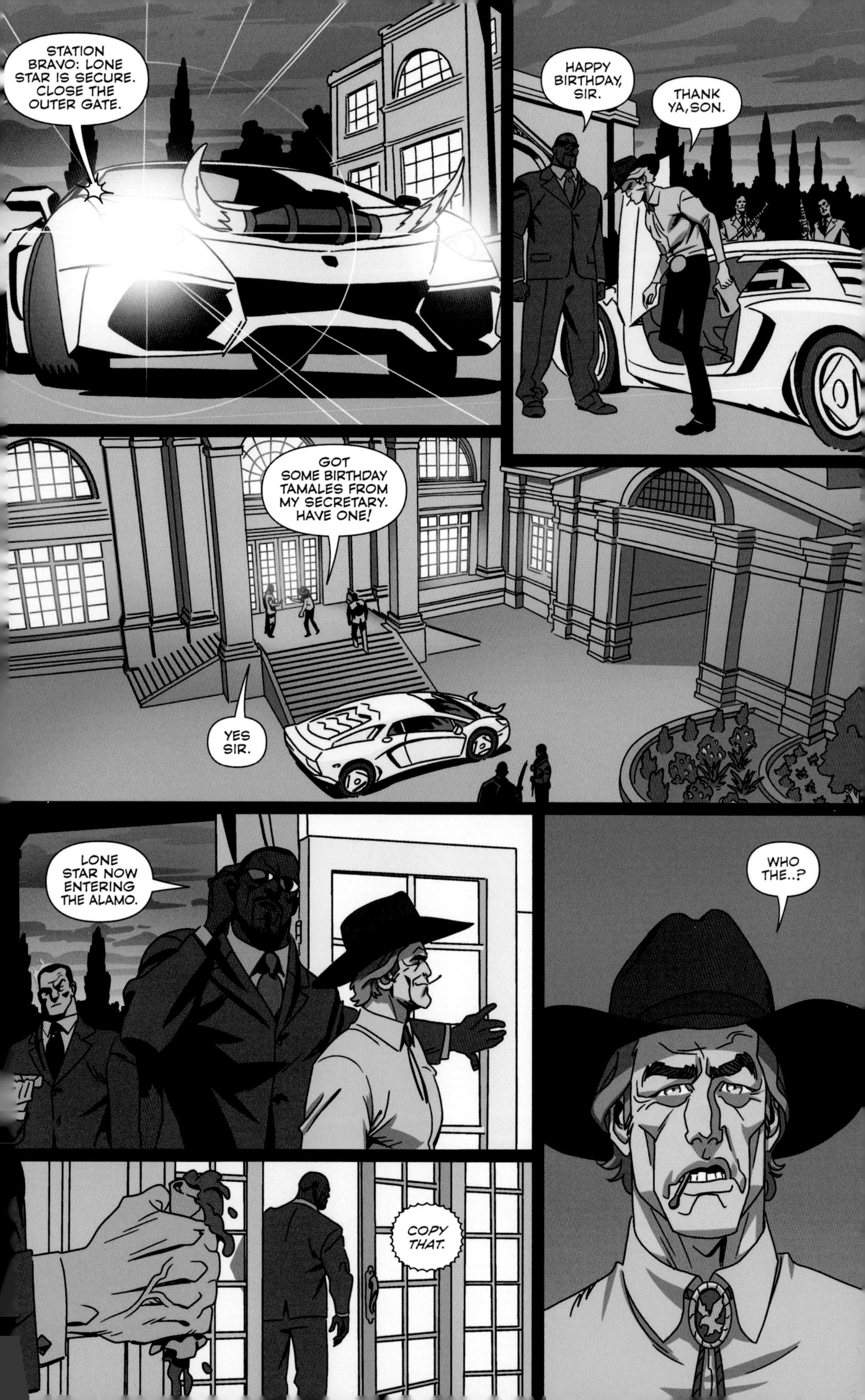
STATION BRAVO: LONE STAR IS SECURE. CLOSE THE OUTER GATE.
HAPPY BIRTHDAY, SIR.
THANK YA, SON.
GOT SOME BIRTHDAY TAMALES FROM MY SECRETARY. HAVE ONE!
YES SIR.
LONE STAR NOW ENTERING THE ALAMO.
WHO THE..?
COPY THAT.

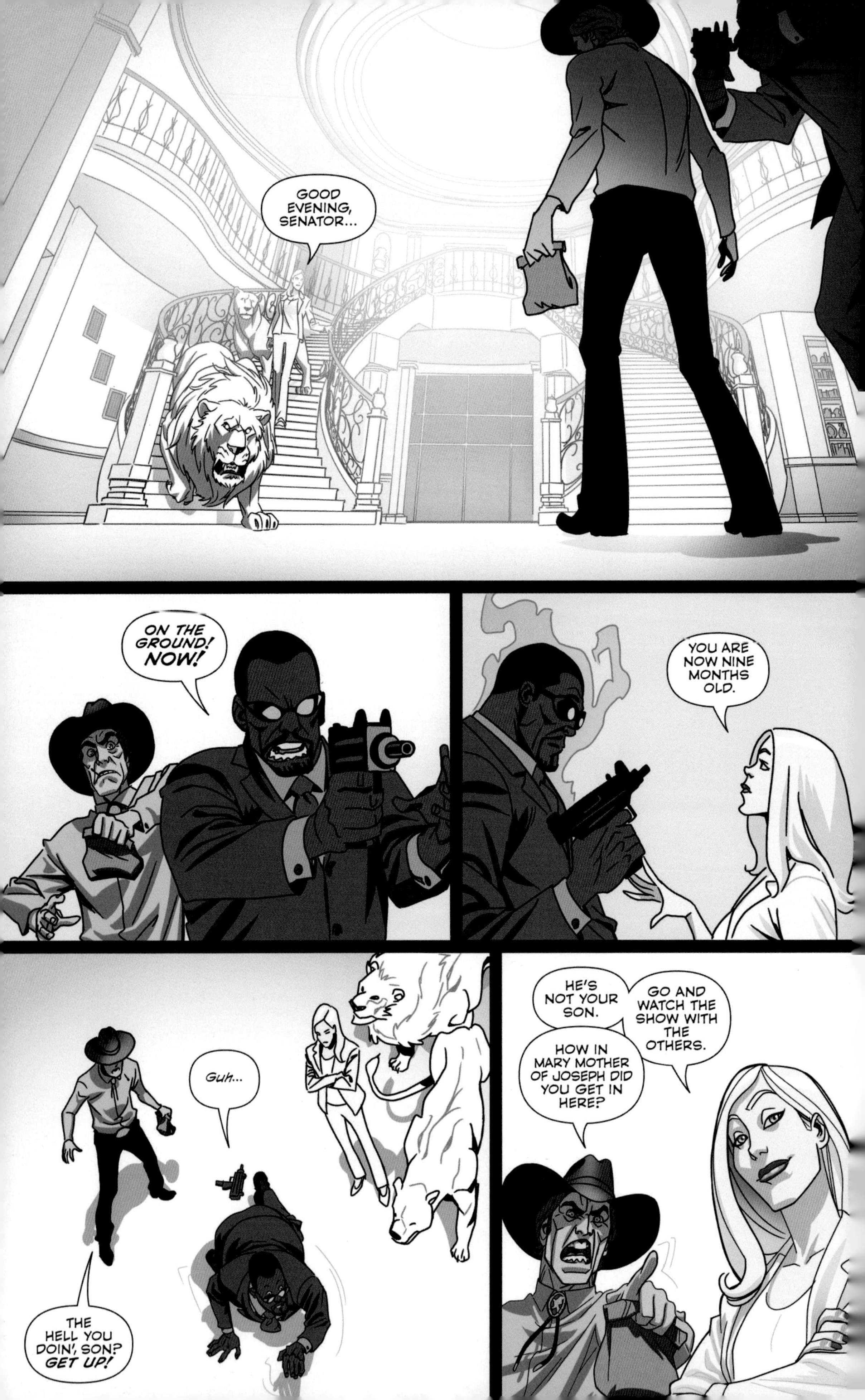
GOOD EVENING, SENATOR...
ON THE GROUND! NOW!
YOU ARE NOW NINE MONTHS OLD.
Guh...
THE HELL YOU DOIN', SON? GET UP!
HE'S NOT YOUR SON.
HOW IN MARY MOTHER OF JOSEPH DID YOU GET IN HERE?
GO AND WATCH THE SHOW WITH THE OTHERS.

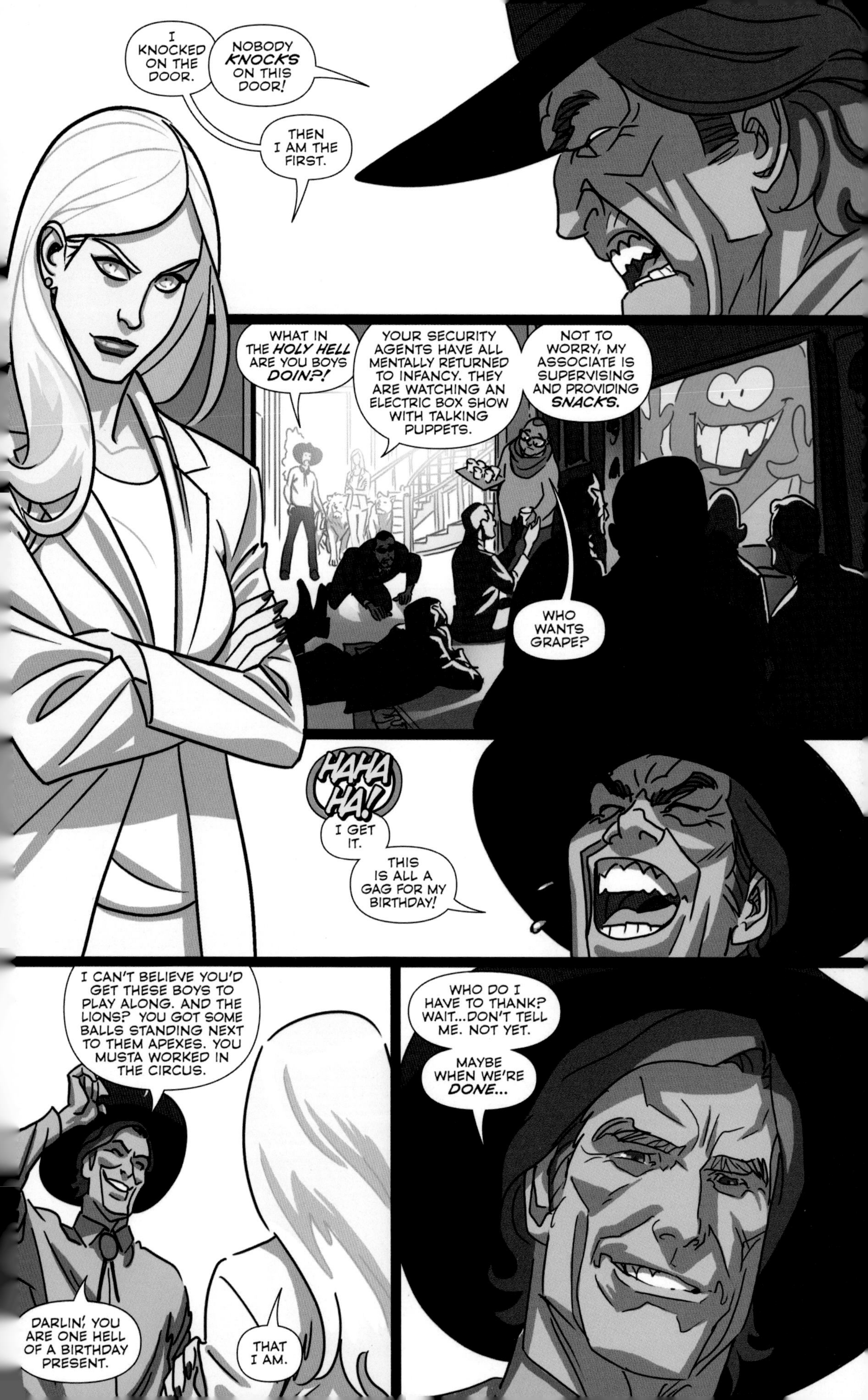
I KNOCKED ON THE DOOR.
NOBODY *KNOCKS* ON THIS DOOR!
THEN I AM THE FIRST.
WHAT IN THE *HOLY HELL* ARE YOU BOYS *DOIN?!*
YOUR SECURITY AGENTS HAVE ALL MENTALLY RETURNED TO INFANCY. THEY ARE WATCHING AN ELECTRIC BOX SHOW WITH TALKING PUPPETS.
NOT TO WORRY, MY ASSOCIATE IS SUPERVISING AND PROVIDING *SNACKS*.
WHO WANTS GRAPE?
HAHA HA!
I GET IT.
THIS IS ALL A GAG FOR MY BIRTHDAY!
I CAN'T BELIEVE YOU'D GET THESE BOYS TO PLAY ALONG. AND THE LIONS? YOU GOT SOME BALLS STANDING NEXT TO THEM APEXES. YOU MUSTA WORKED IN THE CIRCUS.
DARLIN', YOU ARE ONE HELL OF A BIRTHDAY PRESENT.
THAT I AM.
WHO DO I HAVE TO THANK? WAIT...DON'T TELL ME. NOT YET.
MAYBE WHEN WE'RE *DONE*...

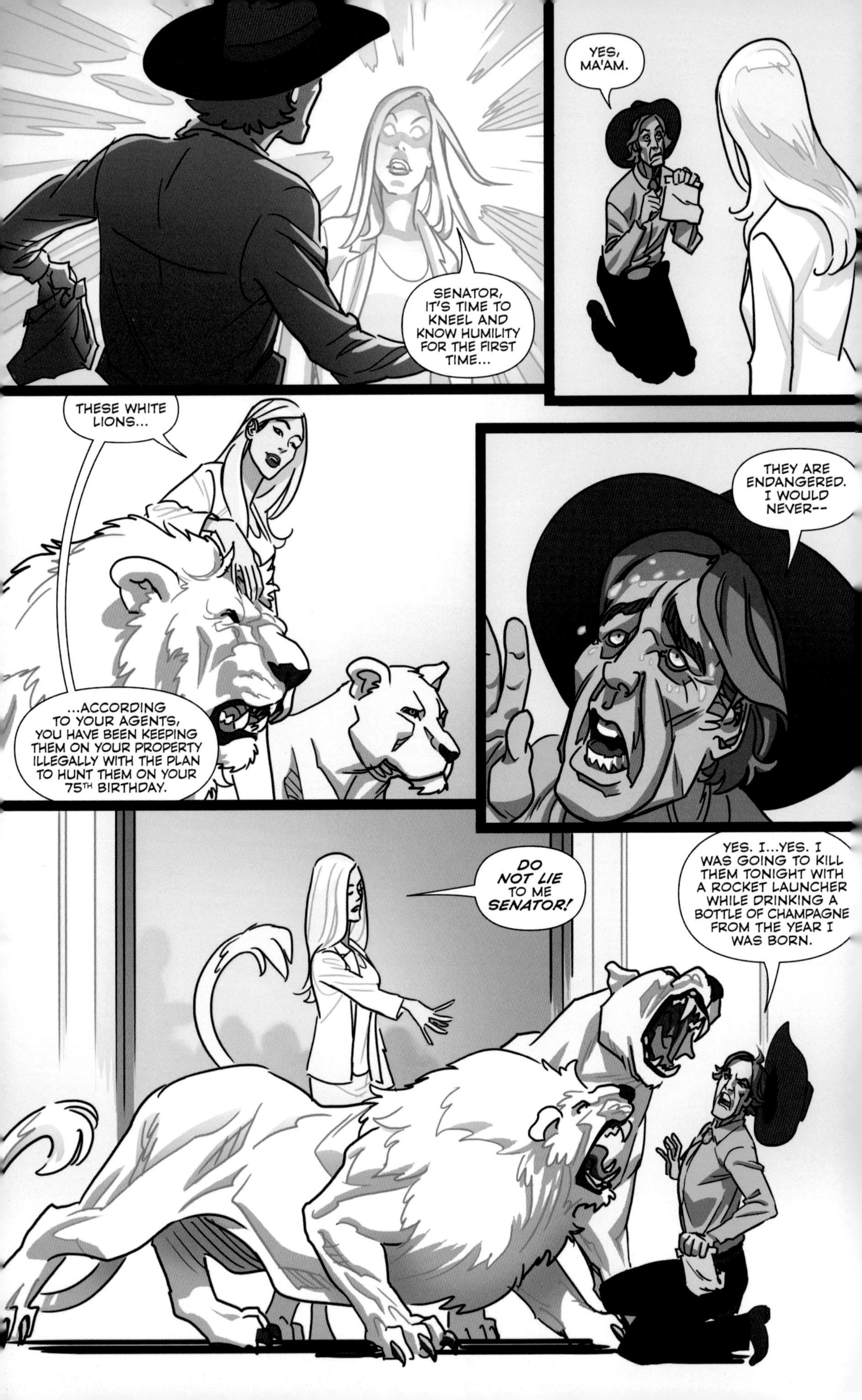
SENATOR, IT'S TIME TO KNEEL AND KNOW HUMILITY FOR THE FIRST TIME...
YES, MA'AM.
THESE WHITE LIONS...
...ACCORDING TO YOUR AGENTS, YOU HAVE BEEN KEEPING THEM ON YOUR PROPERTY ILLEGALLY WITH THE PLAN TO HUNT THEM ON YOUR 75TH BIRTHDAY.
THEY ARE ENDANGERED. I WOULD NEVER--
DO NOT LIE TO ME SENATOR!
YES. I...YES. I WAS GOING TO KILL THEM TONIGHT WITH A ROCKET LAUNCHER WHILE DRINKING A BOTTLE OF CHAMPAGNE FROM THE YEAR I WAS BORN.

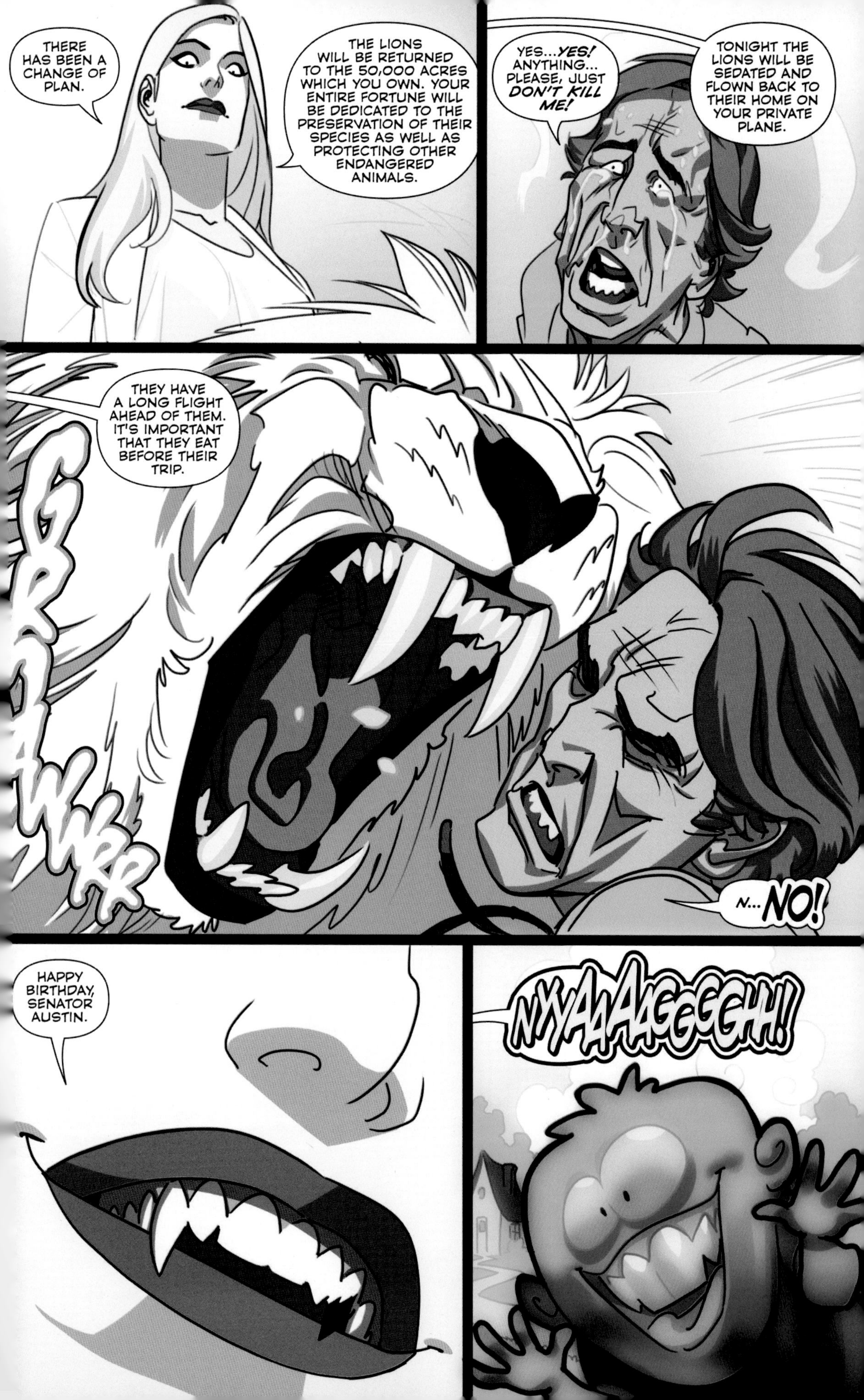

THERE HAS BEEN A CHANGE OF PLAN.
THE LIONS WILL BE RETURNED TO THE 50,000 ACRES WHICH YOU OWN. YOUR ENTIRE FORTUNE WILL BE DEDICATED TO THE PRESERVATION OF THEIR SPECIES AS WELL AS PROTECTING OTHER ENDANGERED ANIMALS.
YES...*YES!* ANYTHING... PLEASE, JUST *DON'T KILL ME!*
TONIGHT THE LIONS WILL BE SEDATED AND FLOWN BACK TO THEIR HOME ON YOUR PRIVATE PLANE.
THEY HAVE A LONG FLIGHT AHEAD OF THEM. IT'S IMPORTANT THAT THEY EAT BEFORE THEIR TRIP.
GRRAWRR
N...NO!
HAPPY BIRTHDAY, SENATOR AUSTIN.
NYYAAAAGGGGHH!!

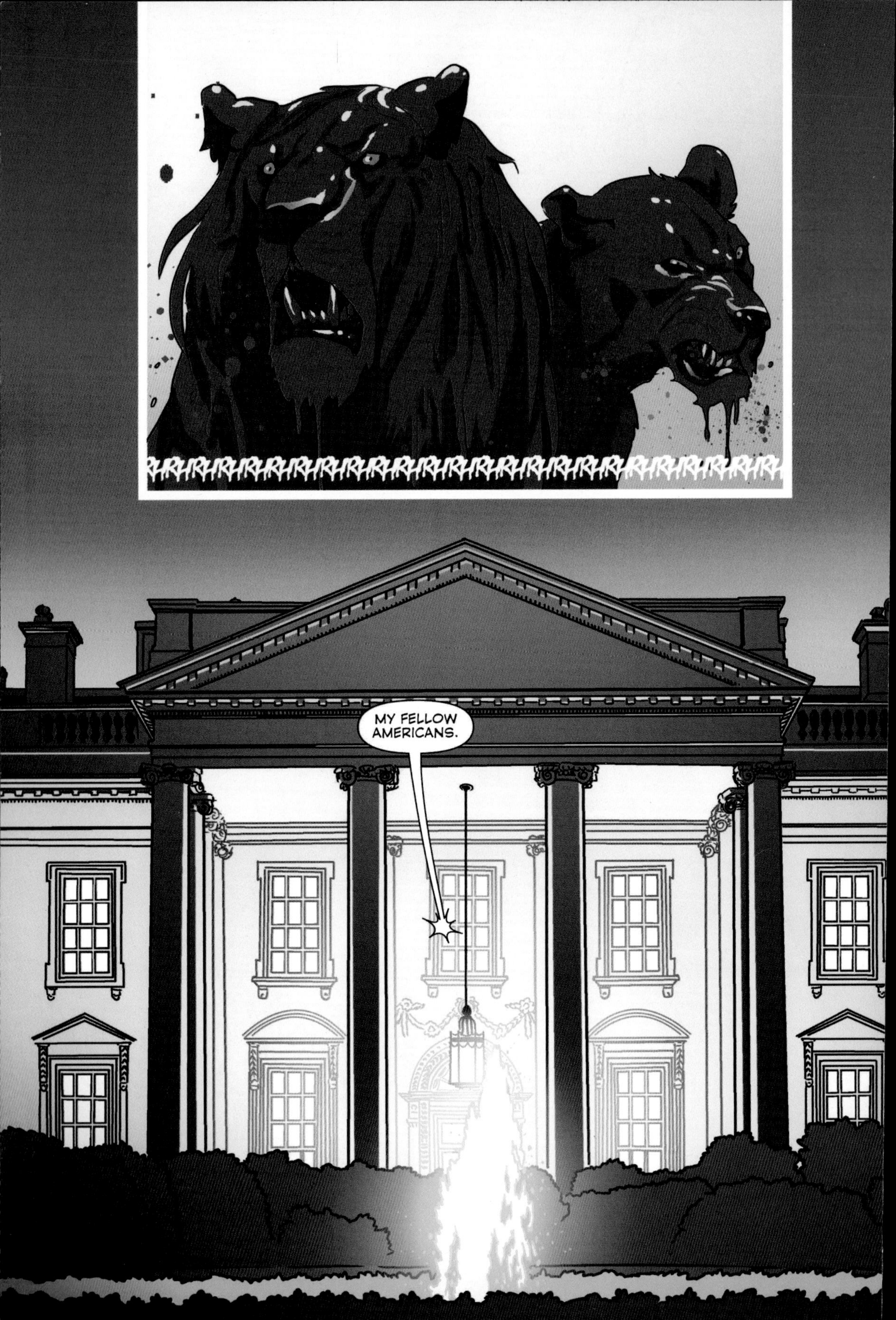
MY FELLOW AMERICANS.

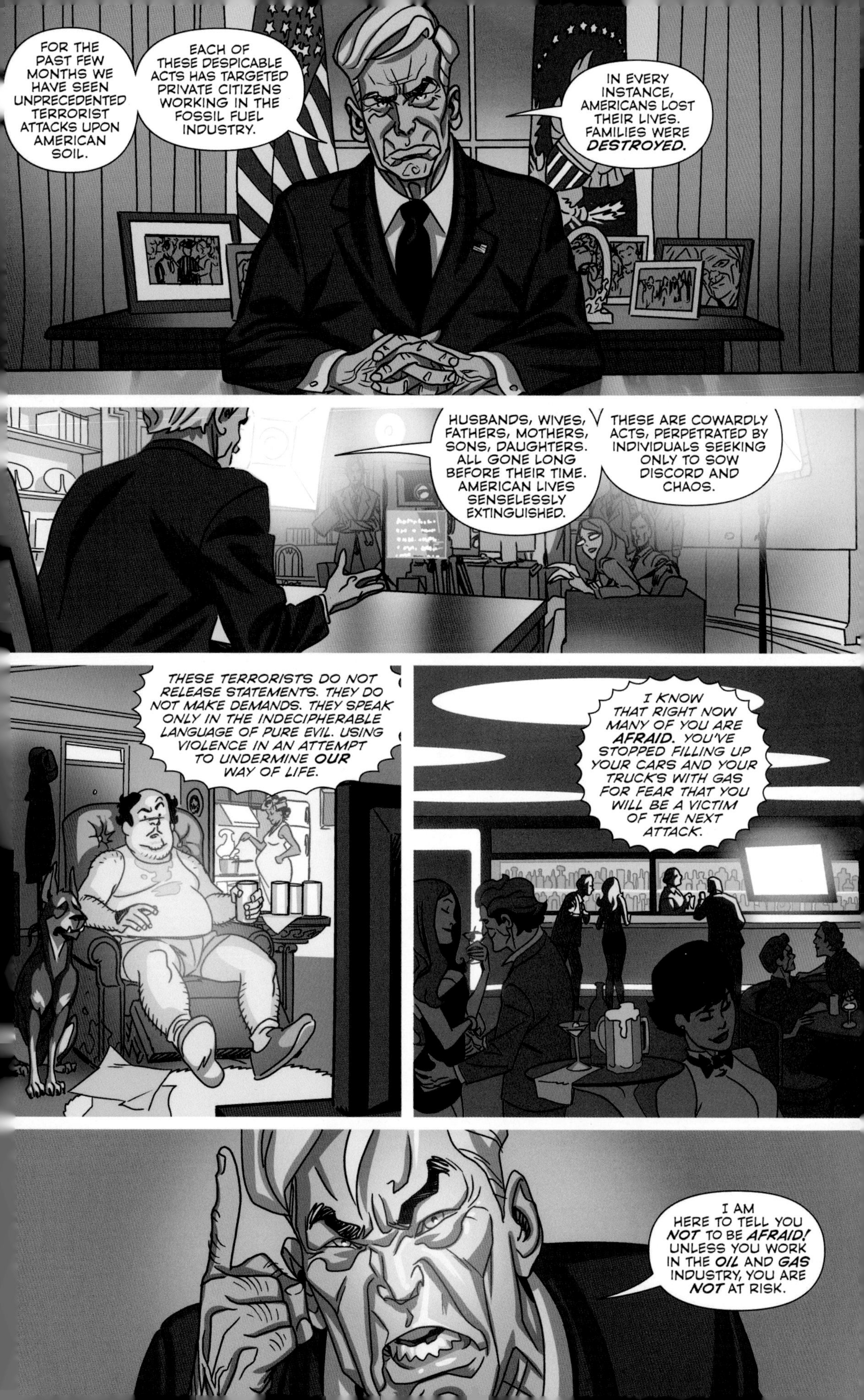
FOR THE PAST FEW MONTHS WE HAVE SEEN UNPRECEDENTED TERRORIST ATTACKS UPON AMERICAN SOIL.
EACH OF THESE DESPICABLE ACTS HAS TARGETED PRIVATE CITIZENS WORKING IN THE FOSSIL FUEL INDUSTRY.
IN EVERY INSTANCE, AMERICANS LOST THEIR LIVES. FAMILIES WERE **DESTROYED.**
HUSBANDS, WIVES, FATHERS, MOTHERS, SONS, DAUGHTERS. ALL GONE LONG BEFORE THEIR TIME. AMERICAN LIVES SENSELESSLY EXTINGUISHED.
THESE ARE COWARDLY ACTS, PERPETRATED BY INDIVIDUALS SEEKING ONLY TO SOW DISCORD AND CHAOS.
*THESE TERRORISTS DO NOT RELEASE STATEMENTS. THEY DO NOT MAKE DEMANDS. THEY SPEAK ONLY IN THE INDECIPHERABLE LANGUAGE OF PURE EVIL. USING VIOLENCE IN AN ATTEMPT TO UNDERMINE **OUR** WAY OF LIFE.*
*I KNOW THAT RIGHT NOW MANY OF YOU ARE **AFRAID.** YOU'VE STOPPED FILLING UP YOUR CARS AND YOUR TRUCKS WITH GAS FOR FEAR THAT YOU WILL BE A VICTIM OF THE NEXT ATTACK.*
I AM HERE TO TELL YOU ***NOT*** TO BE ***AFRAID!*** UNLESS YOU WORK IN THE ***OIL*** AND ***GAS*** INDUSTRY, YOU ARE ***NOT*** AT RISK.

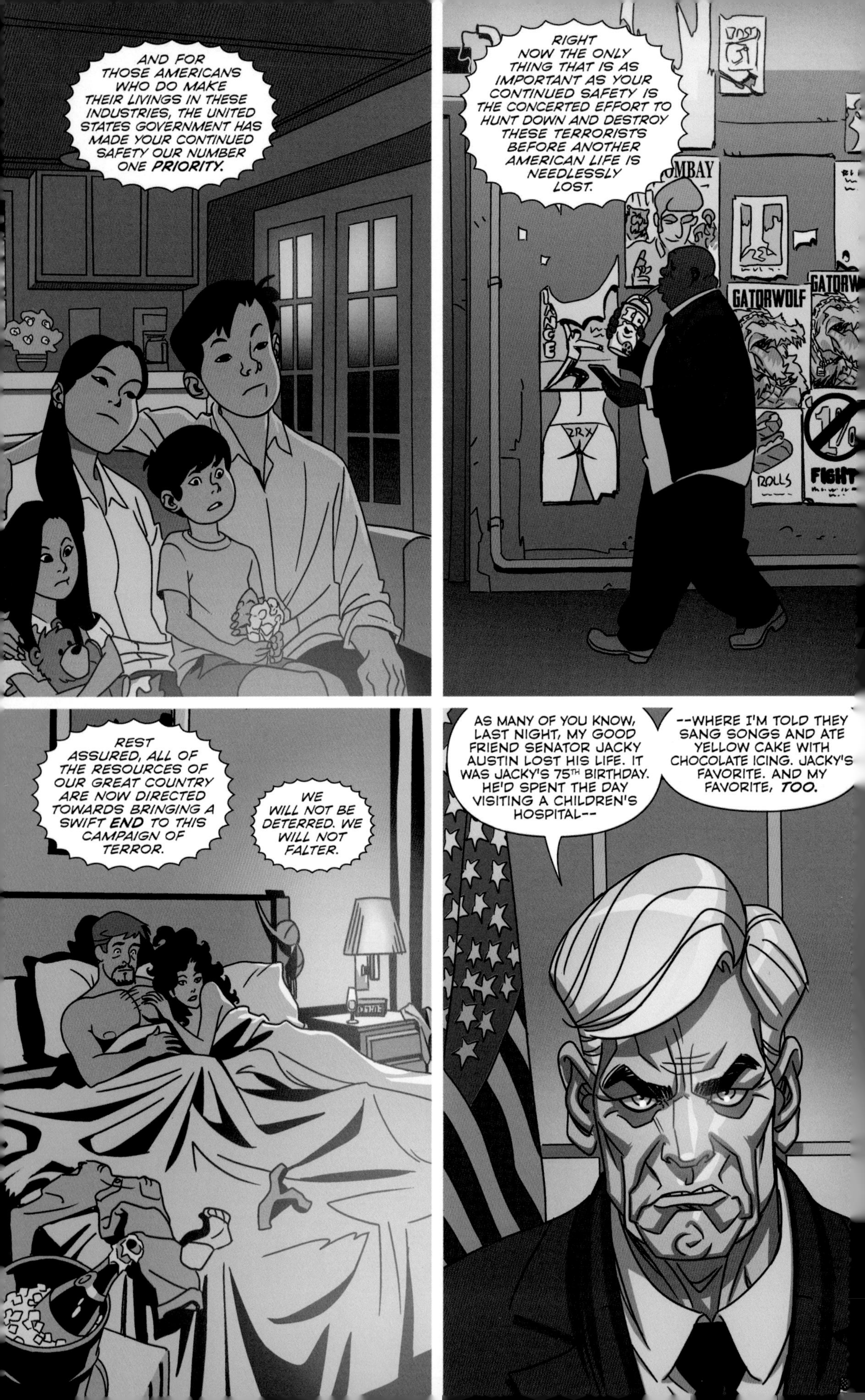
AND FOR THOSE AMERICANS WHO DO MAKE THEIR LIVINGS IN THESE INDUSTRIES, THE UNITED STATES GOVERNMENT HAS MADE YOUR CONTINUED SAFETY OUR NUMBER ONE *PRIORITY.*
RIGHT NOW THE ONLY THING THAT IS AS IMPORTANT AS YOUR CONTINUED SAFETY IS THE CONCERTED EFFORT TO HUNT DOWN AND DESTROY THESE TERRORISTS BEFORE ANOTHER AMERICAN LIFE IS NEEDLESSLY LOST.
GATORWOLF
ROLLS
FIGHT
REST ASSURED, ALL OF THE RESOURCES OF OUR GREAT COUNTRY ARE NOW DIRECTED TOWARDS BRINGING A SWIFT **END** TO THIS CAMPAIGN OF TERROR.
WE WILL NOT BE DETERRED. WE WILL NOT FALTER.
AS MANY OF YOU KNOW, LAST NIGHT, MY GOOD FRIEND SENATOR JACKY AUSTIN LOST HIS LIFE. IT WAS JACKY'S 75TH BIRTHDAY. HE'D SPENT THE DAY VISITING A CHILDREN'S HOSPITAL--
--WHERE I'M TOLD THEY SANG SONGS AND ATE YELLOW CAKE WITH CHOCOLATE ICING. JACKY'S FAVORITE. AND MY FAVORITE, ***TOO.***

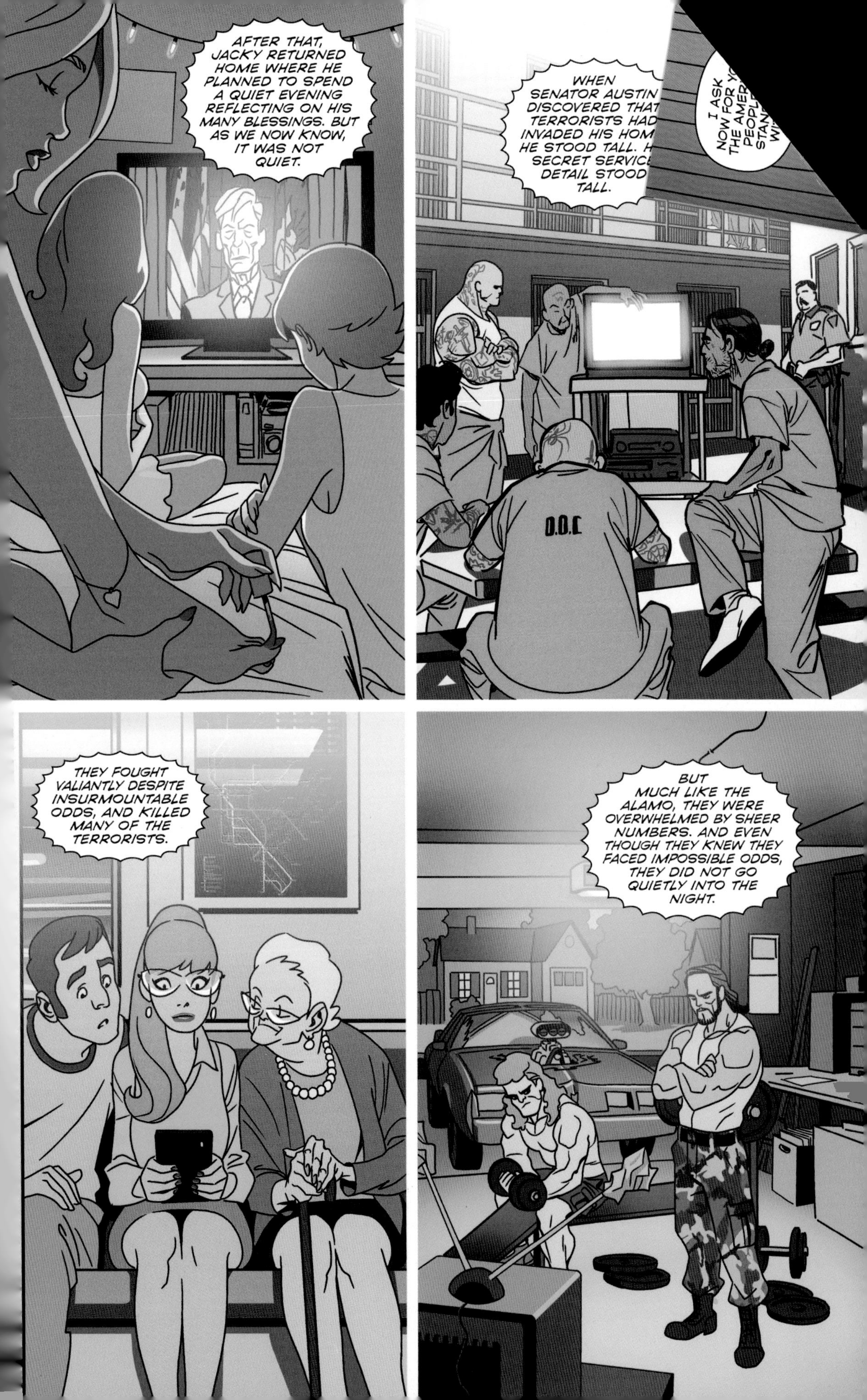
AFTER THAT, JACKY RETURNED HOME WHERE HE PLANNED TO SPEND A QUIET EVENING REFLECTING ON HIS MANY BLESSINGS. BUT AS WE NOW KNOW, IT WAS NOT QUIET.
WHEN SENATOR AUSTIN DISCOVERED THAT TERRORISTS HAD INVADED HIS HOM HE STOOD TALL. H SECRET SERVIC DETAIL STOOD TALL.
I ASK
D.O.C
THEY FOUGHT VALIANTLY DESPITE INSURMOUNTABLE ODDS, AND KILLED MANY OF THE TERRORISTS.
BUT MUCH LIKE THE ALAMO, THEY WERE OVERWHELMED BY SHEER NUMBERS. AND EVEN THOUGH THEY KNEW THEY FACED IMPOSSIBLE ODDS, THEY DID NOT GO QUIETLY INTO THE NIGHT.

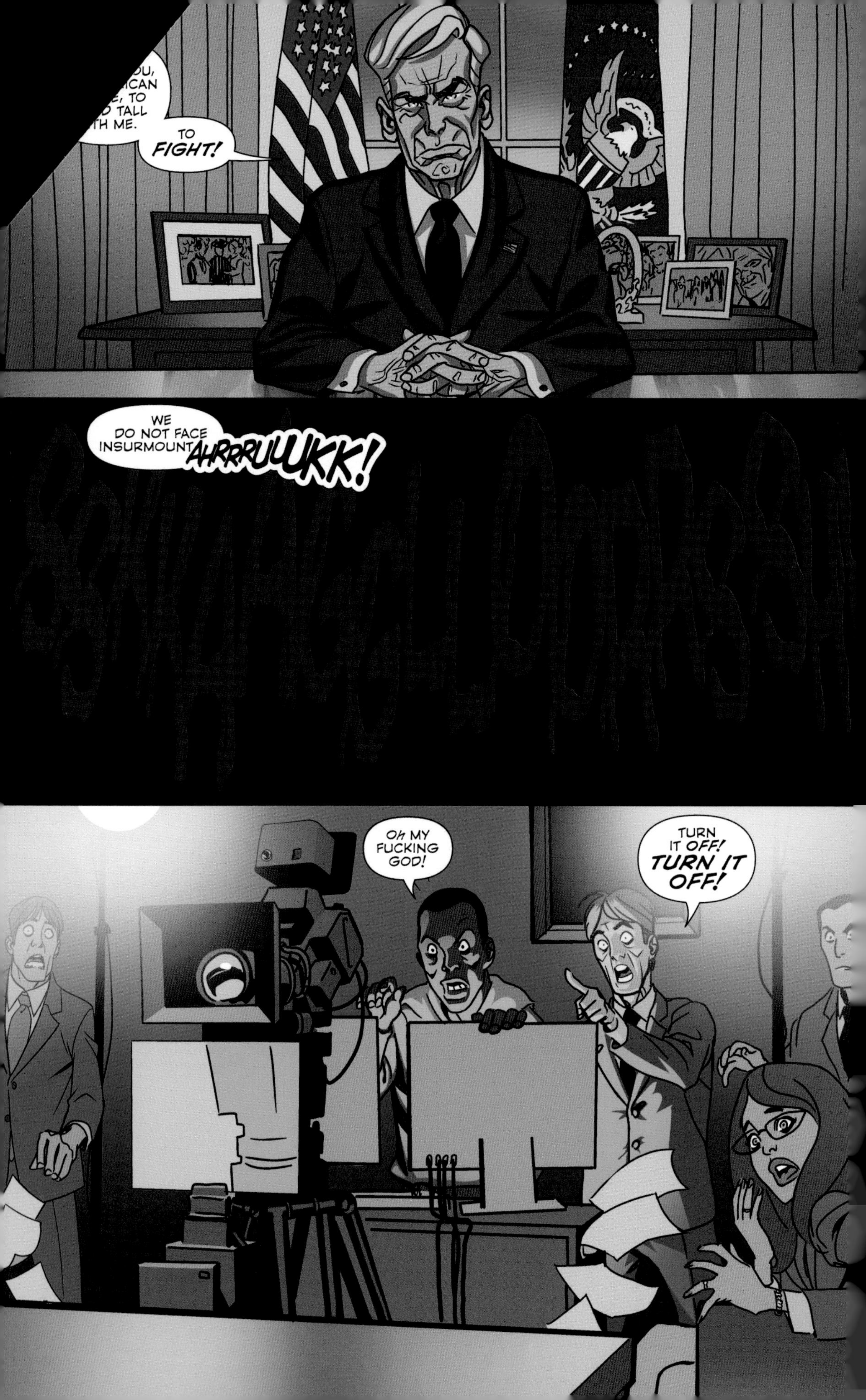
TO FIGHT!
WE DO NOT FACE INSURMOUNTAHRRRUUUKK!
OH MY FUCKING GOD!
TURN IT OFF! TURN IT OFF!

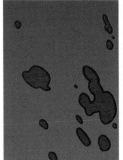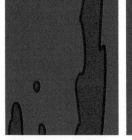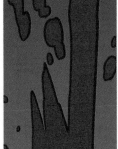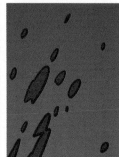

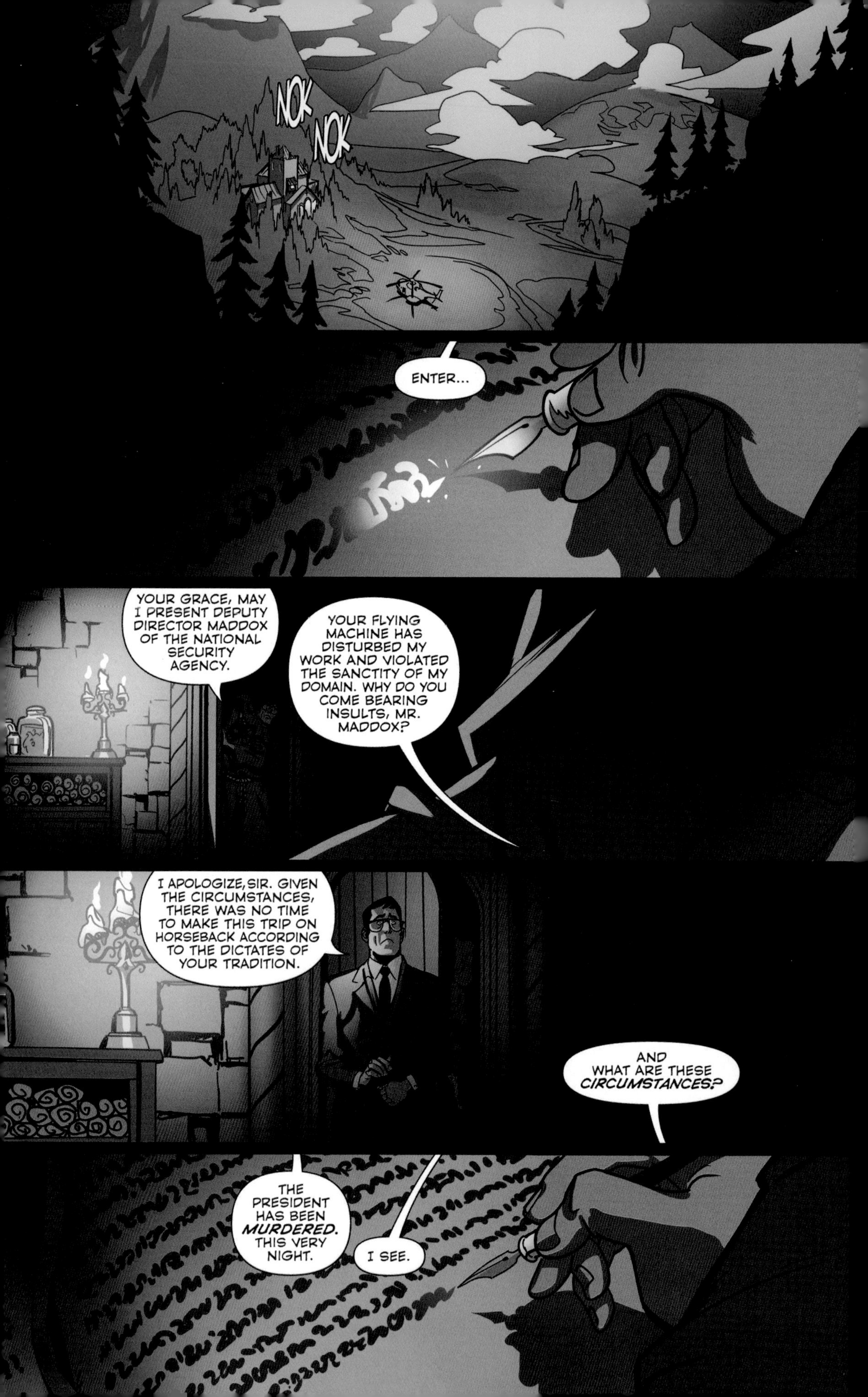
NOK
NOK
ENTER...
YOUR GRACE, MAY I PRESENT DEPUTY DIRECTOR MADDOX OF THE NATIONAL SECURITY AGENCY.
YOUR FLYING MACHINE HAS DISTURBED MY WORK AND VIOLATED THE SANCTITY OF MY DOMAIN. WHY DO YOU COME BEARING INSULTS, MR. MADDOX?
I APOLOGIZE, SIR. GIVEN THE CIRCUMSTANCES, THERE WAS NO TIME TO MAKE THIS TRIP ON HORSEBACK ACCORDING TO THE DICTATES OF YOUR TRADITION.
AND WHAT ARE THESE *CIRCUMSTANCES?*
THE PRESIDENT HAS BEEN *MURDERED.* THIS VERY NIGHT.
I SEE.

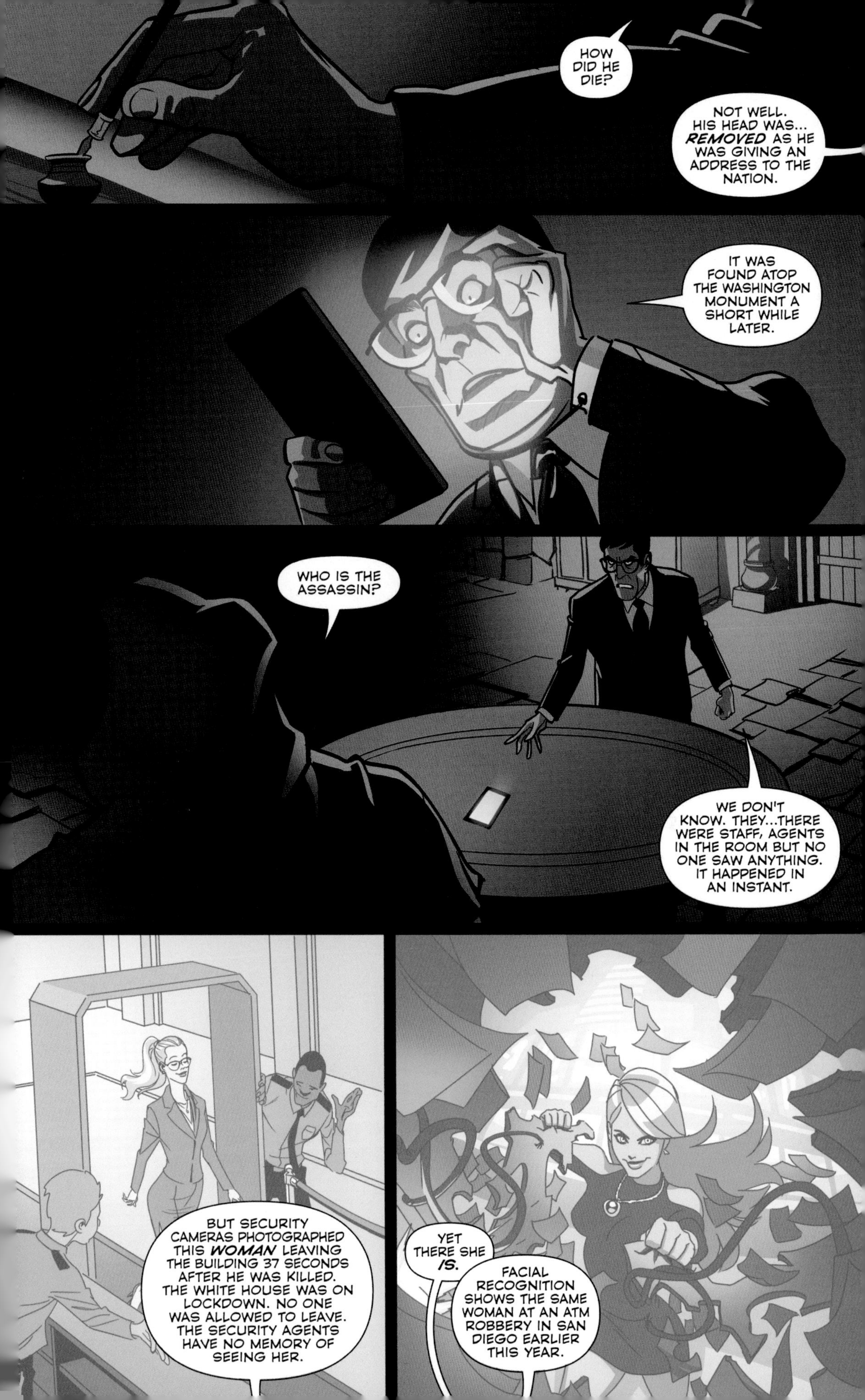
HOW DID HE DIE?
NOT WELL. HIS HEAD WAS... *REMOVED* AS HE WAS GIVING AN ADDRESS TO THE NATION.
IT WAS FOUND ATOP THE WASHINGTON MONUMENT A SHORT WHILE LATER.
WHO IS THE ASSASSIN?
WE DON'T KNOW. THEY...THERE WERE STAFF, AGENTS IN THE ROOM BUT NO ONE SAW ANYTHING. IT HAPPENED IN AN INSTANT.
BUT SECURITY CAMERAS PHOTOGRAPHED THIS *WOMAN* LEAVING THE BUILDING 37 SECONDS AFTER HE WAS KILLED. THE WHITE HOUSE WAS ON LOCKDOWN. NO ONE WAS ALLOWED TO LEAVE. THE SECURITY AGENTS HAVE NO MEMORY OF SEEING HER.
YET THERE SHE *IS.*
FACIAL RECOGNITION SHOWS THE SAME WOMAN AT AN ATM ROBBERY IN SAN DIEGO EARLIER THIS YEAR.

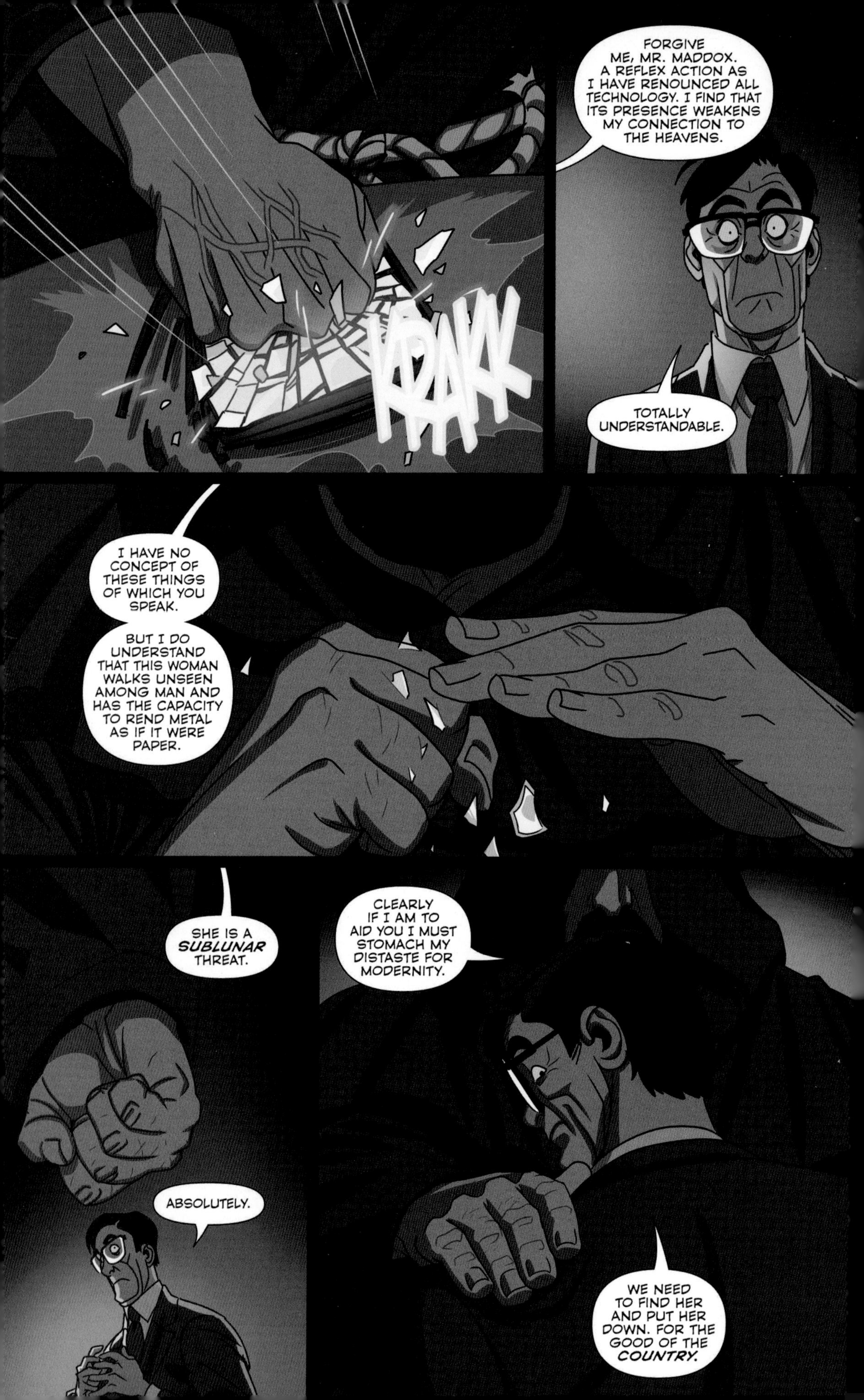
KRAKK
FORGIVE ME, MR. MADDOX. A REFLEX ACTION AS I HAVE RENOUNCED ALL TECHNOLOGY. I FIND THAT ITS PRESENCE WEAKENS MY CONNECTION TO THE HEAVENS.
TOTALLY UNDERSTANDABLE.
I HAVE NO CONCEPT OF THESE THINGS OF WHICH YOU SPEAK.
BUT I DO UNDERSTAND THAT THIS WOMAN WALKS UNSEEN AMONG MAN AND HAS THE CAPACITY TO REND METAL AS IF IT WERE PAPER.
SHE IS A *SUBLUNAR* THREAT.
CLEARLY IF I AM TO AID YOU I MUST STOMACH MY DISTASTE FOR MODERNITY.
ABSOLUTELY.
WE NEED TO FIND HER AND PUT HER DOWN. FOR THE GOOD OF THE *COUNTRY.*

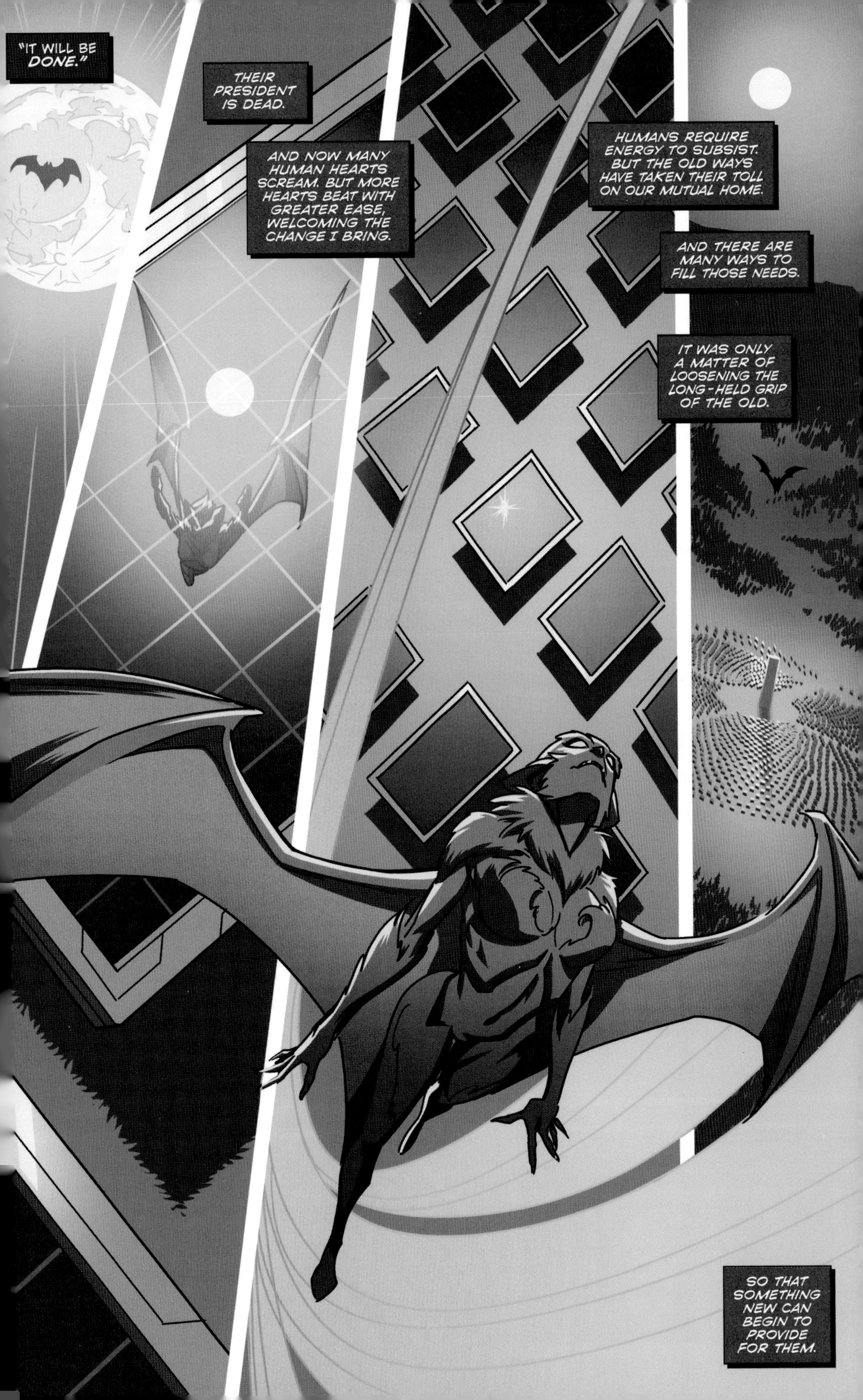
"IT WILL BE DONE."
THEIR PRESIDENT IS DEAD.
AND NOW MANY HUMAN HEARTS SCREAM. BUT MORE HEARTS BEAT WITH GREATER EASE, WELCOMING THE CHANGE I BRING.
HUMANS REQUIRE ENERGY TO SUBSIST. BUT THE OLD WAYS HAVE TAKEN THEIR TOLL ON OUR MUTUAL HOME.
AND THERE ARE MANY WAYS TO FILL THOSE NEEDS.
IT WAS ONLY A MATTER OF LOOSENING THE LONG-HELD GRIP OF THE OLD.
SO THAT SOMETHING NEW CAN BEGIN TO PROVIDE FOR THEM.

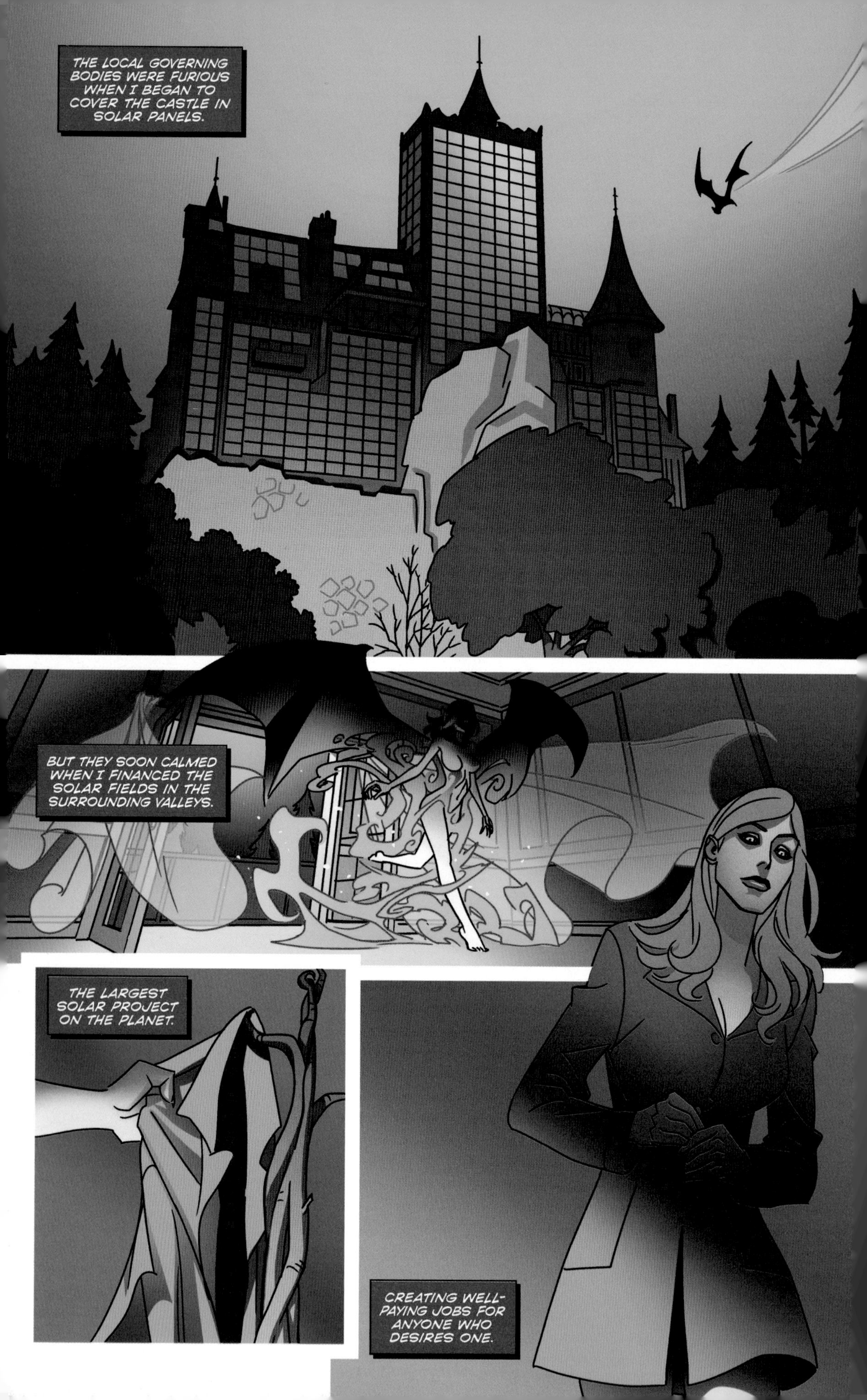
THE LOCAL GOVERNING BODIES WERE FURIOUS WHEN I BEGAN TO COVER THE CASTLE IN SOLAR PANELS.
BUT THEY SOON CALMED WHEN I FINANCED THE SOLAR FIELDS IN THE SURROUNDING VALLEYS.
THE LARGEST SOLAR PROJECT ON THE PLANET.
CREATING WELL-PAYING JOBS FOR ANYONE WHO DESIRES ONE.

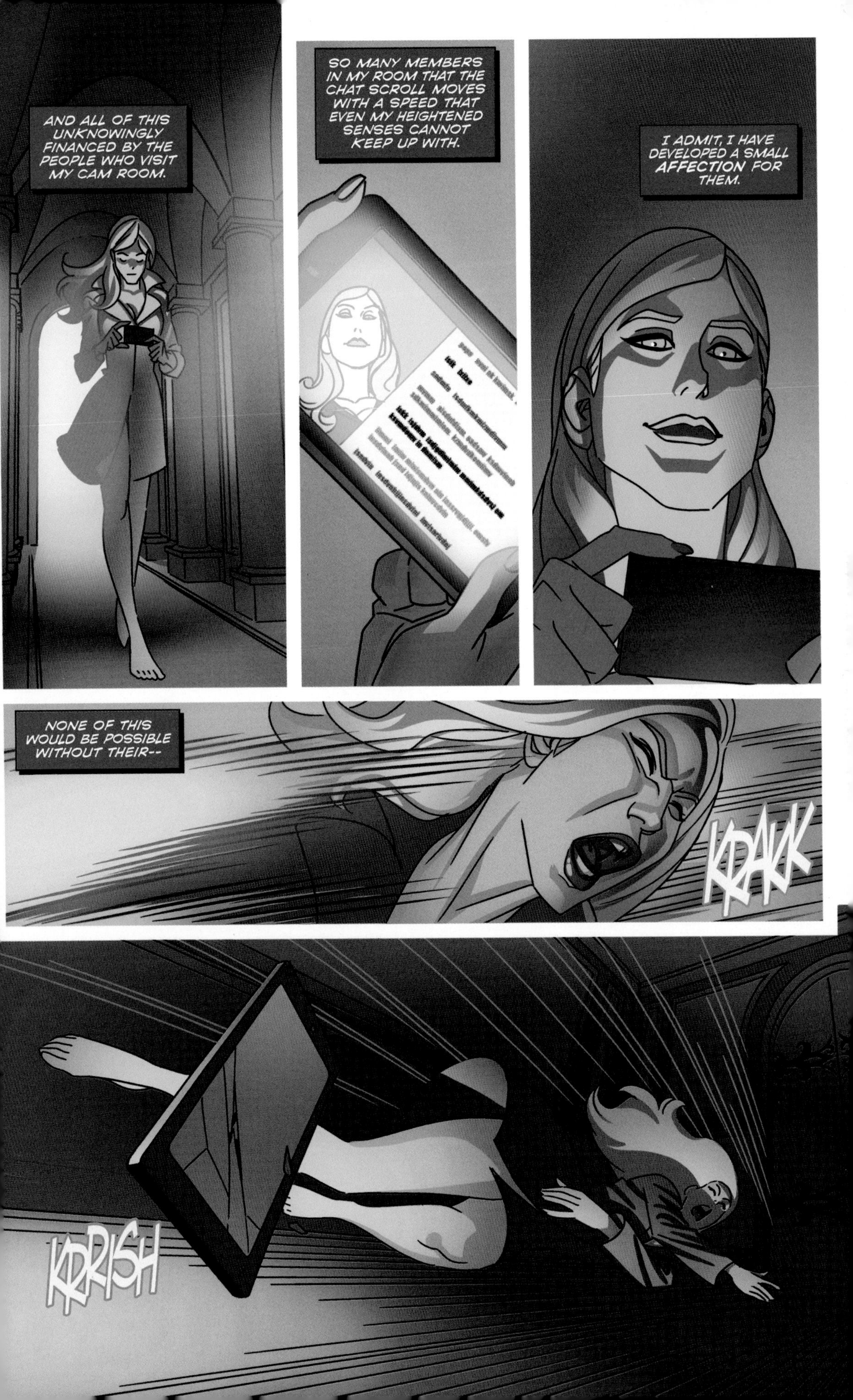
AND ALL OF THIS UNKNOWINGLY FINANCED BY THE PEOPLE WHO VISIT MY CAM ROOM.
SO MANY MEMBERS IN MY ROOM THAT THE CHAT SCROLL MOVES WITH A SPEED THAT EVEN MY HEIGHTENED SENSES CANNOT KEEP UP WITH.
I ADMIT, I HAVE DEVELOPED A SMALL AFFECTION FOR THEM.
NONE OF THIS WOULD BE POSSIBLE WITHOUT THEIR--
KRAKK
KRRISH

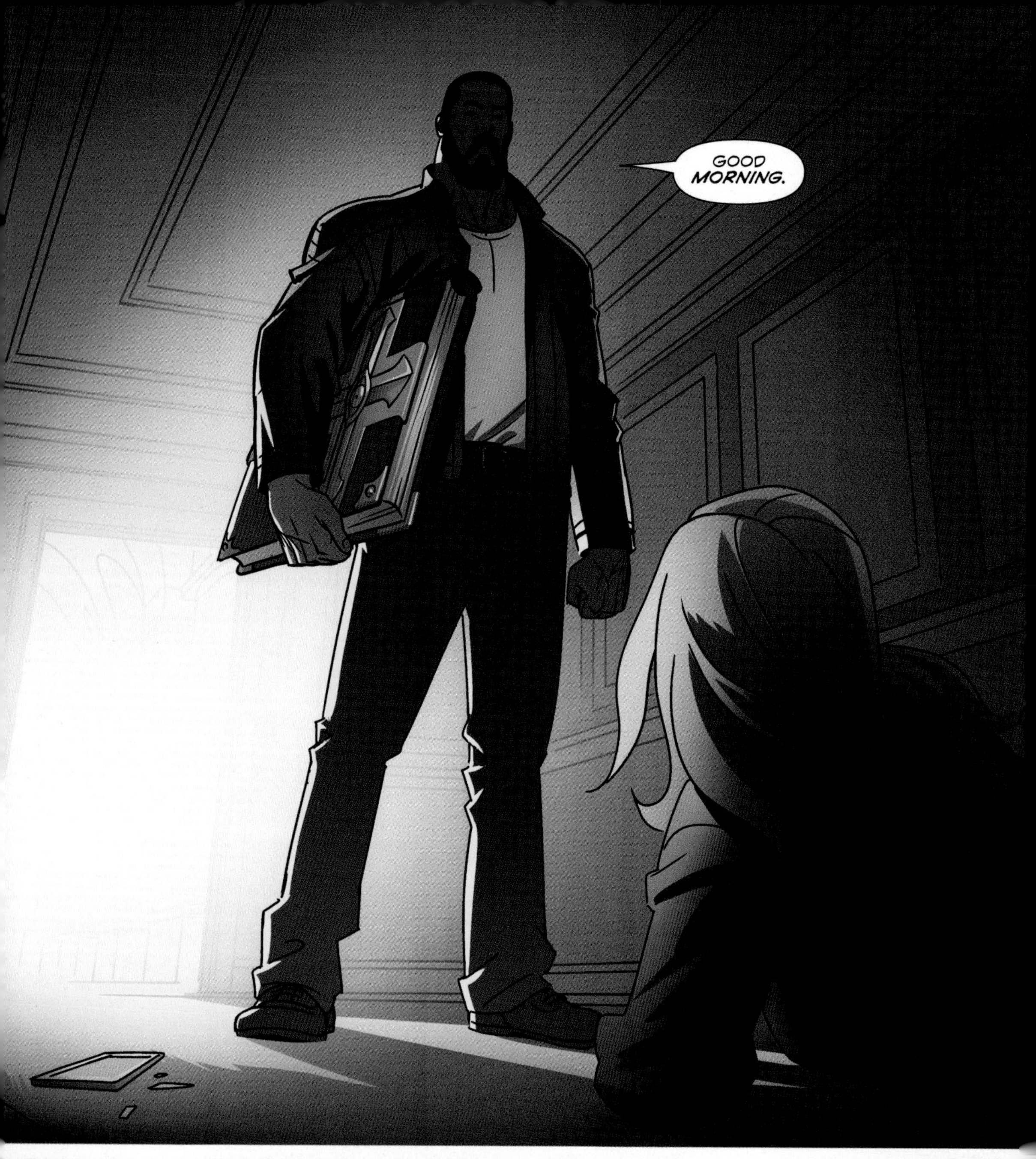
GOOD MORNING.

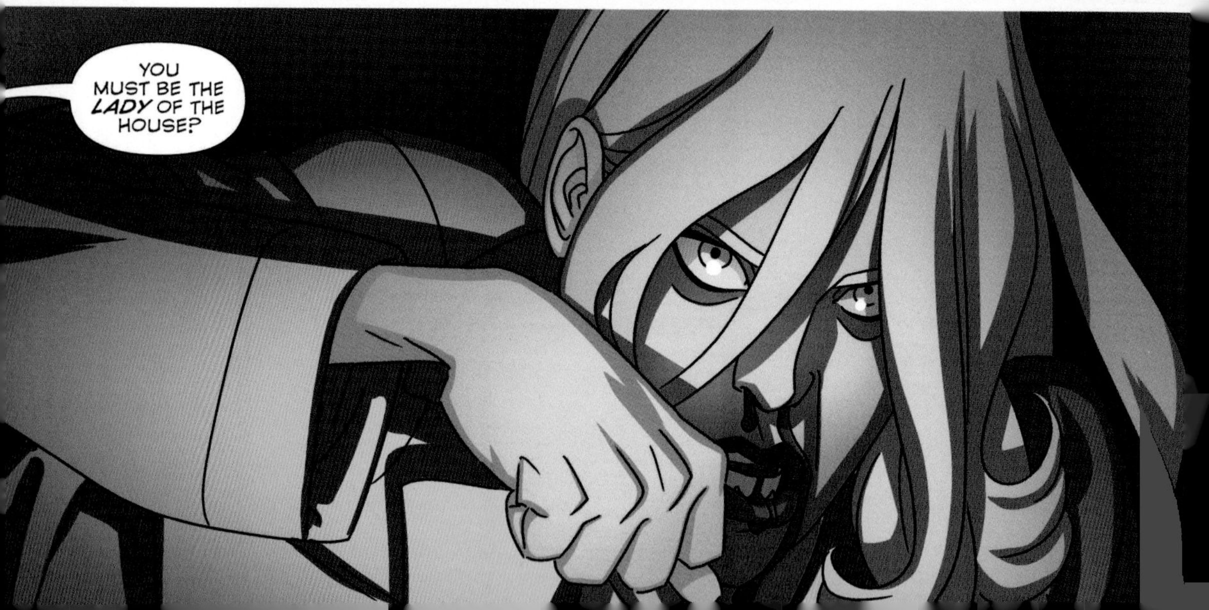
YOU MUST BE THE LADY OF THE HOUSE?

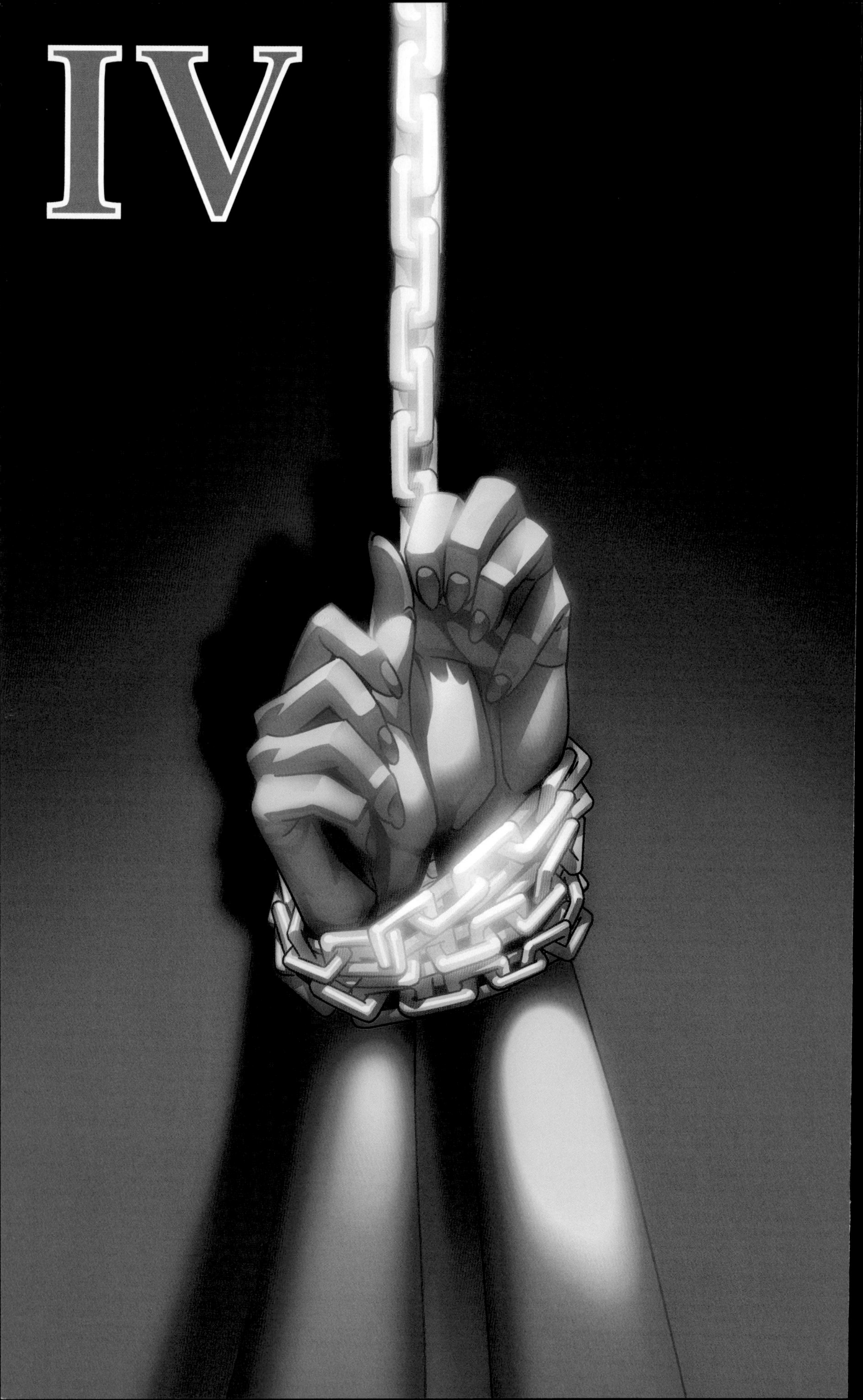
IV

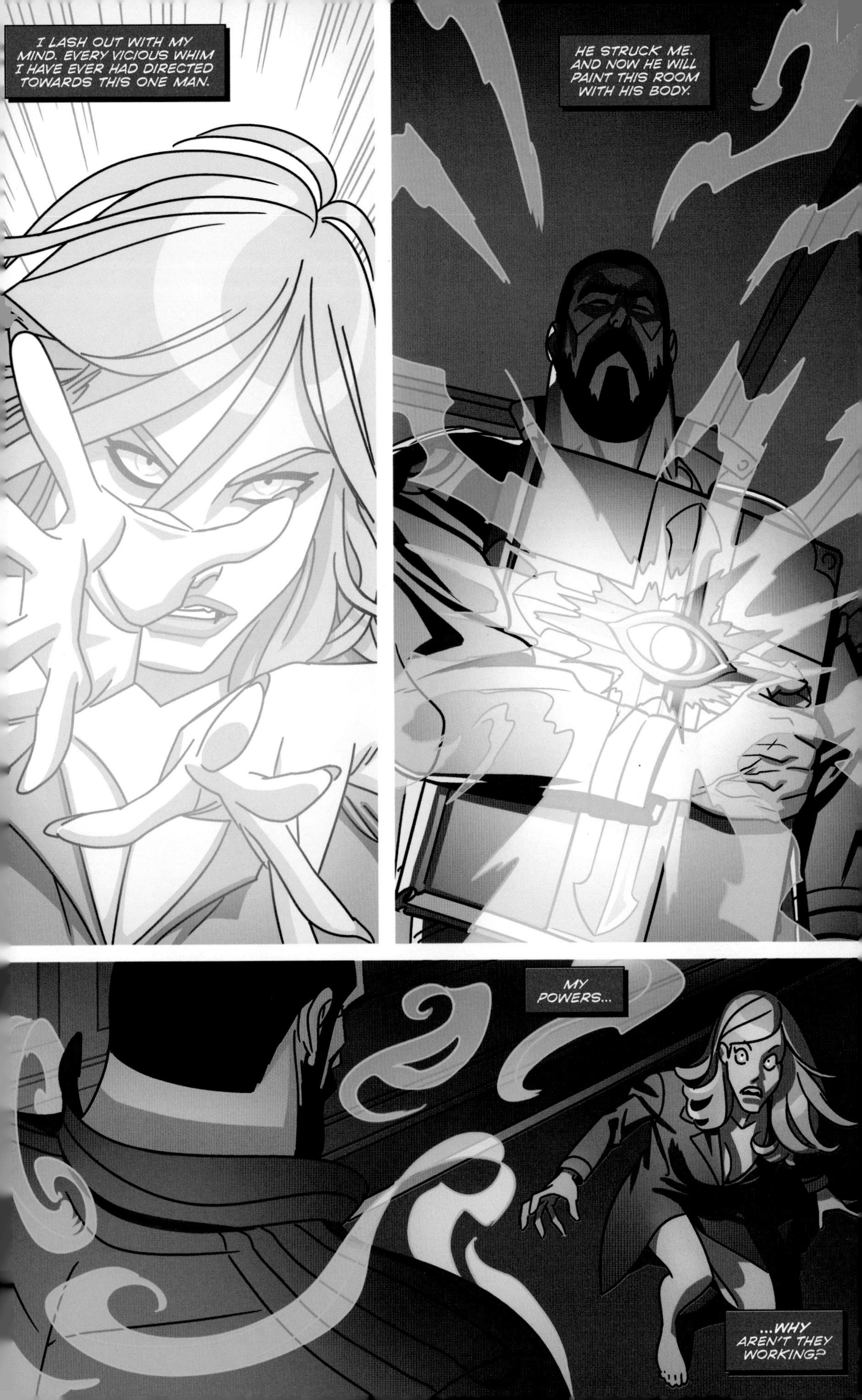
I LASH OUT WITH MY MIND. EVERY VICIOUS WHIM I HAVE EVER HAD DIRECTED TOWARDS THIS ONE MAN.
HE STRUCK ME. AND NOW HE WILL PAINT THIS ROOM WITH HIS BODY.
MY POWERS...
...WHY AREN'T THEY WORKING?

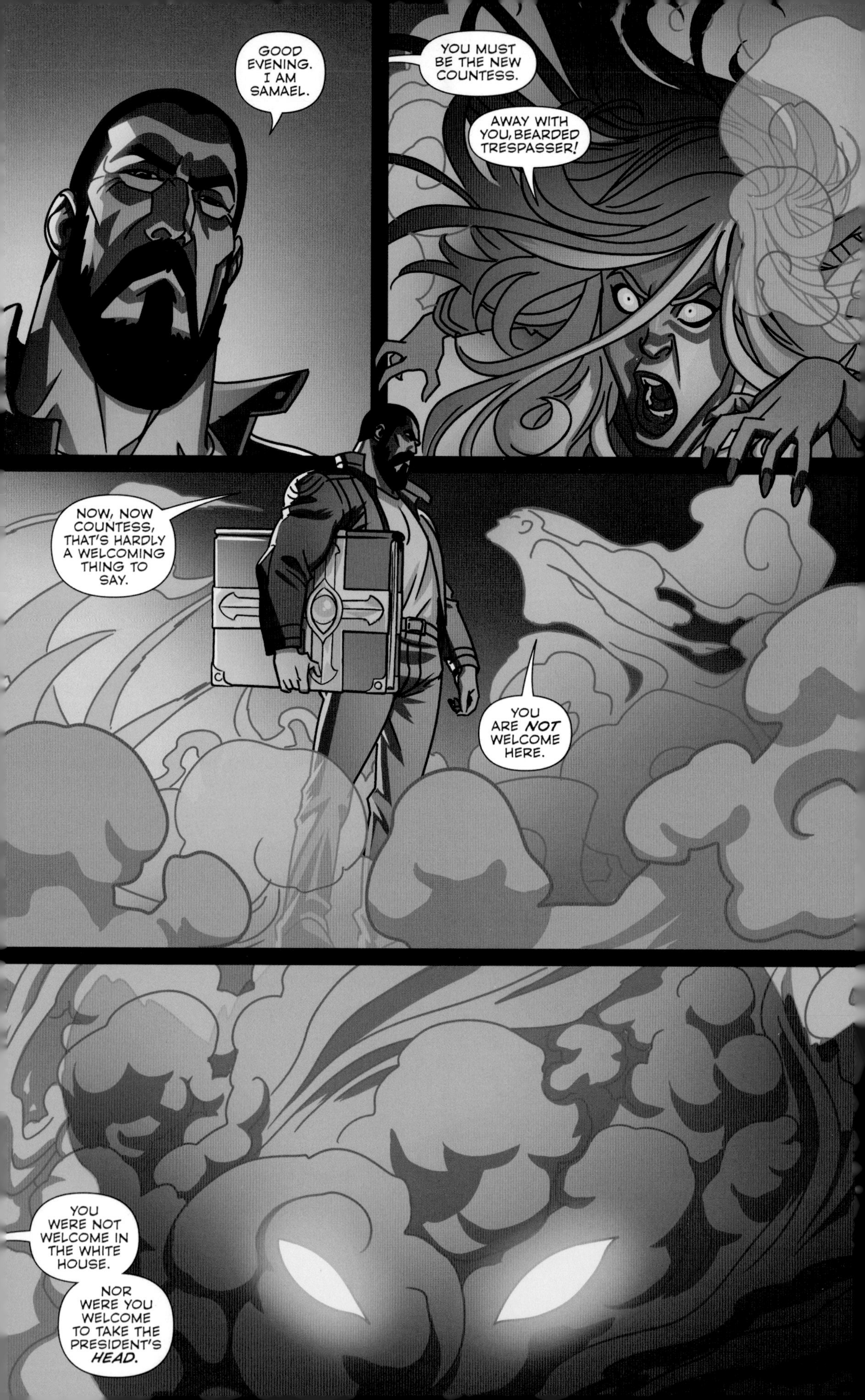
GOOD EVENING. I AM SAMAEL.
YOU MUST BE THE NEW COUNTESS.
AWAY WITH YOU, BEARDED TRESPASSER!
NOW, NOW COUNTESS, THAT'S HARDLY A WELCOMING THING TO SAY.
YOU ARE *NOT* WELCOME HERE.
YOU WERE NOT WELCOME IN THE WHITE HOUSE.
NOR WERE YOU WELCOME TO TAKE THE PRESIDENT'S *HEAD*.

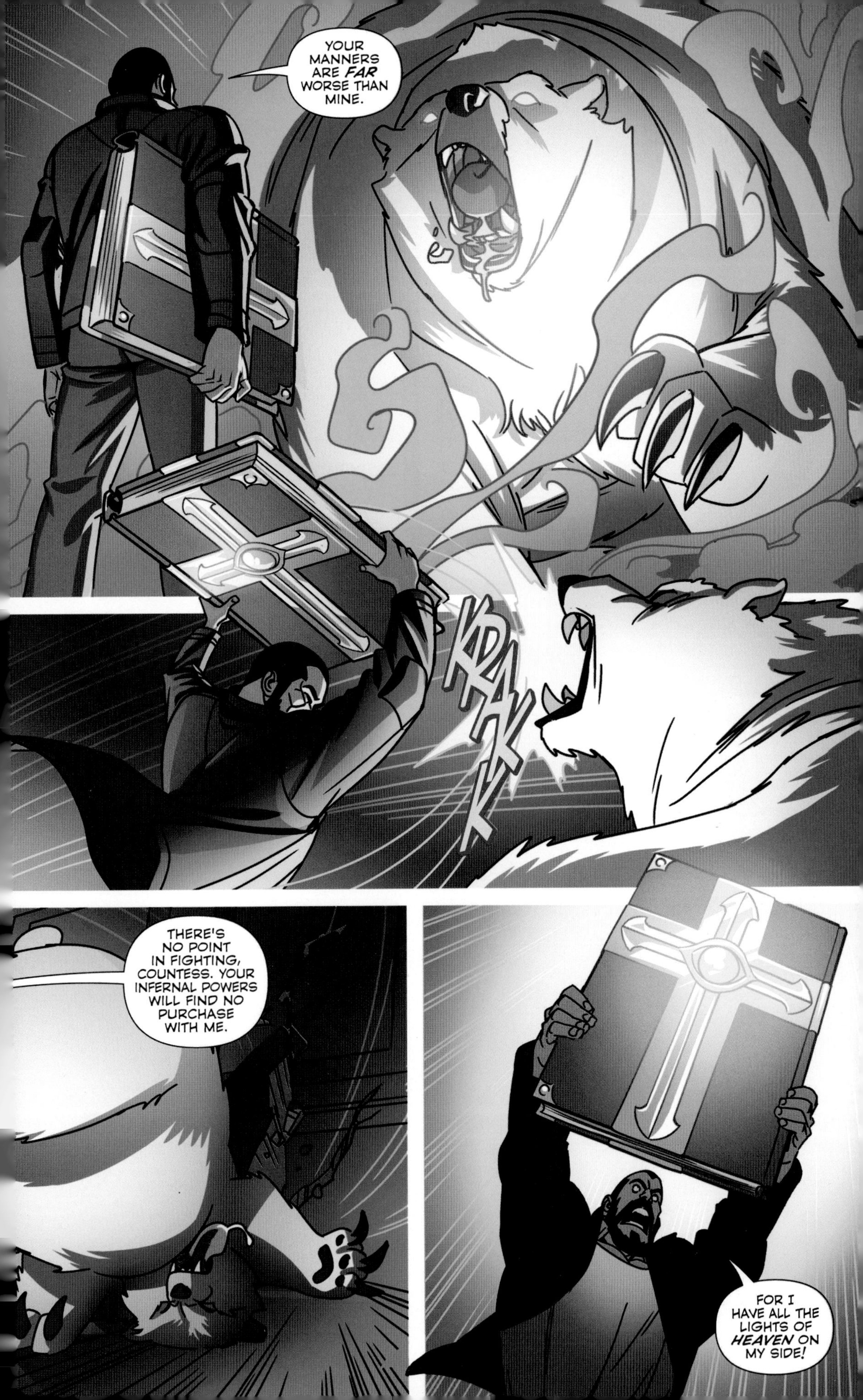
YOUR MANNERS ARE *FAR* WORSE THAN MINE.
KRAKKK
THERE'S NO POINT IN FIGHTING, COUNTESS. YOUR INFERNAL POWERS WILL FIND NO PURCHASE WITH ME.
FOR I HAVE ALL THE LIGHTS OF *HEAVEN* ON MY SIDE!

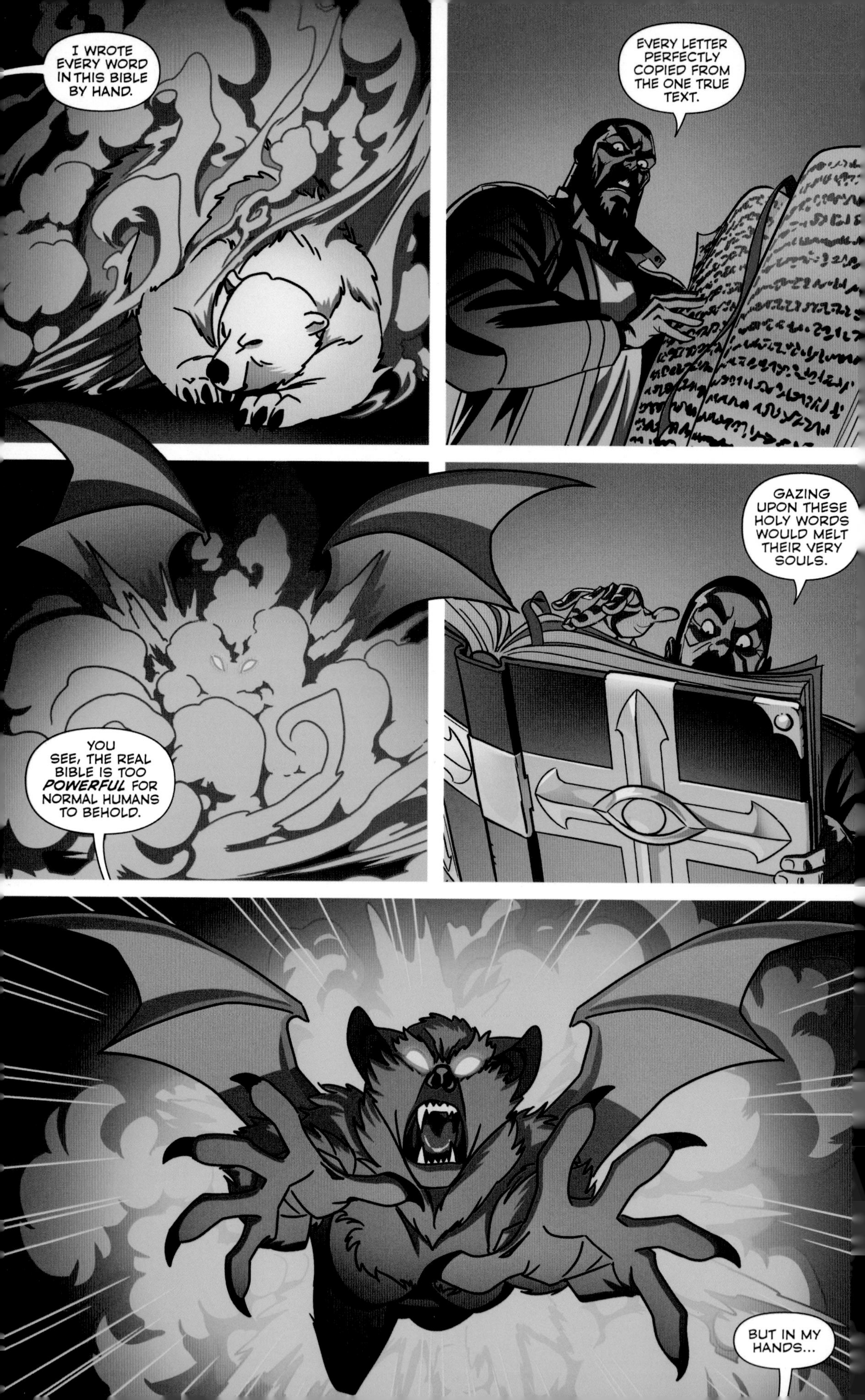
I WROTE EVERY WORD IN THIS BIBLE BY HAND.
EVERY LETTER PERFECTLY COPIED FROM THE ONE TRUE TEXT.
YOU SEE, THE REAL BIBLE IS TOO *POWERFUL* FOR NORMAL HUMANS TO BEHOLD.
GAZING UPON THESE HOLY WORDS WOULD MELT THEIR VERY SOULS.
BUT IN MY HANDS...

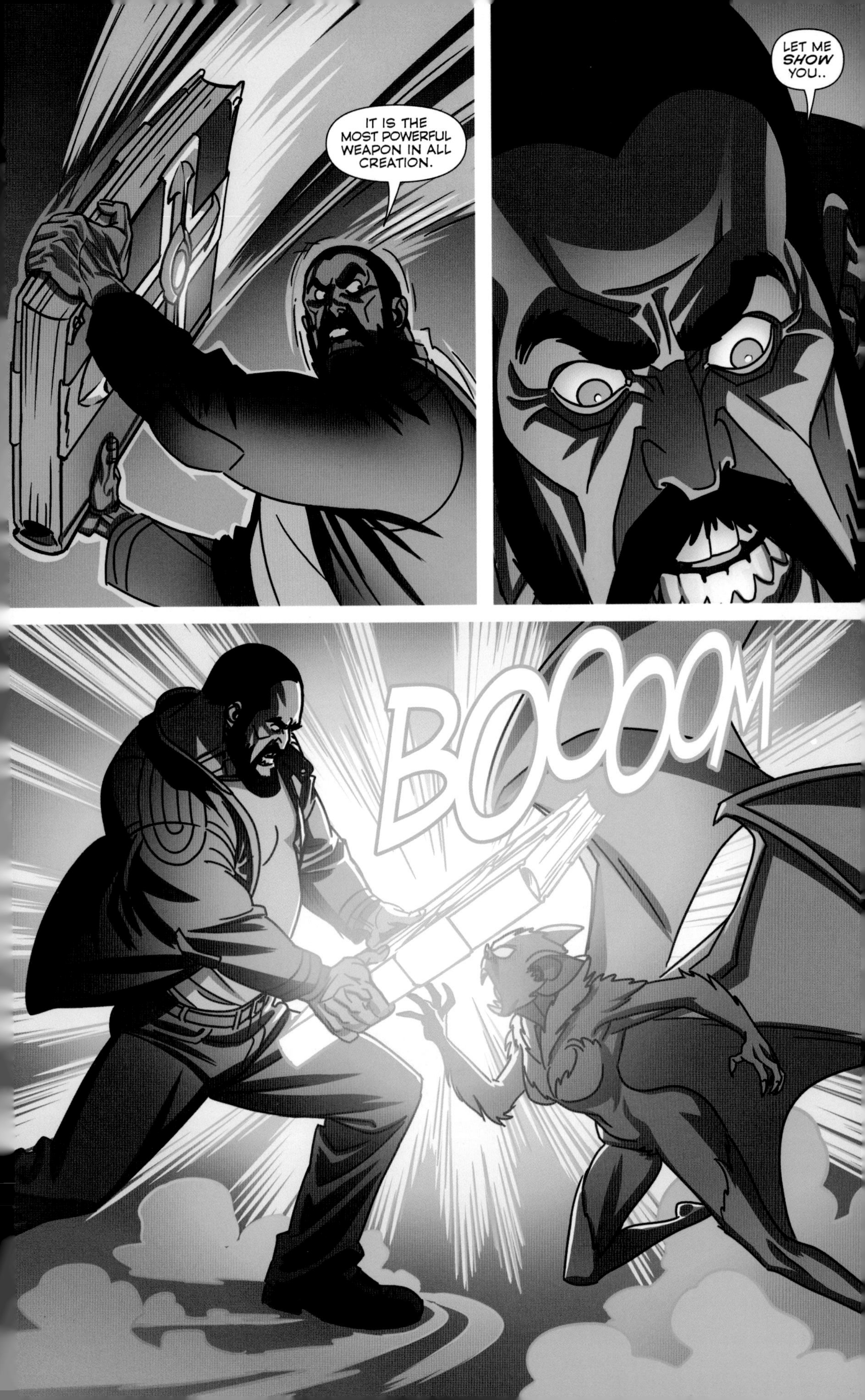
IT IS THE MOST POWERFUL WEAPON IN ALL CREATION.
LET ME SHOW YOU..
BOOOOM

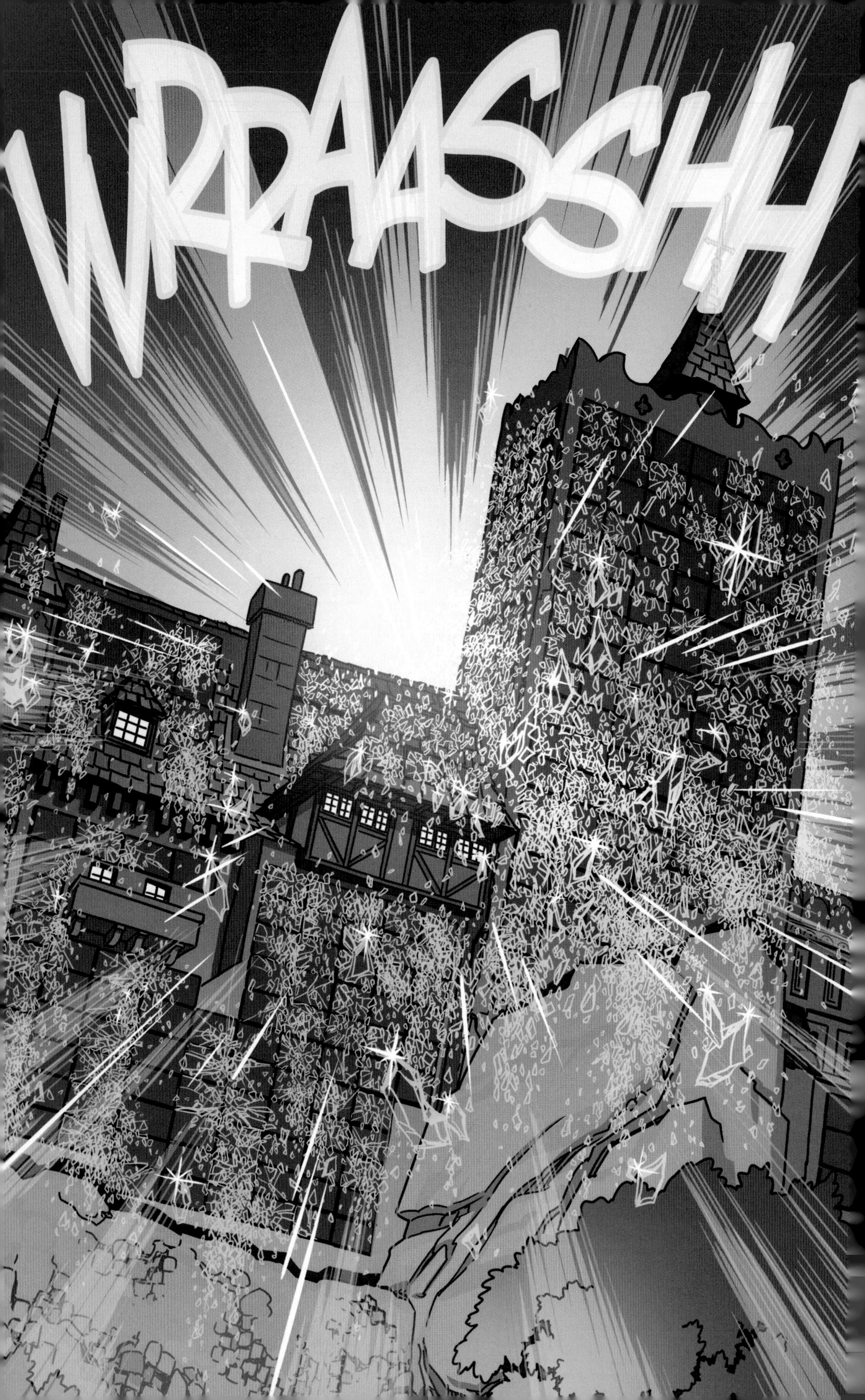
WRRAASHH

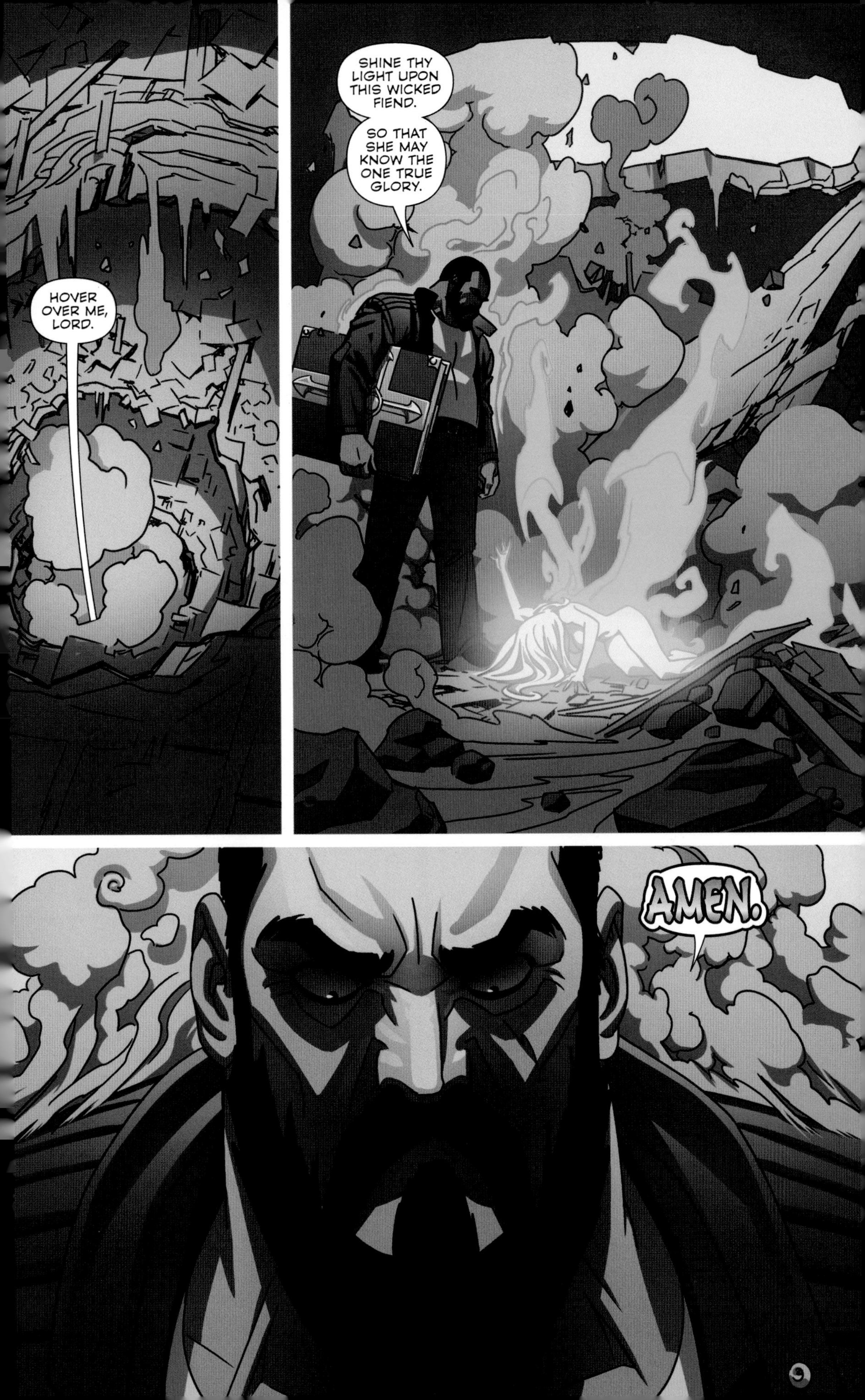
HOVER OVER ME, LORD.
SHINE THY LIGHT UPON THIS WICKED FIEND.
SO THAT SHE MAY KNOW THE ONE TRUE GLORY.
AMEN.

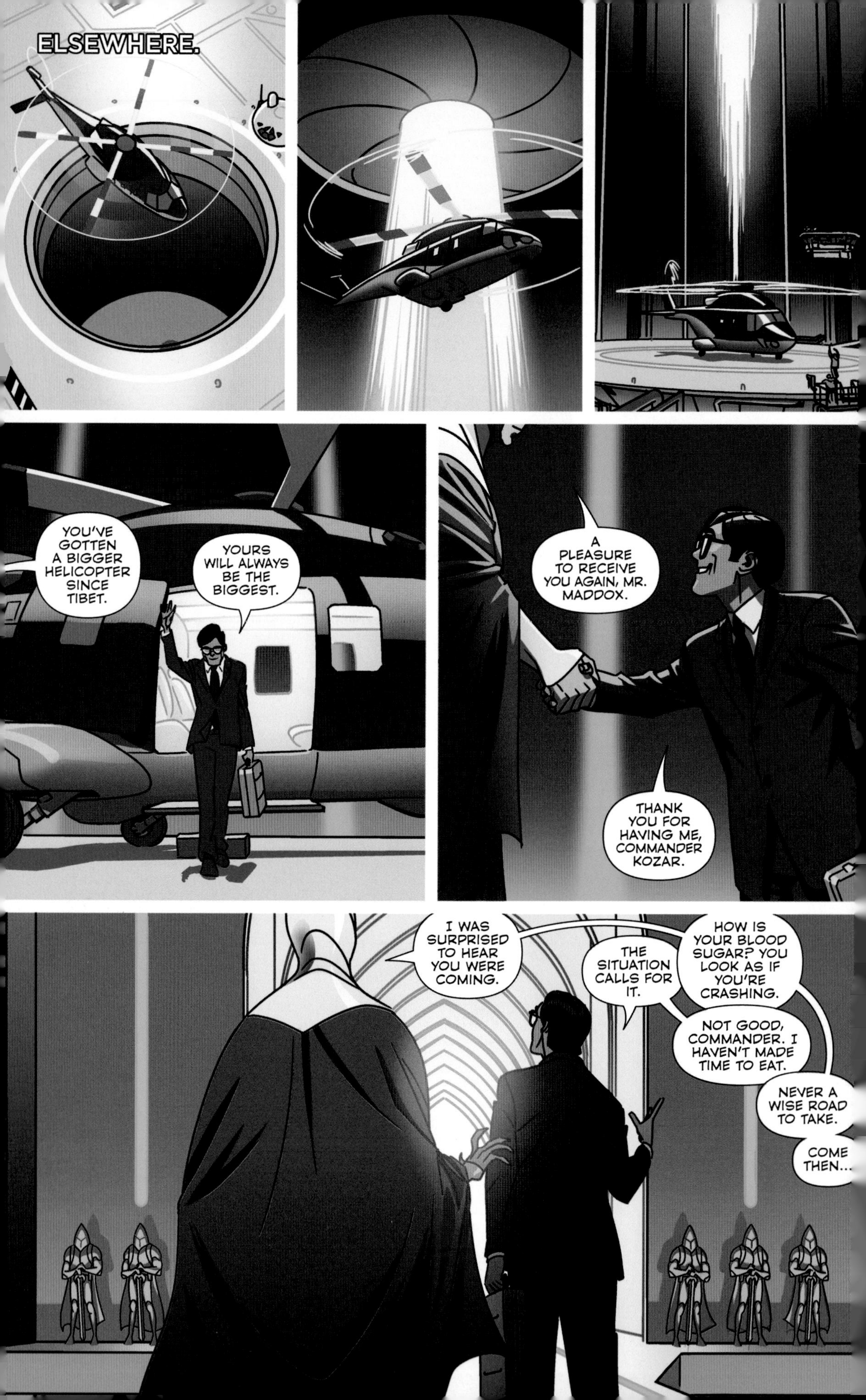
ELSEWHERE.
YOU'VE GOTTEN A BIGGER HELICOPTER SINCE TIBET.
YOURS WILL ALWAYS BE THE BIGGEST.
A PLEASURE TO RECEIVE YOU AGAIN, MR. MADDOX.
THANK YOU FOR HAVING ME, COMMANDER KOZAR.
I WAS SURPRISED TO HEAR YOU WERE COMING.
THE SITUATION CALLS FOR IT.
HOW IS YOUR BLOOD SUGAR? YOU LOOK AS IF YOU'RE CRASHING.
NOT GOOD, COMMANDER. I HAVEN'T MADE TIME TO EAT.
NEVER A WISE ROAD TO TAKE.
COME THEN...

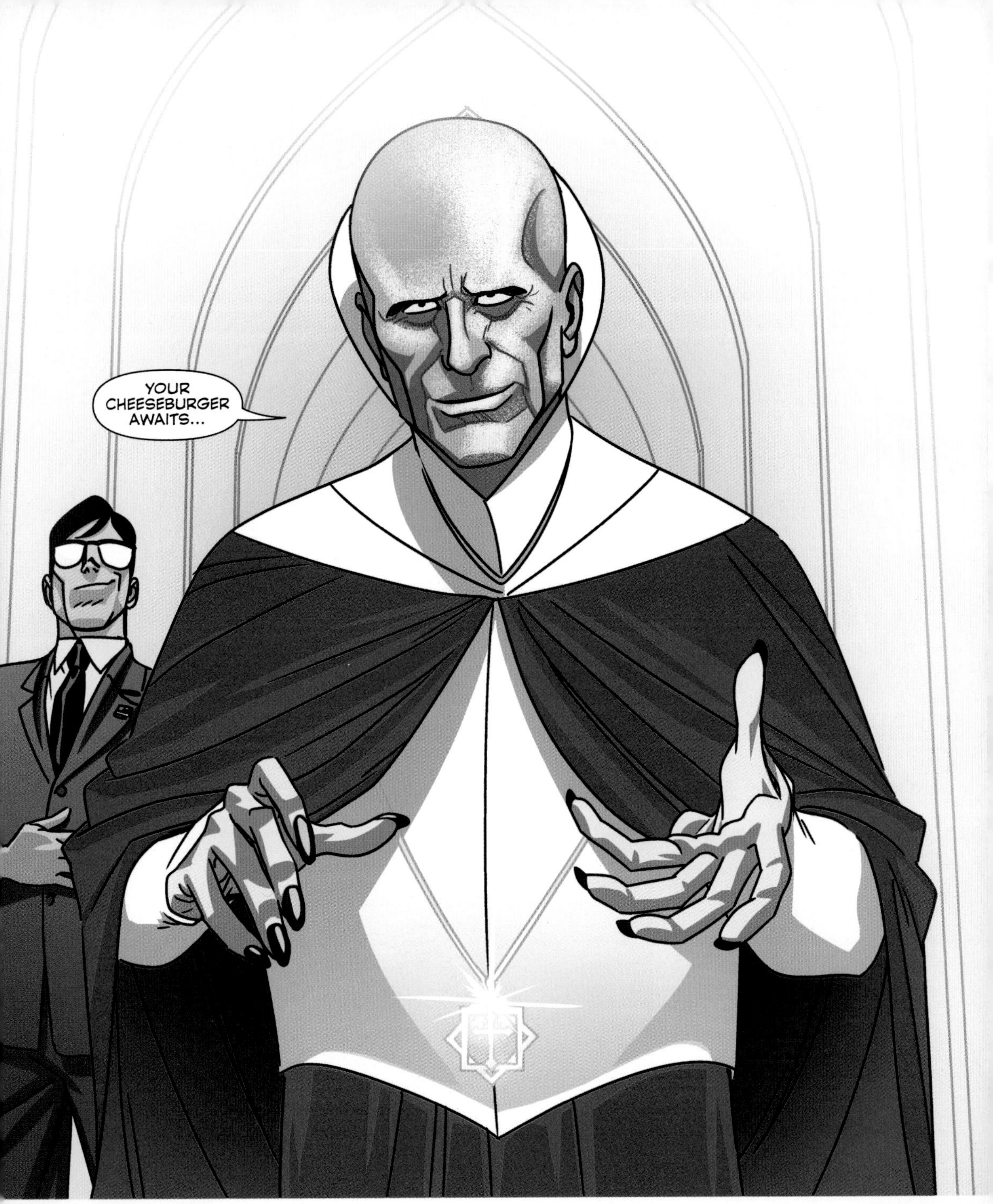
YOUR CHEESEBURGER AWAITS...

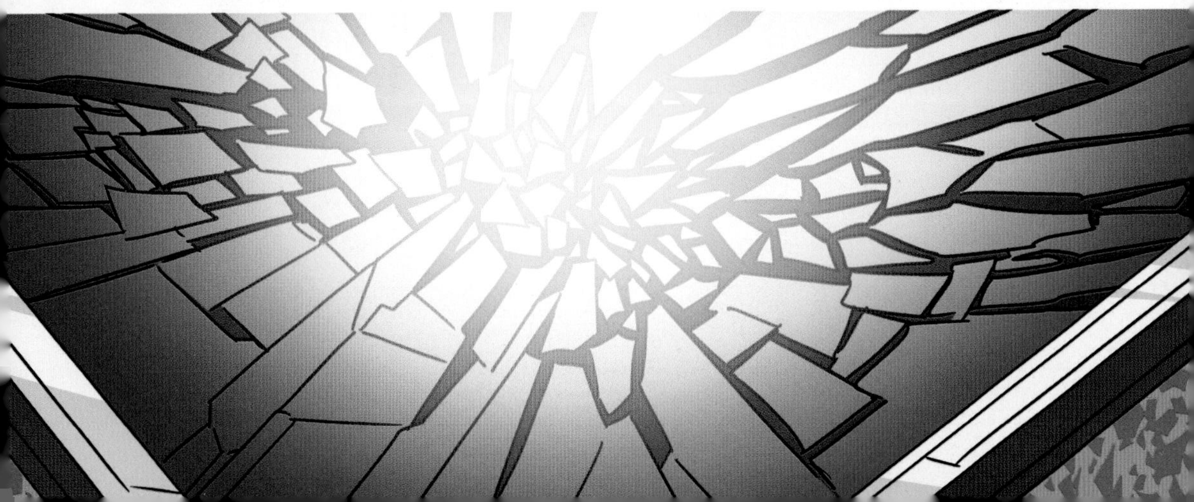

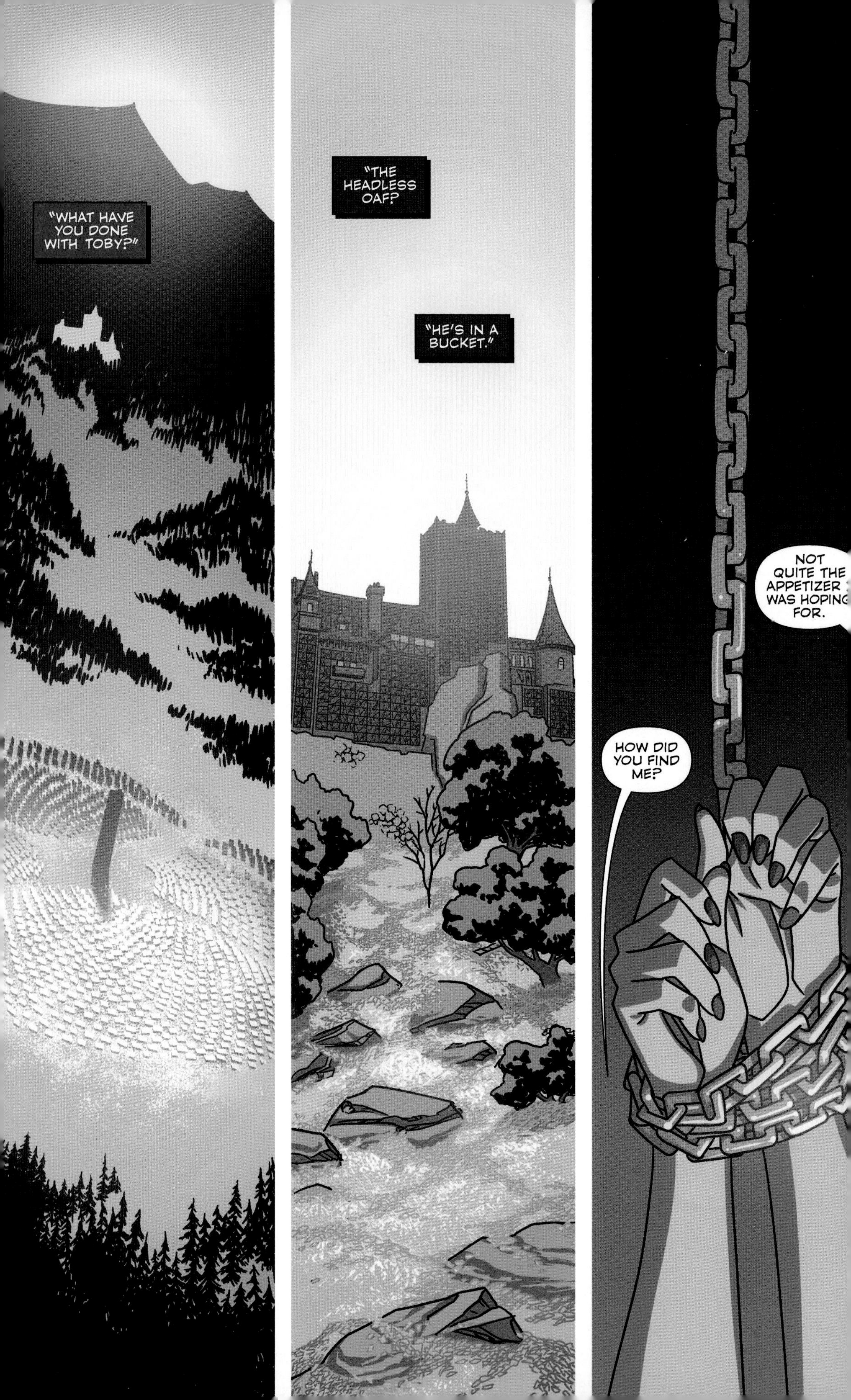
"WHAT HAVE YOU DONE WITH TOBY?"
"THE HEADLESS OAF?
"HE'S IN A BUCKET."
NOT QUITE THE APPETIZER WAS HOPING FOR.
HOW DID YOU FIND ME?

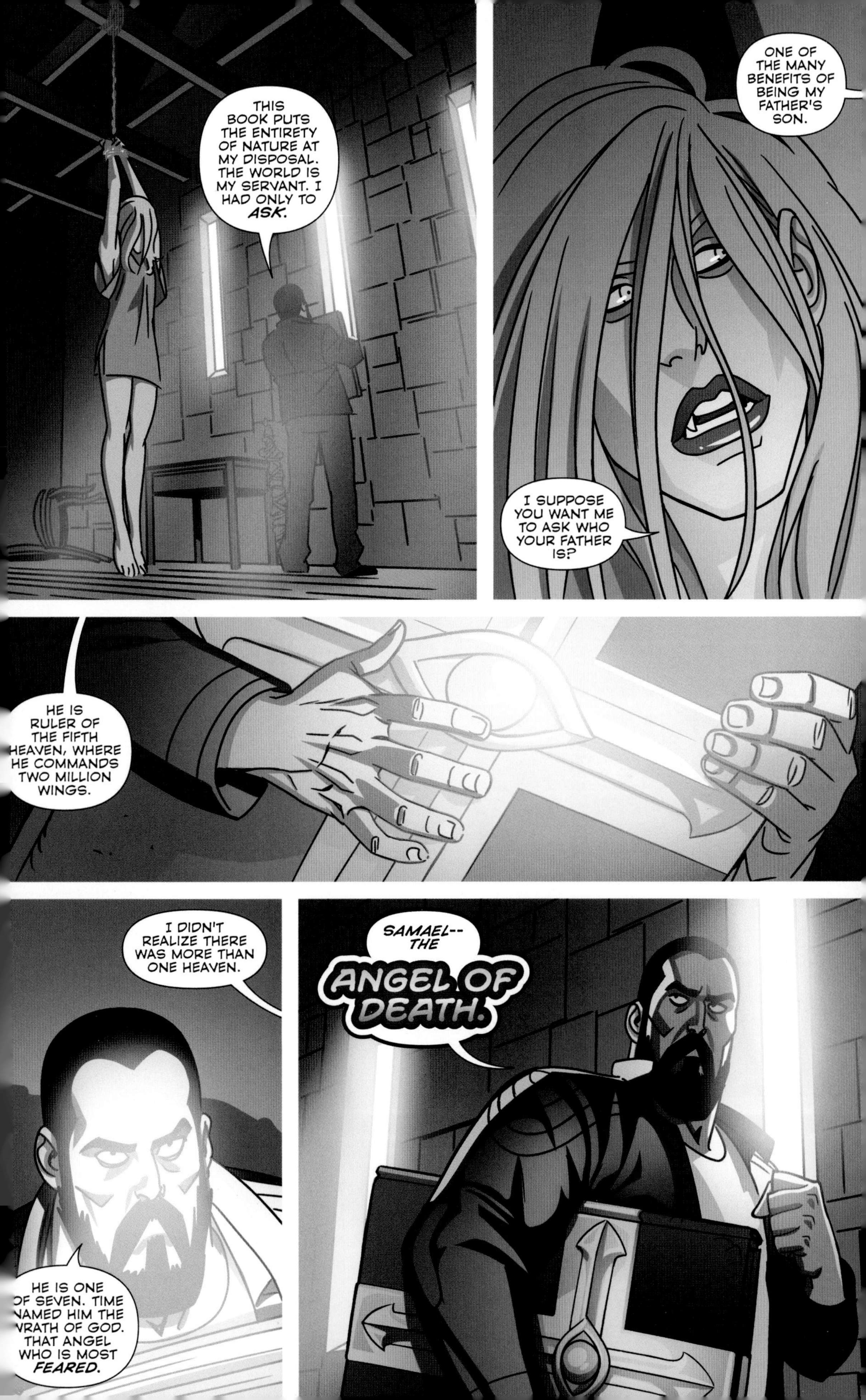

THIS BOOK PUTS THE ENTIRETY OF NATURE AT MY DISPOSAL. THE WORLD IS MY SERVANT. I HAD ONLY TO *ASK*.
ONE OF THE MANY BENEFITS OF BEING MY FATHER'S SON.
I SUPPOSE YOU WANT ME TO ASK WHO YOUR FATHER IS?
HE IS RULER OF THE FIFTH HEAVEN, WHERE HE COMMANDS TWO MILLION WINGS.
I DIDN'T REALIZE THERE WAS MORE THAN ONE HEAVEN.
HE IS ONE OF SEVEN. TIME NAMED HIM THE WRATH OF GOD. THAT ANGEL WHO IS MOST *FEARED*.
SAMAEL-- THE
ANGEL OF DEATH.

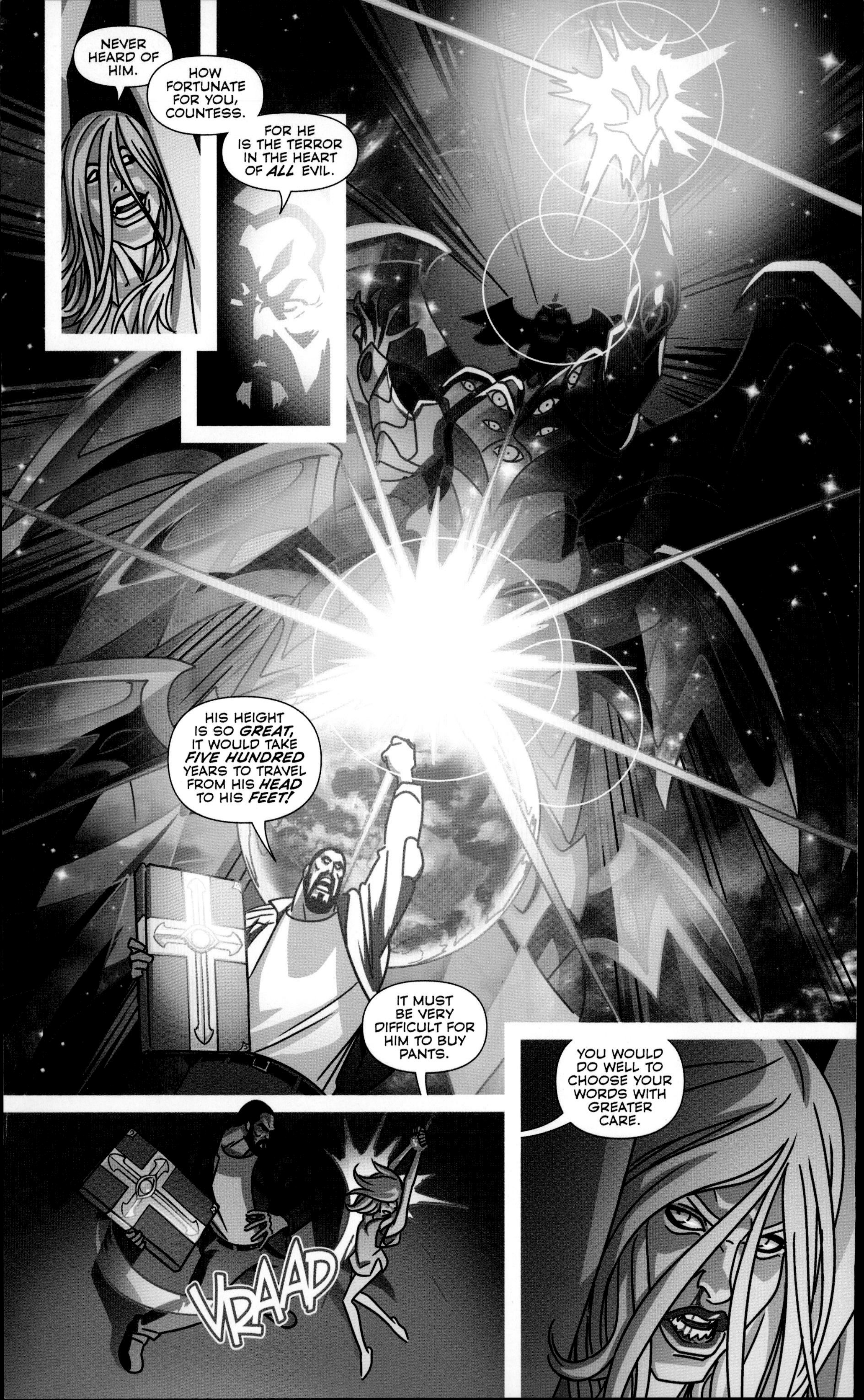
NEVER HEARD OF HIM.
HOW FORTUNATE FOR YOU, COUNTESS.
FOR HE IS THE TERROR IN THE HEART OF ALL EVIL.
HIS HEIGHT IS SO GREAT, IT WOULD TAKE FIVE HUNDRED YEARS TO TRAVEL FROM HIS HEAD TO HIS FEET!
IT MUST BE VERY DIFFICULT FOR HIM TO BUY PANTS.
YOU WOULD DO WELL TO CHOOSE YOUR WORDS WITH GREATER CARE.
VRAAAP

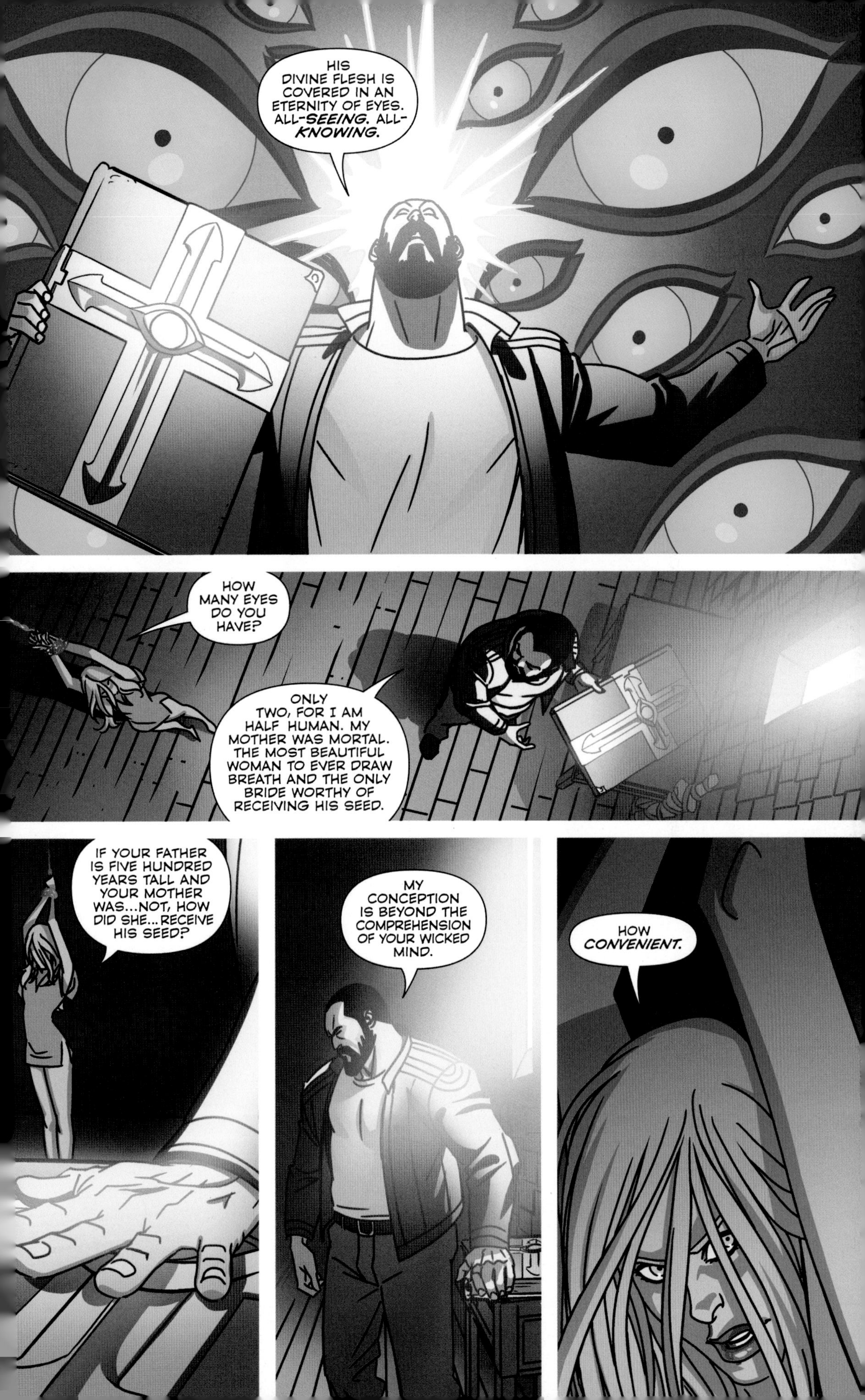
HIS DIVINE FLESH IS COVERED IN AN ETERNITY OF EYES. ALL-*SEEING*. ALL-*KNOWING*.
HOW MANY EYES DO YOU HAVE?
ONLY TWO, FOR I AM HALF HUMAN. MY MOTHER WAS MORTAL. THE MOST BEAUTIFUL WOMAN TO EVER DRAW BREATH AND THE ONLY BRIDE WORTHY OF RECEIVING HIS SEED.
IF YOUR FATHER IS FIVE HUNDRED YEARS TALL AND YOUR MOTHER WAS...NOT, HOW DID SHE...RECEIVE HIS SEED?
MY CONCEPTION IS BEYOND THE COMPREHENSION OF YOUR WICKED MIND.
HOW *CONVENIENT*.

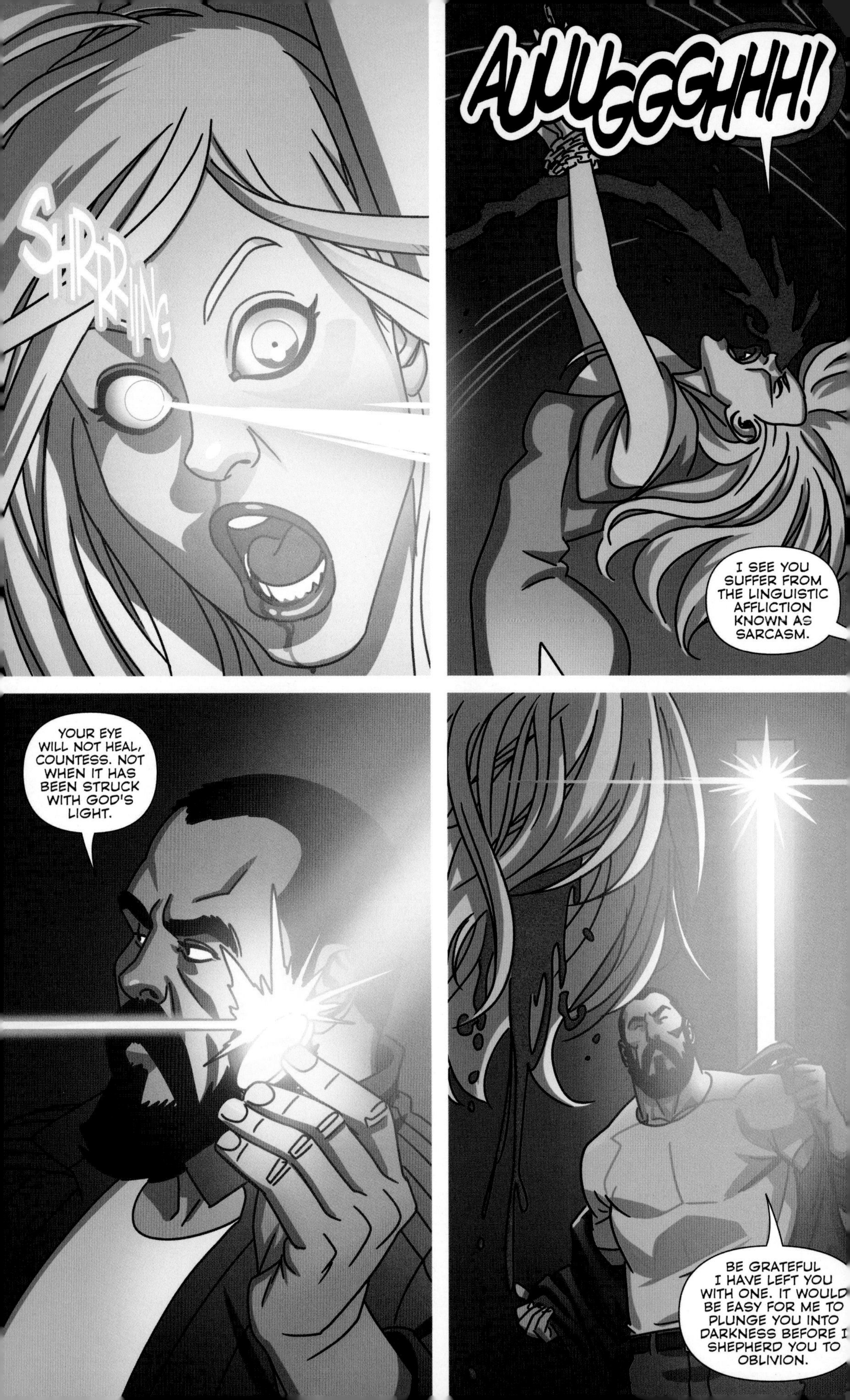
SHRRRIING
AUUUGGGHHH!
I SEE YOU SUFFER FROM THE LINGUISTIC AFFLICTION KNOWN AS SARCASM.
YOUR EYE WILL NOT HEAL, COUNTESS. NOT WHEN IT HAS BEEN STRUCK WITH GOD'S LIGHT.
BE GRATEFUL I HAVE LEFT YOU WITH ONE. IT WOULD BE EASY FOR ME TO PLUNGE YOU INTO DARKNESS BEFORE I SHEPHERD YOU TO OBLIVION.

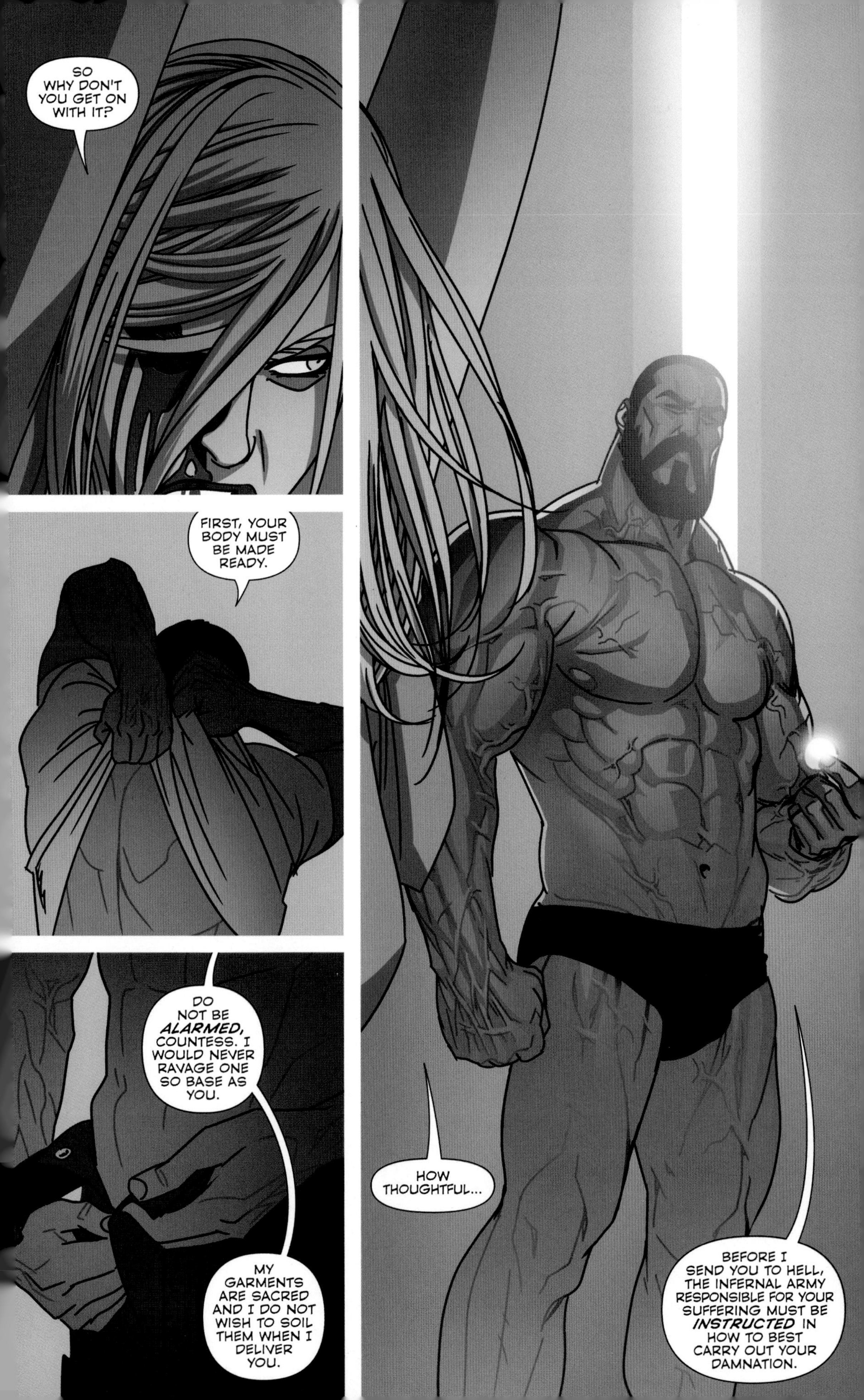
SO WHY DON'T YOU GET ON WITH IT?
FIRST, YOUR BODY MUST BE MADE READY.
DO NOT BE ***ALARMED,*** COUNTESS. I WOULD NEVER RAVAGE ONE SO BASE AS YOU.
MY GARMENTS ARE SACRED AND I DO NOT WISH TO SOIL THEM WHEN I DELIVER YOU.
HOW THOUGHTFUL...
BEFORE I SEND YOU TO HELL, THE INFERNAL ARMY RESPONSIBLE FOR YOUR SUFFERING MUST BE ***INSTRUCTED*** IN HOW TO BEST CARRY OUT YOUR DAMNATION.

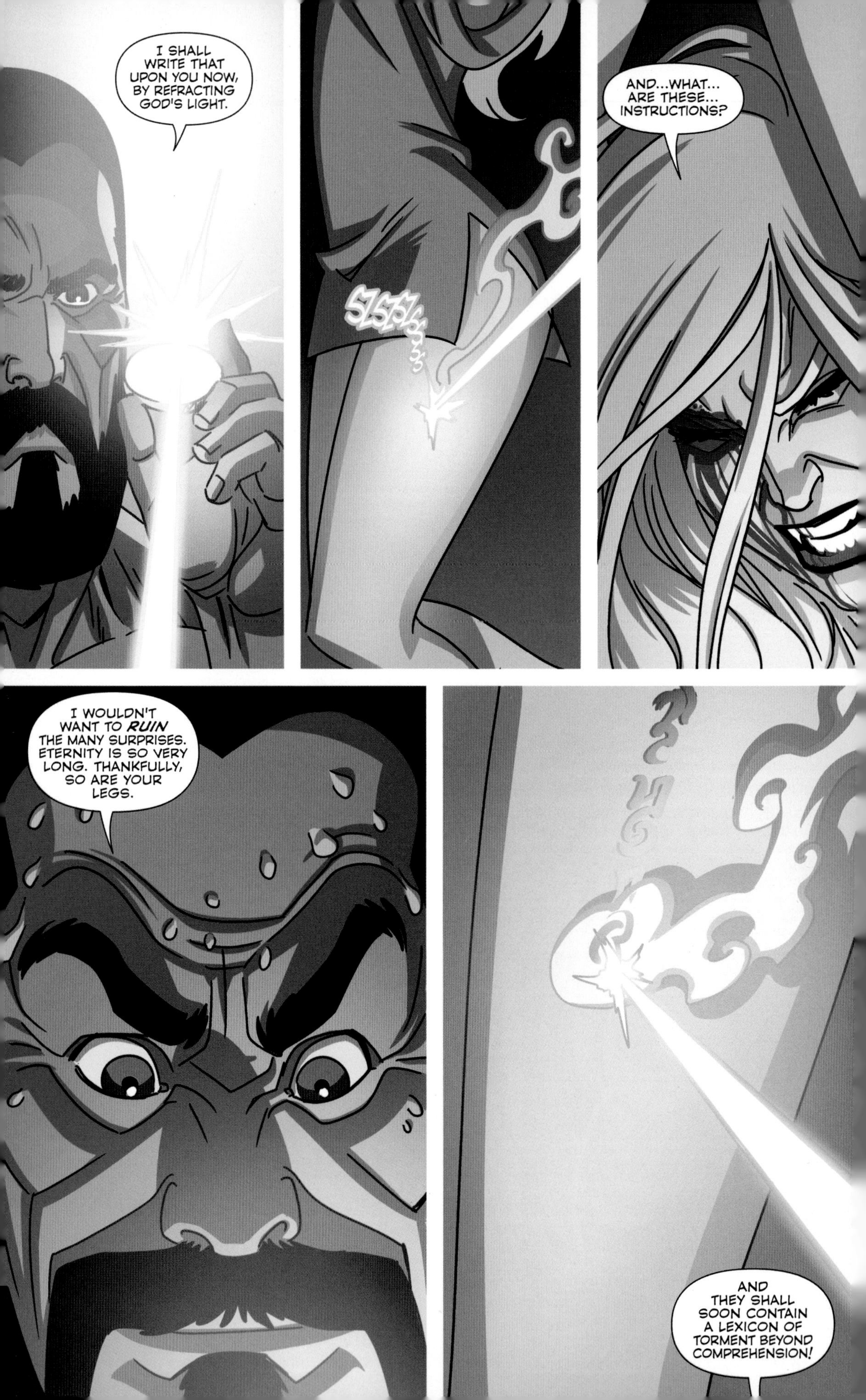
I SHALL WRITE THAT UPON YOU NOW, BY REFRACTING GOD'S LIGHT.
SZSZSZ
AND...WHAT... ARE THESE... INSTRUCTIONS?
I WOULDN'T WANT TO *RUIN* THE MANY SURPRISES. ETERNITY IS SO VERY LONG. THANKFULLY, SO ARE YOUR LEGS.
AND THEY SHALL SOON CONTAIN A LEXICON OF TORMENT BEYOND COMPREHENSION!

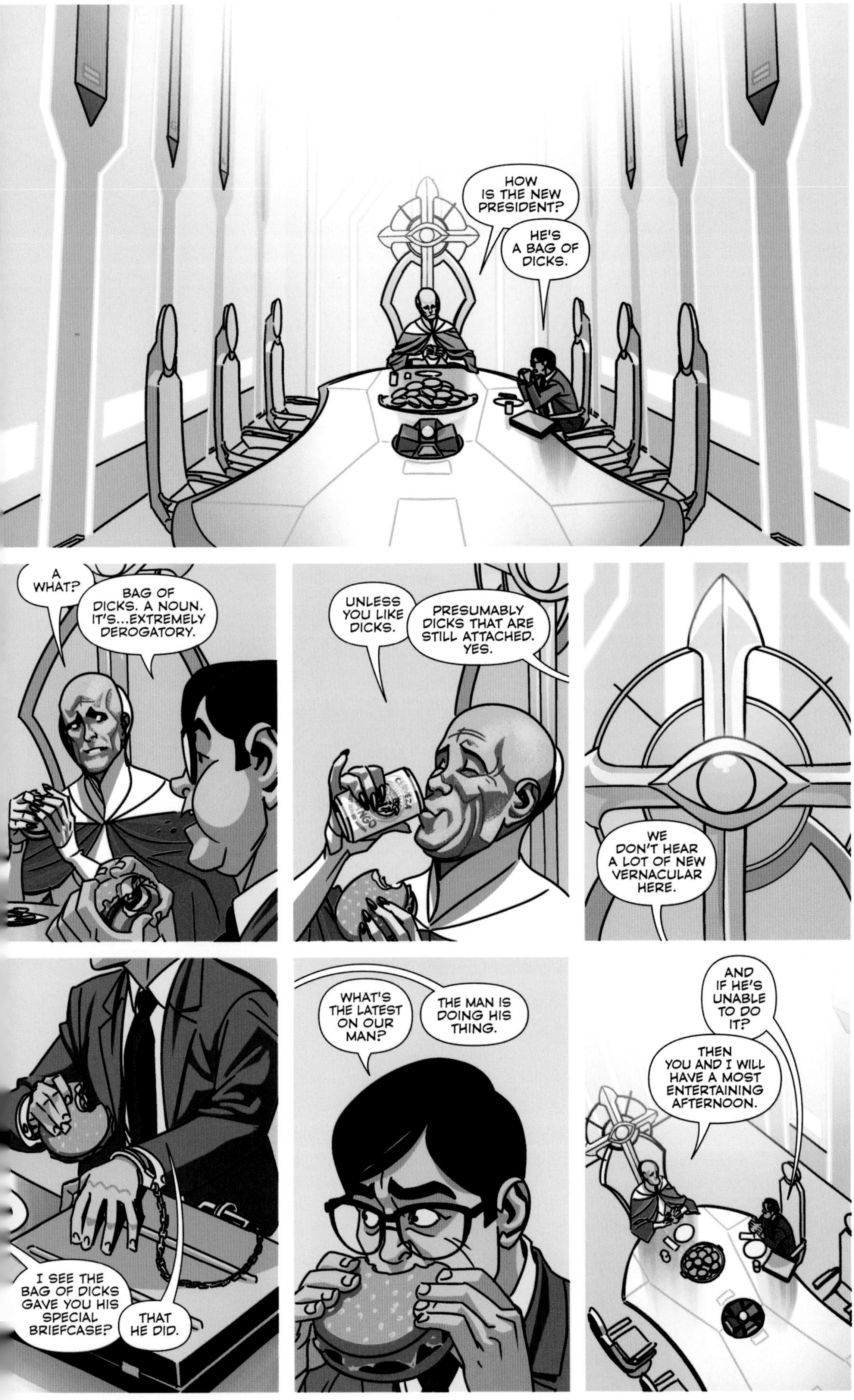
HOW IS THE NEW PRESIDENT?
HE'S A BAG OF DICKS.
A WHAT?
BAG OF DICKS. A NOUN. IT'S...EXTREMELY DEROGATORY.
UNLESS YOU LIKE DICKS.
PRESUMABLY DICKS THAT ARE STILL ATTACHED. YES.
WE DON'T HEAR A LOT OF NEW VERNACULAR HERE.
I SEE THE BAG OF DICKS GAVE YOU HIS SPECIAL BRIEFCASE?
THAT HE DID.
WHAT'S THE LATEST ON OUR MAN?
THE MAN IS DOING HIS THING.
AND IF HE'S UNABLE TO DO IT?
THEN YOU AND I WILL HAVE A MOST ENTERTAINING AFTERNOON.

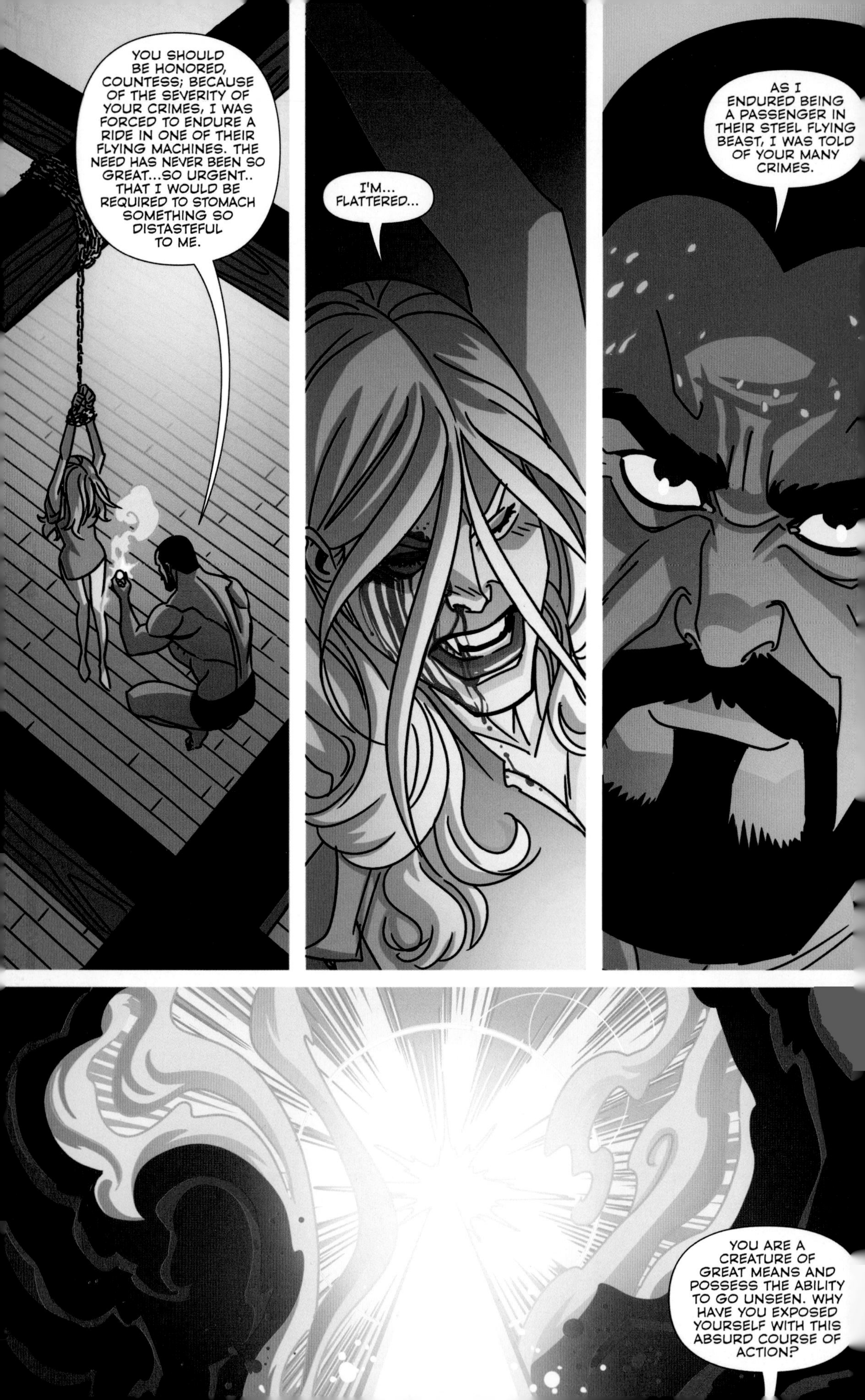
YOU SHOULD BE HONORED, COUNTESS; BECAUSE OF THE SEVERITY OF YOUR CRIMES, I WAS FORCED TO ENDURE A RIDE IN ONE OF THEIR FLYING MACHINES. THE NEED HAS NEVER BEEN SO GREAT...SO URGENT.. THAT I WOULD BE REQUIRED TO STOMACH SOMETHING SO DISTASTEFUL TO ME.
I'M... FLATTERED...
AS I ENDURED BEING A PASSENGER IN THEIR STEEL FLYING BEAST, I WAS TOLD OF YOUR MANY CRIMES.
YOU ARE A CREATURE OF GREAT MEANS AND POSSESS THE ABILITY TO GO UNSEEN. WHY HAVE YOU EXPOSED YOURSELF WITH THIS ABSURD COURSE OF ACTION?

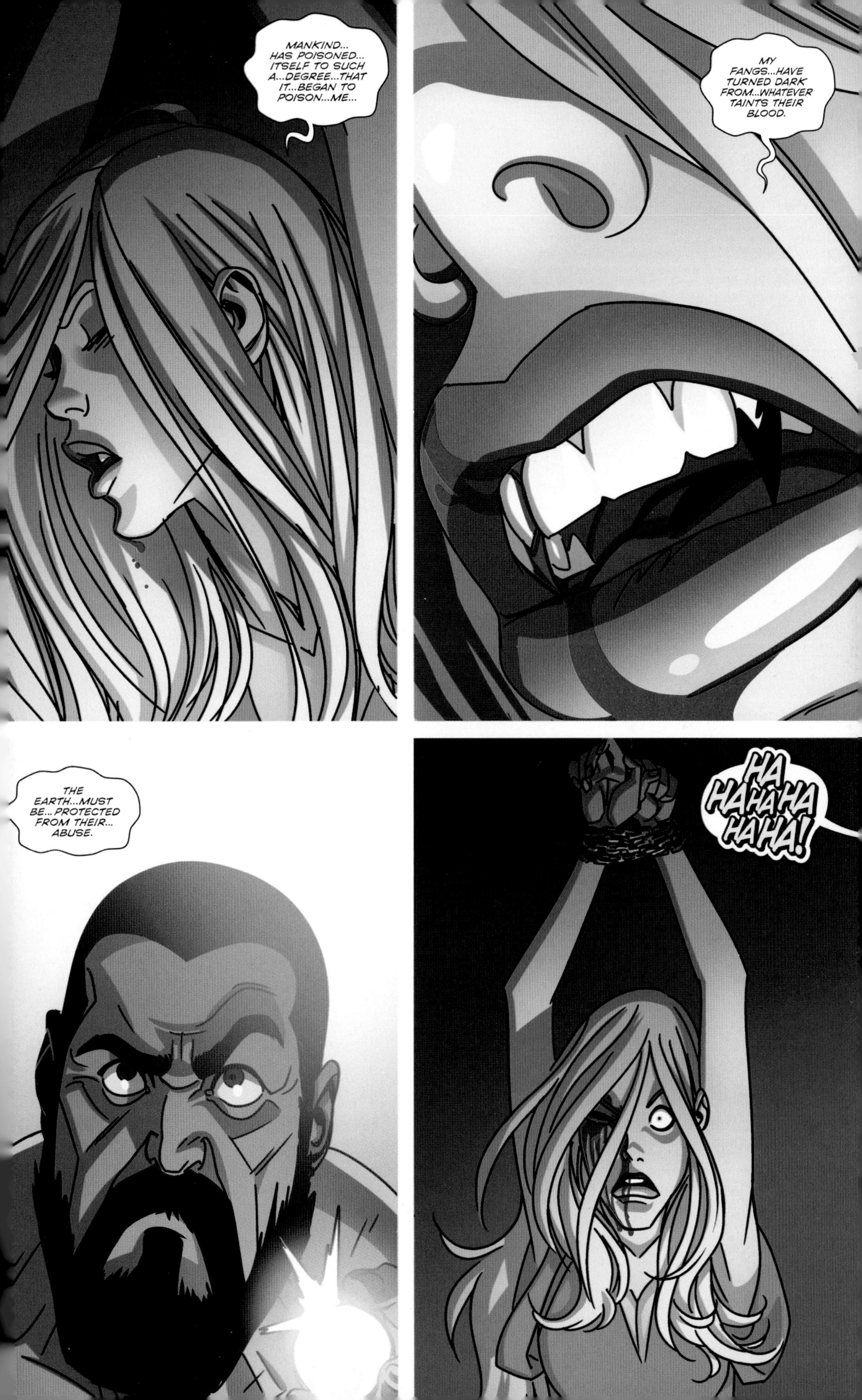
MANKIND... HAS POISONED... ITSELF TO SUCH A...DEGREE...THAT IT...BEGAN TO POISON...ME...
MY FANGS...HAVE TURNED DARK FROM...WHATEVER TAINTS THEIR BLOOD.
THE EARTH...MUST BE...PROTECTED FROM THEIR... ABUSE.
HA HAHAHA HAHA!

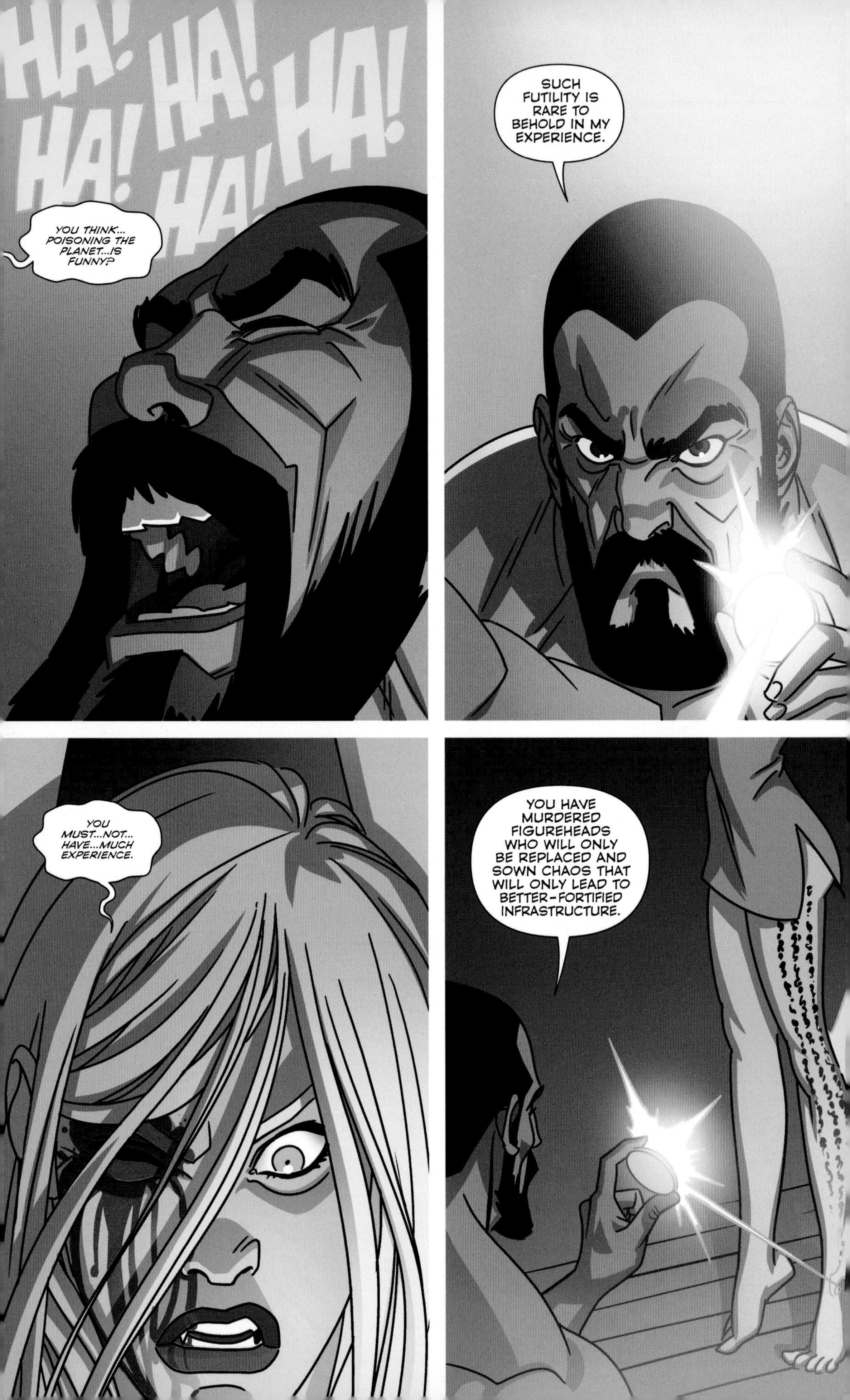
HA! HA! HA! HA! HA! HA!
YOU THINK... POISONING THE PLANET...IS FUNNY?
SUCH FUTILITY IS RARE TO BEHOLD IN MY EXPERIENCE.
YOU MUST...NOT... HAVE...MUCH EXPERIENCE.
YOU HAVE MURDERED FIGUREHEADS WHO WILL ONLY BE REPLACED AND SOWN CHAOS THAT WILL ONLY LEAD TO BETTER-FORTIFIED INFRASTRUCTURE.

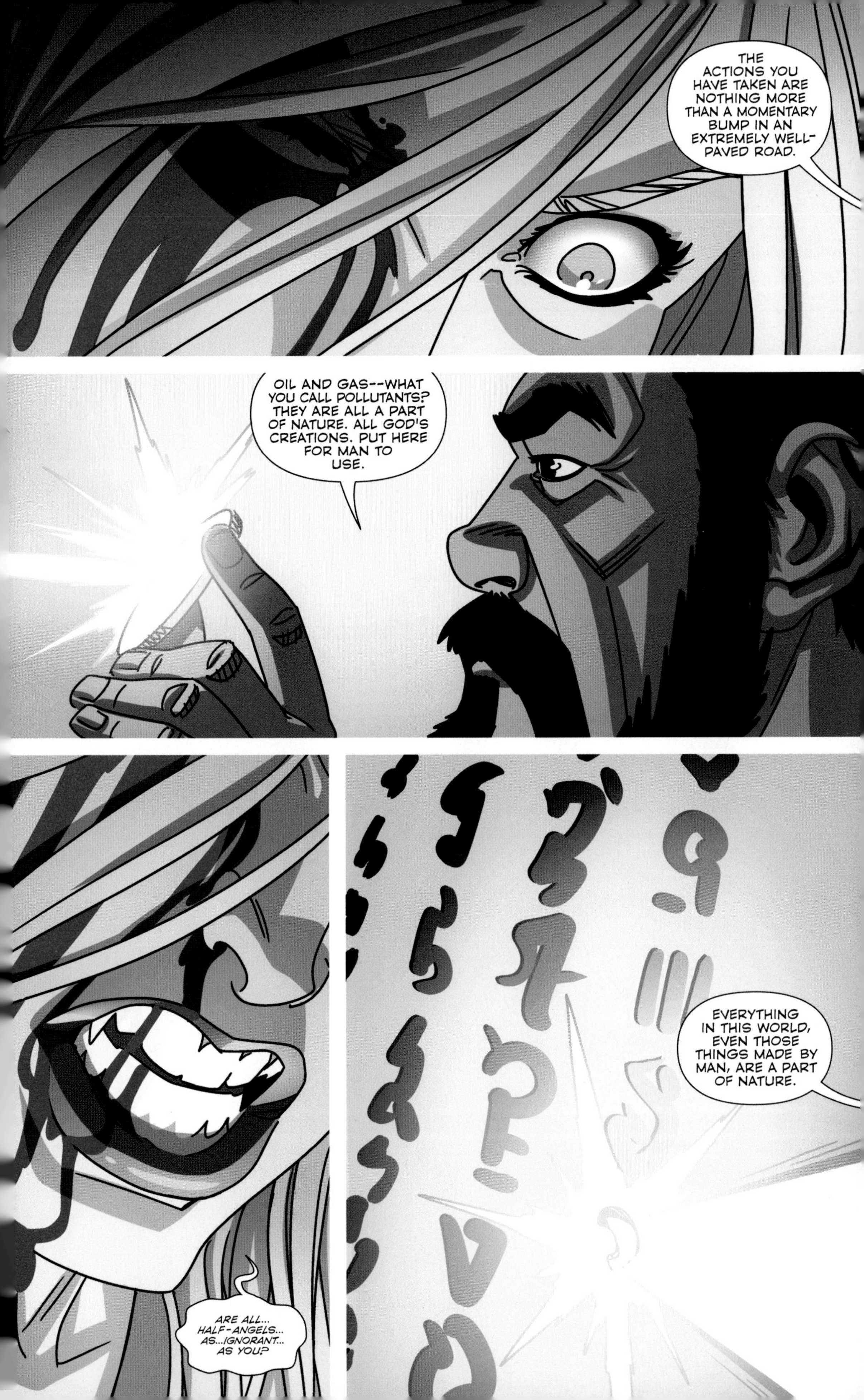
THE ACTIONS YOU HAVE TAKEN ARE NOTHING MORE THAN A MOMENTARY BUMP IN AN EXTREMELY WELL-PAVED ROAD.
OIL AND GAS--WHAT YOU CALL POLLUTANTS? THEY ARE ALL A PART OF NATURE. ALL GOD'S CREATIONS. PUT HERE FOR MAN TO USE.
ARE ALL... HALF-ANGELS... AS...IGNORANT... AS YOU?
EVERYTHING IN THIS WORLD, EVEN THOSE THINGS MADE BY MAN, ARE A PART OF NATURE.

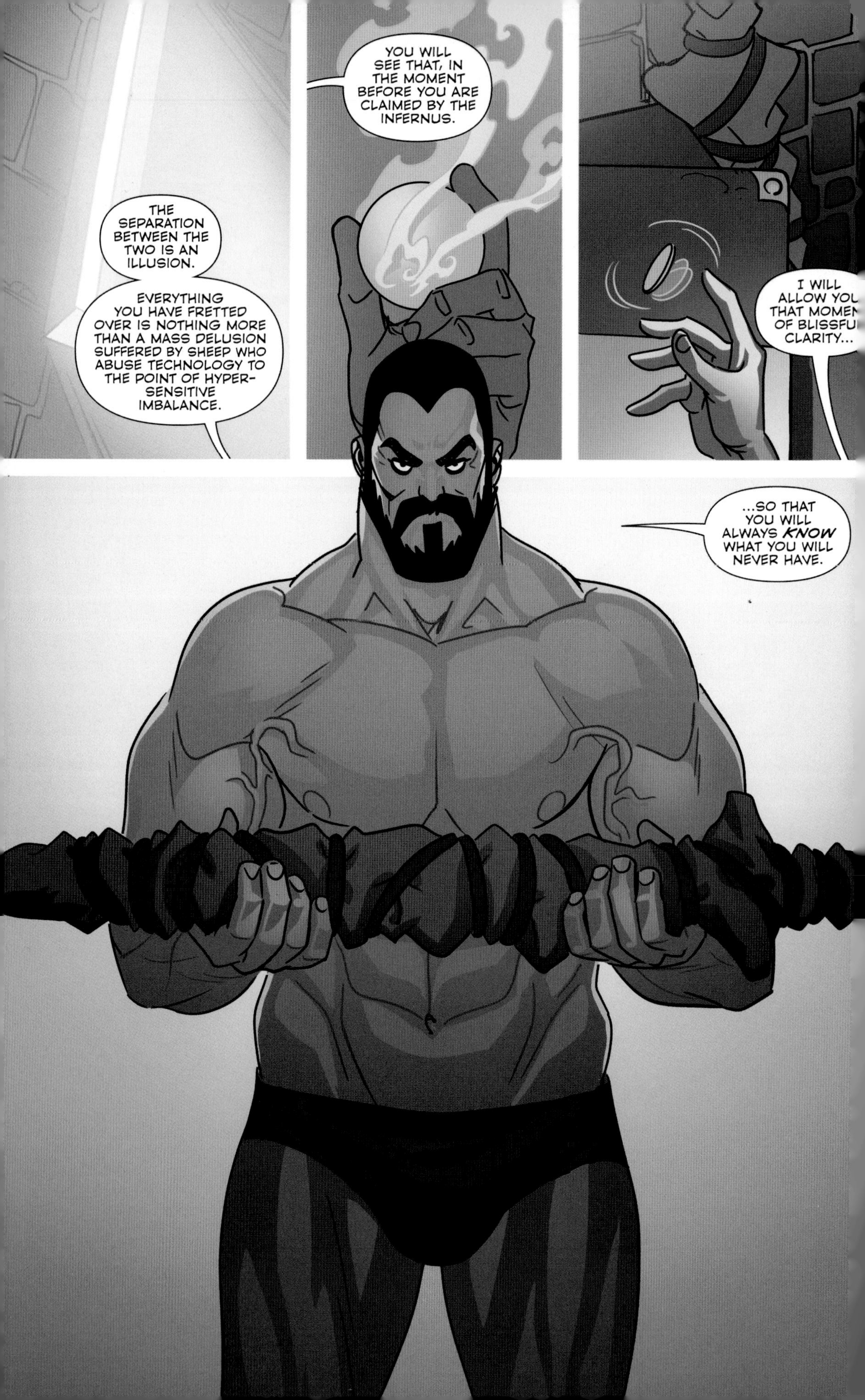
THE SEPARATION BETWEEN THE TWO IS AN ILLUSION.
EVERYTHING YOU HAVE FRETTED OVER IS NOTHING MORE THAN A MASS DELUSION SUFFERED BY SHEEP WHO ABUSE TECHNOLOGY TO THE POINT OF HYPER-SENSITIVE IMBALANCE.
YOU WILL SEE THAT, IN THE MOMENT BEFORE YOU ARE CLAIMED BY THE INFERNUS.
I WILL ALLOW YOU THAT MOMEN OF BLISSFU CLARITY...
...SO THAT YOU WILL ALWAYS *KNOW* WHAT YOU WILL NEVER HAVE.

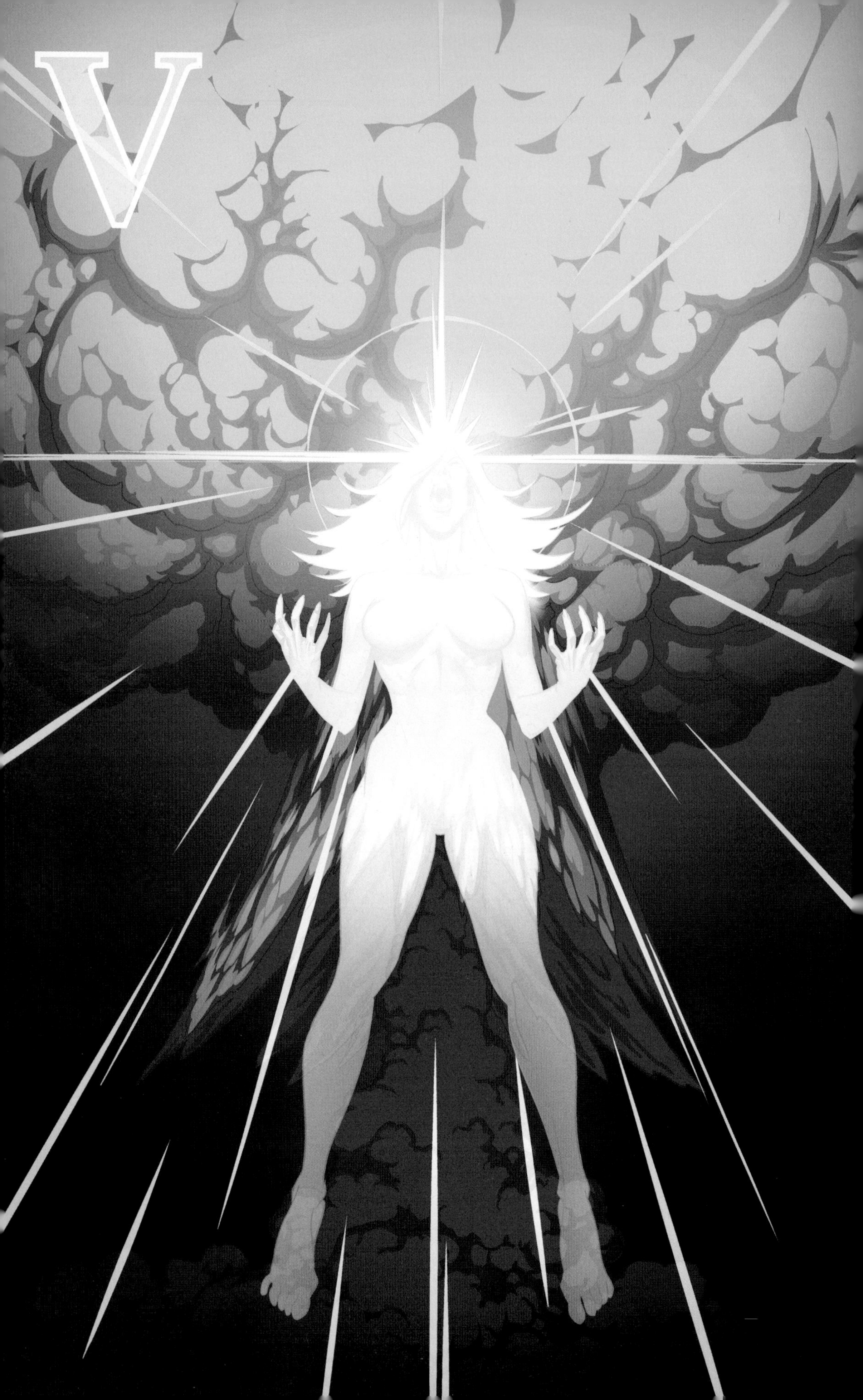
V

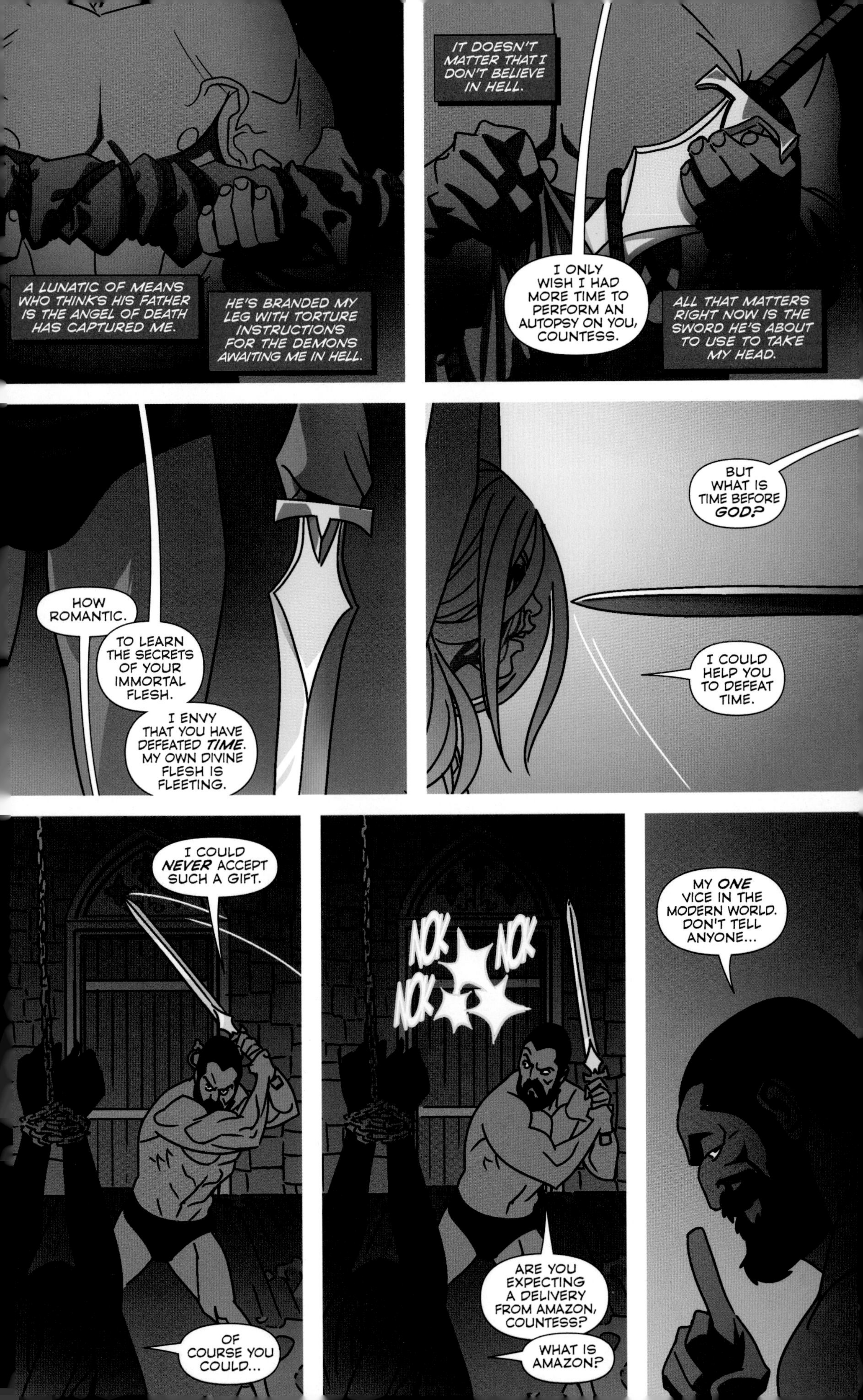
A LUNATIC OF MEANS WHO THINKS HIS FATHER IS THE ANGEL OF DEATH HAS CAPTURED ME.
HE'S BRANDED MY LEG WITH TORTURE INSTRUCTIONS FOR THE DEMONS AWAITING ME IN HELL.
IT DOESN'T MATTER THAT I DON'T BELIEVE IN HELL.
I ONLY WISH I HAD MORE TIME TO PERFORM AN AUTOPSY ON YOU, COUNTESS.
ALL THAT MATTERS RIGHT NOW IS THE SWORD HE'S ABOUT TO USE TO TAKE MY HEAD.
HOW ROMANTIC.
TO LEARN THE SECRETS OF YOUR IMMORTAL FLESH.
I ENVY THAT YOU HAVE DEFEATED TIME. MY OWN DIVINE FLESH IS FLEETING.
BUT WHAT IS TIME BEFORE GOD?
I COULD HELP YOU TO DEFEAT TIME.
I COULD NEVER ACCEPT SUCH A GIFT.
OF COURSE YOU COULD...
NOK NOK NOK
ARE YOU EXPECTING A DELIVERY FROM AMAZON, COUNTESS?
WHAT IS AMAZON?
MY ONE VICE IN THE MODERN WORLD. DON'T TELL ANYONE...

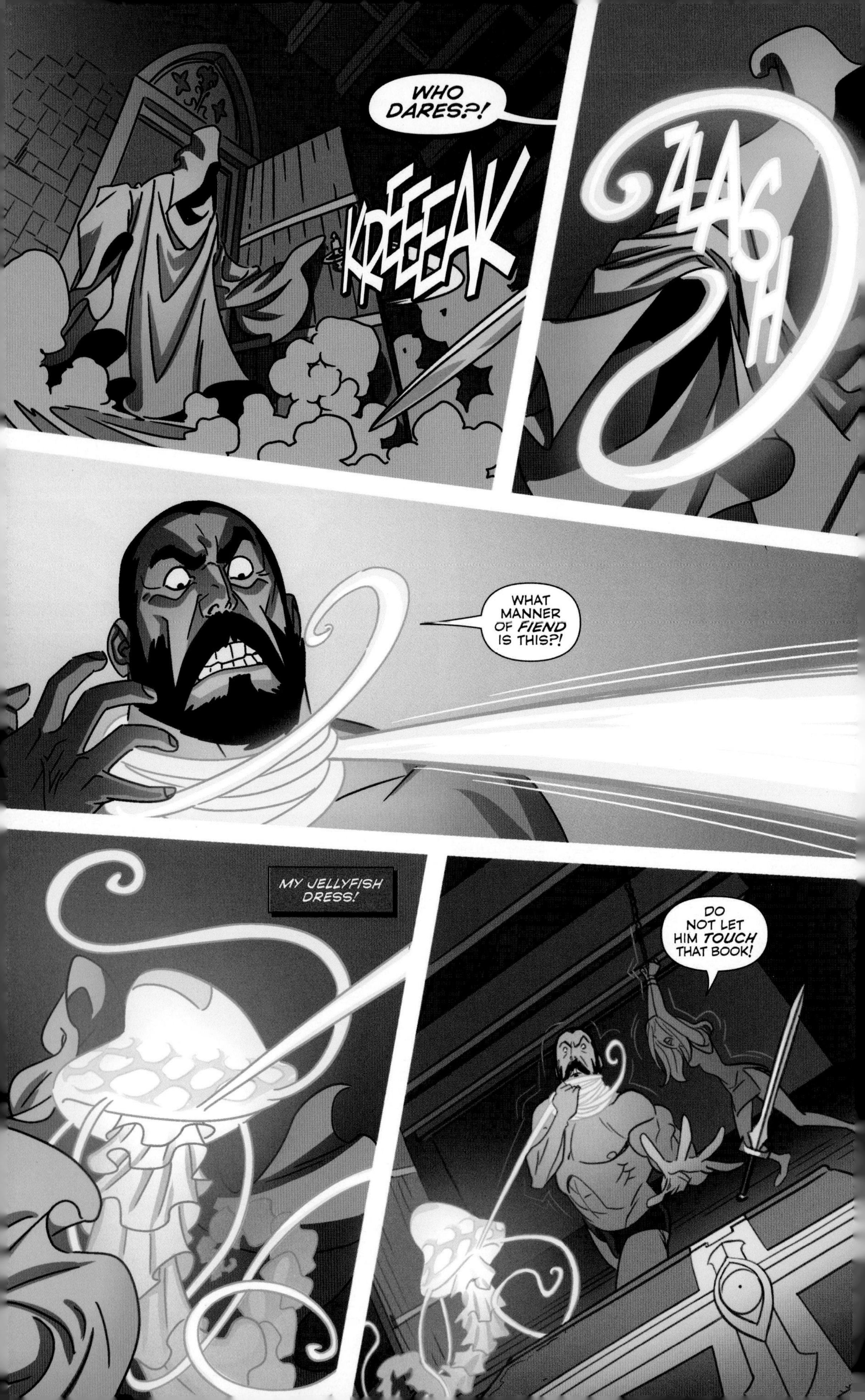
WHO DARES?!
KREEEAK
ZLASH
WHAT MANNER OF *FIEND* IS THIS?!
MY JELLYFISH DRESS!
DO NOT LET HIM *TOUCH* THAT BOOK!

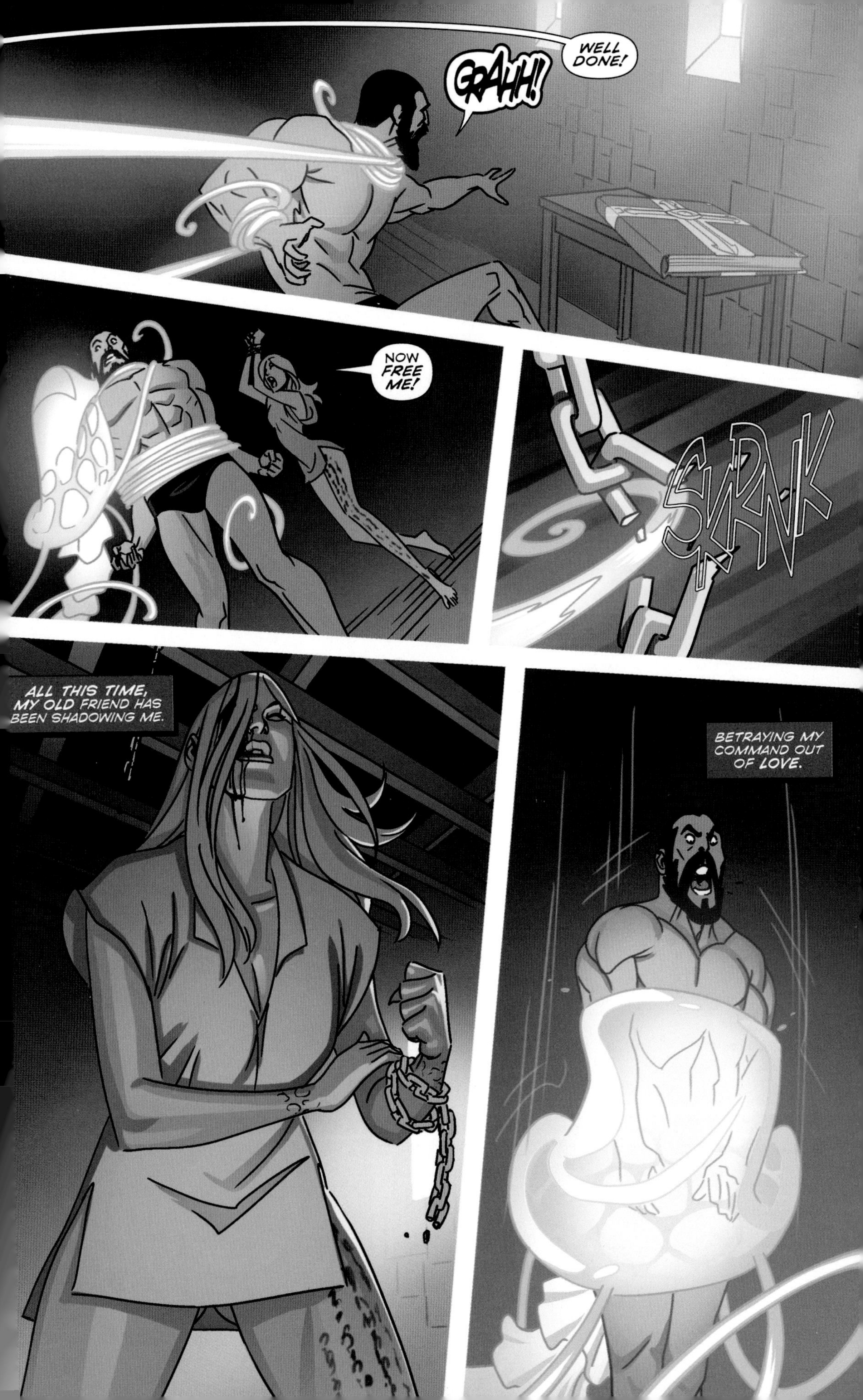
WELL DONE!
GRAHH!
NOW FREE ME!
SKRNK
ALL THIS TIME, MY OLD FRIEND HAS BEEN SHADOWING ME.
BETRAYING MY COMMAND OUT OF LOVE.

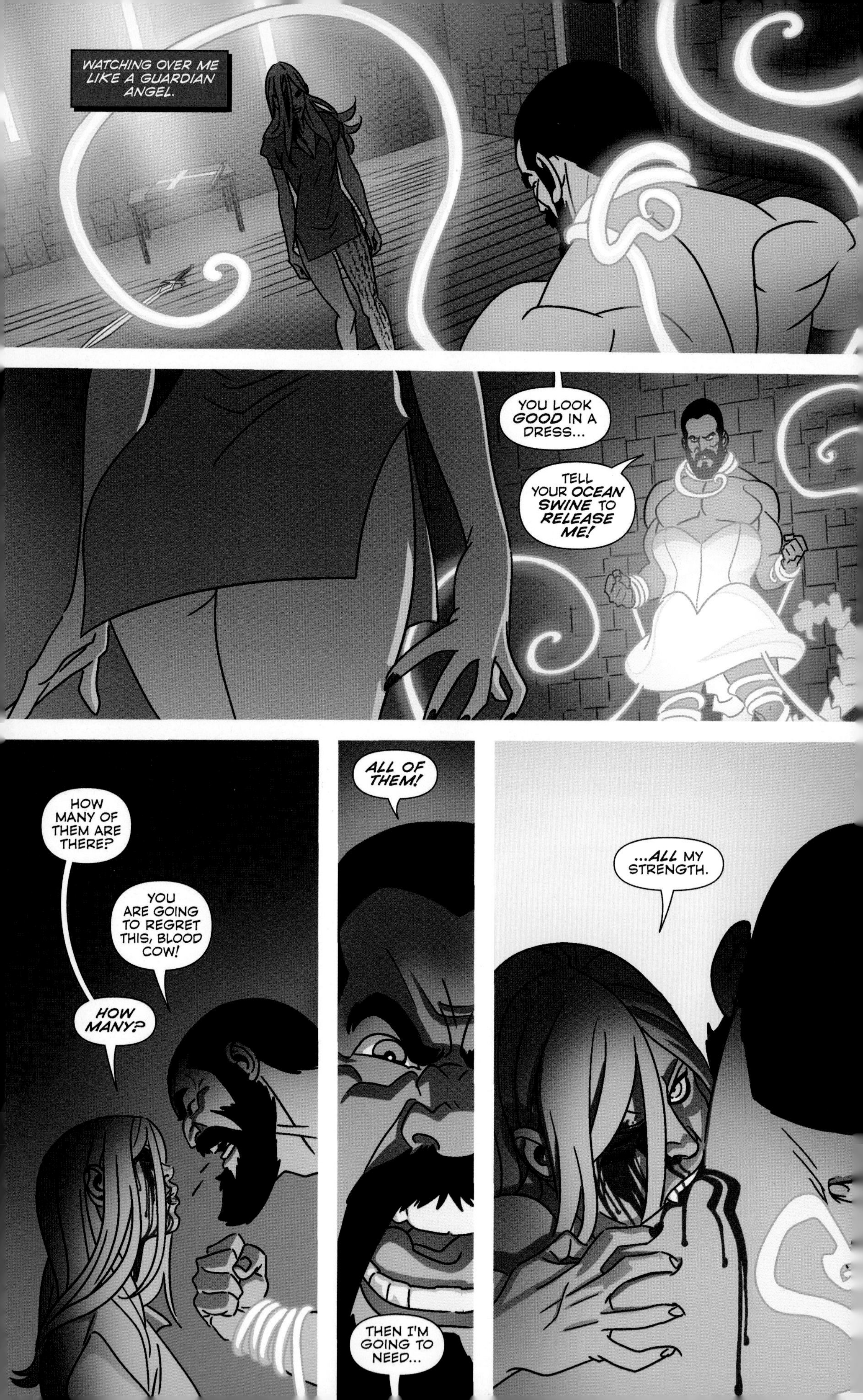
WATCHING OVER ME LIKE A GUARDIAN ANGEL.
YOU LOOK GOOD IN A DRESS...
TELL YOUR OCEAN SWINE TO RELEASE ME!
HOW MANY OF THEM ARE THERE?
YOU ARE GOING TO REGRET THIS, BLOOD COW!
HOW MANY?
ALL OF THEM!
THEN I'M GOING TO NEED...
...ALL MY STRENGTH.

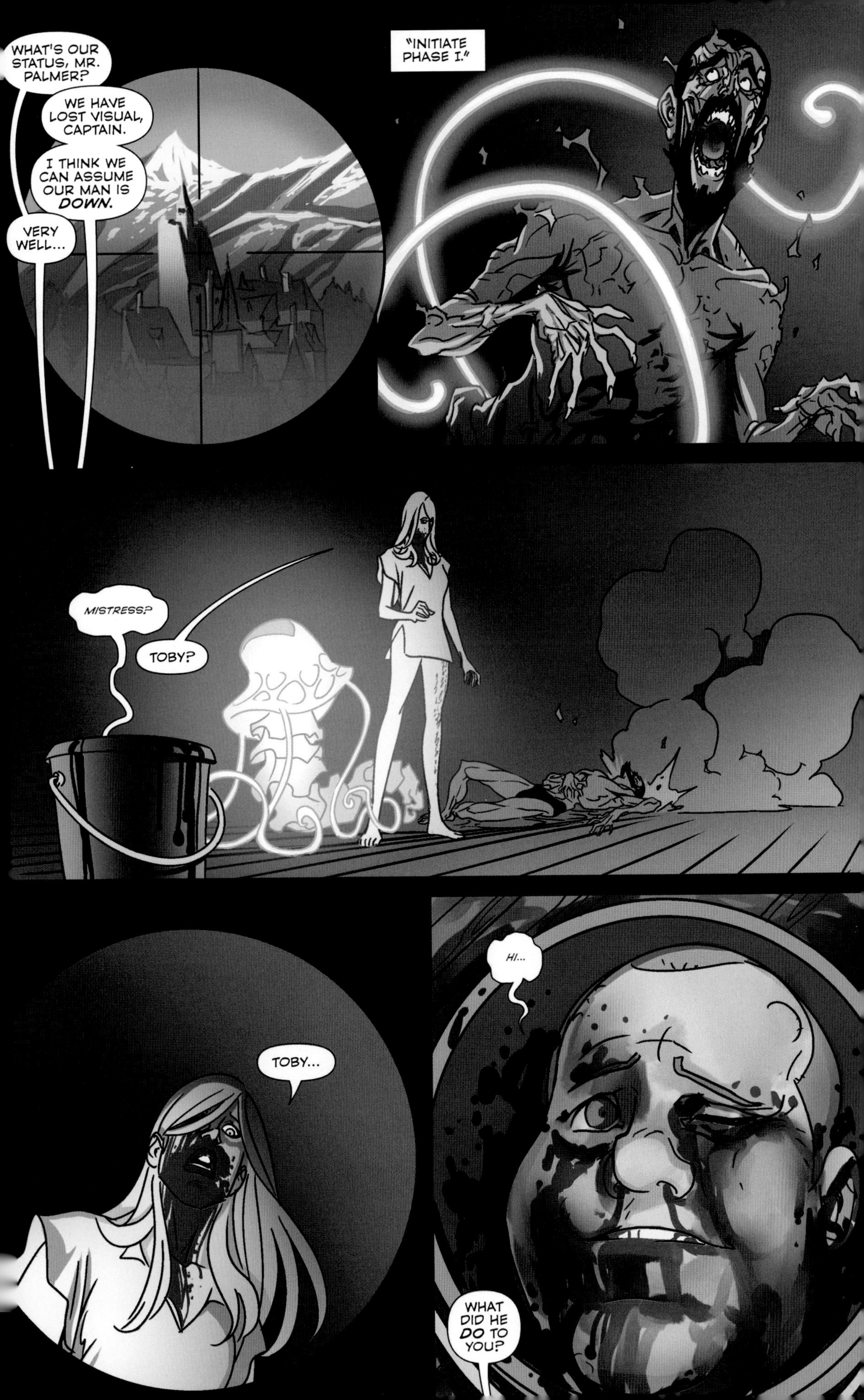
WHAT'S OUR STATUS, MR. PALMER?
WE HAVE LOST VISUAL, CAPTAIN.
I THINK WE CAN ASSUME OUR MAN IS *DOWN.*
VERY WELL...
"INITIATE PHASE I."
MISTRESS?
TOBY?
TOBY...
HI...
WHAT DID HE *DO* TO YOU?

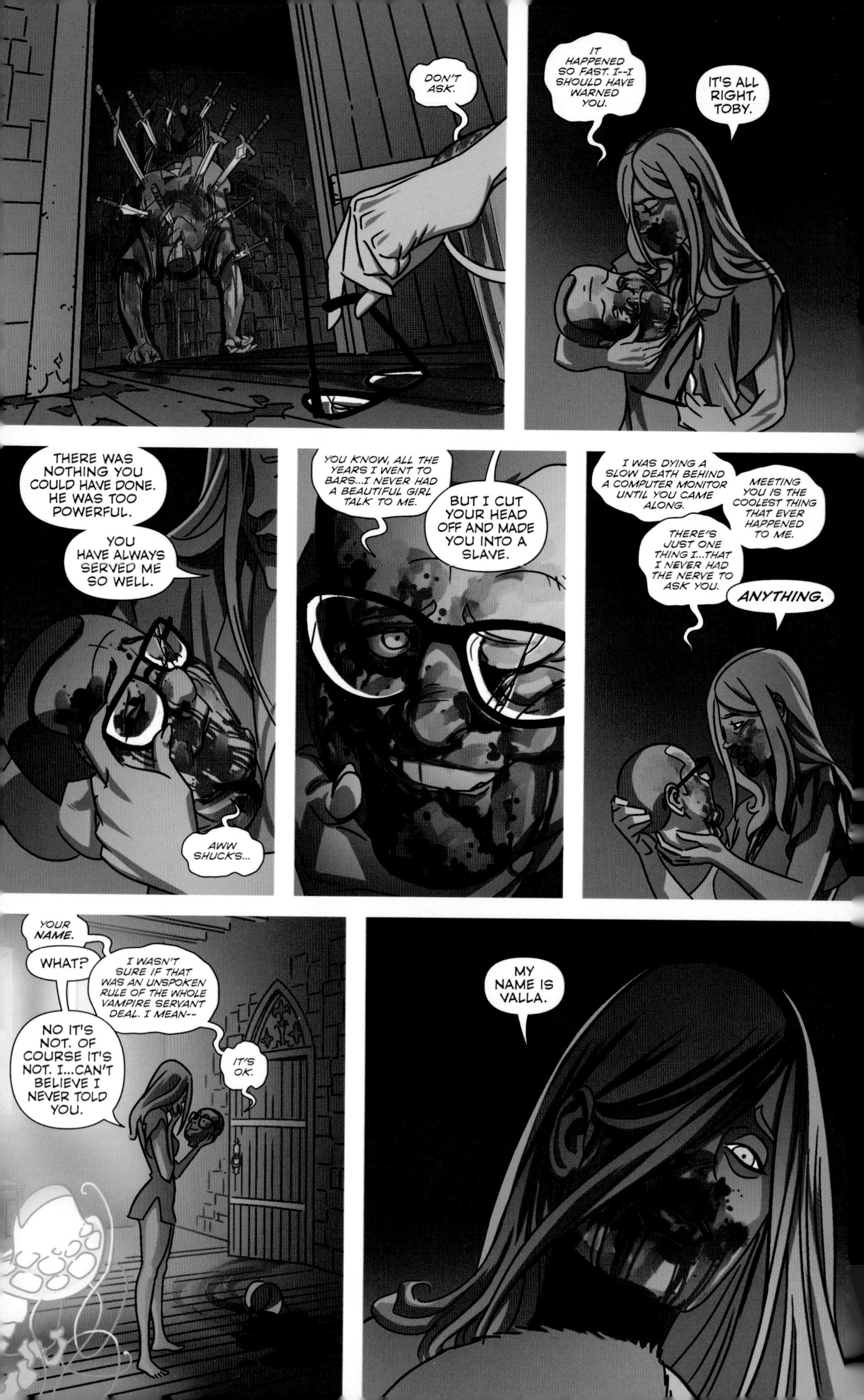
DON'T ASK.
IT HAPPENED SO FAST. I--I SHOULD HAVE WARNED YOU.
IT'S ALL RIGHT, TOBY.
THERE WAS NOTHING YOU COULD HAVE DONE. HE WAS TOO POWERFUL.
YOU HAVE ALWAYS SERVED ME SO WELL.
AWW SHUCKS...
YOU KNOW, ALL THE YEARS I WENT TO BARS...I NEVER HAD A BEAUTIFUL GIRL TALK TO ME.
BUT I CUT YOUR HEAD OFF AND MADE YOU INTO A SLAVE.
I WAS DYING A SLOW DEATH BEHIND A COMPUTER MONITOR UNTIL YOU CAME ALONG.
MEETING YOU IS THE COOLEST THING THAT EVER HAPPENED TO ME.
THERE'S JUST ONE THING I...THAT I NEVER HAD THE NERVE TO ASK YOU.
ANYTHING.
YOUR NAME.
WHAT?
I WASN'T SURE IF THAT WAS AN UNSPOKEN RULE OF THE WHOLE VAMPIRE SERVANT DEAL. I MEAN--
NO IT'S NOT. OF COURSE IT'S NOT. I...CAN'T BELIEVE I NEVER TOLD YOU.
IT'S OK.
MY NAME IS VALLA.

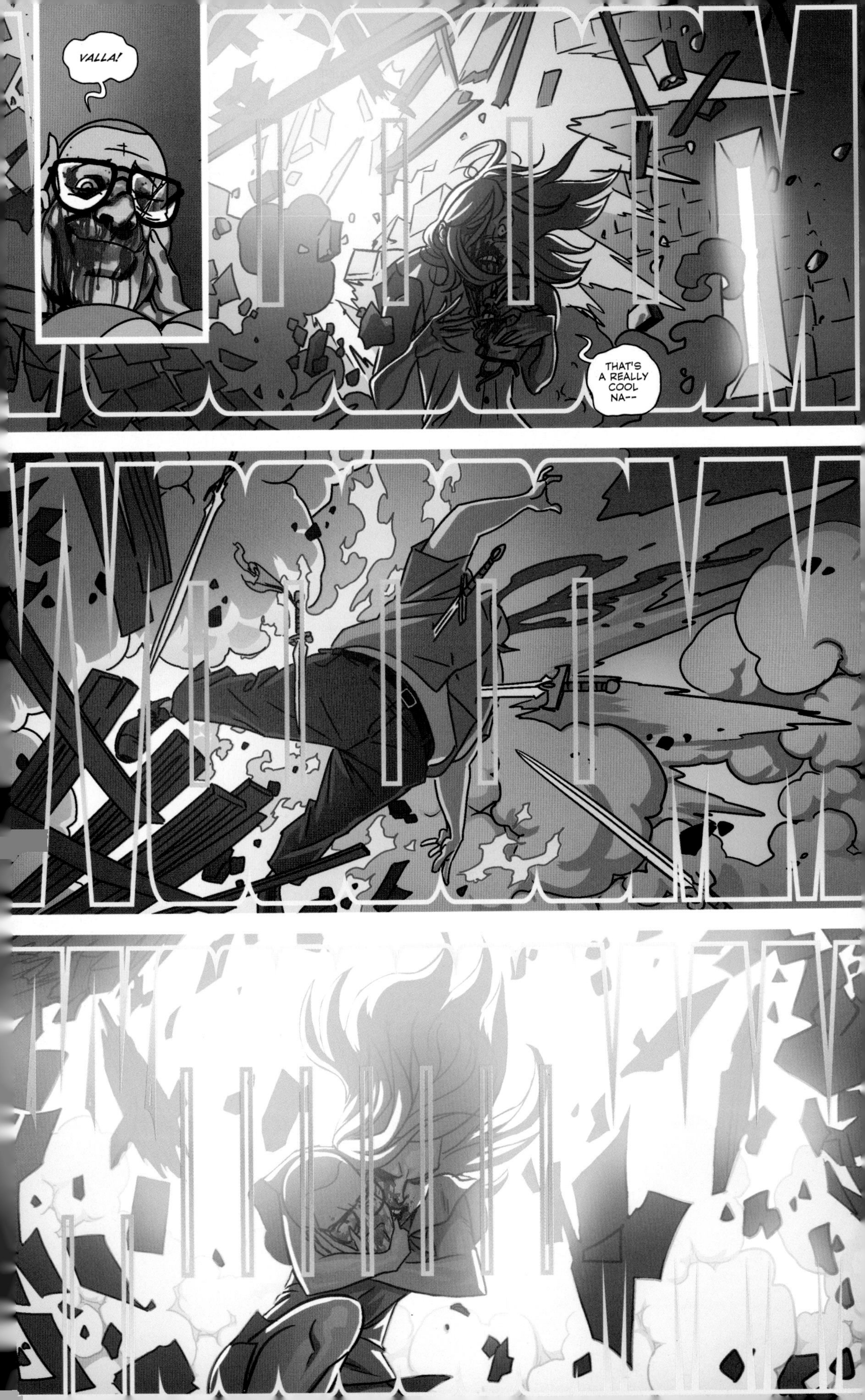
VALLA!
THAT'S A REALLY COOL NA--

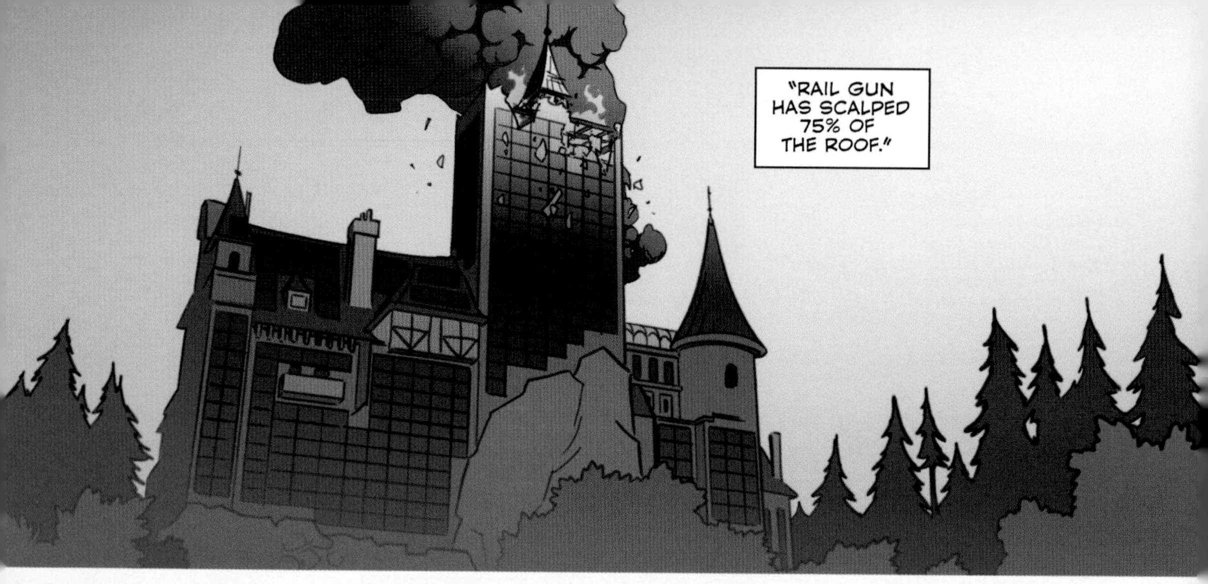
"RAIL GUN HAS SCALPED 75% OF THE ROOF."

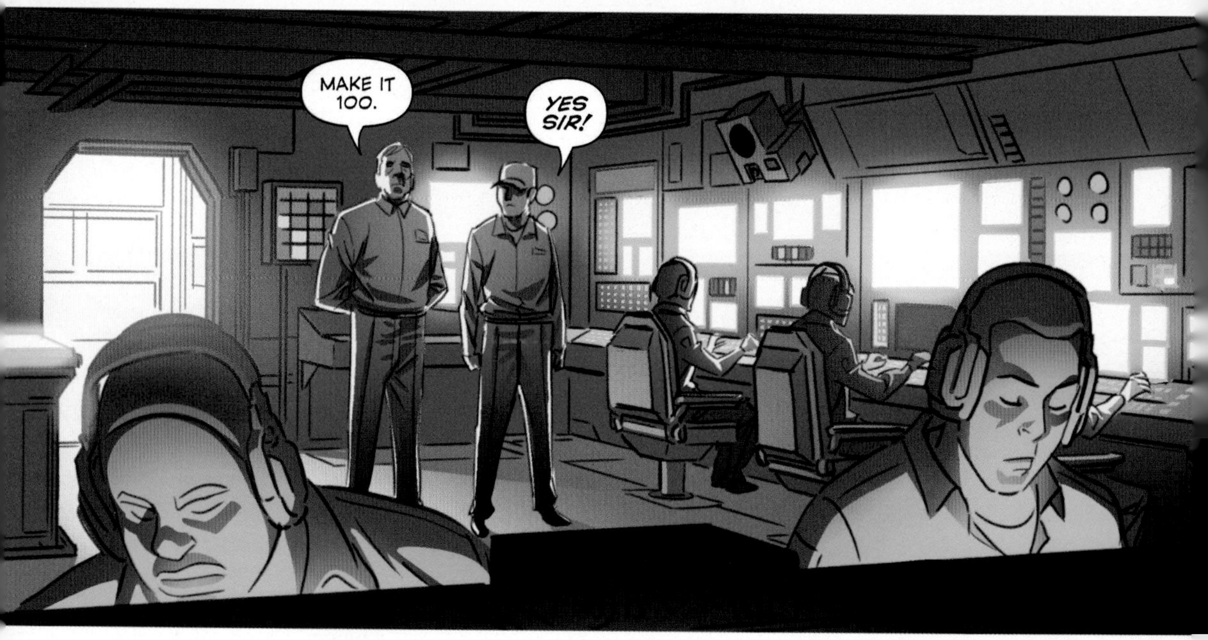
MAKE IT 100.
YES SIR!

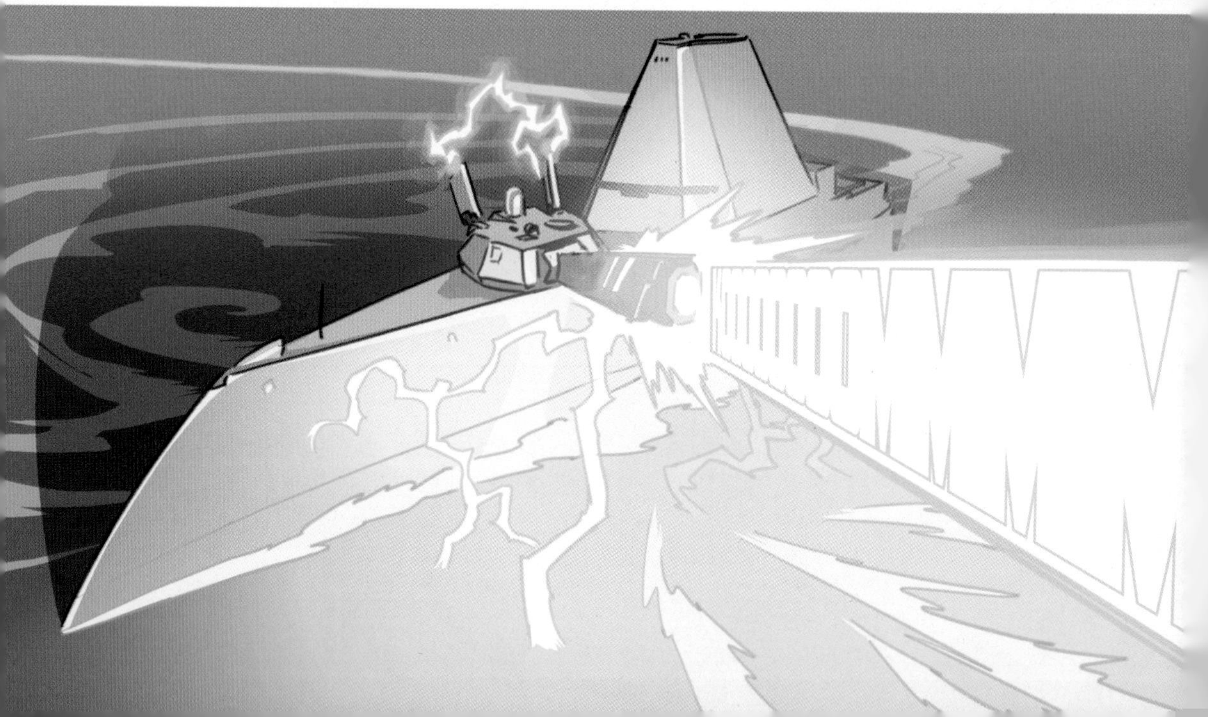

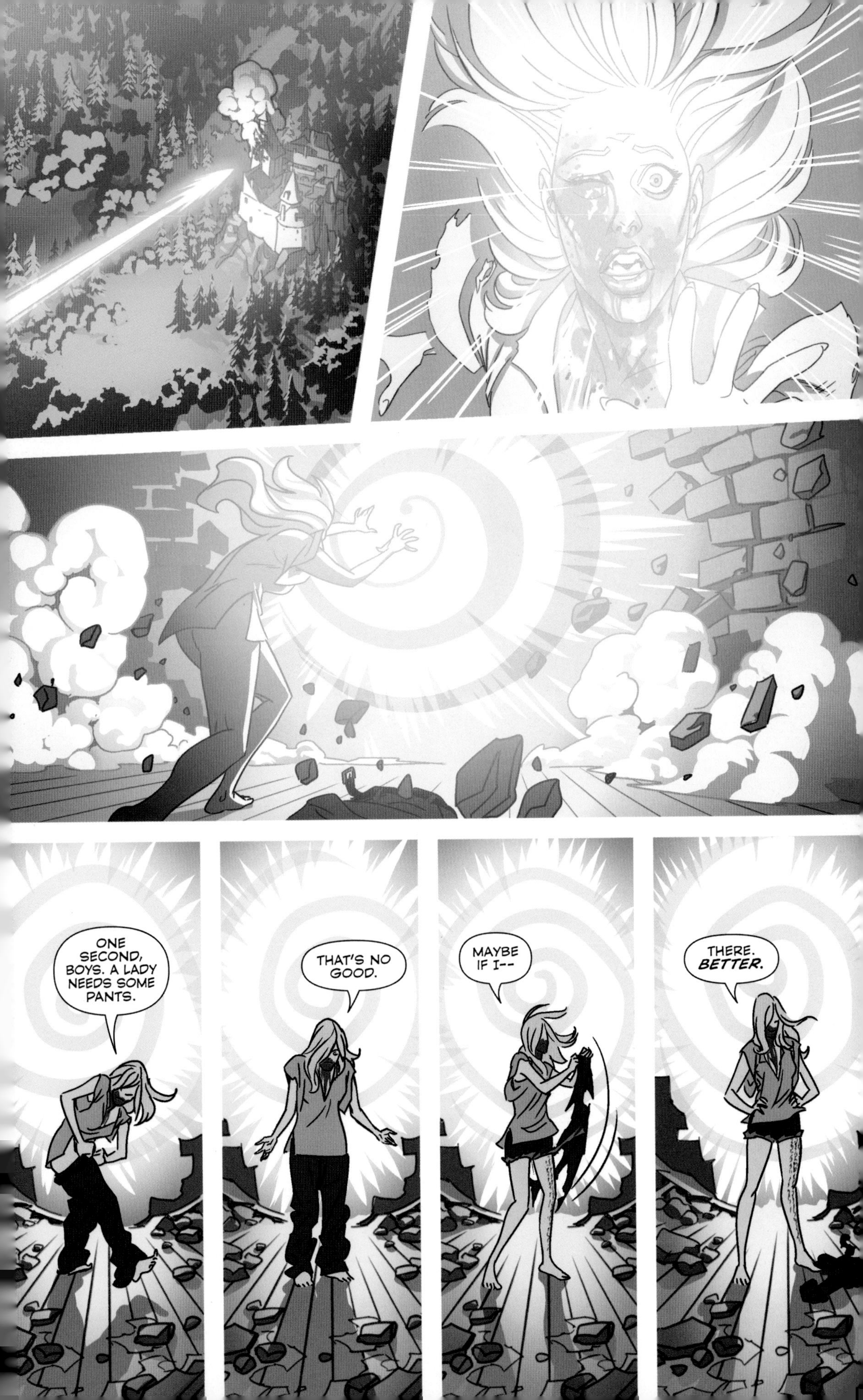
ONE SECOND, BOYS. A LADY NEEDS SOME PANTS.
THAT'S NO GOOD.
MAYBE IF I--
THERE. *BETTER.*

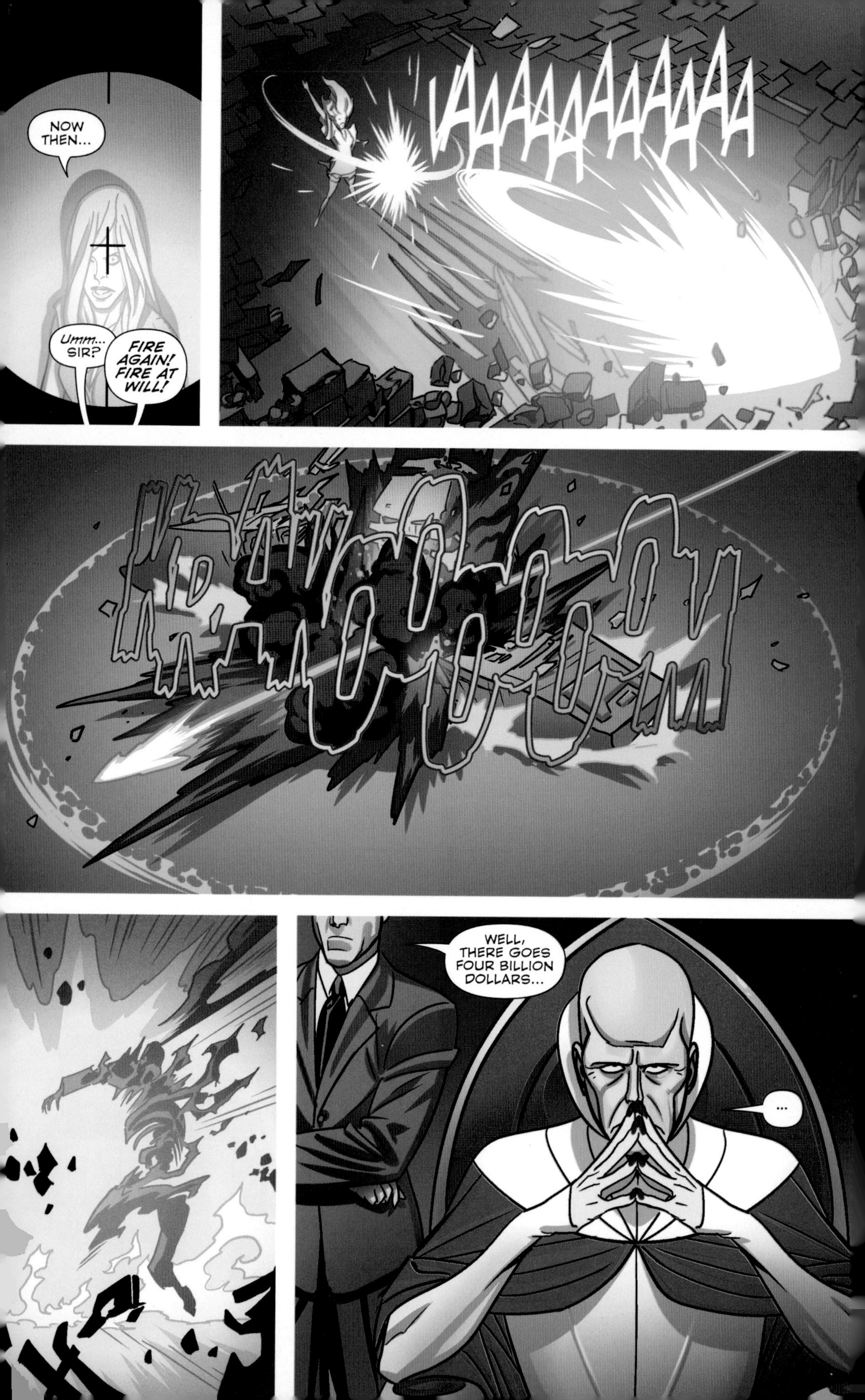
NOW THEN...
Umm... SIR?
FIRE AGAIN! FIRE AT WILL!
WELL, THERE GOES FOUR BILLION DOLLARS...
...

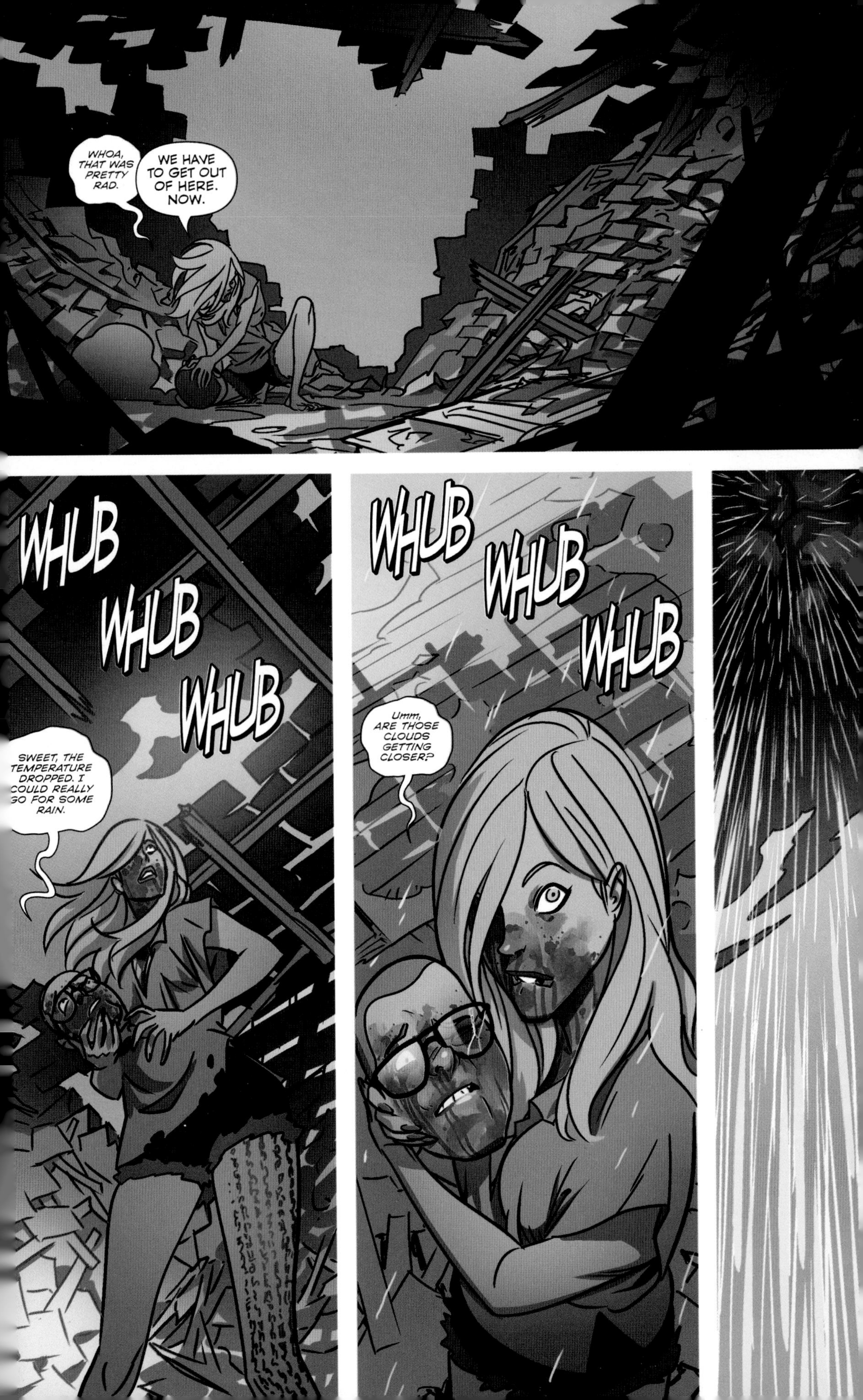
WHOA, THAT WAS PRETTY RAD.
WE HAVE TO GET OUT OF HERE. NOW.
WHUB WHUB WHUB
SWEET, THE TEMPERATURE DROPPED. I COULD REALLY GO FOR SOME RAIN.
WHUB WHUB WHUB
UMM, ARE THOSE CLOUDS GETTING CLOSER?

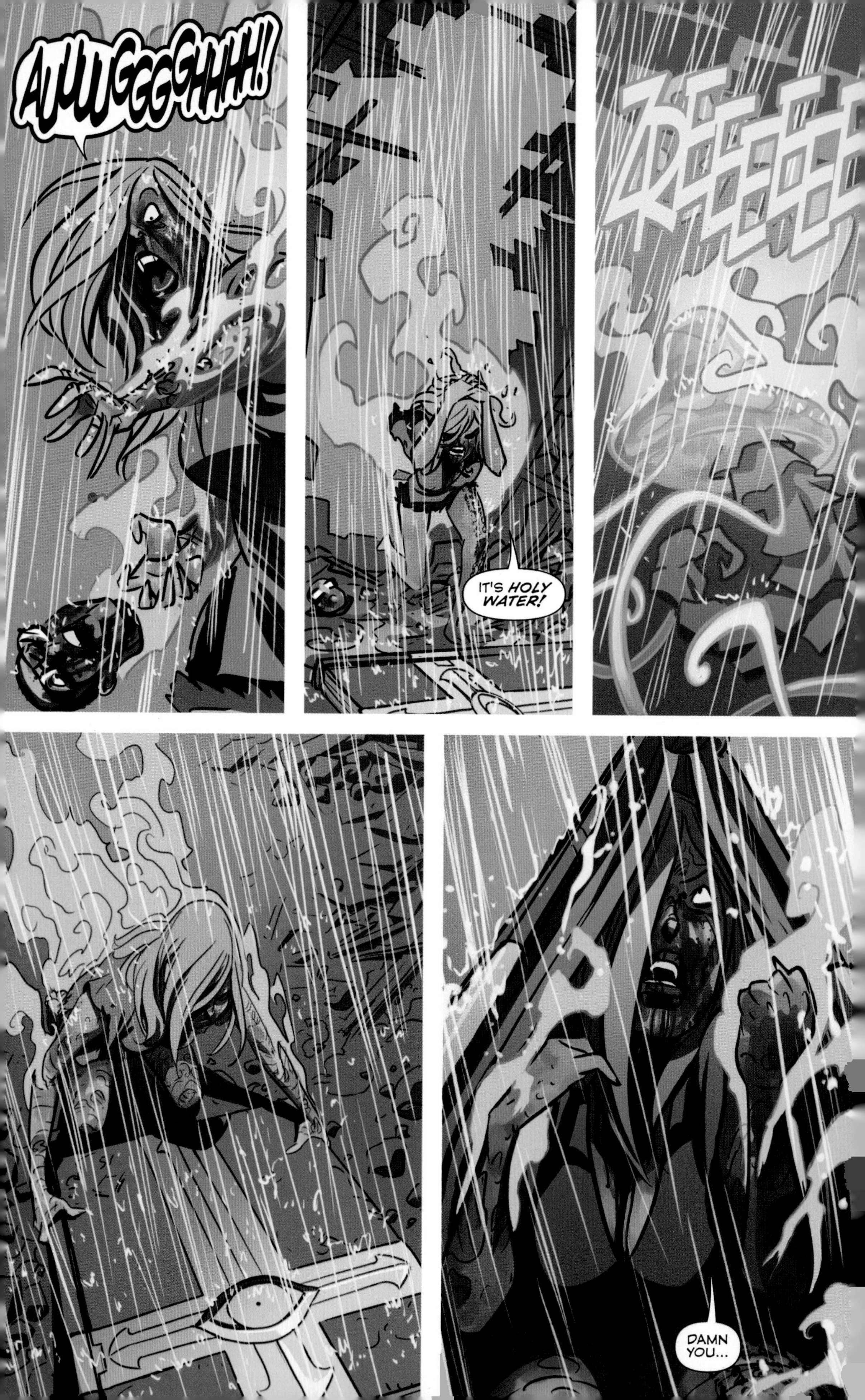
AUUUGGGGHHHH!!
IT'S HOLY WATER!
DAMN YOU...

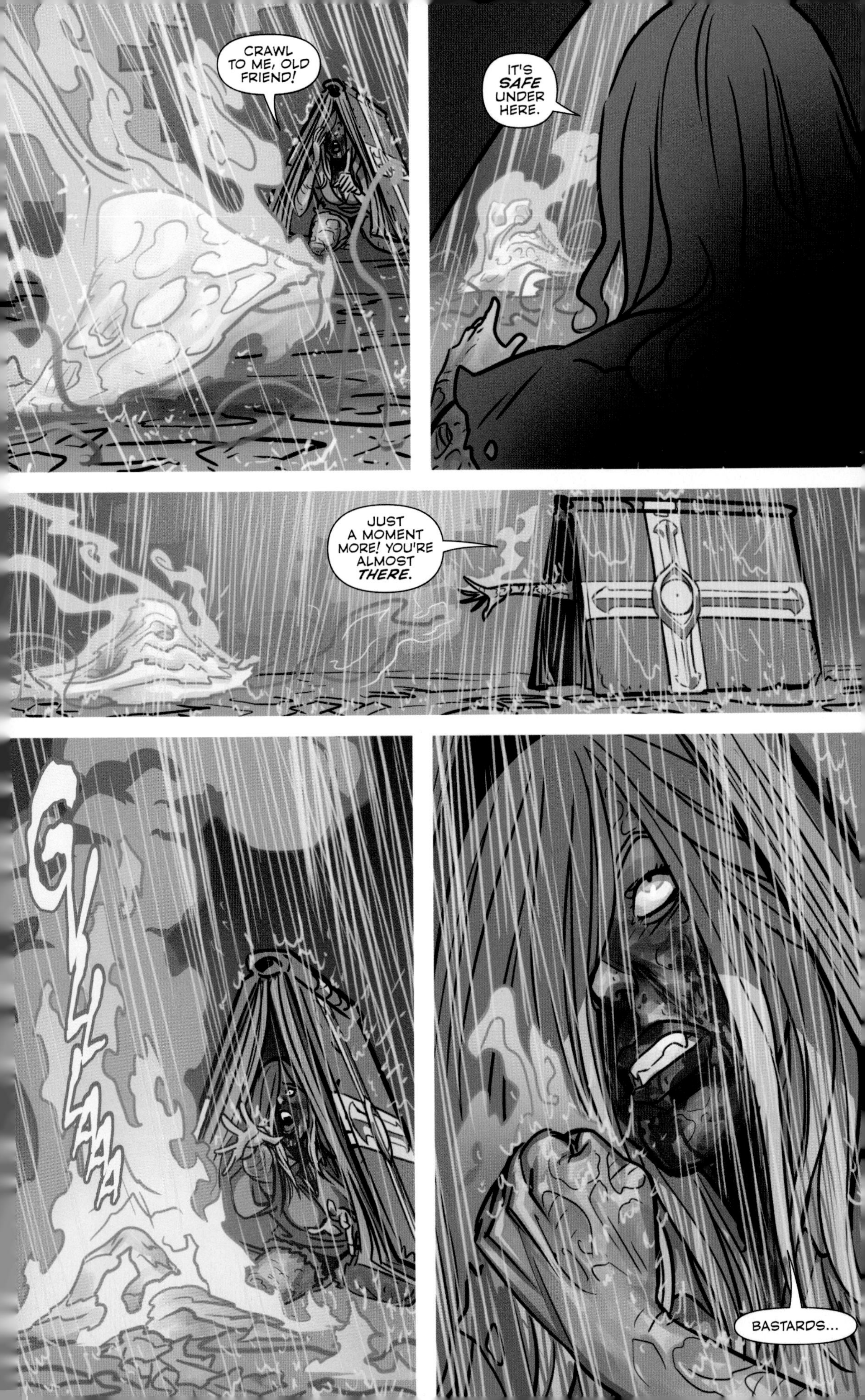

CRAWL TO ME, OLD FRIEND!
IT'S *SAFE* UNDER HERE.
JUST A MOMENT MORE! YOU'RE ALMOST *THERE.*
GHLLAAA
BASTARDS...

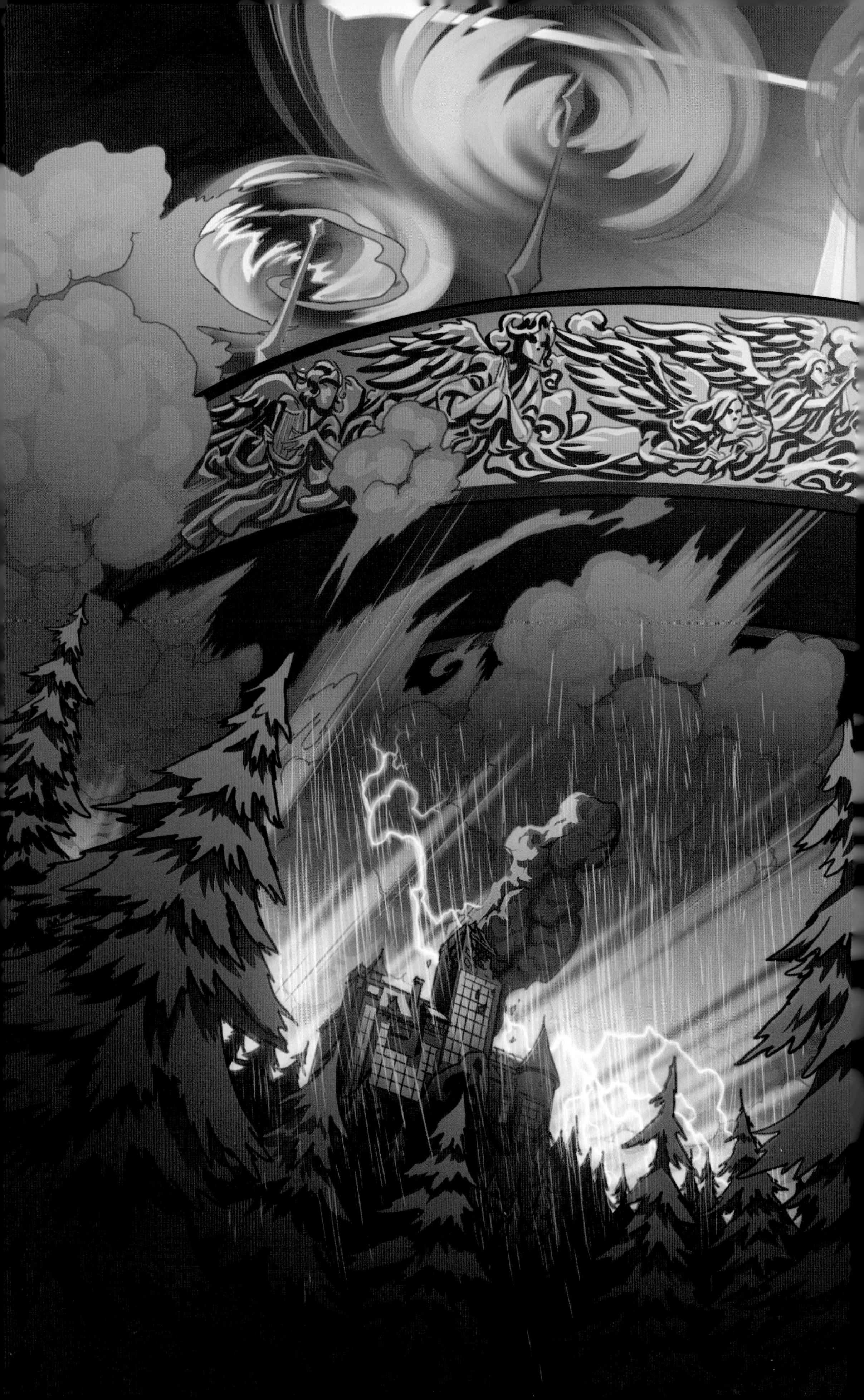

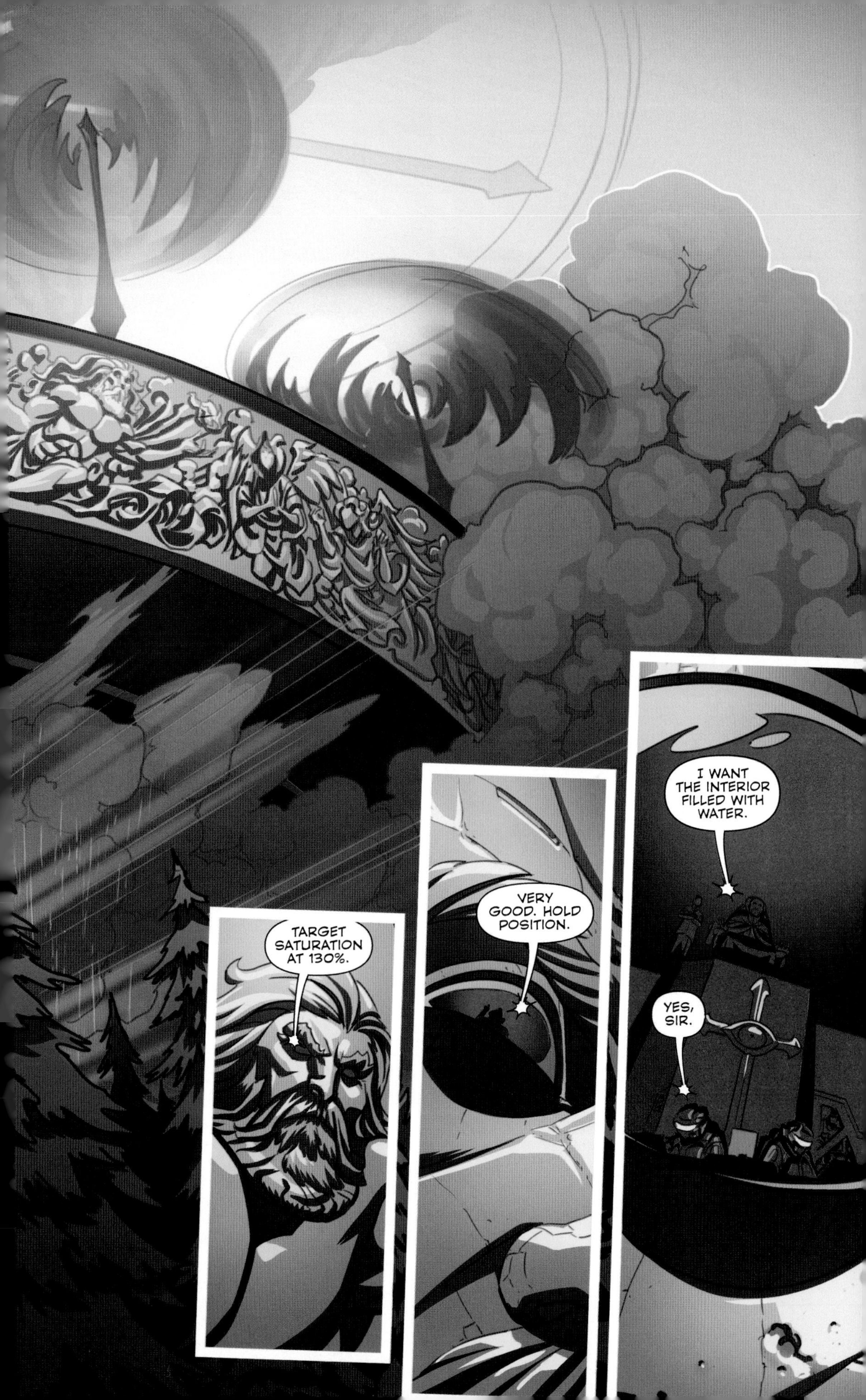
TARGET SATURATION AT 130%.
VERY GOOD. HOLD POSITION.
I WANT THE INTERIOR FILLED WITH WATER.
YES, SIR.

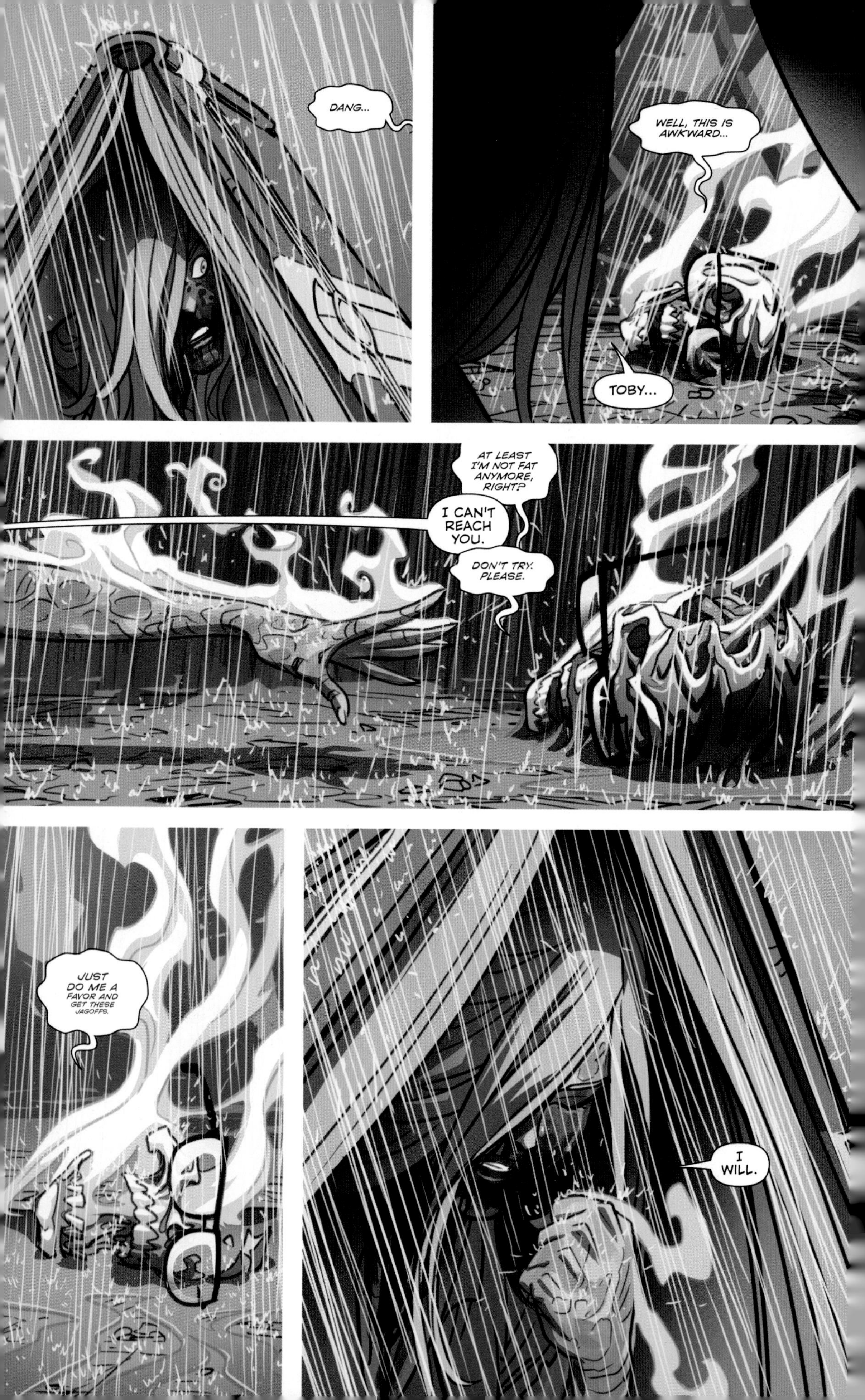
DANG...
WELL, THIS IS AWKWARD...
TOBY...
AT LEAST I'M NOT FAT ANYMORE, RIGHT?
I CAN'T REACH YOU.
DON'T TRY. PLEASE.
JUST DO ME A FAVOR AND GET THESE JAGOFFS.
I WILL.

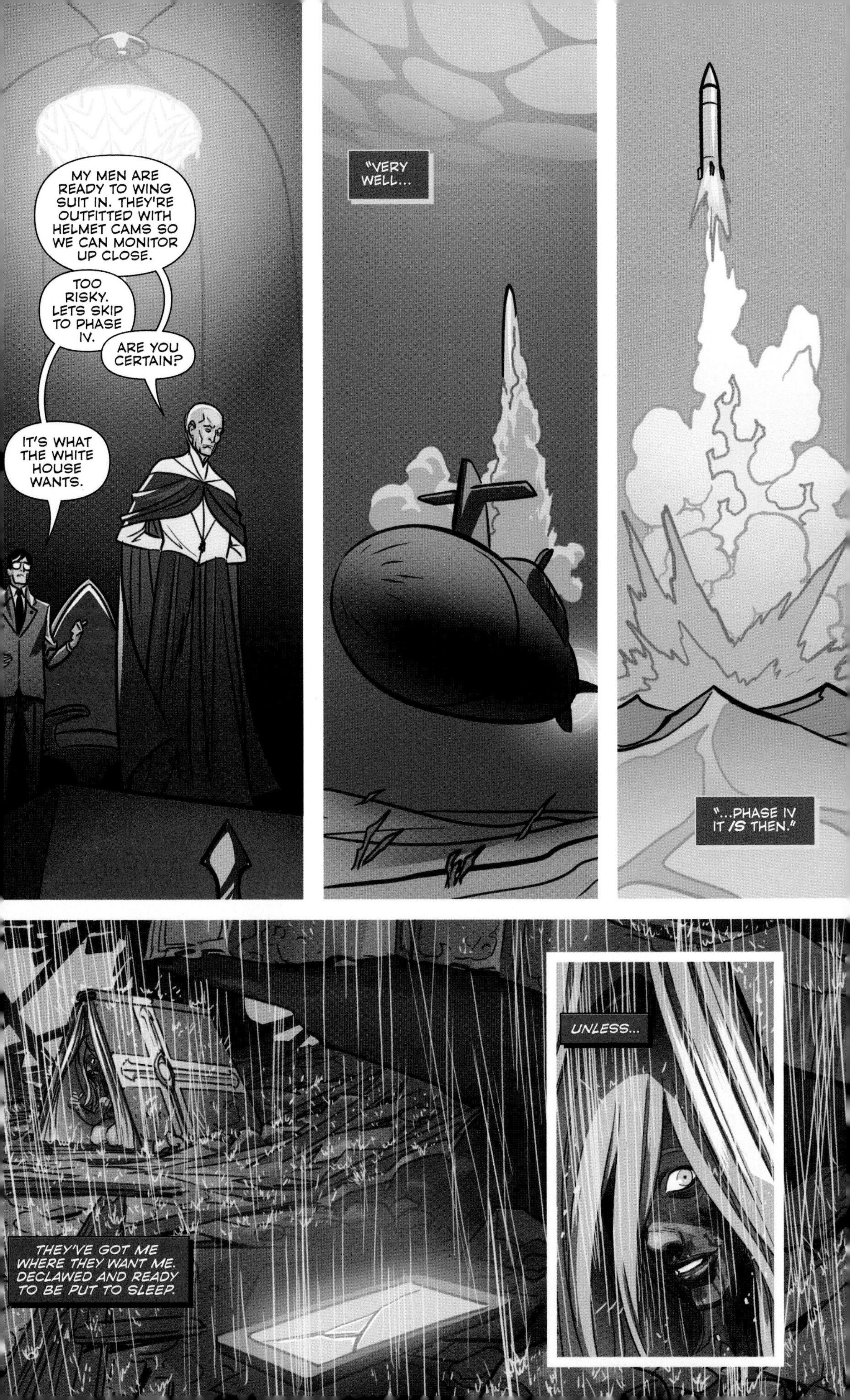
MY MEN ARE READY TO WING SUIT IN. THEY'RE OUTFITTED WITH HELMET CAMS SO WE CAN MONITOR UP CLOSE.
TOO RISKY. LETS SKIP TO PHASE IV.
ARE YOU CERTAIN?
IT'S WHAT THE WHITE HOUSE WANTS.
"VERY WELL...
"...PHASE IV IT IS THEN."
THEY'VE GOT ME WHERE THEY WANT ME. DECLAWED AND READY TO BE PUT TO SLEEP.
UNLESS...

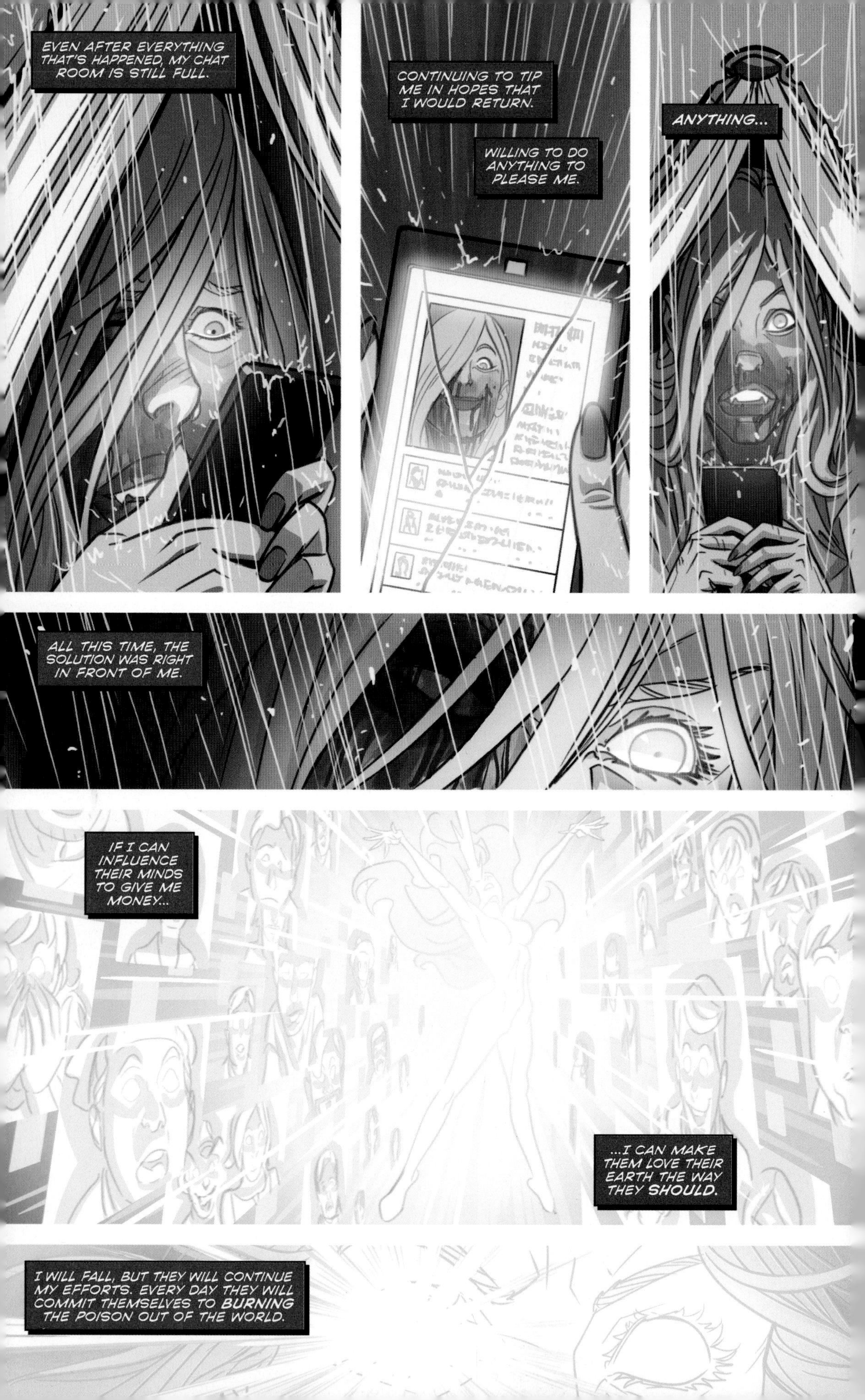
EVEN AFTER EVERYTHING THAT'S HAPPENED, MY CHAT ROOM IS STILL FULL.
CONTINUING TO TIP ME IN HOPES THAT I WOULD RETURN.
WILLING TO DO ANYTHING TO PLEASE ME.
ANYTHING...
ALL THIS TIME, THE SOLUTION WAS RIGHT IN FRONT OF ME.
IF I CAN INFLUENCE THEIR MINDS TO GIVE ME MONEY...
...I CAN MAKE THEM LOVE THEIR EARTH THE WAY THEY **SHOULD**.
I WILL FALL, BUT THEY WILL CONTINUE MY EFFORTS. EVERY DAY THEY WILL COMMIT THEMSELVES TO **BURNING** THE POISON OUT OF THE WORLD.

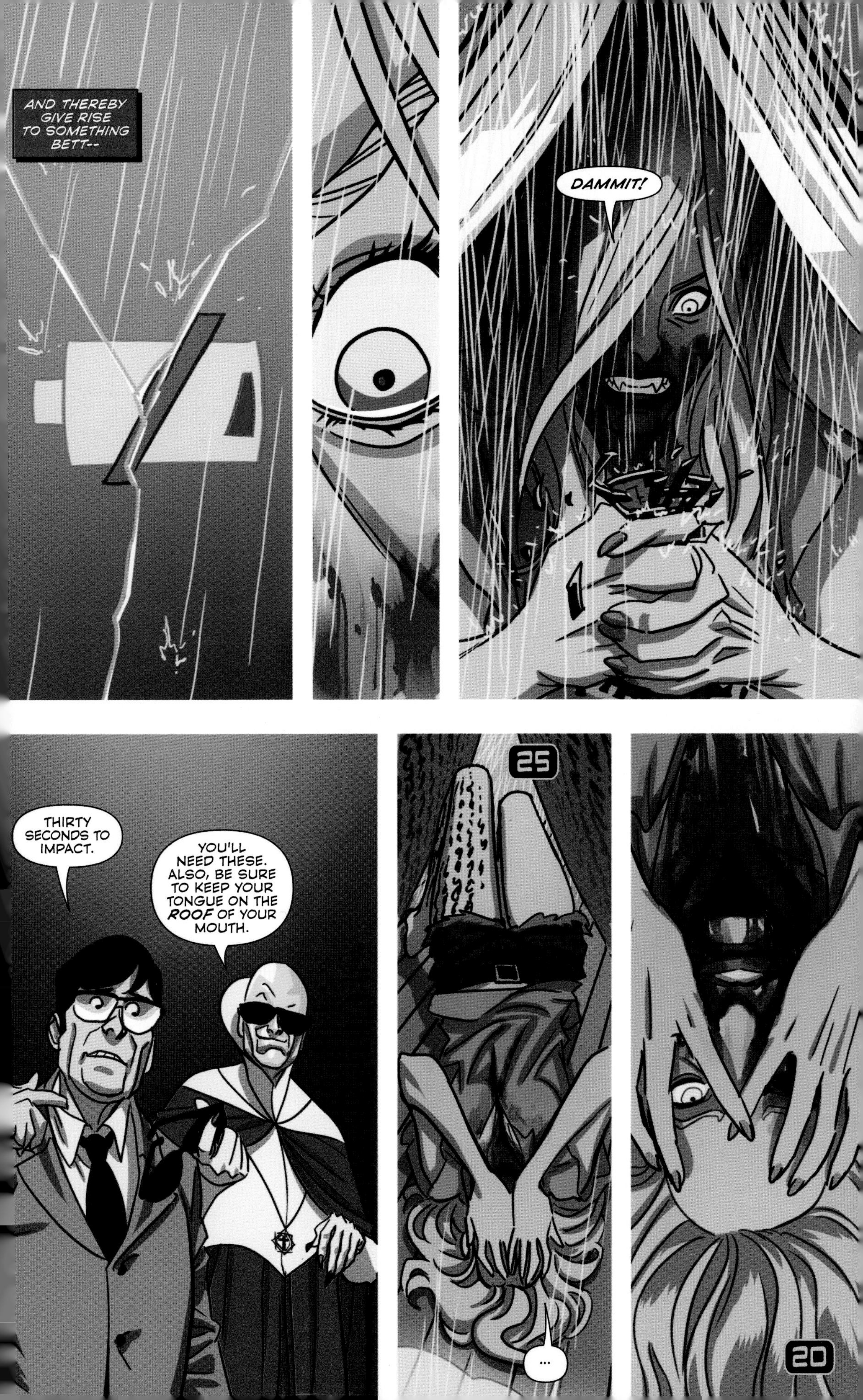
AND THEREBY GIVE RISE TO SOMETHING BETT--
DAMMIT!
THIRTY SECONDS TO IMPACT.
YOU'LL NEED THESE. ALSO, BE SURE TO KEEP YOUR TONGUE ON THE ROOF OF YOUR MOUTH.
25
...

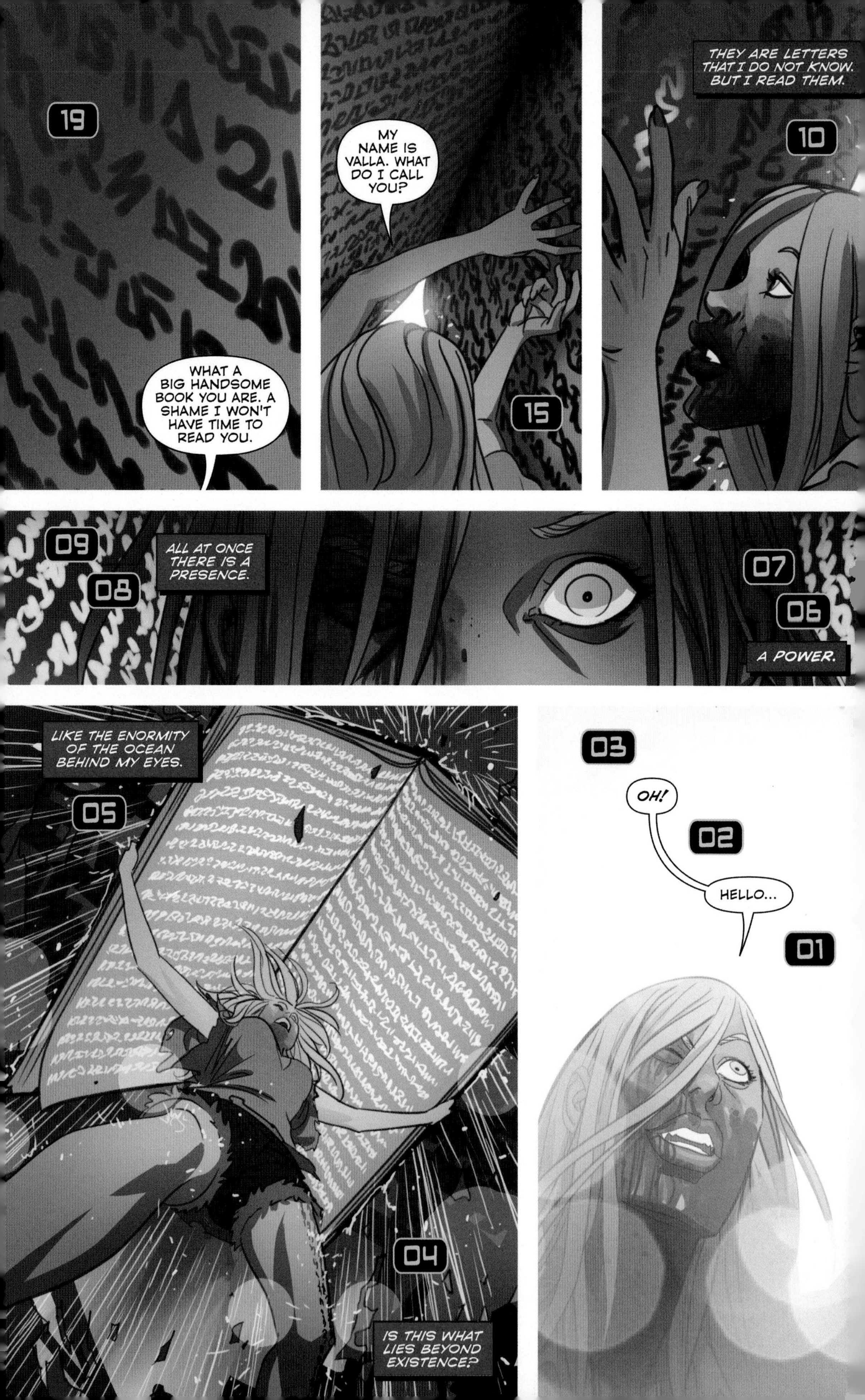
19
WHAT A BIG HANDSOME BOOK YOU ARE. A SHAME I WON'T HAVE TIME TO READ YOU.
MY NAME IS VALLA. WHAT DO I CALL YOU?
15
THEY ARE LETTERS THAT I DO NOT KNOW. BUT I READ THEM.
10
09
08
ALL AT ONCE THERE IS A PRESENCE.
07
06
A POWER.
LIKE THE ENORMITY OF THE OCEAN BEHIND MY EYES.
05
04
IS THIS WHAT LIES BEYOND EXISTENCE?
03
OH!
02
HELLO...
01

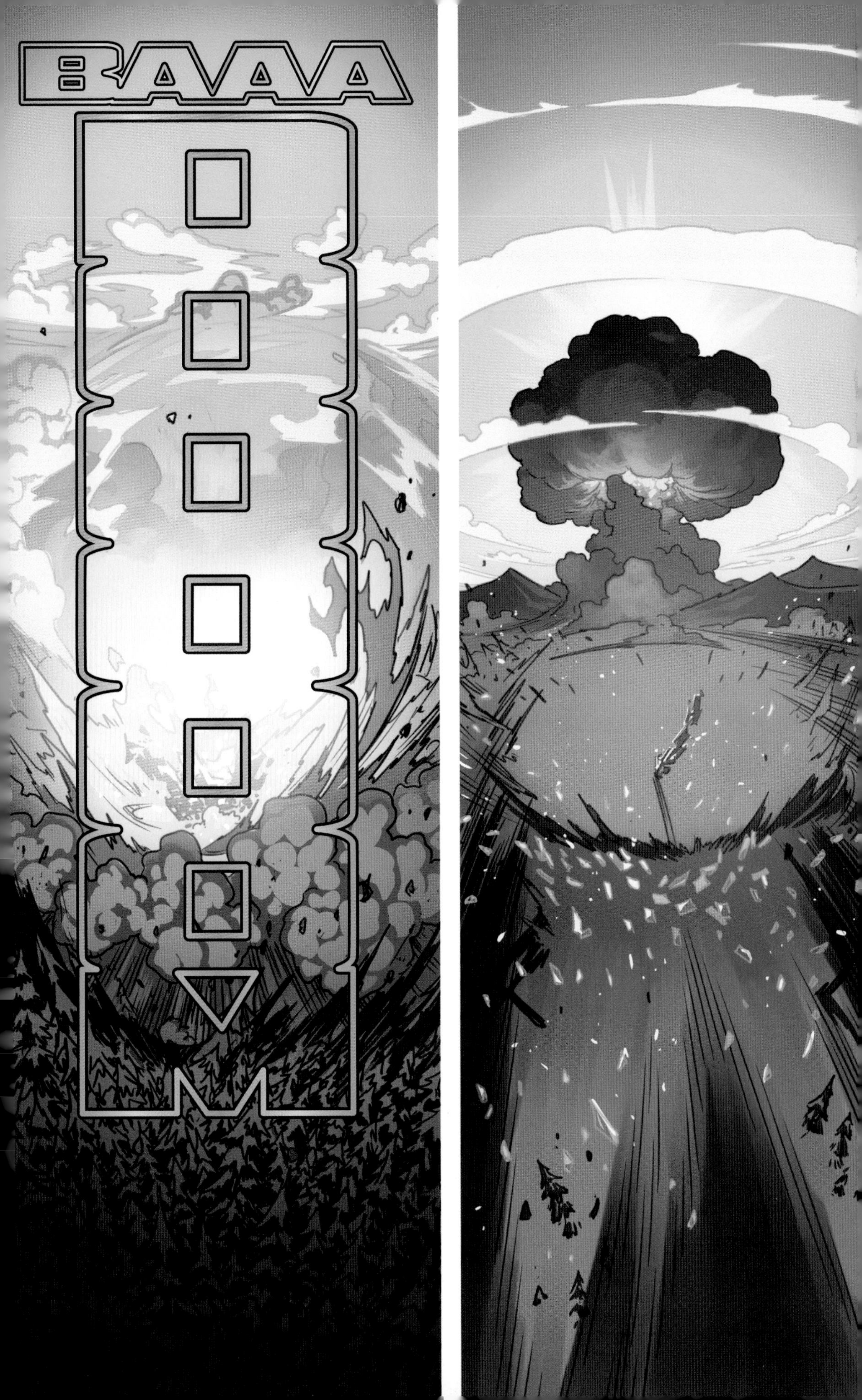
BAAA

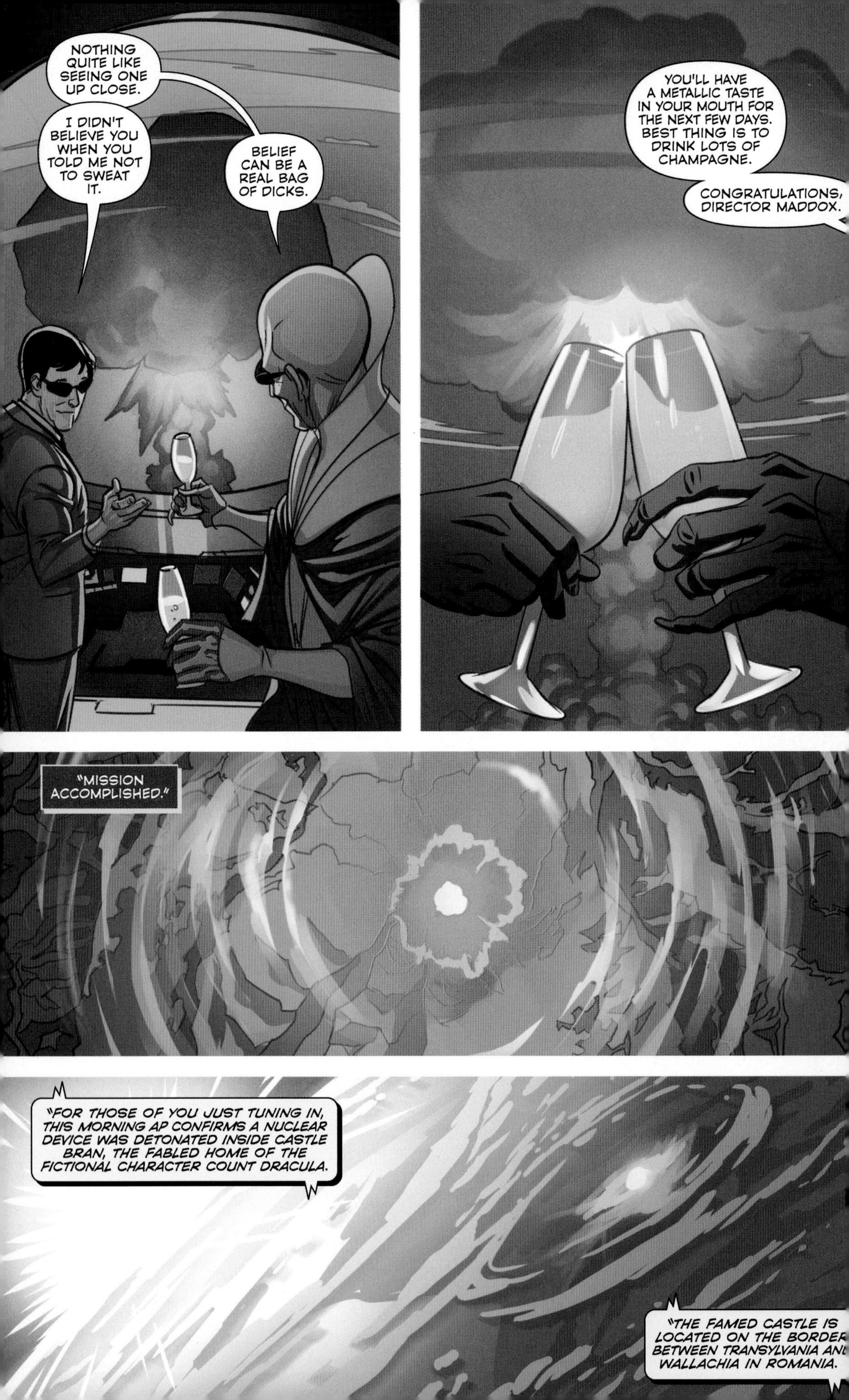
NOTHING QUITE LIKE SEEING ONE UP CLOSE.
I DIDN'T BELIEVE YOU WHEN YOU TOLD ME NOT TO SWEAT IT.
BELIEF CAN BE A REAL BAG OF DICKS.
YOU'LL HAVE A METALLIC TASTE IN YOUR MOUTH FOR THE NEXT FEW DAYS. BEST THING IS TO DRINK LOTS OF CHAMPAGNE.
CONGRATULATIONS, DIRECTOR MADDOX.
"MISSION ACCOMPLISHED."
"FOR THOSE OF YOU JUST TUNING IN, THIS MORNING AP CONFIRMS A NUCLEAR DEVICE WAS DETONATED INSIDE CASTLE BRAN, THE FABLED HOME OF THE FICTIONAL CHARACTER COUNT DRACULA.
"THE FAMED CASTLE IS LOCATED ON THE BORDER BETWEEN TRANSYLVANIA AND WALLACHIA IN ROMANIA.

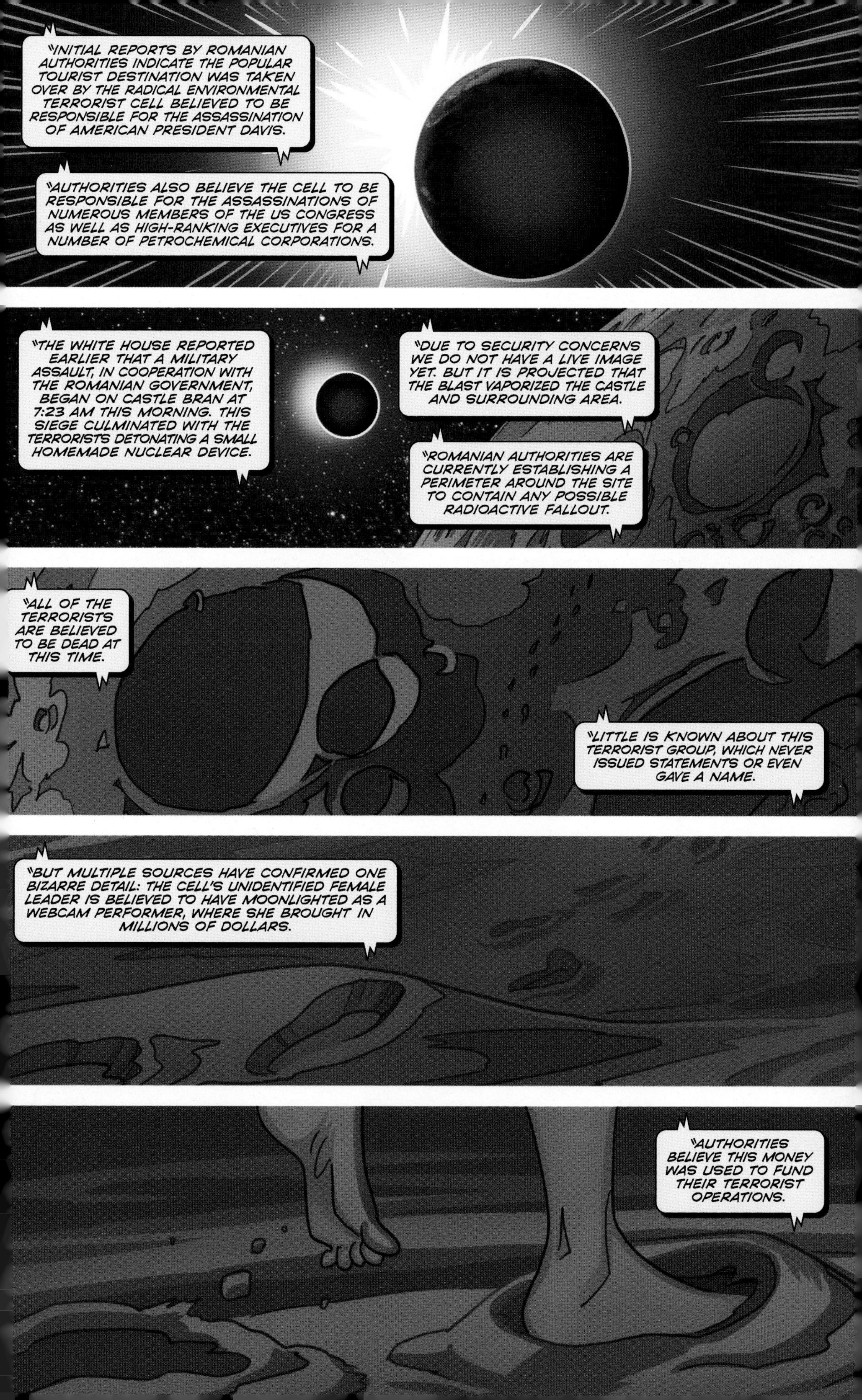
"INITIAL REPORTS BY ROMANIAN AUTHORITIES INDICATE THE POPULAR TOURIST DESTINATION WAS TAKEN OVER BY THE RADICAL ENVIRONMENTAL TERRORIST CELL BELIEVED TO BE RESPONSIBLE FOR THE ASSASSINATION OF AMERICAN PRESIDENT DAVIS.
"AUTHORITIES ALSO BELIEVE THE CELL TO BE RESPONSIBLE FOR THE ASSASSINATIONS OF NUMEROUS MEMBERS OF THE US CONGRESS AS WELL AS HIGH-RANKING EXECUTIVES FOR A NUMBER OF PETROCHEMICAL CORPORATIONS.
"THE WHITE HOUSE REPORTED EARLIER THAT A MILITARY ASSAULT, IN COOPERATION WITH THE ROMANIAN GOVERNMENT, BEGAN ON CASTLE BRAN AT 7:23 AM THIS MORNING. THIS SIEGE CULMINATED WITH THE TERRORISTS DETONATING A SMALL HOMEMADE NUCLEAR DEVICE.
"DUE TO SECURITY CONCERNS WE DO NOT HAVE A LIVE IMAGE YET. BUT IT IS PROJECTED THAT THE BLAST VAPORIZED THE CASTLE AND SURROUNDING AREA.
"ROMANIAN AUTHORITIES ARE CURRENTLY ESTABLISHING A PERIMETER AROUND THE SITE TO CONTAIN ANY POSSIBLE RADIOACTIVE FALLOUT.
"ALL OF THE TERRORISTS ARE BELIEVED TO BE DEAD AT THIS TIME.
"LITTLE IS KNOWN ABOUT THIS TERRORIST GROUP, WHICH NEVER ISSUED STATEMENTS OR EVEN GAVE A NAME.
"BUT MULTIPLE SOURCES HAVE CONFIRMED ONE BIZARRE DETAIL: THE CELL'S UNIDENTIFIED FEMALE LEADER IS BELIEVED TO HAVE MOONLIGHTED AS A WEBCAM PERFORMER, WHERE SHE BROUGHT IN MILLIONS OF DOLLARS.
"AUTHORITIES BELIEVE THIS MONEY WAS USED TO FUND THEIR TERRORIST OPERATIONS.

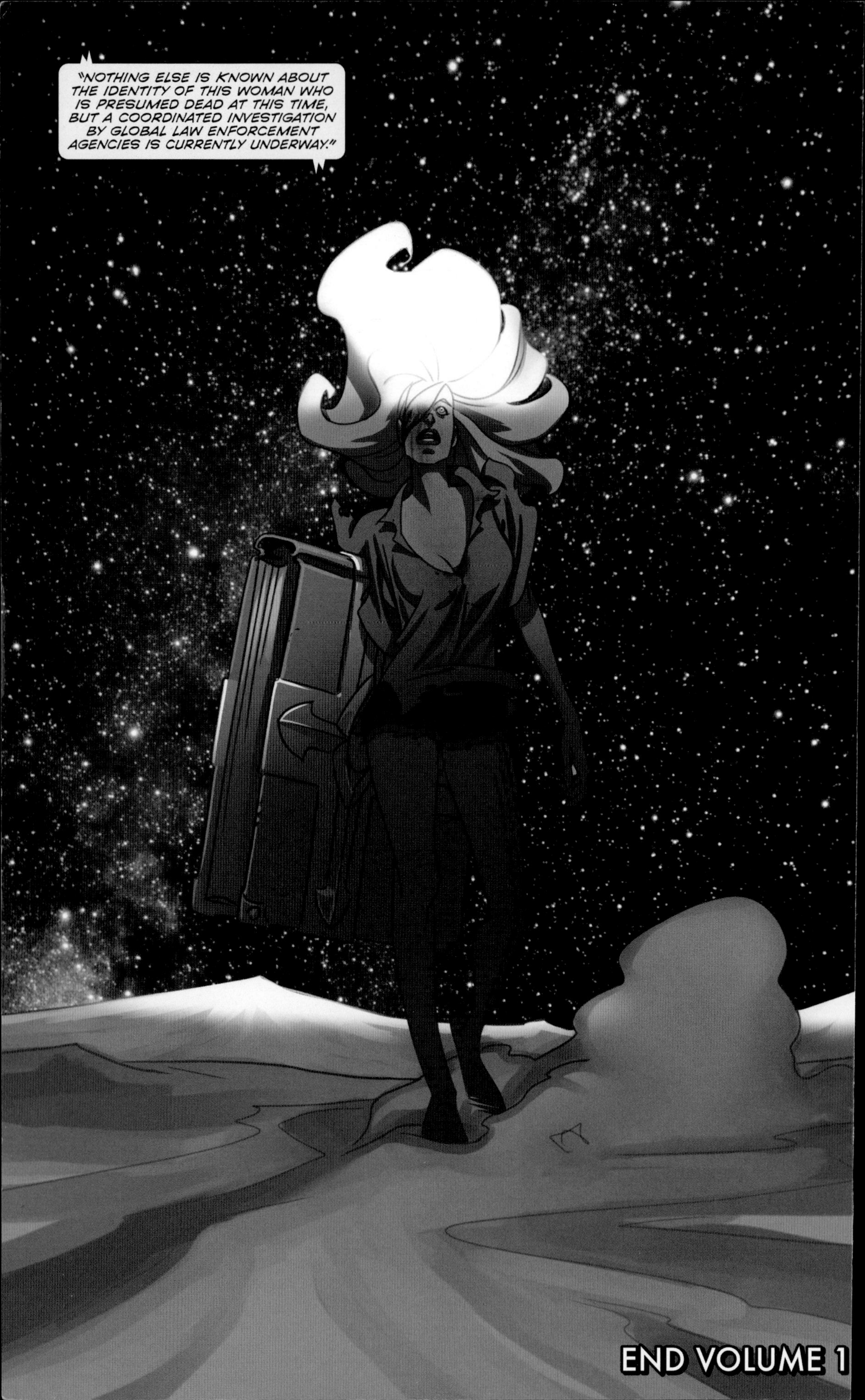
"NOTHING ELSE IS KNOWN ABOUT THE IDENTITY OF THIS WOMAN WHO IS PRESUMED DEAD AT THIS TIME, BUT A COORDINATED INVESTIGATION BY GLOBAL LAW ENFORCEMENT AGENCIES IS CURRENTLY UNDERWAY."
END VOLUME 1

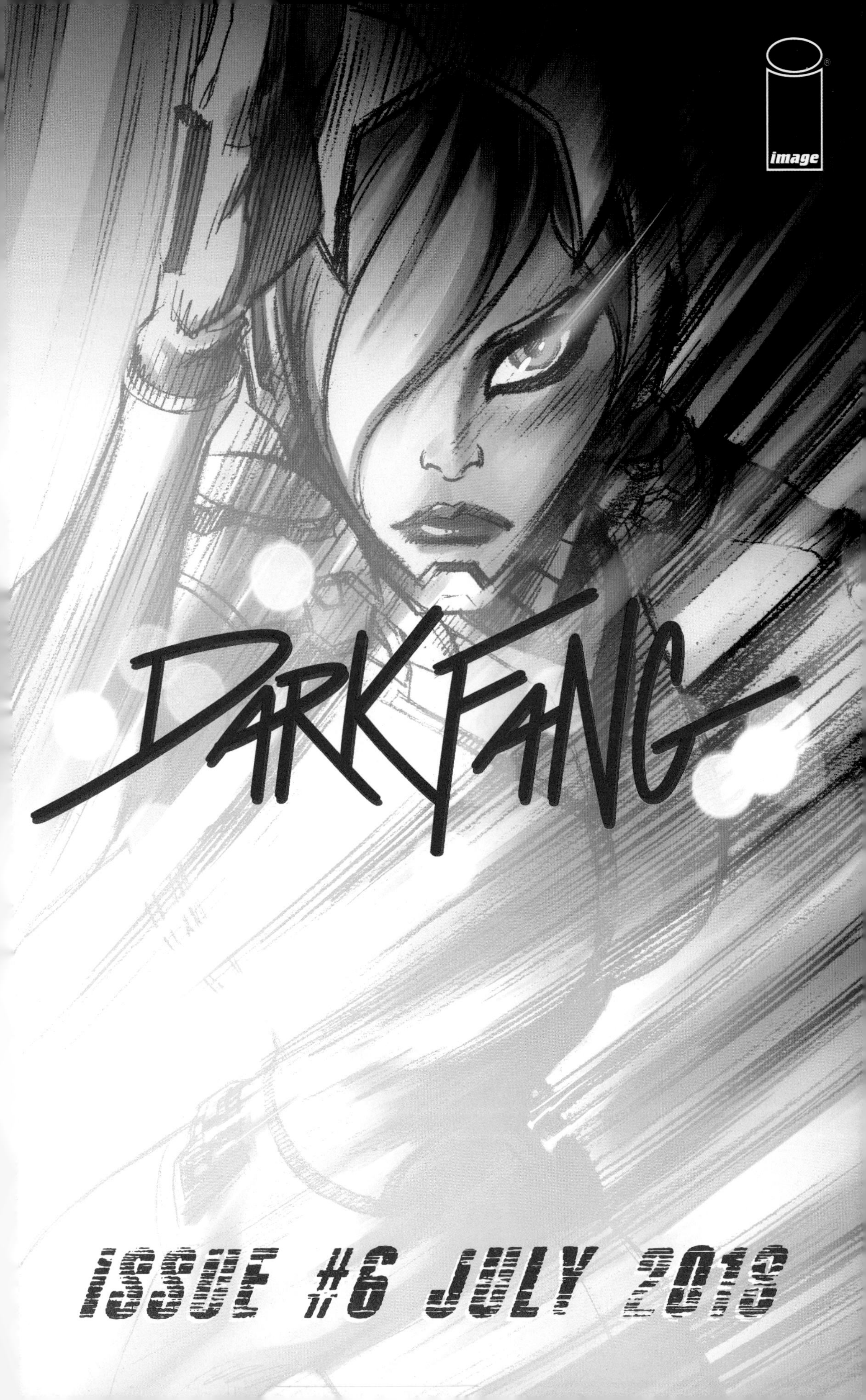
image
DARK FANG
ISSUE #6 JULY 2018

My so-called "creators" have been yammering incessantly for me to provide you with a means by which to contact them. You think it would be enough that I have lent my likeness to this publication? And so, I have very generously decided to relate their pathetic social media handles at this time: **@milesgunter**, **@comickelsey**, **@TaylorEspo.** They can be found on **instagram** and **facebook** as well. I'd write them out but I despise repetition!

But why would you waste time writing them, when you could shower me with adulation at **vallaholla@gmail.com**? Be sure to mark your letters **OK TO PRINT**.

Until next time my dears...

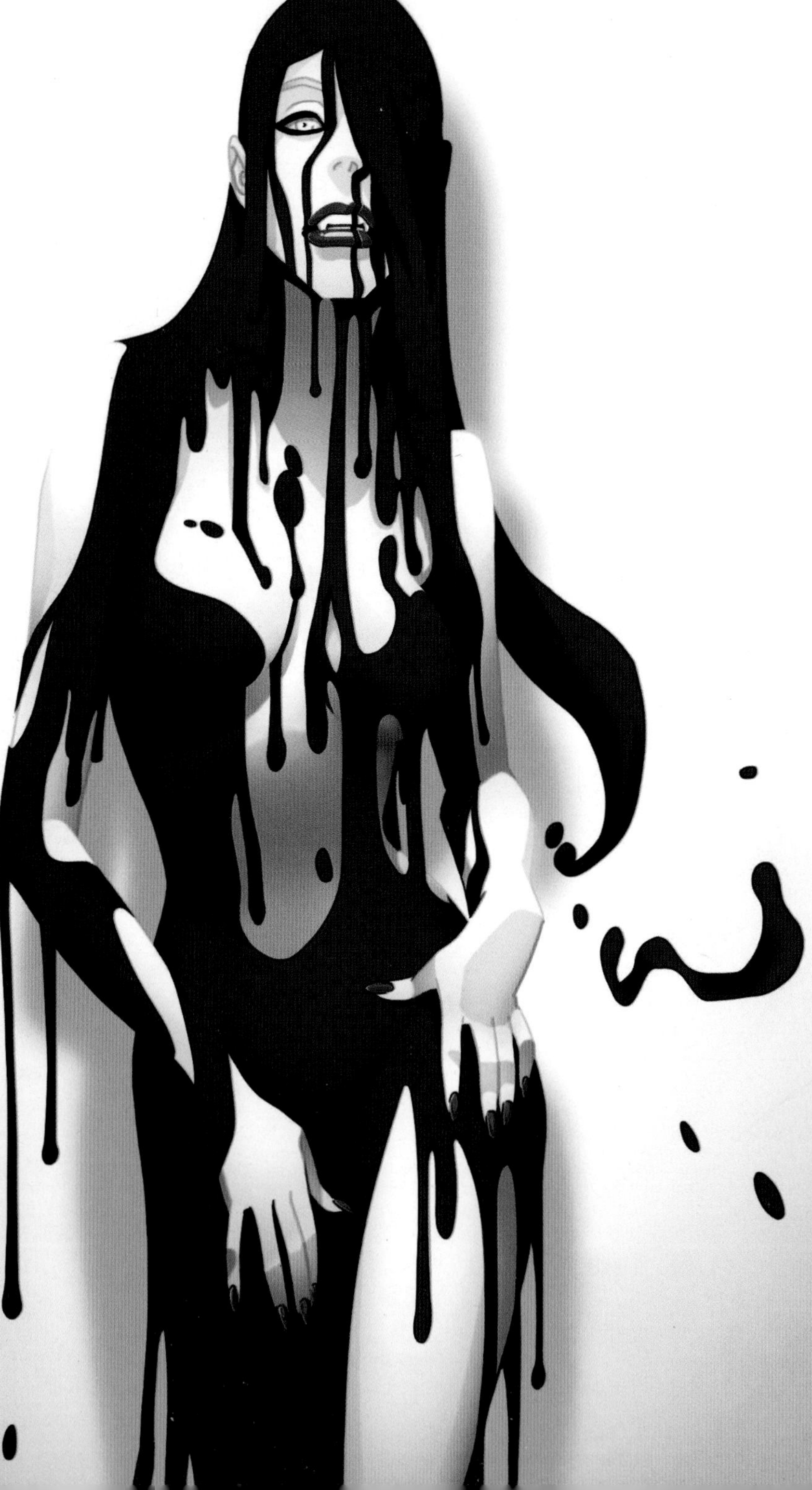